ESPERANCE

PRAISE FOR HEATHER FROST

"Riveting! The slow-burn romance, the compelling
mystery, and twists I never saw coming, made this
book unforgettable. I can't wait for more!"
- I Love Books And Stuff Blog (Ashley) on *Esperance*

"*Esperance* is a brilliant read! Packed with deadly and
dangerous schemes, hidden magic, betrayals and lies,
chemistry-laden romances, and characters you can't help
but root for, this layered and suspenseful fantasy
is one of my favorite books of the year."
-One Book More (Julie) on *Esperance*

"A tapestry of compelling setting, intriguing premise, and
captivating characters, Esperance is nothing short of magic."
- Author Rebecca McKinnon on *Esperance*

"I was instantly captivated by this book.
The characters, the setting, the deception and intrigue!
Esperance is a true page turner and an amazing story.
I can't wait to see what happens next.
- Min Reads and Reviews (Mindy) on *Esperance*

"*Royal Captive* is a standout in its genre!
Full of heart-pounding romance, high-stakes action, and
intricate court politicking, this book lives up to its title...
it holds you captive from start to finish!"
- Author Renee Dugan on *Royal Captive*

"Heather Frost is fabulous at telling enthralling tales!
From the very beginning, you are swept into the

world of Eyrinthia and may never want to leave."
- The Reading Pantry (Anna) on *Royal Captive*

"Once you start [reading], you won't be able to stop, and you'll
thank ~~the fates~~ Frost for creating this captivating world!"
- Darkest Sins (Silvia) on *Royal Captive*

"Frost has a gift — not only for stories, but for creating
characters that leap off the page...This series has [...] quickly
become one of my favorites in the entire genre."
- Author Kate Renae on *Shield & Blade*

"Heather Frost is a force to be reckoned with! ...So many twists,
turns and puzzle pieces, it makes Frost one of my favorite authors!"
- Author Sarah Hill on *Royal Spy*

"Everything was perfect about this book. If you haven't
started reading the [series] then I have no idea what you are
doing. Perfect for those who love royals and Sarah J. Mass."
- Thindbooks on *Royal Spy*

"Heather Frost can write complex characters like nobody's
business! ...[This] series is a hidden gem that I want to
shout from the rooftops."
- Book Briefs on *Royal Spy*

"Every page pulls you in and keeps you trapped until
suddenly the book is over and you're begging for more."
- Author Dana LeCheminant on *Royal Spy*

"This is a story that completely captured my attention from
the very beginning and didn't let go the whole way through
... I've been craving a book like this."
- Getting Your Read On (Aimee) on *Royal Decoy*

Also by Heather Frost:

Fate of Eyrinthia Series
Royal Decoy
Royal Spy
Royal Captive

Fate of Eyrinthia Novellas
Fire & Ash
Shield & Blade

The Seers Trilogy
Seers
Demons
Guardians

Asides: A Short Story Collection

ESPERANCE

Book 1 of the Esperance Trilogy

HEATHER FROST

Summary: Amryn and Carver are strangers brought together by an arranged marriage. Now, they must live in Esperance for a year with other couples to create peace in the empire.

ISBN: 978-1-959122-01-2
Kindle ISBN: 978-1-959122-00-5

For Becky,
Thanks for seeing the magic in this story
from the very beginning.

N
THE CRAETHEN EMPIRE
Sibet
Ferradin
Kalmar
Wendahl
Palar
Cael
Daersen
Vadir
Hafsin
Craethen
Westmont
Xerra
Harvari
Esperance

THE ÆMPIRE'S CHOSEN

Carver Vincetti *Westmont*	**Amryn Lukis** *Ferradin*
Argent Vayne *Craethen*	**Jayveh Umbar** *Xerra*
Rivard Quinn *Daersen*	**Tam Ja'Kell** *Kalmar*
Ivan Baranov *Sibet*	**Cora Amin** *Hafsin*
Darrin Fythen *Vadir*	**Marriset Navarre** *Palar*
Samuel Kenton *Wendahl*	**Sadia Kavel** *Cael*

1

AMRYN

The name rang in Amryn's ears as the tall double doors swung open, revealing a long aisle that stretched the length of the vaulted chapel. Bright tropical flowers and emerald fronds in large gold pots brought splashes of color to the otherwise dull, tan stone room. Wooden pews creaked as spectators craned their necks to look at her, though her eyes were drawn to the altar at the end of the aisle, and the dark-haired man who stood waiting for her. She had only learned his identity a moment before those doors opened, but Carver Vincetti was about to become her husband.

If he didn't discover her secrets and kill her, she just might live long enough to see him die.

In the corner, a string quartet played the empirical anthem, the notes resonant and strong as they echoed against the stone columns that ringed the chapel.

She hated every note.

Sheathed in her wedding dress, beads of sweat gathered

along her spine. Even this deep in the temple, surrounded by stone, the oppressive heat of the jungle was stifling. The style and weight of her gown was impractical in this climate, and the humidity had wreaked havoc on her hair. Her maids had made a valiant effort to tame the uncontrollable crimson waves, but they'd soon had no choice but to admit defeat. Instead of the Ferradin bridal tradition of loose hair, they'd twisted and pinned until her flaming locks were piled into an elaborate bun atop her head. In truth, it was a mercy; she wouldn't have been able to stand feeling anything against her neck when it felt like her skin was melting. The fitted bodice was too tight across her chest, and the very air felt different as it entered her lungs. Nothing like the cool mountain air of home.

If she'd been getting married in Ferradin, she would have held wildflowers in varying shades of purple, blue, and white. The bouquet she held instead was filled with tropical flowers with sharp edges, in vibrant colors of pink, orange, and yellow. The foreign flowers trembled in her hands. She tightened her grip until her knuckles were as white as her dress.

She could not afford to show weakness.

Amryn lifted her chin. Despite the pounding of her heart and the twisting in her gut, she forced herself to step forward. The thinly carpeted floor was cold and hard beneath the thin soles of her elegant shoes, and her long gown dragged at her legs, but she kept moving.

Behind her, the chapel doors thudded softly closed. The sound was hauntingly final.

Too many emotions churned in the room for Amryn to decipher anything specific, but she felt a familiar pulse from her uncle Rix. He was the only face in the crowd she knew, and she picked him out easily. He sat about halfway down the aisle on the left side of the chapel. His green eyes were fixed on her, and though he was only in his late thirties, his brown hair had been rapidly replaced by gray when the emperor's edict had arrived. He wore the expected empirical black, but a sash of blue, white, and gold plaid draped over one shoulder and across his chest. It was a little bit of Ferradin, and Amryn needed that reminder of home.

Her focus shifted to the front pew, where four couples sat side by side. That meant, after Amryn's wedding, there would be only one more today.

Twelve strangers. Six marriages. One year in Esperance. That was the emperor's decree, and none of them had any choice in it.

Amryn was halfway down the long aisle now, and she could no longer avoid studying her future husband.

Carver Vincetti stood at strict attention before the altar, his feet planted shoulder-width apart and his spine rigidly straight as he faced the room. He was younger than she'd expected, probably twenty-five or so—only a few years older than her twenty years. He looked as dark as his reputation, though, with black hair that fell over his brow and bronzed skin that hinted at his southern heritage. His nose was long and straight, his jaw angular and covered with dark stubble. That shadow of a beard seemed at odds with his military uniform, which was empirical black and immaculately tailored to fit his wide shoulders, long arms, and tapered waist. While he had no visible weapons, there was no doubt he was a capable killer. Even from this distance she could see the piercing blue of his eyes—the lightest of his features by far. And when those aquamarine eyes sharpened on her, raking her from head to toe and marking every detail, every hair on her body lifted.

Then their gazes locked, and there was no fighting her shiver. In the coldness of his eyes, she saw the Carver Vincetti that was whispered about throughout the empire. The emperor's favorite general. The heir to the throne of Westmont. The man that many simply called *the Butcher*.

She refused to break this stare. Instinct screamed that doing so would be a critical mistake. So, even though her pulse skipped faster, she didn't look away.

Carver's expression didn't alter, which made it impossible to guess his thoughts. And with so many people in the room, Amryn couldn't get a read on his emotions.

If the man even had any.

Finally—and yet far too soon—she stood before him. He was taller than her by nearly a head, but she lifted her chin in order to keep his gaze.

He held out a hand, and under the watchful eyes of the high cleric and a chapel full of witnesses, she set her palm against his.

Carver's long fingers curled around hers, his grip strong, yet surprisingly careful. As if he feared his larger hand could crush hers. His skin was rough with callouses, and he wore a silver ring with a simple band on his forefinger. He smelled of warm sandalwood with a hint of spice. Standing this close to him, she could see a pale scar that traced over his chin, nearly hidden by the black stubble that coated the lower half of his face.

Carver turned, pulling her with him to face the altar and the high cleric. The older man had a shaved head, as all clerics did, though his robes were more elaborate and colorful than the simple brown ones the low-ranking clerics wore. He gave them a small smile and gestured for them to kneel at the altar.

The music faded as they knelt together on the narrow cushioned bench, their hands still joined. The high cleric began to recite the marriage prayer. It was filled with promises of love, care, trust, and fidelity, and Amryn let the meaningless words float over her.

Now that she was closer to Carver, she might be able to discern his emotions from all the other chaotic feelings in the room. She glanced sideways, relaxing slightly when she saw his attention riveted on the high cleric.

His jaw was set firmly, but not harshly. A soldier, accepting orders. As she studied his profile, it truly appeared that Carver felt nothing. So she reached out with her empathic sense, gently probing the space between them until, finally, she felt him.

Carver Vincetti was not emotionless. Seething just below the surface of his unwavering expression, she felt frustration, surprise, irritation, determination, impatience . . . and fear.

Shock rippled through her, and she must have made some sound or tightened her hold on his hand, because his blue eyes darted to hers. This time, she was prepared for the intensity of his stare. But she was not prepared for the slight twist of his lips.

The smile was small, but it altered his entire bearing. The remoteness, the cold intensity—it vanished in an instant, replaced with a half-smile so devastatingly handsome there was an unwanted flutter in her stomach.

Unwilling to process that, she sternly reminded herself who he was. *The enemy.*

Though she hadn't returned his smile, his grew into a smirk, and Amryn felt his sudden spike of amusement. He was mocking her somehow, though she hadn't done or said anything.

She jerked her eyes away, pretending to focus on the high cleric. But the color in her cheeks grew as Carver continued to watch her.

It was time for the oaths.

"Do you, Amryn Lukis, swear before the Divinities that you will love, protect, and cherish Carver Vincetti until death, and revere him as your husband?"

Her stomach cramped, and her voice came out a little hoarse as she responded to the cleric. "I swear."

Carver still eyed her profile, and his hand tightened around hers; an unconscious tic, she thought.

"And do you, Carver Vincetti, swear before the Divinities that you will love, protect, and cherish Amryn Lukis until death, and revere her as your wife?"

"I swear." Carver's voice was deep and smooth, and without hesitation.

The high cleric easily continued his practiced words. "Then before the All-Seeing Divinities and these witnesses, you are now married. Please rise."

They stood. Carver only released her hand long enough for them to turn to face the chapel, and then his fingers wrapped around hers once more.

Applause rang dully in the stone chapel, but the audience blurred as Amryn stared out at them. A tremble shook her legs, and her palms began to sweat as reality sank in.

She was married. And she was about to be trapped in this temple for a year—cut off from everything and everyone she had ever known.

Carver didn't wait for the applause to die out. He tugged her away from the altar, and Amryn had no choice but to follow him. Her pulse thumped too loudly in her ears, and when they reached the first pew that held the other married couples, Carver withdrew his hand. She did not miss the way his fingers flexed—as if even the ghost of her touch bothered him.

They joined the couples on the first pew, and Amryn slid a fraction away so their shoulders wouldn't accidentally brush. She wanted to bolt from the room, but instead she braced herself for the last marriage.

She was not prepared to see the man who took Carver's place at the altar.

Prince Argent Vayne, heir to the Craethen Empire. She never would have imagined that he would take part in his grandfather's scheme for peace. And she was clearly not alone.

Murmurs broke out as shock pulsed through the room, dominating all other emotions. Witnesses straightened sharply, and the whispering only died when the music started once more and the double doors swept open to reveal the final bride.

She was beautiful, with long black hair and rich brown skin. Her wedding gown was as long as Amryn's, but her train stretched out far behind her. Her smile was shy as she met Prince Argent's gaze across the chapel, and despite the sea of emotions that clouded everything, Amryn could feel the spark of the woman's love and joy. And—surprisingly—Amryn felt it echoed in Argent as he grinned at his bride.

As the high cleric began the marriage ceremony for the empirical prince, dread rippled through Amryn. Had the Rising known he would be here? Did the rebels plan to assassinate the future emperor while he was stuck in Esperance with the rest of them?

She supposed in the end it didn't matter.

The emperor had summoned them all to this temple in an

effort to save the empire. Instead, Esperance would be its undoing.

Amryn was here to make sure of it.

2

CARVER

CARVER STOOD ON THE EDGE OF the large banquet hall, studying the milling crowd as he sipped his wine. The emperor's guest list had been minimal, for purposes of security. Each of the newlyweds had been allowed only one escort and a limited guard for the journey to the remote temple of Esperance, and the rest of the spectators were made up of nobles, politicians, and key church leaders from the capital.

Carver wondered how many of them were enemies.

Positioned by the towering archways that led to an open balcony, Carver could hear the sounds of the jungle that surrounded the temple compound. The screeching calls of birds, the chattering of monkeys, the chirp and thrum of countless insects. Rolling hills, thick vegetation, and distant jagged mountain peaks were all he could see. Gnarled vines strangled the tan stone railing of the balcony, which spanned the length of the dining hall. Sticky heat clung to Carver's skin, but he wasn't exactly uncomfortable. He had been in jungles before. He'd fought and bled in them.

He had never thought to be married in one, though.

His father came to stand beside him. The wineglass he held looked ridiculously small in his large hand. Cregon Vincetti, the High General of Craethen, was tall and imposing, but Carver knew the lines around his blue eyes were from smiling with his family, and that his booming laugh was louder than any shouted commands. He didn't have a single weapon on his belt; every entourage had been thoroughly searched when they'd entered Esperance. Only the guards were allowed to have weapons.

Cregon looked just as strange without his customary blades as Carver felt without his own.

"Your mother may never forgive the emperor for this," his father said. His father"s voice was pitched low, though they stood apart from the crowd and the buzz of other conversations would drown out his words before they had a chance of being overheard.

Carver still forced a smile, just in case anyone was watching. "She *did* offer to be my escort."

Cregon leveled Carver a look. "I wasn't about to send your mother here."

"You were worried about her if a fight broke out?"

"No. I was worried she might *start* a fight."

Carver huffed a short laugh. His mother's skills with a blade were rivaled only by her temper, once flared.

She didn't approve of Carver's arranged marriage, or of being cut off from him for a year. But then, she hadn't stopped hovering since he'd returned from Harvari—bloody, broken, and barely alive. His parents worried that the wounds that had nearly killed him ran deeper than his skin.

They were right, though Carver would never admit it aloud.

Cregon Vincetti took a swallow of wine and winced.

Carver's mouth curved. "Westmont's orchards have spoiled you."

His father grunted as he eyed the red liquid. "Nothing tastes quite as good as home."

Home. The word elicited all sorts of conflicted feelings, and the stiff collar of Carver's uniform was suddenly too tight around his throat. Family, duty, honor, war—they were all entwined with *home.* As was the feeling of being trapped.

When the emperor had summoned him to the palace weeks ago, he'd assumed it was to send him back to Harvari. And despite everything, he was itching to do *anything* after convalescing at home for six months. Even return to war.

He just hadn't anticipated this particular war.

His eyes sought his new bride, who stood on the far side of the banquet hall. As if she wanted to be as far away from him as possible.

Amryn Lukis—Vincetti now, he supposed—was a puzzle. She had been his wife—*Saints,* that was a terrifying word—for nearly an hour, yet they hadn't actually spoken to each other. The moment the ceremonies ended, they'd all been ushered from the chapel and into this hall. Amryn had stepped away from Carver without a backward glance and moved to stand by her uncle.

She was beautiful. There was no denying that. Carver knew he would always remember the moment those chapel doors had opened and he'd first glimpsed her. The fire of her hair paired with her porcelain skin was a striking contrast, and the stark white of her dress only enhanced the stunning effect. Her sea green eyes were pale and depthless.

She was moderately tall, and though her build was slender,

the clinging dress revealed distracting curves. It wasn't until she stood before him that he noticed the light dusting of freckles scattered across her pert nose and curved cheekbones. Instead of marring her beauty, the markings enhanced it. They made her look real. Her round face was softened further by the crimson ringlets that brushed her cheeks.

Saints, that hair. Even now, standing with a room between them, those locks were distractingly vibrant. He wondered how long they fell when unpinned.

A stupid thing to wonder, considering circumstances.

As if she felt his attention, Amryn's focus slid to him.

There was nothing pale or delicate in the way she looked at him. Her strange green eyes bored into him, firm and unafraid. Few dared meet his gaze like that. Not with his reputation. But she didn't flinch away. She challenged him with that stare.

For the life of him, he didn't know why that made his pulse thrum faster. Or why he could still feel her hand in his.

"She's very beautiful," his father commented lowly.

"She might be a traitor," Carver said. It was a good reminder for them both.

"There is that." The corner of his mouth suddenly lifted. "A red-haired girl from Ferradin. I should have taken the bet when Ford offered it to me."

Carver rolled his eyes, but his mouth twitched, just as it had when the thought of his friend's bet had crossed his mind at the altar. "You should never encourage Ford and his bets."

"I didn't. But I can't speak for your brothers and sisters. Or your grandparents."

Carver barely hid in a snort. His large family could be exasperating, but he would do anything for them. "I'm grateful my life can provide such entertainment for the family," he said drolly.

"You've always been entertaining, Carve." Cregon lifted his glass and took another sip of wine—and grimaced.

Carver chuckled while his father glanced around for a place to put the offending drink, but the servants were busy making final adjustments to the table settings. No one wanted to be the reason the wedding feast didn't run smoothly. Not with the emperor reigning over it.

Cregon finally sighed in defeat and simply lowered his glass. "I'm not sure your pairing with Amryn Lukis was a good idea. Ferradin has many personal grievances against the empire—Westmont, specifically."

Which was exactly why Carver had insisted the emperor match him with whoever the king of Ferradin chose to send. The kingdom's troubled history with the empire made them a prime suspect for dissention.

They knew the Rising had planted rebels in Esperance; they just didn't know *who*. Identifying their enemies was Carver's first priority. Although, since his best friend had also insisted on coming to Esperance for a year, protecting Argent had also moved to the top of Carver's list.

The prince stood with his new wife, Jayveh. They were grinning as they held hands and talked with the emperor. They were the only newly married couple still standing beside each other, and Carver couldn't remember ever seeing Argent look so happy.

"If anyone needs your worry," he said to his father, "it's Argent."

"He loves her," Cregon said.

That was the problem; Argent wouldn't see a threat in Jayveh. Meanwhile, Carver saw a threat in everything and everyone—especially her.

"I know you'll keep an eye on him," his father said. "Just make sure you guard your back as well."

Carver tipped his head in acknowledgement, but his attention was once again drawn to Amryn. But instead of meeting her green-eyed gaze again, he intercepted a glare from her uncle.

Lord Rix Varden, chief advisor and best friend to King Torin Halvin of Ferradin. Definitely a man with grievances against the empire. The man's face tightened as he studied Carver. There was a warning there, along with unmistakable disapproval.

Lifting his wineglass in a silent salute, Carver flashed the man a grin.

Rix's thick eyebrows slammed down.

His father sighed. "You shouldn't provoke him."

Carver lifted one shoulder. "Maybe he'll snap and betray himself as a rebel. That would make things easier."

Cregon was silent for a short moment. Then, "I know how he feels."

Surprised by his suddenly subdued tone, Carver shot his father a look.

The older man shook his head slowly. "It's not easy, letting you come here. Watching you marry a stranger. A potentially dangerous stranger, at that." He let out a slow sigh. "Your mother and I only ever wanted our children to marry for love. As we did."

"Life rarely turns out how we wish." Carver thought he'd kept his tone light, but he regretted saying anything as his father eyed him with cautious concern.

"Are you sure you're up to this?" his father asked.

Carver's fingers tightened around the stem of his glass. "I'm fine."

It looked like Cregon might press, but a call for everyone to begin taking their seats interrupted him. Carver seized the excuse, bidding a quick farewell to his father so he could escort Amryn to the head table, where the newlyweds were to sit with the emperor.

Crossing the floor with long, purposeful strides, he soon stood before Amryn and her uncle.

Rix's look was withering, but Carver tried to ignore that. It was time to adopt his role: charm his wife into revealing her secrets. Failing that, he would have to resort to other means to determine her allegiance.

He hiked his lips into a wide smile and addressed Amryn directly for the first time. "It's unfortunate we didn't have an opportunity to meet before the ceremony. I'm Carver Vincetti." He stuck out a hand, but Amryn didn't take it—or the subtle invitation to join him in disparaging the emperor and his choice of keeping the arranged pairings secret until right before the ceremonies. It was probably a weak test of her allegiance to the empire anyway, but maybe it would pave the way for a future conversation in which she'd let her guard down.

For now, she simply gazed at him steadily with those unsettling, fathomless eyes. Finally, her pink lips moved. "I know who you are."

Her voice was lower than he expected; certainly not as airy and insubstantial as her appearance. Standing this close to her again, he wondered if she presented herself this way on purpose. The elegant gown that washed out her already pale skin, the wide neck that revealed fragile collarbones—even the way her hair was piled on her head, leaving her neck bare. Was it all an effort to look slight and delicate, so her deadly strike could be all the more unexpected?

He let his offered hand fall, then flashed her a smile. "Well, you have me at a disadvantage. But I look forward to getting to know you, Amryn."

The skin around her eyes tightened, and in no way did she return his smile.

So much for charm. Perhaps he was simply out of practice.

Amryn glanced at her uncle. "We should take our seats."

Rix didn't look at all inclined to leave her with Carver. But since everyone else in the room was winding their way toward their assigned tables, he didn't have much of a choice.

His guarded eyes slid to Carver, and his jaw flexed as he clearly fought for words. Since the emperor had decreed that all escorts would depart before dark, this could be the only time Amryn's uncle had with Carver.

Finally, the man spoke, and his voice was surprisingly rough. "Don't hurt her."

The unexpected order was edged with a plea, and Carver's shoulders tightened. "I won't."

It wasn't exactly a lie; Carver would never personally hurt a woman. But if Amryn was a traitor to the empire, he would do his duty.

Rix's expression hardened, but he didn't say anything else as he turned to Amryn and pressed a quick kiss to her temple. He whispered something indistinct, then—with a last look at Carver—he strode away.

Carver turned to escort Amryn, but she was already moving for the head table, which was raised on a dais and set perpendicular to the other three long tables in the hall. He followed after her, walking briskly enough that he easily caught up to her. He said nothing as they found their seats.

Carver was relieved to see that Rivard had been placed some distance away with his own new bride. The emperor had asked if there would be any trouble between him and Rivard, and Carver had assured him there would be none.

As long as Rivard kept his distance, that might actually remain true.

Carver set down his wineglass and pulled back Amryn's chair for her.

She visibly stiffened, but gathered her long skirt and sank onto the cushioned seat. Once she was settled at the table, he sat beside her.

The grating sound of chairs being pulled across the stone floor echoed across the banquet hall until everyone was seated.

The emperor stood at the end of the long head table, his bodyguards behind him as he faced the room.

Emperor Lorcan Vayne's hair was thin and white, and his blue eyes were watery with age. He was seventy-six years old, and his frailties had begun to show. Looking at him, one might find it difficult to believe he had actually been the man to envision an empire, and then fight to make it happen. Before the empire existed, Lorcan Vayne had been the king of Craethen. But he had risen to unite eleven other kingdoms, establishing unmitigated peace across the greater part of the continent. He was committed to keeping that peace alive—no matter the cost.

The emperor beamed as he lifted his age-spotted hands. "Welcome to Esperance!" His gaze skated over the couples seated at the table, his eyes shining. "This temple is a place of peace and light, and you are the bright future of our great empire. You—the Empire's Chosen—will lead us into a new age of unmitigated peace. You have each been selected by the rulers of your individual kingdoms, and I am grateful for your willingness to embrace this unique task." He straightened a little, and though he was still clearly speaking to the newlyweds, his voice projected throughout the room. "For one year, you will be sealed together on these temple grounds. Guards will secure the gates, and they will not admit anyone inside the compound, nor will they permit anyone to leave. There will be no messages sent or received.

"Sealing Esperance is for your safety. It is also for your growth. You will have uninterrupted time to strengthen your marriages as well as foster friendships with the other chosen. There will be no outside distractions, influences, or biases. You will learn to rely on and trust each other. Through marriage, you will mend the rifts of previous generations. Working together, you will solidify the peace that was the inspiration for this empire. Because there is strength and peace in unity."

The motto of the empire was echoed by the spectators seated at the other tables: "Strength and peace in unity!"

Emperor Lorcan's face softened. "The empire began in the kingdom of Craethen, and has since spread to become the strongest power in the world. We united so no more senseless blood would be spilled between neighbors. So that our kingdoms could come together for peace, not war." He looked to Argent, and then Jayveh, and his smile broadened. "My grandson, the future emperor of Craethen, and his beautiful wife, the future empress, will lead us into a new age. With their support, and the leadership of one of my best advisors, Chancellor Aaron Trevill, these newly wedded couples will form the first Craethen Council. Together, you will debate important decisions that face our empire and help construct new laws that will shape our joined nations. Each kingdom in the empire will always have a voice on the council. By merging the high families of each kingdom, we have assured that your future children will bind all of us even more irrevocably together. Because of the efforts of the twelve of you, the Craethen Empire will live forever!"

Applause began somewhere—probably from the clerics in the room—and the witnesses and escorts soon joined in. Amryn clapped with the rest of them, though the motion was stilted.

Carver couldn't really fault her for her rigidness. His own clapping rang false in his ears.

Then something else rang out: the snap and twang of a fired crossbow.

The sound was nearly drowned out by the crowd, but Carver would have known it anywhere.

His stomach dropped. "Get down!" he shouted, but it was too late.

A cry pierced the room and the emperor fell, a bolt buried high in his chest.

3

AMRYN

CARVER'S SHOUT JOLTED AMRYN, but it was feeling the emperor's agony that made her gasp.

The room exploded into chaos.

Guards shouted. Across the floor, men and women leapt up from their chairs and bolted toward the exits. The emperor's bodyguards rushed to surround him, and screams echoed as more crossbows were fired.

Amryn was frozen. Her heart seized in her chest, the emperor's pain lancing through her.

A bolt slammed into the arm of the newly married man seated next to her, and his gut-wrenching howl snapped her out of her frozen state. She shoved to her feet, but almost immediately Carver snagged her wrist. He hauled her down to the floor behind the table, the shivering black tablecloth a feeble shield from the rest of the room.

Her new husband's jaw was tight as he crouched beside her. "Stay down," he ordered tersely, "or you're going to get yourself killed."

Amryn's stomach clenched. The fear in the room was a raging storm. The man who'd just been shot—she thought his name was Ivan—was stumbling to his feet, blood dripping from the bolt stuck in his arm. His face was set in a silent snarl and he grabbed up his dinner knife before darting out of view.

Still hunched beside her, Carver reached blindly onto the table, and when his hand came back down, he clutched a dinner knife as well. Palming the cutlery, he cursed under his breath. "Saints, I miss my blades," he muttered. He looked to her, his blue eyes severe. "Stay here."

He didn't wait for a response, just vaulted onto the table. Dishes clattered as he leaped to the other side, charging in the direction the shots had come from.

Amryn's fingers dug into the stone floor, a knot tightening her throat. Was this the Rising?

Immediately, she dismissed that possibility. Why would the rebels recruit her for a mission in Esperance, only to attack now?

The chaos in the room nearly robbed her of breath. She looked up and down the length of the table, noting that some of the couples had scattered, though a few of the newlyweds remained huddled beside the table. One of the brides made eye contact with Amryn—she thought she'd heard someone at the table call her Tam—and the woman's shock and fear punched into Amryn with near physical force.

Amryn hadn't known many empaths; after being hunted for years and executed by order of the church, most empaths were either dead, or too good at hiding to reveal their secret. But even without the ability to compare, Amryn was certain she felt things more intensely than most empaths. Sometimes, if she had warning, she could brace herself and better handle the emotions that slammed into her. But in a sudden and violent situation like this, the emotions were crippling.

Terror, shock, rage, bloodlust, horror, and pain. It was everywhere. Overwhelming. And when she felt the first death, she shuddered.

Feeling a life end was an indescribable horror. She'd experienced it before, and feeling it now brought her back to that long ago night. The helplessness she'd experienced. The fear. The grief.

She would not be that terrified little girl again.

Gritting her teeth, Amryn pinched her eyes closed. In her mind, she sat behind her cello. Her hand encircled the smooth wooden neck, and her fingers pressed against the taut strings as her bow dragged out deep, resonant notes. As always, the act of imagining the creation of a familiar song—willing it from memory—soothed the tension in her muscles. Created a buffer between her and the emotions that tried to flood her. It was a trick Rix had taught her. Something that her mother had done, when her empathic gifts had become too much to bear.

When Amryn opened her eyes, she could breathe. She could think. The emotions in the room were still frenzied, but she'd created a shield of sorts.

Still crouched by the table, Amryn twisted, searching for the nearest exit. Carver had told her to stay in place, but every instinct screamed to flee the room.

She trusted her instincts far more than she trusted him.

Across the dais on her left, she spotted an open doorway. There was no one between her and that escape, so she gathered her flowing skirt in one hand, but hesitation caught her before she ran. She glanced toward the surface of the table.

As an empath, fighting was nearly impossible. Even if she

had time to brace herself, hurting someone would still cause her pain.

Pain, however, was survivable. Death wasn't.

Keeping her head ducked behind the table, Amryn blindly searched for a knife. Her fingertips brushed the cool, rounded edge of a plate, then the crisp fold of a linen napkin. With a little fumbling, she finally grasped the thin blade she wanted.

The shouting in the room had reached a fevered pitch. She thought she heard Rix bellow her name, but her uncle was too far from the head table; she couldn't wait for him, and it would be foolish to risk plunging into the seething crowd to reach him.

She tightened her grip on the knife and looked toward the doorway again. From the corner of her eye, she saw the other huddled bride—Tam—suddenly lurch to her feet. The woman was small and fast, but she only made it a few steps before she was tackled by a large man. He wore the garb of a servant, but he wielded a large dagger in one hand and grabbed a fistful of her brown hair with the other, jerking her head back to expose her throat.

Tam's scream was swallowed in the other battle sounds, but Amryn felt her spike of pain. The brutal claws of her fear.

Amryn darted forward, the knife burning her palm as she stabbed the man's back.

The blade didn't penetrate as easily as she thought it would; the tip pierced his flesh, but he was already whipping around with a roar, and the dinner knife clattered to the floor.

The slash of his echoed pain nearly brought Amryn to her knees. She stumbled back a step, her pulse hammering.

The man glared at her, a silent snarl twisting his features.

Tam kicked the man's cheek, knocking him back. The woman scrambled away from him, her white skirt spilling over the floor as she fought to gain her feet.

Amryn darted forward and grabbed Tam's hand, jerking her up. "The door!" she gasped.

Tam was already running with her, but they'd only made it a few steps before Amryn's skirt was snagged from behind. She barely managed to let go of Tam as she fell. Her knees slammed into the stone floor with jarring force, and then her chest hit, driving the rest of the air from her lungs. Her chin knocked off the stones, and her vision blurred.

Harsh fingers clamped down on Amryn's ankle, and she was dragged backward.

Tam screamed.

Amryn couldn't breathe as she was flung onto her back. The furious man straddled her, his knees digging into her hips.

Tam charged him, but one backhand sent her spinning to the ground.

Amryn was still dazed, but adrenaline rushed through her when the large man's attention turned back to her, his dark eyes blazing. Rage, despair, desperation, pain—it all stabbed into her.

She thrashed beneath him, but the heavy skirt restricted her movements, and he pinned her easily. Once he had both of her hands manacled in one of his larger ones, he lifted his dagger, the tip aimed for her heart.

She didn't have enough air to scream.

His body suddenly jerked. His hold on the knife clenched, but his body was already sagging. As he swayed, the knife slipped from his fingers and clattered to the floor beside Amryn. His grip on her wrists loosened, and he slumped to the side.

Behind him stood Carver Vincetti. He held a bloody knife—not the table knife she'd last seen him with, but a dagger he must have taken from someone else. A scowl darkened his face as he stared down at her. "I told you to stay down."

Amryn trembled. Her attacker was dying on the floor beside her. She could feel it. She kicked away from him, gasping for air as she scrambled backwards.

Carver's eyes narrowed. He stepped forward, and Amryn cringed back.

He stilled at once, a furrow growing between his dark brows. "Are you all right?"

Her attacker expelled his last rattling breath, and the sudden loss of life—of all feeling—made Amryn double over.

She threw up on her new husband's boots.

The fight was over. While guards called the room to order, Carver fetched a napkin so Amryn could wipe her mouth, and then he extended a hand to help her up.

He didn't say anything about his boots. She hadn't expected such courtesy, and for some reason it made her cheeks burn more than if he'd cursed her.

He studied her intensely, which only increased her blush. "Are you all right?" he asked again, his eyes boring into hers. "Did you hit your head?"

She swallowed hard, still tasting the acidic bile. "No."

He eyed her chin.

She knew it must be red, because it was throbbing from hitting the floor. Her flush deepened. "I hit it a little," she admitted. "But I'm fine."

She wasn't fine. Her stomach still churned, and all she wanted to do was escape this room and all the emotions in it.

Carver looked like he might press the issue of her injury, but his father arrived—as did Rix.

Her uncle grasped her arms, tugging her away from Carver. His eyes were frantic as he studied her. "Are you hurt?"

"I'm all right," she assured him.

High General Cregon Vincetti frowned. "Are you sure?"

Saints, she could barely breathe, surrounded by three towering men. "I'm *fine*," she insisted.

Rix's brow grew lined. "Let's get you out of here."

"You can't leave."

Rix stiffened at Carver's words. "She's been attacked. She's clearly distressed."

Cregon Vincetti frowned, and in that chiseled expression she could see an echo of Carver. "He's right," the high general said. "The emperor was attacked. No one can leave the room."

"Is the emperor still alive?" a new voice asked.

Amryn twisted, and Rix released her so they could all face one of the newly married couples. She recognized Tam at once, and she was relieved to see the woman standing, though dark bruising had already started on her cheek. Her husband was the one who had spoken.

Amryn hadn't heard his name yet, though she guessed from his lightly toned complexion that he was from one of the central kingdoms. He looked to be Carver's age, and he was nearly as tall, but he had a thinner build. His dark brown hair matched his eyes, and he had a prominent nose and high cheekbones. While he was handsome, Amryn immediately disliked the feel of him. It was hard to know exactly why, especially with such high emotion in the crowded room, but just the fact that he had a constricting hand clasped around Tam's upper arm made Amryn stiffen.

"The emperor will be fine," Carver's father said. "The bolt hit near his shoulder, and his guards attended him immediately."

The man's shoulders fell a little as he released a sigh. "That's fortunate."

A sudden wave of loathing made Amryn shiver, and she glanced toward Carver. His gaze was fastened on Tam's husband, and the remoteness on his face was as telling as any glare.

Carver hated this man.

Cregon Vincetti glanced at his son. "We should assist Argent."

Amryn looked over her shoulder and saw that the empirical prince was issuing rapid orders to guards, as well as a physician who had been rushed in for the emperor.

Carver's deep voice brought her attention back around as he addressed Rix. "Will you stay with her?"

Surprise filtered through her, and that was all her own.

Rix's eyes narrowed. "Of course."

Carver nodded once, then strode toward Prince Argent.

The high general lingered, his gaze on Tam's husband. "Rivard, why don't you make sure all of the couples are all right?"

It was phrased as an invitation, but the air of order couldn't be missed. Rivard dipped his pointed chin and released Tam.

None of them missed how she rubbed at her arm as he walked away.

Anger flared from Rix.

Cregon's concern was just as potent. He made an effort to moderate his voice as he addressed Tam. "My dear, are you all right?"

Her eyes shined with moisture, but she nodded. "Just a little bruised." Her brown eyes darted to Amryn. "You saved my life. Thank you."

Before Amryn could respond, there was a piercing shout. "*Kian!*"

They all turned, and Amryn saw several guards had forced three men to kneel on the dais.

One of the brides darted forward. Fear, confusion, and grief hit Amryn as the bride was held back by a guard.

"Kian!" she gasped.

The man who knelt in the middle lifted his head. His features were too similar to the bride's for coincidence. Based on their ages, Amryn guessed they were siblings. Blood trickled from the corner of his mouth, and his eyes were sharp. "Stay back, Cora."

The young woman's entire body shook as the guard held her back. "What have you done?" she cried.

Kian didn't answer, and his expression didn't alter. Not even when Prince Argent stepped forward and the entire room quieted.

The prince's face was a stoic mask, but his eyes betrayed his rage. "You attempted to kill the emperor. You failed."

"Esperance will fail!" The man beside Kian spat at Argent's feet and was abruptly kicked by one of the guards.

Argent raised a hand, staying further violence. He opened his mouth to speak, but an older voice cut him off.

"The peace will not fail," the emperor said, his voice wavering only a little. His skin was pale, nearly as white as his hair, and the haphazard bandage on his shoulder was blood-stained. His guards remained close, but the emperor walked of his own volition to stand beside his grandson and face the three surviving attackers. "There is strength and peace in unity," the emperor intoned. "That is why Esperance will succeed, no matter what you or anyone else attempts to do to stop it."

Kian's chest rose and fell as he glared at the emperor. "Death to the conqueror and all who support him!"

The emperor's eyes tightened. "There will be no peace with men like you." He nodded to the guards, and a sword was raised.

Cora shrieked, and Amryn's gut dropped as a blade was rammed through Kian's back.

4

CARVER

CARVER AND ARGENT STOOD IN the large sitting room of the emperor's apartment. The physician was in the bedroom watching over the emperor as he slept. Carver's father was elsewhere in the temple, conferring with High Cleric Zacharias and Chancellor Trevill, the man appointed to oversee the newlyweds as they formed the first Craethen Council.

Argent's arms were crossed over his chest, his breaths low and rigidly even. He'd finally stopped pacing. He was staring at the brightly decorated room, but Carver knew he wasn't actually seeing the patterned rugs, the oil paintings, or the antique furniture. He was definitely not aware of the stunning jungle sunset happening outside the arched windows, even though they stood beside the balcony.

"He's all right," Carver said quietly.

Argent's stance didn't relax. "He could have been killed."

"But he wasn't."

Argent's jaw flexed. "He's older than he'll ever admit. He shouldn't have even made the journey here."

"He wouldn't have missed this."

His friend said nothing to that. But his shoulders lowered, though his arms remained folded across his chest, and his voice was soft as he asked, "Do you think this is a mistake?"

Carver shoved a hand through his dark hair. How to tactfully answer that? "I think the idea of political marriages and the formation of a council are solid ideas. But since we know the Rising has infiltrated Esperance, coming here may not have been the wisest course." Having Argent here was *definitely* not wise. Argent was the only heir to the empirical throne. If he died . . .

Saints, he couldn't die.

"This was the only way," Argent said. "Tension has been rising among the kingdoms, and the war with Harvari isn't over. Craethen must be united or we will be destroyed—either from without, or within."

"I know."

The Rising was an organized rebellion, but they weren't the only internal threat. Today's attack had been made by a few insurgents from Hafsin—not connected with the Rising at all. Kian—Cora's older brother, and her escort for the wedding—had not had the opportunity to give them answers before his execution. But his death had loosened the tongues of his friends. Despite the added mess for the servants to clean up, spilling his blood so abruptly had been a calculated choice. Kian's friends were still breathing after their confessions, and Carver's father would personally oversee their transfer to a prison in the capital.

They were not the first men to strike out against the empire, and they would not be the last.

Argent exhaled, moving suddenly for the windows. Carver

moved with him, the two of them overlooking the courtyard below.

Esperance was a sprawling temple with multiple buildings. It had once been a palace, but when the emperor had conquered the region, he had given the compound to the church. It was deep enough in the jungle that it was a constant battle to keep the foliage from growing back and covering the buildings and grounds. Esperance had many purposes. It was the stronghold of the church; a place where clerics were trained in the prayers and ceremonies of the Divinities, and a place to store their holy records.

Not being religious, Carver could at least see the more practical uses of Esperance. It was a place where the emperor had deposited a great deal of gold, jewels, and expensive relics from all the kingdoms, to keep the empire's wealth safely divided among multiple, defensible treasuries. The temple had multiple galleries of priceless art, and it was also a place where men and women could find refuge from the world. Anyone could petition for a place in Esperance. Some chose to live in the outbuildings, away from the temple and all others. Some took vows of silence, but served in the temple archives and galleries. All of them sought healing in some way.

Of course, no petition would be granted this year. Esperance would belong to the new Craethen Council—the Empire's Chosen. The newlyweds wouldn't be alone, though. They would have all the clerics to keep them company.

That didn't exactly comfort Carver.

"Rivard will investigate the clerics," Argent said, as if following his thoughts. "With his family ties to the church, he'll be able to determine who is friend and who is foe. You will uncover the rebels among the couples."

"And Jayveh?"

Argent frowned—probably at his tone.

They'd had this conversation before.

Jayveh claimed to have learned about the Rising when her uncle, King Jamir Umbar, had summoned her to the Xerra throne room about two months ago. He told her of the emperor's edict—that the most notable, marriageable woman of Xerra must be presented to Esperance for an arranged marriage—and then he had told her that he'd received a letter from the Rising. The missive had detailed the beginnings of a plan, and she was told in no uncertain terms that she would join their ranks in Esperance and help bring down the empire with whatever mission she was given. If she refused, her younger brothers would be tortured until she changed her mind.

Jayveh could have bent to those threats. Instead, she'd secretly made her way to the capital so she could warn the emperor of the threat, and gain protection for herself and her brothers. The emperor had been grateful for her loyalty, and he'd asked her to tarry for a short time at the empirical palace as plans were made. That's when she and Argent—once childhood friends—had become reacquainted, and it hadn't taken long before they'd fallen in love.

At least, Argent had. Carver still wasn't sure if Jayveh's actions thus far were anything more than an act.

It didn't matter that she'd been the one to warn them, or that she'd come to Esperance to infiltrate the Rising and be an informant for the empire. She had a dark history with Argent and the empire—a history the emperor and Argent had both set aside, apparently—and Jayveh now had unrivaled access to Argent.

What if she was actually loyal to the rebels, and her plan all along had been to seduce Argent and feed false information to them? It wasn't such a stretch, considering she was already playing double agent for the empire; her uncle and the rebels thought she was on their side, and Argent was just a besotted prince, unaware of the Rising's plot. Argent's performance was convincing. Probably because it wasn't a performance. He *was* totally besotted.

And that meant he wouldn't be on guard with her.

Argent had bodyguards, of course. They were the only guards or servants in Esperance that wouldn't be supplied by the church, but even if they were unerringly vigilant, Jayveh could kill Argent before any bodyguard could hope to reach them.

The thought made Carver's gut clench. Until he understood Jayveh's motivations, he would wonder if she was manipulating Argent. Manipulating *all* of them.

"She's not one of them," Argent said quietly. "She's never been one of them, Carve."

He met his best friend's stare. "Can we really know that for certain? She has reasons to carry a grudge against the empire."

Lines drew across his forehead. "That's all in the past. We've discussed it, and it's not an issue."

Carver barely held back a sigh.

Argent smiled faintly, though his tone remained serious. "I know this is difficult for you. But I need you to trust me."

"I *do* trust you."

The corner of his mouth lifted. "And I trust her. So . . ."

Carver gave him a dark look. "You're not as clever as you think you are."

"Ah, but I'm far more clever than *you* think I am."

He rolled his eyes.

Argent's flash of amusement faded. "Carver, I didn't want her to risk playing double agent for us. But she insisted on doing her part to protect the empire. To protect me."

Carver exhaled slowly. "I know." *But all of that could have been a manipulation, too.*

He bit his tongue to keep the words from escaping. He'd expressed all of this and more to Argent before, and his friend would not be swayed.

"Jamir told her that the Rising will give her specific instructions once Esperance is sealed," Argent said. "Until she can prove herself to you, perhaps you can extend a little faith."

Faith was not something he had a lot of these days, but he nodded once.

Argent straightened a little. "Your father is still planning to collect Jayveh's brothers on his way back to the capital?"

"Yes. They'll be safe in Westmont soon enough."

Argent grunted. "Unless that miserable excuse for an uncle refuses to let them go."

"Jamir won't have a choice." Most noble sons who lived in the south spent at least one year at Westmont, which was known for training the best soldiers in Craethen's military. By many, it was considered a rite of passage. The fact that Jayveh's brothers had not been allowed to go was just one more sign of their uncle's negligence.

According to Jayveh, there had been many other abuses.

Carver's father was a general and a politician; he would be able to successfully maneuver King Jamir into such a position that he would have to let his nephews go to Westmont or risk looking petty to his peers—or worse, miserly. With Jayveh successfully ensconced in Esperance, Jamir would be confident that she wouldn't be the wiser about the location of her brothers.

Carver looked to Argent. "You haven't mentioned your role yet."

The corner of his mouth lifted. "I thought it was obvious. I'm supposed to keep all of you safe."

"No. That's *my* role. You just need to keep yourself safe."

Argent's gaze softened. "I know you didn't want me to come. But I had to, Carve. Please understand."

He did. At least, in theory. He imagined that if he loved a woman—no matter how foolishly—he couldn't stand by and watch her marry someone else. Still . . . "I know you trust Jay-veh," Carver said quietly. "But I need you to be careful around her, just in case."

Argent laid a hand on Carver's shoulder. "She's on our side. Not everyone is an enemy." His eyes narrowed. "Speaking of enemies . . ."

Carver lifted a hand. "I don't want to talk about Rivard."

Argent sighed. "I'm going to have a hard time keeping you two from killing each other, aren't I?"

"Not if he stays away from me."

Argent's lips pressed together, but he didn't argue. "At least we know he's not a rebel."

That was fair. Rivard's family was as old and loyal as Carver's own, and they'd known each other for years—which only made Rivard's sins that much more unforgiveable to Carver. Still, his betrayal had been personal—nothing against the emperor.

"What about Ford?" Argent asked.

Carver appreciated the change in topic. "He's in position." Ford had been a part of Carver's life since they were children, and he'd been with him during the worst battles in Harvari. While he wasn't of noble birth, Ford was willing to do anything to help the empire. For the next year, he would live in one of Esperance's many outlying cabins, alone in the jungle, so he could serve as a messenger. They couldn't afford to be totally cut off from the rest of the empire; not with the battle they waged against the rebels. The emperor was unwilling to publicly send messages into Esperance, as that would break his own rule. So, Carver, Argent, and Rivard would all rely on Ford to get any necessary messages in and out of Esperance for the next year.

"Do you think Ford can stand being alone for so long?" Argent asked.

It was a reasonable question, since Ford was a man of high spirits and always in need of people and laughter. "He won't be totally alone. He'll have contact with me and the messengers." He glanced at Argent. "Harvari left its mark on him. A little solitude will benefit him."

Argent loosed a slow breath. "War is ugly."

He had no idea. As much as Carver loved and respected his friend, Argent had never experienced the true horror of war. He thought he understood. He saw from afar the damage, the cost. But he had never been covered in blood. He had never held a sword until his hands were numb. He'd never been surrounded on all sides, deep in the enemy line, wondering which faceless man would succeed in killing him. He had never had to climb over piles of bodies—men he had personally killed. He had never fought all day and all night, only to spend the next day and night visiting his broken men. He hadn't sat with them as they cried and died. Buried them, along with the countless innocent women and children who—

He cut off his thoughts before the memories could assault him, overwhelm him.

It was the only way he managed to stay sane.

Argent eyed him. "Are you all right?"

No. Not even close.

Carver's hands fisted. "I'm fine." Maybe if he kept saying it, he'd one day believe it.

The main door to the suite swept open, and his father strode in. The high general looked tired as he crossed the room to join them. He bowed to Argent, then gave his report. "The escorts are making their preparations to depart. Some have already left."

The emperor had intended to leave as well, but after his injury, he would be in Esperance for as long as his recovery took.

Carver dreaded his father's departure. He hated to lose an ally.

"That's good," Argent said. "I feared some would resist leaving, after what happened."

"I think that fear was merited," Cregon said. "I can attest to the fear it places in a parent's heart to leave a child here."

"What have you overheard in your talks with the other escorts?" Argent asked. He clasped his hands behind his back as he spoke, looking effortlessly regal. He'd mastered the look by the time he was five years old.

"Most are concerned about the security of Esperance, but I heard no one outright disparage the empire." Cregon frowned. "I don't know all of them personally, but a few seemed nervous whenever I approached."

"You *are* the Bloody General," Carver said his father's well-known—and well-feared—moniker blithely.

His father rolled his eyes, but his tone was grim. "It makes it hard to know if my reputation is what intimidated them, or if they have something to hide."

"You'll have eyes on them after they go home," Argent said. "If they commit treason, we'll catch them."

"True enough. Until then, we must be patient, I suppose." He glanced at Carver. "High Cleric Zacharias and Chancellor Trevill know nothing of the Rising being present in Esperance. If you deem it necessary at any time to inform them, they could be allies."

It was Argent who spoke. "Until we're assured they're not involved in the rebellion, we can't risk showing our hand. Especially not before Jayveh's brothers are safe."

Cregon tipped his head, acknowledging this. Then he looked at both of them, his gaze serious. "Both of you must exercise extreme caution. Be slow to trust, and keep your eyes sharp. Until Jayveh is contacted and given orders, we have no idea what the Rising has planned." He focused on Carver. "Do not miss your check-ins with Ford. If I don't hear from you when expected, I can't guarantee your mother won't storm the temple to rescue you."

He could easily picture his mother doing just that.

Cregon set a hand on each of their shoulders, and in that moment it was clear that he wasn't speaking as High General of Craethen, and he wasn't viewing Argent as his prince or Carver as his general. Argent had spent every summer of his formative years in Westmont, training with Cregon. Argent was family in all ways that mattered.

"Protect each other," Cregon said, his voice uncharacteristiccally rough. He tightened his hold on their shoulders. "No matter what else happens here, I need you to promise me that you'll both come home."

Carver's throat tightened.

Argent was the one who managed to speak first. "We will."

Cregon's eyes slid to Carver.

"We'll come home," he promised.

It was also an echo of what he'd said before going to Harvari, and he knew his father noted that, because the skin around his eyes tensed.

They both knew all too well that, even if you came home from the war, you were never the same.

5

AMRYN

AMRYN SQUEEZED RIX TIGHTLY, her heart aching as he embraced her in return.

They stood in the center of a small sitting room in their shared suite. This had been their temporary apartment since arriving in Esperance, and though it was as foreign and impersonal as the rest of this temple, at least she'd had Rix.

Her maids had helped her change out of her wedding dress as soon as they'd retreated from the banquet hall. The white gown had been in rough shape after everything that had happened, so she now wore a dark green dress with light gold accents. Rose and Elsie had fussed over her, and Amryn had to fight back a sudden rush of tears. She didn't have many friends; as an empath, it wasn't safe for her to have confidantes. But Rose and Elsie had helped care for her since she was a little girl. Their compassion, worry, and kindness was familiar, their rolling Ferradin accents comforting. And she was about to lose them.

They'd been told that guards and servants would be assigned

to them during their stay in Esperance. It was supposed to keep them from possible biases, or prejudices. Keep them safer.

It would only further their isolation.

Rose and Elsie hadn't touched her hair. They didn't have the time, because they had to finish packing and remove all the trunks, because the emperor's edict was that, after the weddings, none of the escorts could stay overnight again in Esperance. They had to leave soon so they could make it to the nearest town before full dark.

So, Amryn's hair was still elaborately pinned, but that was the only physical reminder that she had not somehow imagined this horrible day.

She was married to Carver Vincetti. She was a newly recruited rebel with no idea of what the Rising would ask her to do here. And Rix was leaving.

"This is so much harder than I thought it would be," her uncle whispered.

Amryn closed her eyes, her head buried against his strong chest. Being held by him reminded her of all the times she'd curled up in his arms to escape the horrible nightmares that had plagued her for years. She wasn't a child anymore, but this nightmare she faced was real, and that made it all the more terrifying.

Rix's arms tightened around her. "Trust no one. Especially *him*."

No need to specify who he meant.

She swallowed hard. "I won't."

Her uncle pulled back, just enough to view her with a serious gaze. "Whatever mission the rebels assign you, your first goal is to protect yourself. Take no overt risks. Don't let anyone close."

She could feel his fear, and it melded with her own.

When Torin had received the emperor's letter that demanded the most noteworthy woman from his court be sent to Esperance as a bride, they all knew Amryn was the only choice. She had grown up in the castle, and she was Rix's niece—and he was Torin's chief advisor, and the king's best friend since childhood. Picking anyone else in Ferradin could be seen as non-compliance to the emperor, if Lorcan Vayne knew anything of their court.

And since he only allowed the kings and queens to rule their kingdoms as *he* saw fit, Lorcan Vayne knew everything about every court in the empire.

Despair, fear, anxiety—Amryn had felt all that and more. But she had never once thought of telling Torin no. The man was her uncle's best friend. To her, he had been another uncle and guardian. These two men had raised her when she had no one else. She would do anything for them.

When another letter had followed a couple of weeks later, offering an invitation to join the Rising . . . Amryn had easily agreed to that as well. This was an unprecedented chance to strike back at the empire that had stolen so much from so many. From her.

Rix worried about her being asked to do something violent, and in truth, Amryn had worried about that, too. But Torin had reasoned that the risks would be minimal. "She won't be alone," he'd said to Rix. Then to her: "You will have allies, even if they aren't known to you. And if Ferradin can play a part in tearing down the Craethen Empire . . ."

Rix had remained worried, even after she agreed. Amryn knew his complicated mix of emotions stemmed from the fact that Torin didn't know the full risk Amryn was taking.

Torin had helped raise her, but he didn't know she was an empath. That's how dangerous her secret was. When she'd first come to live with Rix all those years ago, he'd told her in soft whispers that she must never tell *anyone*. Not even Torin. The risk of betrayal was far too great—whether intentional or not.

They both knew only too well that betrayal could come from the most trustworthy of places.

So Torin didn't know that when he asked her to join the Rising and come to Esperance, she would be surrounded by clerics who would kill her in a heartbeat if they discovered she was an empath.

The fear she felt now, standing in this room with her uncle, was not all her own.

Knowing Rix needed reassurance, Amryn forced a small smile. "You've taught me well. I'll be fine."

Her uncle did not look convinced. "If your mother were still here . . . She would never forgive me for this."

"I agreed to do this," she reminded him gently. "It's a way to get justice for her. For all of us."

He nodded once, but his eyes remained tortured.

There was a light rap on the door, and Rix cleared his throat before calling, "Enter."

It was Rix's bodyguard, Bram. He was a burly man with graying temples, and he had been Rix's personal guard for years. "My lord, the horses are ready. We must leave now if we wish to reach the village by nightfall."

"I'll be down in a moment," Rix said.

Bram bobbed his head, shot Amryn a gentle, if slightly forced, smile, then retreated back into the corridor. Beyond him, Amryn could see a female cleric. The woman wore the traditional brown robes and her head was shaved. Amryn had never understood why clerics—both male and female—shaved their heads. It could make it hard to discern the gender of a cleric, but the woman had spoken to her earlier. She was waiting for Amryn to finish her goodbyes so she could escort Amryn to the rooms she would share with Carver.

Her stomach pitched at the thought.

In all of her preparations, she'd tried not to dwell on her inevitable wedding night, but that was like walking the edge of a cliff and trying to convince herself the drop didn't exist.

The last time she had seen Carver, he'd been splattered with blood. She didn't know what to expect from the emperor's favored general tonight, but anyone known as *the Butcher* wouldn't be kind or gentle. Oh, he'd been congenial enough at the wedding feast. But as soon as the attack came, he'd been brutally efficient. She wasn't sure which version of Carver to expect tonight, but once they were alone, his true colors would certainly emerge.

Rix must have caught her sudden turmoil, because concern pulled at his features. "Are you still feeling sick?"

She knew he was asking about the fight earlier; the violence had been overwhelming, and the effects had lingered long after she'd left the banquet hall. But that wasn't what caused her nausea now.

Before leaving Ferradin, Rix had—blushingly—told her what to expect on her wedding night. It had been uncomfortable for both of them, and she'd hurried to assure him that her maids had shared some things as well. If the situation hadn't been so terrifying, Rix's flood of relief that the excruciating conversation could end might have been amusing.

She smiled a little now. "I'm fine. Truly."

Rix didn't look like he fully believed her. He wasn't an empath—even though the ability ran through families, it was unpredictable. No, Rix just knew her well.

He pulled her into a last, hard embrace. "You are strong, and so incredibly brave," he whispered. "I'm in awe of you."

Emotion heated her veins, and her throat tightened. "This isn't goodbye."

"I know." He pulled back, and Amryn's heart hammered as she felt the waves of his rioting emotions crashing into her own. His focus was absolute as he met her gaze. "I love you."

Her heart squeezed. "I love you, too."

The words felt painfully final, but there was nothing else to say. Rix gave her a short nod and strode from the room.

The female cleric who had been waiting in the hall offered a tentative smile. "Are you ready to go to your new rooms?"

In no way was Amryn ready, but there was no point in lingering. She couldn't avoid her new husband forever—much as she wanted to.

She followed the woman into the corridor, and they made their way toward the large stone staircase that ascended to the next floor. They passed a few servants and several guards. Their presence made Amryn's skin tighten. "Are there usually so many guards?" she asked.

"Not usually, but the emperor insisted that the high cleric guard Esperance well while you're all here."

Considering what had happened at the wedding feast, it wasn't a bad idea. But an increase in guards could prove an obstacle if the rebels wanted Amryn to sneak around the temple. That was a worry for another day, though.

Her long green skirt trailed behind her on the steps as they climbed, and Amryn noted that they hadn't seen any of the other couples. When she asked if they'd all share the same wing, the cleric shook her bald head. "Not all of you, no. The high cleric thought it would be best to grant you some space and privacy, so you are spread over three wings. You'll be given a tour tomorrow."

Amryn nodded, but made no other response as they entered a long corridor and came to a stop before two large, intricately carved wooden doors. The cleric prodded them open. "Welcome to your room," she said, gesturing for Amryn to enter.

The suite was larger than the temporary rooms she and Rix had shared; the sitting room alone was quite grand. A brightly colored rug sectioned off the chairs and settees that created a visiting space. Threads of vivid red, green, yellow, and blue patterned the rug, and were repeated in the tapestries that hung on the wall. Vibrant potted flowers and dark green fronds were scattered around the room. Carved stone columns bracketed a balcony, but while the double doors stood open, there was a fine netting cast over the doorway—no doubt to keep the insects out. Perhaps it also deterred the monkeys she could hear, screeching and chattering nearby. Every lamp in the room was lit, and the windows and balcony revealed the jungle beyond, its emerald hue slowly being overtaken by the shadow of coming night.

Everything about this place—the décor, the smells, the sounds of the jungle, the heavy air that clung to her skin—it all screamed that she was far from home, and the homesickness hurt far more than she would ever admit.

"The bedroom is just down the hall," the cleric said from her place near the doors. "You'll find all of your belongings there, along with a washroom. If you're in need of anything at any time, simply pull the bell here, by the doors, and a servant will be alerted." Her eyes darted behind Amryn. "Ah! Your maid is ready to attend you."

Amryn turned and spotted a middle-aged woman emerge from the short hall. Her long black hair was bound in a tight braid that hung over one shoulder, and her skin was a rich brown. She wore a simple gray dress, and she had some lines around her eyes and mouth, but her gaze was friendly as she bobbed a curtsy. "Lady Vincetti, it's an honor to serve you. I'm Ahmi, and I'll be your maid during your stay at Esperance."

Amryn only managed a nod before the female cleric asked the maid, "Is General Vincetti here?"

"No," Ahmi said. "I believe he's still with the emperor and Prince Argent."

"Ah." The cleric clasped her hands in front of her. "Well, I'm sure he'll be along soon." She turned to Amryn. "The high cleric is holding a breakfast tomorrow for all of you at seven bells. Is there anything else you require before I leave?" When Amryn shook her head, the cleric beamed. "Very well. Have a pleasant night, Lady Vincetti."

Unlikely.

Her throat was dry as she watched the cleric leave, and then she faced Ahmi.

The maid's smile was soft. "I'm sure you must be exhausted after such a long day. I've prepared some tea that will help revive you a little, if you'd like."

"Thank you," she said, accepting the kindness. Maybe the hot tea would help settle her nerves, or bolster her. If nothing else, it would give her shaking hands something to hold.

She followed Ahmi back into the large bedroom, which was dominated by a wide four-poster bed. The quilt was done in shades of turquoise, gold, and cream, which matched the rug on the floor and the curtains that hung beside the darkening windows. Lamps glowed on the bedside tables as well as atop the long, dark wood dresser. Her trunks were stacked in a corner, next to unfamiliar trunks that must belong to Carver. In the opposite corner, a dressing table with a large mirror stood waiting for her, the cushioned chair pulled out and a variety of perfumes, brushes, and combs set out.

It was a beautiful room, but even though it held some of her things, it didn't feel like hers. She'd had to leave most of her belongings in Ferradin; clothes, keepsakes, books—her cello. None of it was practical for her time in Esperance, but she was wishing now that she'd found a way to bring more of home with her.

The tea tray waited on a low table. Ahmi deftly poured a cup and passed it over.

The next half hour was a blur. Amryn sipped her tea while Ahmi prepared her for the evening, and soon she was seated before the mirror with an empty cup and wearing a long white nightdress that was sheer beneath her blue silk wrapper. Her wrists, arms, neck, and legs had been carefully perfumed, and her lips had been painted a dark shade of red. Her riotous curls—made even more unruly by the jungle's humidity—flowed over her shoulders and back, loose and free from the pins that had constrained them all day.

"You are beautiful," Ahmi told her.

Amryn's cheeks burned as she eyed herself in the mirror. She remembered when Rose and Elsie had packed her trunk in Ferradin, and she'd glimpsed this nightgown. The sight of it then had made her eyes widen, but that moment was nothing compared to the panic she felt now while wearing it.

She'd never been intimate with a man. She'd never even been kissed by one. She'd never allowed anyone that close, because she had far too much to lose. Vulnerability flared in her chest, and she had to remind herself to breathe.

Ahmi took a step back. "I've unpacked most of your things, and I'll do the rest tomorrow. Is there anything else you require tonight?"

Amryn shook her head, and Ahmi quietly excused herself.

The moment the maid closed the bedroom door, Amryn stood, turning her back on the mirror.

She thought seriously of locking the bedroom door, but as tempting as that was, it wasn't an option. She doubted a simple lock would deter General Carver Vincetti. Besides, she couldn't afford to fall under his suspicion. That meant she couldn't withdraw, or let him believe she had anything to hide.

Her hands shook a little as she paced, her bare feet scuffing the carpet. Her heart hammered as she imagined that door opening to reveal Carver. What would his expression be as he took in the sight of her—in this nightdress? What would he say? Or would he say nothing, just press her down on the bed?

She could already feel the weight of him, crushing her. His hot breath against her skin. His hands on her body.

Her stomach churned.

She could hear every sound beyond the bedroom, so she knew the moment Ahmi left the apartment. Silence descended within the suite, but it only made the night cries of the jungle louder. She prayed Rix had made it safely to the nearby village; that nothing out there had eaten him.

Amryn finally tired of pacing and stood in the center of the floor, wondering if she should remain standing, or be on the bed when Carver arrived.

The lamps flickered and burned. Her heartbeat eventually evened out, though tension remained in her shoulders as time dragged on. An hour. Two.

Carver did not appear.

Exhaustion had made her sit on the edge of the bed, and—despite her fear and anxiety—her eyelids grew increasingly heavy. This day had been exhausting in every way possible, and she couldn't help but curl up at the end of the bed, her tired eyes on the door as she tried to stay awake.

She must not have succeeded, because when the bedroom door clicked, she jolted awake.

She scrambled to sit up, clutching a blanket to her chest as she watched the door ease open.

Carver stepped carefully inside, and his eyes darted instantly to the bed. When he met her gaze, he froze. "Apologies. I didn't mean to startle you."

His voice—though pitched low—sounded loud in the silence of the shadowed room. It raised every hair on Amryn's body, making her painfully aware of how isolated she was.

He was staring at her. Waiting for a response, she realized belatedly. "You didn't startle me," she said.

He arched a dark brow, but didn't comment on her obvious lie as he stepped fully into the room. "I just came to grab my things."

She blinked, her heart still pounding. "Your . . . things?"

He tipped his head. "I'll be sleeping in the sitting room."

"Oh." It was the only response she could manage as she watched him cross the room to his nearest trunk.

Clearly his things hadn't been fully unpacked yet, either. After some brief riffling, he withdrew a bundle of clothes before he shut the wooden lid and twisted back to her. "Goodnight."

"Goodnight," she echoed, stunned. Confusion and sheer relief battled for dominance inside her as Carver retreated without another word, and the door latched behind him. His footsteps carried him back down the hall and away from her.

Was it some kind of cruel trick? Would he be back in a moment? His emotions, strangely subdued, hadn't given her any clues. He was weary. Surprised to have awoken her . . . could he truly not mean to share her bed?

She waited with bated breath, but his footsteps never came back down the hall.

Slowly, she eased out of bed and padded softly to the door. After a slight hesitation, she twisted the lock, then returned to the bed.

She fell asleep almost instantly.

6

CARVER

CARVER STOOD IN FRONT OF THE balcony, the glow of morning light permeating the sitting room as he held his pose. He hadn't bothered to put on a shirt, as the warmth of the climate didn't necessitate it. With his arms outstretched, he focused on his posture and breathing. The motions of these stretches and accompanying meditation came to him without thought. His grandfather had taught him these exercises when he was just a boy. They were as much a part of him as his own skin.

These days, he actually felt more like himself during these exercises than he did *in* his own skin.

As he went through the motions and paused in the well-practiced stances, he tried to ignore the uncomfortable pull of old scars, and the newer wounds that now marred his body.

Instead of the calming silence he normally endeavored to achieve, he heard his grandfather's voice in his mind.

You won't hold a blade until you can hold these poses, boy. Anyone who wants to master a weapon must first master themselves. You cannot fight an enemy until you have fought off all the internal distractions. You cannot solve the discord outside yourself until you have silenced the war within.

Carver forced his shoulders to ease down, even as he kept his arms in position. He ignored the stiffness in his neck—that's what came from sleeping on a settee—and banished the strain building in his muscles as he held the pose.

Imagine yourself on a bridge, his grandfather had told him. *In any battle, in any of life's stresses, you must imagine you are standing on a bridge. Don't let panic override the truth—that you stand on firm ground. Let the fear, the doubt, all rush beneath you, like a river. There, then gone. Never touching you. Never throwing you off course.*

The image of Amryn sitting in the bed—*their* bed—with her flaming hair falling in riotous waves all over her shoulders as she clutched a blanket to her chest, slammed into his mind.

Saints, her hair was long when unpinned.

Of course, it was the fear in her eyes that had truly stuck with him.

He gritted his teeth and forced all thoughts of his new wife away.

All those distracting thoughts belong in the river. Let them wash away beneath you. Don't let them distract you. Don't give them the power to shake you.

Carver moved to the next pose; arms spread wide to either side, remaining level with his shoulders, as he sank into a crouch with one bare foot balanced forward, the other braced behind him. He could feel the spot near his left shoulder protest, and he knew the scar was stretching.

These poses had become even more important after Harvari. If he didn't do them, he ran the risk of his body locking up. He needed to keep loose, despite his injuries.

He needed to prove that his body wasn't as broken as the rest of him.

In the quiet of the morning, the chatter of monkeys was loud. The call of birds, the chirping of insects—all of the sounds reminded him of Harvari. The tents he'd slept in, the battles he'd fought. The people he hadn't been able to save.

You're standing on a bridge . . .

He heard movement in the bedroom, and his meager attention snapped. He didn't rise from his pose, but tension stiffened his spine.

Amryn was awake.

With strained ears, he tracked her as she slid from the bed and moved around the room. A closet door creaked open, then fell closed. A chair shifted over the floor.

By the time the bedroom door opened and her footsteps tread up the hall, Carver had grabbed his shirt and tugged it on.

She wore a blue robe, and her hair was an untamed mess that tumbled over her shoulders and back. She held the robe closed with both hands, and her pale green eyes were wary as they found him. She stopped just inside the sitting room, keeping a good twenty paces between them.

"Good morning," he said.

Her fingers tightened on her robe. "Good morning." Her eyes darted over the room. "I was wondering if my maid was out here."

"I think she's waiting for us to call for her." No maid would want to show up too early after a wedding night.

Amryn seemed to follow his thoughts, because her cheeks reddened. Her eyes caught on the settee closest to the balcony and the tangle of blankets there. She then looked to the double doors of their suite, and the connected bell.

She was acting so skittish, he expected her to dart to the bell like it was a lifeline, but she surprised him by squaring her shoulders and facing him. "Why did you sleep out here?"

Carver leaned back against the nearest stone column, his hands sinking into his pockets. "Did you want me to join you?"

Her cheeks flooded with color, but she didn't blink. "I expected you to."

She'd dodged the question, hadn't she? "I expected you to be asleep, since I was so late."

"And yet you woke me."

"I'm sorry for that." His chin lowered, his eyes fastened on hers. "I never planned on us sharing a bed last night."

His words clearly caught her off guard. She eyed him with a slight frown. "Is there some strange Westmont tradition I should be aware of?"

Once again, the corner of his mouth lifted. Her humor was unexpected. "Probably, but not in this case. I simply don't know you, and I'm not ready to sleep with you."

Amryn stared at him, her expression carefully neutral. Her unique green eyes were truly mesmerizing. They were the oddest eyes he'd ever seen. He wondered if—

"You're not what I expected," she said, breaking into his thoughts. The way her pink lips abruptly clamped made him think she hadn't meant to voice that particular thought.

Carver pushed off from the pillar and walked slowly forward. Amryn tensed, but didn't draw back from his approach.

Definitely not as skittish as she'd seemed yesterday.

He stopped a few paces away, granting her some space. He wasn't trying to frighten her, after all. Quite the opposite.

"There's something you need to know about me," he told

her, his voice low and steady. "I will never touch you against your will."

She stared at him, and he couldn't tell if she believed him.

It didn't matter if she was a rebel or not, he didn't like the thought that any woman would be afraid of him.

Besides, things would be easier if she could relax around him. She might let her defenses fall. So he smiled. "If I did, my mother would kill me."

The words surprised a short, somewhat hoarse laugh out of her. "She would?"

"My father would help her."

The corner of her mouth lifted, however slightly.

He pressed that advantage by taking a couple steps forward and extending a hand.

She eyed it, confused.

"Hello," he said. "I'm Carver." When she still hesitated, he ducked his head so they were eye-level, his hand still hanging between them. "Don't you think this will be easier if we attempt to get to know each other?"

Her brow furrowed, but she slipped her small hand into his broader one. Her palm was soft, but there were callouses on her fingertips. He wondered what had made them.

He squeezed her long fingers gently, pushing his curiosity aside for now. "This is the part where you tell me your name," he mock-whispered.

Her mouth twitched. "Amryn."

"It's a pleasure to meet you, Amryn."

Her eyes traced his face. "And you . . . Carver."

Hearing his name spoken in her low tone and the rolling Ferradin accent made something low in his abdomen clench. It was an unexpected physical reaction, and not altogether pleasant.

He could not afford to be thrown by her.

Amryn's maid prepared her with a speed Carver had never seen his sisters accomplish, and so it wasn't long before he and Amryn began their walk to the designated breakfast hall.

She wore an emerald green dress that made her fiery hair all the more vivid. Her curls had been wrestled into a thick braid that trailed down her back. Even though the dress was made of probably the most breathable fabric available in the cold climes of Ferradin, sweat was already beading along Amryn's brow, and her cheeks were flushed.

"Your body will adapt," he said.

She glanced over at him as they made their way down a wide stone staircase. "Excuse me?"

"To the climate. The humidity is brutal, but you will adapt over time."

Amryn snorted. "If I don't melt first."

He felt a smile tug into place. "I felt the same in Harvari. But you *will* get used to it."

"Forgive me if I don't believe you. Isn't Westmont unconscionably hot as well?"

"Compared to Ferradin, I suppose it might be considered that. I just think of it as the warmth of home."

"Ferradin can be warm," Amryn said, swiping a quick hand over her hairline. "*This* rivals the Scorched Plains."

He chuckled. "I suppose it's a matter of perspective."

They reached the base of the stairs and turned right, following the directions they'd been given. Other than a handful of guards and servants, they didn't see anyone else in the long corridor.

Wanting to keep her talking, Carver said, "I miss the ocean, and the sandy beaches of Westmont. What do you miss from home?"

"Everything," she whispered.

Her melancholy was like a barb against his skin, and he winced. A poor choice of topic on his part, when she was clearly homesick.

She peeked over at him. "I miss the mountains."

The admission was unexpected after her previous one-word response, but he grasped at it gratefully. "Westmont doesn't have many mountains, at least not near my home. I remember the first time I traveled with my father and we came across a true mountain range. I was terrified."

She shot him a look. "Why?"

"I thought it would fall on top of me and crush me flat." He shrugged. "I was only a child, so it seemed a valid fear at the time."

The ghost of a smile lifted her lips. "So mountains no longer scare you?"

"I didn't say that. Frankly, I always feel a little trapped whenever I find myself surrounded by them." Her smile was proof that she was relaxing around him, but that fact alone wasn't what kept him talking. He found he enjoyed talking with her—liked coaxing those rare smiles from her. "Mountains also steal the sunlight prematurely, and they block the view of the rest of the world. And have you ever *climbed* one?"

"Don't tell me that the emperor's favored general is afraid of heights," she said, one eyebrow raised.

He scoffed. "As if *I'm* the one with an issue if I have a rational fear of falling off a cliff and plunging to my death?"

"You know," she said a bit drolly, "I grew up playing on mountains."

"Then it's a blessing from the Divinities that you're still alive."

She rolled her eyes at that, but she wore an amused smile. "Has anyone ever told you that you're overly dramatic?"

"Yes. Just about *everyone*," he added, making his tone as dramatic as possible.

He didn't get a full laugh out of her, but she made a sound in her throat that could have been the beginnings of one.

Perhaps charming his wife wouldn't be as difficult as he'd feared.

He glanced over at her. "Why do you miss the mountains?"

His more serious tone chased away her smile, but she didn't miss a step as they neared the end of the corridor. "I feel lost without them," she said, and he was surprised by the honesty in her voice. "They've always surrounded me. Given me landmarks. When I'm surrounded by mountains, I feel . . . safe."

Something she clearly didn't feel here.

Not that he blamed her. Esperance had already been a place of death, and they'd only been married for a day.

She peeked over at him. "Why do you miss the ocean?"

He shrugged. "I hadn't really thought about it . . . but I suppose I miss everything about it. The sound of it, the smell of it—the way it goes on forever." The ocean comforted him. Reminded him of better days. Sometimes, in Harvari, he would close his eyes and try to picture it. The salty air, the spray hitting his face, the gritty sand clinging to his bare feet. The glitter of the water.

Sometimes, he could almost imagine the sweat and blood on his skin was water. Only water.

"You miss it because the ocean is home," she said quietly.

He glanced at her. "And that's why you miss the mountains."

Her steps slowed as they reached the breakfast room. Beyond the arched doorway, Carver could hear the hum of voices, and the scents of breakfast wafted into the hall. But he paused with Amryn, the two of them standing alone in the hall.

This moment felt weighted, and he wanted to say the right thing.

"My father described the mountains of Ferradin," he found himself sharing. "How snow can top the peaks even in summer, making them a vivid blue and white on top, but covered in trees and cliffs and wildflowers everywhere else. They sound breathtaking."

Amryn stared at him, and as her eyes slowly narrowed, he felt a sinking in his gut.

"Your father has only been to Ferradin once, I think," she said quietly. "To conquer it."

She stepped around him and entered the breakfast room, leaving him standing alone in the hall.

7

AMRYN

AMRYN TOOK A SEAT AT THE long table, her pulse skittering. All around her, couples laughed, talked, or had already begun eating. The brown-haired woman on her left barely looked at her, though a cool haughtiness came from her, barbed with jealousy. Amryn didn't know her name, and she didn't understand her jealousy—until it spiked when Carver settled on Amryn's other side.

Perhaps her jealousy came from not gaining *him* as her husband?

You can have him, she thought sourly.

Carver was handsome, it was true. And he was certainly high-ranking in the empire. But she wanted nothing to do with him.

He'd taken her by surprise at nearly every turn, and she was beginning to think that was deliberate on his part. It was almost as if he were trying to catch her off guard, just so he could pry into her mind and learn her secrets.

Despite the unexpected kindness he'd shown in not claiming what was his by law, she still didn't feel safe around him. Not when the only man in Esperance more loyal to the emperor was Prince Argent.

"Your father has only been to Ferradin once, I think. To conquer it."

She shouldn't have said that. Nothing about those words—or her pointed tone—could do anything but paint her in a negative light. Something she really shouldn't risk, considering all she was hiding.

Carver reached for the wooden bowl of figs in front of her, and his increased nearness made her skin prickle.

He didn't seem to notice her sudden stillness. He piled figs, cubed melon, fried eggs, ham, and some kind of brown, crusty bread onto his plate, and began to eat.

Amryn picked at a few items that seemed palatable, though once again she was reminded that the food here was wholly different from that found in Ferradin.

A bitter-smelling drink was poured for her by a servant, and she wrinkled her nose. It was thicker and darker than tea, and steam rose from the cup. Considering how overheated she already was, she had no desire to try it.

Carver leaned in, his voice low. "It's coffee. It's made from beans. We have it in Westmont as well."

"I'm not thirsty." But she did eye the pitcher of juice across the table. It was just a bit too far for her to politely reach.

"It's delicious," Carver assured her. "Probably an acquired taste, though." He lifted his own cup and took a sip. He cracked a smile when he saw she was watching, and she hated that heat touched her cheeks.

His words, combined with that half-smile, was like a challenge. After stumbling so much around him, she wasn't willing to back down now.

She lifted the cup, blew on it gently, then sipped cautiously.

The brew burned her tongue, but it was the taste that had her fighting a gag. She set it aside. "I suppose my palette is a little more discerning than yours."

"You can add milk to it," Carver said.

"I can also *not* drink it."

He huffed a short laugh. "True." He surprised her once more by reaching for the pitcher of juice that she'd been eyeing, and pouring her a glass.

"Thank you," she said, a bit grudgingly.

This time when he flashed a smile, she saw a dimple appear. "You're welcome."

The light from the windows along the back wall caught in his dark hair, which had fallen over his tanned brow. She didn't realize she was staring until movement from the arched doorway snagged her attention.

Tam and Rivard walked into the breakfast room. Rivard's walk was oddly stiff, and Tam's head was down. With all the people in the room, it was hard to pick up on Tam's emotions, but it helped that Amryn had felt her yesterday, during the fight.

Today, she radiated sadness, tinged with hopelessness. And there was a distinct edge of disdain as she glanced toward her new husband.

As the two settled in their seats across the table, Amryn caught Tam rubbing her wrist, as if it hurt her.

Beside Amryn, Carver stiffened, and she noted his cold stare fixed on Rivard. His flash of hatred was potent, reminding her of their brief encounter after the fight yesterday. Clearly, there was history between them—and not a good one.

A door on the other end of the room opened, and the high

cleric strode in. "Good morning," he called out, his robe rippling as he walked at a purposeful clip. His bald head seemed to make the wrinkles on his face all the more prominent as he studied them. "I see we're missing some of our number. The Divinities do not appreciate tardiness. We will need to work on your punctuality while you're here."

"Clearly *our* punctuality isn't in question," the woman beside Amryn muttered. The pitch of her voice was loud enough that the entire room must have heard.

Her new husband snorted in amusement.

The high cleric stopped at the head of the table, where there were four empty chairs. "I don't intend to fall behind in our schedule just because others are late. So, I shall begin by sharing that the emperor is resting well and healing quickly, despite the egregious attack yesterday."

Amryn glanced across the table, to where Cora sat. The girl's eyes were rimmed red from recent tears, and the cut of pain she still felt from her brother's brutal execution was acute.

"Now, we have a full day ahead of us," High Cleric Zacharias continued. "As you are all aware, your time spent in Esperance will be filled with many important tasks, and I have no intention of letting your duties go undone, no matter the distractions that married life can supply." His gaze grew pointed on the open doorway, and Amryn twisted in her chair along with everyone else to see Prince Argent and Jayveh enter, arm-in-arm. Both were beaming, and the adoration, love, and excitement sparking between them was potent enough that it tore through every other emotion in the room.

Including the high cleric's thread of annoyance.

Argent finally glanced away from his wife to scan the room, and his grin widened. "Apologies for being late," he said. "I'm afraid my wife and I became . . . distracted."

Jayveh's dark cheeks colored, but her smile broadened.

The high cleric cleared his throat. "I don't mean to censure you, Prince Argent, but I'm afraid your duties in Esperance cannot be superseded by anything else. All of you have an obligation to—"

"Be married and make peace?" a new voice interrupted.

Amryn looked once more to the open doorway and spotted a man she'd glimpsed yesterday standing near the emperor. He looked to be in his mid-thirties, and his smile reminded her of Uncle Rix. He strode forward with confidence, walking behind Argent and Jayveh as they all approached the head of the table.

The man continued to talk as he walked, his gaze fixed on the high cleric. "Really, Zacharias, wasn't the emperor's goal to see these marriages succeed? I believe the prince and princess were simply following orders."

The high cleric visibly bristled. "Chancellor Trevill. There's no need to twist my words."

Trevill cracked a smile. "What else are politicians good for?"

High Cleric Zacharias did not look amused by the quip.

Trevill didn't seem to notice, or care. He took a slight step back, allowing Argent access to the seat at the head of the table.

The prince lifted a declining hand. "No need, I'll sit beside my wife."

That sparked some whispers, from servants and newlyweds alike, but Argent and Jayveh didn't seem to hear.

Once they were settled at the table, the high cleric took the seat at the head, leaving Trevill to sit on his other side.

The high cleric cleared his throat. "Well, now that we're all here, I would like to properly introduce myself. I am Zacharias,

High Cleric in the Church of the Divinities, and the Caretaker of Esperance. I have been charged by the emperor to oversee this next year, and I take that responsibility seriously. The emperor has given me the authority to act in his name. That means, regardless of the titles you hold outside these walls, you will defer to me. In Esperance, my word is law." He looked far too delighted at the prospect, though his features were carefully neutral as he turned to the chancellor on his left. "Trevill, would you like to introduce yourself?"

"Of course. Thank you, Zacharias." The high cleric's mouth tightened at the informality, even though he'd treated Trevill the same. But the chancellor didn't seem to notice as he took a turn surveying the table. "I'm Chancellor Trevill. The emperor has tasked me with overseeing the new ruling council, of which you are now all a part. I will carry no vote, but I will be your mediator and advisor. This is a new political structure, and it will require all of us to work together. During our sessions, I ask that you be unafraid to speak your mind, but always treat other views with respect."

"When you are not fulfilling your new council duties," the high cleric said, "you will be participating in other ventures. A weekly schedule will be given to you, because we do not want to squander the time we have. You can expect to participate in a variety of exercises that will help you bond as couples and friends, and you will also have lessons that will broaden your minds. Additionally, you will have ample time for prayer and self-reflection to feed your souls. If you have any concerns or difficulties during our time here, you may come meet with me, and I shall be happy to offer counsel."

He slowly scanned the table, looking at each of them in turn. "Esperance is an ancient word that means *hope*. This is fitting, as you are our hope for a brighter future. People journey from all across the empire to be here. To bask in the light and hope of the Divinities. Esperance is a place of healing, and that is what we will do together. *Heal.* Your individual souls, your new marriages, and the empire as a whole."

Amryn's heart pounded as the cleric's focus landed on her, and a shiver tracked down her spine.

"There will be no secrets between us," Zacharias said. "Before this year is out, I will know everything about you."

Amryn wasn't sure if he meant the words as a threat, but that's exactly how it felt.

After breakfast, they were all led on a tour of Esperance, starting with the main temple they would be living in for the next year.

The couples walked in pairs, so Amryn followed Carver as he shifted into a position directly behind the empirical heir. Even without a weapon on his belt, Carver's stance was protective as they followed the prince and his new princess.

The sprawling temple had several floors and multiple wings and towers. They didn't see every part of the main building, but they were briefly shown a vast library, an art gallery, and a museum. In one of the narrower corridors, Amryn's arm brushed Carver's as they walked. The brief contact shot awareness through her whole body. She was quick to shift away, and her darting eyes noticed Carver's hand roll into a fist, though he didn't spare her a glance.

She made a concerted effort for the rest of the tour to avoid any more accidental touches.

In addition to everything they'd seen so far, the temple

also contained offices for the high-ranking clerics, at least a hundred guest suites, and a few dining rooms in various sizes. There were also breakfast rooms, study and meditation rooms, and several sitting rooms. There was a great hall, that had once been a throne room, but now stood empty. And there was a large ballroom that was quite musty from being closed up. The unused rooms felt strangely haunted, and were stark reminders that Esperance, too, had been conquered by the empire. Amryn was glad to leave them behind.

Outside the main temple, the walled compound of Esperance held smaller chapels, as well as quarters for the clerics, guards, and outdoor servants. Amryn knew from what Torin and Rix had told her that servants of the church weren't paid in gold, but in lodging, food, and blessings from the Divinities.

Despite many of the beautiful things in Esperance, Amryn couldn't shake her unease. She found herself rubbing her mother's old prayer coin in her pocket, as if that could ward off the eeriness. The clerics and servants were all polite, but the feeling of being trapped was overwhelming. She also felt extremely isolated, even though she was surrounded by people. She assumed a lot of her unease came from the almost threatening air the high cleric gave off.

The group took their time walking to each new site their guide directed them toward, and Amryn stayed silent as they were shown the features of the vast yard.

There were storage buildings that housed food and supplies, and there were many small huts tucked around the expansive yard of the compound. The huts were all abandoned.

"Many retired soldiers stay here," the male cleric explained. "They come to escape the world and heal from the unseen horrors of war."

Carver, who had remained close to Amryn, tensed a little.

"How awful," one of the new brides whispered. Amryn only caught the words because the woman stood directly behind her. She'd learned during breakfast that the woman's name was Sadia.

Their guide gestured to the nearest outer wall of the compound. "There are even huts beyond Esperance's walls, for those poor souls who truly seek solitude. Of course, they were all emptied for the coming year."

Just ahead of her, Amryn saw Princess Jayveh tighten her hold on Prince Argent's arm, and she felt a wave of the princess's concern. "Where were they sent?"

Their guide was quick to answer. "Those who could be convinced to go home, did so, while some elected to go to a clinic in the capital. Others chose to make their own way back into the world. Some even became servants here."

"Wait," the brown-haired, jealous woman from breakfast—Amryn had overheard her name was Marriset—interrupted, not even trying to check her tone. "There are troubled soldiers here? Walking among us as *servants?*"

"I assure you, only those considered stable were granted such a request," their guide said hurriedly. "They have sworn oaths to never again take up weapons, and their only wish is to serve the Divinities. You are quite safe. Now, on the other side of this garden, there's a training yard that the soldiers used to practice and exercise . . ."

As they changed their course, Amryn peeked at Carver. His tension hadn't ebbed, and considering Marriset's comments, that wasn't really a surprise. But what *did* surprise Amryn was the lack of any strong emotions from him. All she felt was muted calm.

Rix sometimes attempted a forced calm around her, but even at his best, he never managed the level of control Carver was exhibiting. She wondered how he managed it.

Or perhaps she just wasn't attuned to Carver yet, and all the other emotions around her were marring her ability to read him correctly.

The gardens at Esperance were impressive. Some were painstakingly cultivated, while other sections ran wild; like a piece of the jungle itself had been brought into the compound. Monkeys scrambled in the trees above them, chattering away as the group moved from flower gardens to herb gardens, then to fields and orchards growing a variety of foods Amryn didn't recognize. She supposed it made sense that the temple was self-sufficient. How else would they have survived for a year without supplies from the outside world?

They ended their tour at a large stone gazebo located in one of the flower gardens, where they were served a cool, fruity drink. While most of the couples broke into groups to talk, Amryn quietly sipped from her cup. Even though the juice didn't drive away the sweltering heat, or dry the sweat dripping down her spine, it at least made her feel a little better.

A bird shrieked above them and Amryn startled, clutching her glass in a vicelike grip.

"Afraid of the birds?" Carver asked from beside her.

She pinned him a look. "No."

His aquamarine eyes held a hint of amusement. "Liar."

She couldn't really deny it when another bird screeched and she winced.

"It's all right," he told her. "They're harmless. Just loud."

"The whole jungle is loud. I'm never sure which creature is going to call out an attack next."

"Actually, it's the silent predators that are the most dangerous."

She snorted. "Thank you for that reassuring thought."

"Any time." His eyes narrowed a little, then traced over her face. "You look a little flushed. Are you all right?"

The heat in her cheeks mounted under his stare. "Forgive me, but I'm not used to being baked alive."

His dimple flashed as he quirked a smile. "Living on the Scorched Plains *can* be difficult."

The reminder of her earlier quip was unexpected. She wasn't sure if it was a peace offering of sorts, or another attempt to throw her off-balance.

She didn't have a chance to respond, because Prince Argent and Princess Jayveh stepped up to join them. "Ah, the Scorched Plains," Argent said to Carver. "Your eternal resting place."

Carver turned to the prince, his voice even as he said, "I wouldn't want you to get lonely down there."

Amryn's breath caught at the inherent insult. Her attention snapped to Prince Argent, but he only threw back his head and laughed.

Carver flashed a smile.

The empirical princess shook her head, though amusement sparked in her eyes as she turned to Amryn. "It's a pleasure to meet you, Amryn. I'm Jayveh."

Feeling somewhat off-balance, Amryn gave a belated curtsy. "The pleasure is mine, Princess."

"Oh, please, there's no need for such formalities."

"Agreed," Argent said, wrapping one arm around Jayveh's waist. His smile was full as he met Amryn's stare. "You must call me Argent."

She didn't think she'd ever be able to do that. Her heart raced in her chest and her palms were slick. This was Prince Argent Vayne. The only person in the empire more powerful than him was his grandfather.

And Carver had insulted him. And Argent had laughed.

She'd known they were friends, but she never would have believed that she'd see the Heir of the Craethen Empire and the Butcher tease each other. She didn't think men like that were *capable* of it.

"He means it," Carver said from beside her, his tone gentle.

She glanced at her new husband. A man of many contradictions, she was coming to find; he had sensed her unease, and he was attempting to quell it.

"I really do," Argent said. Then he held out a hand, and Amryn had no choice but to take it. He lifted her hand and brushed his lips against her knuckles. "It's wonderful to meet you, Amryn."

Sincerity poured from him, with only a shadow of concern. Or was it doubt?

She withdrew her hand the moment it was polite to do so.

Jayveh's gaze was warm as she addressed Amryn. "I have to admit, I have many questions about Ferradin. My mother used to read me stories about fairies and enchanted lochs. It always sounded so otherworldly."

"Xerra feels much the same to me," Amryn confessed.

"The jungles of southern Xerra are especially overwhelming," Jayveh said. "I grew up on the northern plains, and even I can feel the difference in climate." She eyed some of the flyaway hairs that had curled free of Amryn's braid. "I'd be happy to share a smoothing tincture for your hair, if you'd like. It works wonders for me."

"I would appreciate that," she told her honestly.

She noticed the men had gone silent as she and Jayveh talked. Argent watched them with a small, contented smile on his face.

Carver simply watched.

"It's no trouble," Jayveh said, her genuine kindness threading the air. "I'll have something delivered to your maid tonight."

"Thank you."

"Attention, please," their guide called out. "If you are all properly refreshed, it is time to move on to the next item on the high cleric's agenda. Gentlemen, you will accompany me to the training grounds, which have been readied for some friendly sport. Ladies, you will follow Cleric Hashi to a tearoom in the temple, where you can get to know each other better."

"Will you walk with me, Amryn?" Jayveh asked.

"Of course." There was no other polite answer. Besides, regardless of what mission the Rising assigned her, they would want her to take advantage of getting close to the future empress.

"I can escort you back to the temple," Argent offered.

"No." Jayveh patted his arm. "You need to follow instructions, Your Highness."

"He's never excelled at that," Carver said blithely.

Argent kicked his boot, though not with actual force.

Jayveh slipped out from her husband's arm and handed over her glass.

The prince took it without hesitation and gestured for two bodyguards to come forward.

Jayveh loosed a sigh. "You're a little overprotective, you know."

"I know. But you're deserving of every protection." He leaned in and set a quick kiss on her cheek.

From the corner of her eye, Amryn caught Carver angling toward her. Her stomach plunged and she twisted away, only

to freeze when she realized he wasn't leaning in for a kiss—
he was extending a hand to take her glass.

Face flaming, she passed it to him. "Thank you."

He dipped his chin, his eyes fastened on her as if he worried about her sanity. "You're welcome."

Her face was still burning as she turned to follow Jayveh
and the other women away from the stone gazebo.

She felt Carver's eyes on her long after they left the garden behind.

8

CARVER

"WHAT DID YOU DO TO YOUR WIFE?" Argent asked, his voice pitched low as they trailed behind the other men toward the training grounds.

"What do you mean?" Carver asked.

Argent's stare was pointed. "She flinched away from you, Carve."

So he hadn't been the only one to notice. He sighed. "I haven't hurt her."

"Of course not," Argent said at once. "But is she really so nervous around you?"

"Apparently." He scrubbed the back of his neck and lowered his voice even further. "I've tried to put her at ease. I gave her the bedroom."

"You . . . gave her the bedroom?"

"I don't know her—I'm not going to sleep beside her. Or *with* her," he added pointedly, since Argent's mouth had opened. "She isn't ready for that, and neither am I. Besides, I need to be able to sneak out to Ford."

They'd fallen behind the others, and though Argent's body-guards hovered nearby, Argent and Carver were effectively alone.

The prince took a moment to consider Carver's words. He didn't argue, but he did say, "I like her. She's quiet, but she seems kind. She could be good for you, if you'll give this a real chance."

Carver wasn't sure what to say to that. Because, despite everything, he thought he might like Amryn, too.

And that was dangerous, if she was indeed a traitor.

Argent may have followed his thoughts, because he suddenly lightened his tone. "I know why you're looking a little frustrated. It's because your charm isn't working like it usually does. Amryn Lukis is going to make you actually put forth an effort."

Carver rolled his eyes and changed the subject. "You shouldn't have given up your place at the head of the table this morning. Some could interpret that as a weakness, or you deferring to the high cleric."

"I *am* supposed to defer to him. So are you."

It was really the only way to make sure things in Esperance ran smoothly. The Empire's Chosen were made up of princes, princesses, and other important nobles. Not to mention Carver was a decorated general, and Argent was the future emperor. But they could only have one leader here, and Emperor Lorcan had chosen High Cleric Zacharias. The general in Carver understood that; in a battle, the line of command had to be clear. But the strategist in him understood the importance of Argent keeping at least some of his power.

"You could have kept your rightful seat and brought Jay-veh with you."

"I don't think High Cleric Zacharias would have appreciated

me telling him to scoot down a chair." Argent glanced at Carver. "Besides, my move was calculated."

"It was?"

He nodded. "First, I wanted to see who would try to take the head seat—Trevill, or Zacharias. It wasn't really a surprise that the high cleric took it, but it tells us something about him."

Carver scoffed. "The man's speech told us all about him."

Argent chuckled. "Yes, he's a bit more pompous than I expected. But that wasn't the only thing I was trying to do."

"Do tell."

"Well, I needed to make sure any rebels in the room are convinced I'm enamored with Jayveh—to a foolish degree."

"Your plan is to play the fool?"

He almost looked offended. "I'm quite capable of playing a fool."

"I know. I've seen it. But it's always been unintentional on your part."

Argent's eyes narrowed. "I could have you hanged, you know."

"So you've been saying all our lives."

The prince rolled his eyes. "If I'm wholly besotted with my wife, people will underestimate me. They may get reckless and show their hands prematurely. And it will keep Jayveh safer, because any watching rebels will think she's thoroughly seduced me." He lifted a finger, stalling Carver's response. "Which, admittedly, she has. But I can do my part to make it obvious so our enemies might lower their guard. And besides, you have to admit, by allowing Zacharias to take my seat this morning, I may have emboldened others to attempt to undermine me."

Carver frowned. "That's not a good thing, Argent."

"Isn't it? Don't we want to identify those who might try to bring down the empire?"

"You shouldn't be playing any games. It's too much of a risk."

"So you just expect me to sit back and watch you, Jayveh, and Rivard do everything to flush out the traitors?"

"Yes. Exactly that."

He muttered something under his breath. It didn't sound complimentary.

Carver sighed. "You can't play the spy, Argent. You're a terrible liar."

"Some would consider that a *good* trait."

"Not for a spy." Carver glanced over at him. "I appreciate your desire to help. Really. But we've been over this; your job is to keep yourself safe. Leave the rebels to me."

"You realize there's an argument to be made that the rebels are more my problem than yours, right?" But he let out a sigh, and Carver knew he'd won the argument. For now, at least.

They reached the training yard. The cleric had walked the other men over to a rack of mock weapons. Even though they weren't real, Carver's palm still itched to hold them.

"For those who do not wish to duel," the cleric was saying, "you are more than welcome to simply observe. You will have the use of the yard for the rest of the afternoon."

Carver wanted to move for the stand of weapons immediately, but he forced himself to hang back and observe the other men.

Argent was the first to move to the stand, and as he picked through the faux blades, Darrin was quick to join him.

Carver had never met him before coming to Esperance. Darrin hadn't come to train in Westmont because he'd apparently suffered from many illnesses as a child, which kept him home. He was a high-ranking nobleman in the kingdom of Vadir. He was a top suspect in Carver's mind, purely because he had several family members who had openly professed anti-empirical sentiments. At the moment, the dark-haired man looked especially eager to make inroads with Argent—which only increased Carver's suspicions.

The next person to make a move was Ivan. He took a place at Argent's other side carefully, making an effort not to move his left arm. Carver knew he'd been injured in the attack yesterday. With cool blue eyes, Ivan surveyed the spread of weapons, but he didn't touch anything. His blond hair brushed high cheekbones, making him look even more severe. He was from Sibet, where the winters were harsh and the people harsher. He was not the heir to his father's throne—he was the second son. He'd also never come to Westmont to train, but his reason had been distance related; Sibet and Westmont were on opposite ends of the empire. Some believed that distance created a disconnect from the rest of the empire, and there might be truth to that. Carver would need to make a point to get closer to Ivan.

Samuel hung back. He didn't look altogether excited to be in the training yard, but Carver knew that was because Samuel was a scholarly prince. Wendahl was known for its universities and healers, but even so, Samuel's father had sent him to Westmont for one summer. Carver had crossed paths with him, but Samuel was younger by nearly six years, and that had kept them from forming any real bond.

That left Rivard.

The high-born noble of Daersen stood apart, but it really wasn't a surprise to see him darting a look at Carver. The last time they'd seen each other outside of Esperance, Rivard's face had been covered with blood.

The same blood that had coated Carver's fists.

Rivard was tall and thin, but surprisingly adept with a blade. His black hair was longer now, nearly brushing his shoulders. He came from a family of devout worshipers who had held various positions within the church and in the Daersen government. His family had demonstrated unfailing loyalty to the Craethen Empire from the beginning, which was why the emperor trusted Rivard. While Carver agreed that Rivard was loyal to the empire, trusting him implicitly wasn't a mistake he would ever make again.

Rivard's green eyes landed on Carver's, and then he was walking forward. "Carver," he said, once he was close.

Just hearing his voice made the latent rage in Carver's gut swirl. It took every bit of his self-control to keep his emotions in check. *It's just water flowing under a bridge.* "Rivard." His voice was flat, but that was the best he could manage.

Rivard's expression was neutral. "I was hoping we could speak. Perhaps later, after—"

"I don't think there's any need for that."

"I disagree. I think we should clear the air."

"I'm not interested in anything you have to say."

Rivard's forehead creased. "You're being petty."

Carver took a step forward, sinking as much menace as he could into his stance. "Do you want me to break your nose again?"

Rivard didn't cower. He only jutted out his chin, his gaze narrowed. "I thought war changed men, but you're exactly the same."

A hollow smile curved his mouth, revealing an edge of

threat. "You have no idea how much I've changed."

"Carve!" Argent called, swinging the wooden blade he'd selected. "Come pick a sword so we can spar! It's about time we had another bout."

Without a word, Carver pivoted on his heel and strode away from Rivard. Argent's gaze spoke volumes, but he didn't say anything as Carver moved for the stand of weapons.

Ivan, Darrin, and Samuel had all selected blades. While Ivan and Darrin paired off for a match, Samuel asked Rivard if he wanted to join him.

"Of course," Rivard accepted, his smooth voice only a little tense as he moved toward the stand.

Unwilling to remain near Rivard a second longer than necessary, Carver snatched the closest wooden sword. The blade was weighted with lead, which gave it a comfortable heft. He still missed his own blade, though.

He walked with Argent to a corner of the yard and they took up positions across from each other on the hard-packed dirt. After the customary bow, they began circling. The familiarity of dueling each other was comforting, and Carver could feel his muscles relaxing. He hadn't expected Esperance would have a training yard, but he would now make an effort to come daily.

It would help keep him sane.

Argent struck first, as he usually did, and the crack of their wooden blades split the air. They dealt rapid blows, parrying and twisting to get a better hit. They fell into their old patterns, moving fast and fierce. Though Carver was focused on the mock fight, he was aware of the other fights in progress.

Ivan and Darrin were going at each other with increasing intensity. Rivard had already won against Samuel, but they were squaring off once more. The clerics and guards simply watched.

Argent grunted as he dodged Carver's latest strike. "You've been practicing."

"No. I'm just better than you."

His friend chuckled, even as he swung—Carver jumped back.

Several blows later, Carver had the tip of his blade at Argent's throat.

The prince was breathing hard and sweat coated his brow, but he surrendered with a smile. "I'll let you have this victory."

Carver snorted, going for an unaffected air even though his spine dripped sweat. "I'll let you think you *allowed* me that victory."

Samuel stepped forward. "You're both incredibly skilled," he said. "I wouldn't mind a lesson or two."

Argent nodded to Carver. "He'd be the better teacher."

Rivard rolled his wrist, letting his practice blade swing as he stared at Carver. "Care to spar?"

Carver's grip on the hilt flexed.

Argent spoke before he could. "Perhaps you and I should spar instead, Rivard. Carver and Samuel could—"

"Yes," Carver said, his gaze firmly on Rivard.

Argent muttered a curse, but Carver ignored him as he shifted to face Rivard. His gaze was sharp, and he didn't blink as they dipped into abbreviated bows.

Carver could hear his father's voice in his head, telling him of the stupidity of this, but he ignored the warning as he attacked.

Rivard met him without hesitation, striking back with more force than Carver had expected. He'd been practicing. But then, Carver had, too. He'd fought for his life on a battlefield more times than he could count.

Rivard hadn't.

The fight was brutal. The leaden sword clipped Carver's arm more than once, which would surely leave deep bruises, but he didn't slow. He beat Rivard further and further back, until they left the dirt yard and nearly spun into a group of watching clerics.

Argent yelled something, but Carver's attention was fully on Rivard.

They exchanged a few more blows, then Rivard surprised him with a hit to his jaw.

Carver's head snapped back, his face sparking with pain. His grip on his sword clenched.

Mere seconds later, he shoved Rivard to the ground.

Rivard fell hard in an ungraceful sprawl and his sword bounced away. Carver set his mock blade against Rivard's heaving chest and leaned down.

Rivard flinched as the blunt tip dug into his chest.

Carver enjoyed seeing that spark of pain too much. He kept his voice low as his eyes bored into Rivard's. "It would be wise of you to stay away from me."

The other man's face turned red. "You act as if I'm the only one who made mistakes. I'm not the only one to blame for what—"

"Don't," Carver warned, increasing the pressure of the blade against Rivard's chest.

He hissed in pain. "Let me up."

Carver didn't move.

Rivard's glare sharpened. "Let. Me. *Up.*"

Argent's hand was suddenly on Carver's shoulder. "Stop

this," he ordered quietly. "You're making a scene."

Carver knew Argent was right—he could feel everyone watching him—but his muscles jerked with the effort to draw back his sword. Taking that first step back was even harder, but he managed.

Rivard pushed to his feet, the heel of one hand scrubbing over his chest. "It's been years. Will you never let this go?"

Carver's skin heated. "You destroyed my family."

"And I said I was sorry," Rivard snapped. "What else do you want?"

Carver just turned and walked away.

"He lied to you, Carver."

Carver paused, a deep roar building in his ears.

Rivard knew he had Carver's attention, even if he hadn't turned around. His words seemed to come easier now. "Everything you think you know? It's not the full truth. Berron lied to you. And you never questioned—"

Carver twisted and smashed his fist into Rivard's face. Pain burst over his knuckles, but watching Rivard's head snap back, his eyes wide with shock, was every bit as rewarding as he'd thought it would be.

But as Rivard clutched his blood-spurting nose and staggered back, Carver saw their audience had grown by one member.

High Cleric Zacharias did *not* look pleased.

9

AMRYN

AMRYN CAREFULLY POURED steaming tea into the white porcelain cup, taking her time with every motion. When she finished, she would be expected to join the circle of conversation on the other side of the sitting room.

The female cleric told them this tearoom had been designated for the ladies to use at any time during their stay, and that they'd be passing the afternoon here. The space was large, with wide windows set in the back wall that revealed the dark emerald jungle and the distant, craggy mountains. The room was decorated predominantly in cobalt and gold, set against the by-now-familiar light stone walls. A large tapestry on one wall depicted the Tree of the Living Eternity, which the Divinities watched over. It was undoubtedly a priceless masterpiece, but even the cleric hadn't spared it a second glance before ducking out.

Amryn hoped the high cleric's schedule would eventually ease into something less regimented; she didn't know if she could stand a full year without a free moment to breathe.

From across the room, Marriset's laugh rang out as she talked with Sadia. Jayveh had chatted pleasantly with Amryn as they'd walked back to the temple, but as soon as they'd entered the sitting room, she'd moved to Cora's side. The young woman had been exceptionally quiet this morning. She was probably still in shock and mourning her brother's death.

Tam stood near Amryn, also preparing her cup of tea. The tittering laughter behind them only served as a harsh background to the deep sadness and low anger that vibrated from Tam.

Amryn recalled the way she'd rubbed her wrist at breakfast, and Rivard's heavy-handedness after the attack yesterday. Clearing her throat, she asked quietly, "Your name is Tam, isn't it?"

The woman peeked over at her, her hair dark as night and her eyes looking a little lost. "Yes. And you are . . .?"

"Amryn."

"Ah. That's right." Tam's dusky cheeks pinkened slightly. "Forgive me, I'm not very good at remembering names."

"Well, we haven't been formally introduced."

"You saved my life yesterday," Tam said. "Somehow, that makes it feel like an introduction isn't really necessary."

"Don't forget, you helped save me, too." Amryn lifted a small spoon and stirred in some sugar, the light tinkling of the metal hitting glass sounding strangely loud. "How are you settling in?"

Tam didn't look up as she stirred her own cup, but her misery swelled. "Fine. And you?"

"Fine."

They stood beside each other in silence, the hum of conversation behind them.

"My mother is very ill," Tam said suddenly, her voice low.

Amryn shot her a glance, her fingers tightening on the spoon as she felt the sharp stab of the woman's grief. "I'm so sorry."

Her lips pursed. "So am I." She finally met Amryn's gaze, and the sheen of tears in her eyes was unmistakable. "She won't survive the year. I won't be with her in her final days. I won't even know when she dies, because we can't receive messages. I won't attend her funeral." Her chest lifted sharply as she sucked in a breath and blinked quickly. "Apologies."

"You don't need to apologize." Amryn's heart ached for her. "I'm truly sorry."

"Why should you be sorry? You're not the one who banished me here. My father . . ." Resentment spiked. She looked away and dropped her spoon on the tray with a dull clatter. Amryn could feel the girl's emotions being clamped down and wrestled into submission. When she looked at Amryn again, there was only a low throb of fury and grief now. "What's done is done. I suppose nothing else matters but serving the empire."

Amryn had no idea how to respond, so it was just as well that Marriset, the jealous woman from breakfast, appeared at Amryn's other side.

"What are we gossiping about over here?" she asked, eagerness sparking. Her emotions were edged with jealousy and envy, which dulled her physical beauty somewhat—though she was undeniably beautiful. She had olive skin, chestnut brown hair, and perfectly sculpted features. She stood with confidence, and she carried herself with a superior air that Amryn instantly disliked.

Marriset viewed her with a small smile, and Amryn didn't need to be an empath to feel the barb in her expression. "It's

Amryn, isn't it?" she asked, not waiting for a response to her first question.

"Yes," Amryn said.

Marriset gave a little nod and lifted a small plate and placed two finger sandwiches on it, along with some figs. She popped one into her mouth and chewed. "Does anyone else's skin crawl whenever those clerics talk, or is it just me? I swear by the Divinities, they're going to drive me insane. They act so superior, but they're the ones with shaved heads, dull brown robes, and no individuality." She shook her head. "I'm certain they made the tour as confusing as possible, just so we'd all feel lost. They kept winding around a hundred different corridors!" She lifted one of her sandwiches and took a nibbling bite, which she quickly swallowed. "And why did the high cleric demand such an early breakfast? Honestly, I would have preferred a full day in my room to recover after yesterday. Or even just from last night." She looked to Amryn and Tam. "How were your nights?"

"Fine," Amryn and Tam said together.

"Oh?" Marriset lifted a sculpted eyebrow. "Only *fine*? I'm sorry for you."

No she wasn't. She was positively giddy with gloating.

Marriset ran her fingers through her long brown hair. "I'll say this about Darrin. He may have a disappointing title, but he certainly didn't disappoint behind closed doors. He knows his way around a woman." Her glittering eyes settled on Amryn, who had just pressed her teacup to her lips. "You must tell us what sort of lover the Butcher is."

Amryn choked on her tea, her cheeks suddenly burning.

"Oh come now, there's no need to be shy. We're all married women. You can tell us what he's like. I'm sure Tam is also dying to know."

"I'm fine without knowing," Tam said, her voice almost a mutter.

"You can't expect me to believe you're not curious," Marriset said. "Aside from Prince Argent, he's the most notable person here. General Vincetti is positively infamous. And exceptionally attractive. What is it about dangerous men?" Her tongue darted over her lips. "I certainly wouldn't mind having him. As my husband, I mean." Her flare of passion—not to mention her possessive tone—made it clear she was not lying. She wanted Carver.

Strange, how that made Amryn bristle. She shifted her weight, though it did nothing to make her more comfortable. "Should we join the others?" she asked.

"A great idea," Tam said, already moving.

Amryn followed, and, unfortunately, Marriset was right behind her.

A long, empty settee waited across from Jayveh, Cora, and Sadia. There was a low table between the available couch and the others, and Tam was quick to take the farthest spot. Amryn sat on the opposite end, balancing her tea and saucer carefully as she did so.

Jayveh and Sadia were chatting, and their conversation didn't break as Marriset ignored the chair she'd occupied before and instead sat on the settee between Amryn and Tam.

Saints, this woman was going to drive Amryn mad.

Marriset sat with perfect posture, her back straight and one leg crossed primly over the other. She took another bite of her small sandwich before glancing at Amryn again. "So, how was he?"

Amryn looked at her. "What?"

Marriset's eyes fairly glittered. "How was Carver? They say he takes whatever he sets his mind to on the battlefield. Is it the same in the bedroom?"

Amryn wanted to ignore her—or simply tell her off—but her face seared with heat, and she could feel the woman's determination to get answers. She had to say something, or Marriset would keep pressing for details. "He got back to our room quite late after seeing to the emperor. He was very tired."

Marriset's eyes rounded. "He didn't want you?"

Her words stung. Which was ridiculous, considering how relieved Amryn had been when Carver hadn't touched her last night.

Marriset clicked her tongue. "How horrible. If you need my advice on how to seduce a man, let me know." Her eyes dragged over Amryn. "Just a few little adjustments would make a vast improvement."

Her rudeness wasn't a surprise at this point, but the way this woman made Amryn's own cattiness emerge was unexpected. Her smile was narrow as she met Marriset's gaze. "Oh, I think I've learned enough from you already."

The woman's expression tightened a little, though her smile remained in place as she twisted to Tam. "What about you and Rivard? How was your night?"

"We did our duty," Tam said, her voice as flat as her brown eyes.

"Ah, no more details? You two are positively killing me. What's the point of being married and having this time together if we're not going to share what we've learned from our husbands?" She let out a low groan. "Oh, very well. I suppose I can settle some other curiosities. Tam, your father is the king of Kalmar, correct?"

"Yes." Tam lifted a brow. "And what is your connection to the king of Palar?"

Marriset's smile firmed, making it clear she'd heard the unspoken insult in Tam's words; the mere fact that she had to ask meant Marriset was not as high-ranking as Tam.

Amryn smiled against the rim of her cup.

"I'm the king's second cousin," Marriset said. "And since everyone else in my family was already married, I was chosen." She looked to Amryn. "I'm afraid I don't really know anything about you. Except, of course, that you have a weak constitution."

Amryn blinked. "What do you mean?"

Marriset gestured vaguely with her small sandwich. "Well, after the fight yesterday, none of us were on the floor retching."

Amryn stiffened.

"Leave her alone," Tam said.

"I didn't mean any offense," Marriset said quickly, though her delight at hitting a nerve was obvious. "It just seems to me that, if anyone should have reacted so . . . *violently*, if you'll forgive the word, I would have expected it to be Cora. It was her brother who nearly got us all killed, after all."

Amryn darted a look to Cora, and it was clear from the way the girl broke off talking to Jayveh and Sadia that she'd heard.

Jayveh's head turned slowly toward them, her gaze pinning Marriset. The empirical princess felt many things, all tangled up in a way that made them hard to decipher. It made it impossible to predict what she might say, though Amryn assumed her top priority would be to smooth things over. That's what the emperor would want: peace, no matter the cost.

Her chin jutted out slightly as she faced Marriset. "There's no need for cruelty. Not when we'll all be living together for a year."

The open condemnation surprised Amryn—and everyone else in the room, including Marriset.

She set down her sandwich, annoyance flaring. But she cleared her throat and spoke with a measured tone. "I didn't mean to offend."

"I'm relieved to hear that," Jayveh said. "But you should work harder to avoid doing so in the future."

Marriset's anger was a blistering throb that made Amryn's temples ache.

Jayveh set aside her cup of tea. "I think we should take a moment and get to know each other. Sadia, would you like to introduce yourself first?"

There was a thread of timidity from Sadia, though Amryn wasn't sure if it was because of the tense exchange that had just happened, or the fact that she was perhaps shy by nature. But she shared a smile with them all. "I'm Sadia Kavel. My cousin is the king of Cael, and he asked me to come to Esperance so he didn't have to break off his sister's engagement to a local lord." Her warm affection for her cousin was clear. "I'm now married to Prince Samuel Kenton of Wendahl, and he is . . ." Her cheeks pinkened. "Well, he's very handsome."

Jayveh gave Sadia a smile before she looked to Cora. "Would you like to go next?"

The girl was clearly the youngest of them all, and her grief was still potent, but she nodded. "I'm Cora Amin of Hafsin, and I'm married to Ivan Baranov of Sibet."

She offered nothing more, and Jayveh didn't press. She only looked to Tam.

"I'm Tam Ja'Kell," she said, her voice a little too flat. "Rivard Quinn of Daersen is my husband now."

When the attention shifted to Marriset, she straightened

a little, like she was preening. Her smile was wide, but not wholly sincere as she said, "I'm Marriset Navarre. I'm from Palar, which is the most beautiful place in the empire. My husband is Darrin Fythen of Vadir. He's quite important in Vadir's court."

When she finished and every eye shifted to Amryn, she was grateful to still hold her teacup. It kept her hands from fidgeting under their combined attention.

"I'm Amryn Lukis. I'm from Ferradin, and I'm married to Carver Vincetti, of Westmont."

Just saying the words made her stomach churn. It didn't matter that he'd surprised her with some kindness, some humor—he was still the Butcher. Still her enemy. Would the fact that he was her husband ever *not* terrify her? She doubted it.

"How are you related to the king of Ferradin?" Sadia asked.

"Oh, I'm not." It was only then that she realized all the other women had royal blood; even Marriset, who was far removed, had a link to the throne of Palar. "My uncle is the chief advisor to King Torin," Amryn explained. "That's why I was chosen."

"Were you raised in the palace?" Marriset asked.

"Yes." It was mostly the truth.

Jayveh took her turn. "I'm Jayveh Umbar of Xerra, and I'm married to Prince Argent Vayne." Her smile was unrestrained, and her joy was genuine.

"Is it true you knew the prince when you were children?" Sadia asked.

"Yes," Jayveh said. "When I was young, I spent many summers at the empirical palace, visiting with my family. Argent and I became friends even though he was a few years older than me."

"Isn't that lovely?" Sadia smiled. "I think you're the only ones who knew each other before."

Marriset leaned forward. "Your uncle is the king of Xerra, correct?"

"Yes." Jayveh's tone betrayed nothing, but Amryn sensed a ripple of anger at the mention of her uncle.

"But he wasn't always the king, was he? Your father used to rule Xerra, before the emperor took away his crown." Marriset glanced at the others, who had all gone silent. "I can't be the only one who knows the scandal. Rumors even reached Palar!"

Marriset's words teased free an old memory. Many years ago, Amryn had overheard Rix and Torin talking one night. It was a usual complaint; that the emperor only gave kings the illusion of power within their kingdoms. The king of Xerra, who had been viewed as a loyal friend to the emperor for years, had suddenly lost his throne. It had been given to his younger brother with no explanation to the other nations within the Craethen Empire. The old king hadn't even been arrested, or banished—he'd just lost his crown.

"It's a warning for the rest of us," Torin had concluded grimly. "It's the emperor's way of telling us that he doesn't even need a reason to set us aside. We are forever subject to his whims."

In the tea room, curiosity rippled out from everyone, except Jayveh. The princess felt a mixture of dread, old pain, and shame. "It's true that my father was once the king of Xerra," she said. "But the emperor had his reasons for what he did."

Her tone was final, but Marriset chose to ignore that. "It's strange to me that the emperor chose to match you with Argent." While her tone was conversational, her jealousy of the princess was painfully sharp. "After all, you were really no more than a disavowed princess, relegated to essentially nothing in her uncle's court."

The princess's expression tightened.

"What seems strange to me," Tam said tersely, before Jayveh could, "is that a noblewoman such as yourself has no social graces."

Marriset's eyes flew wide. "Excuse me?"

"Jayveh is the empirical princess of Craethen," Tam said firmly. "Perhaps you should keep that in mind when you address her."

Cora's eyes were wide, and Amryn was just as surprised. Tam had seemed too reserved to speak out like that.

Amryn didn't miss Marriset's spike of resentment; it even sparked in her eyes.

Sadia cleared her throat. "Well. I think this pleasant tea is exactly what the high cleric had in mind when he had us all shut in here."

Cora snorted, and Tam grunted.

Jayveh set aside her tea. "I know this isn't easy for any of us. And I know I'm the lucky one who got to marry a man I know and love, but . . . we all left family behind. We're all facing unknowns. We're sitting with people from other kingdoms— kingdoms that may have wronged our own in the past. But we can't be ruled by our history. No matter our differences, we're all stuck in Esperance. We can choose if we're going to isolate ourselves, or if we're going to make peace with each other and become friends."

The room was silent.

It was Cora that finally shifted in her chair, and her voice was soft. "I want to call all of you my friends, rather than my enemies."

Jayveh nodded once. "I agree. So, since I think we've about exhausted the topic of me . . . What are some of your favorite pastimes?"

As the conversation slowly picked up, Amryn had to wonder if the men were having an easier time making peace.

If not, at least they'd been given swords instead of teacups.

10

CARVER

"WHAT BY ALL THE DIVINITIES possessed you to attack each other?" High Cleric Zacharias hissed, pacing on the other side of his enormous desk. Every item on the dark wood surface was meticulously organized. Stacks of paper were put neatly in their place, along with ink, quill, and a letter opener.

Carver had studied everything on the desk, because if he looked at the man who was reprimanding him, his temper—already riding too close to the surface—might snap.

He sat in a hard-backed chair with his arms folded across his chest. Rivard sat beside him, his face streaked with partially dried blood. His nose was already several different shades of purple.

Neither of them answered the cleric. But for the record, Zacharias didn't seem to need their participation. He'd been going on like this since they'd entered his office several minutes ago. It had been a good hour since the incident in the yard. Before they'd been called into the high cleric's office, Zacharias had interrogated the cleric that had been overseeing them in the training yard, to get his account of what had happened.

Clearly, his words hadn't painted either Rivard or Carver in a good light, because they were both being subjected to this lecture.

"I don't understand how either of you could devolve into such terrible behavior so quickly. Not a full day into this venture, and you're already drawing blood!"

The way the high cleric was treating them was reminiscent of a parent lecturing a child, and that fact alone made Carver bristle. Saints blast it, he was a bloody *general* in the empirical army.

He had to keep reminding himself that the emperor had given the high cleric authority to act in his name, and so he couldn't snap back.

It was hard to show deference to a man he didn't respect, though.

Still, Carver had been reprimanded by domineering commanders before, and he'd learned to control his tongue—even when he disagreed with them. So, while the high cleric railed at him and Rivard, Carver fought to keep his expression neutral.

"Isn't it enough that we had killers break into the temple to enact violence? Was it really necessary for you to do the same? And with the emperor still within these walls!" The tension in the high cleric's voice made it clear he was more worried about the emperor finding out and blaming *him* for what had happened, than any trouble Carver and Rivard might find themselves in.

Carver's first impression of Zacharias was definitely proving correct. The man was excited by the important task he'd been given, and thrilled to have authority over them all, but he didn't actually want to take responsibility for anything negative that might happen here.

Carver's opinion of Zacharias continued to diminish as he continued to rant. "You both know how important this peace is. I am absolutely appalled by your behavior! Any animosity is unacceptable here. Esperance is a place of peace and healing. You will resolve this. *Now*."

There was a beat of silence, and the absence of his booming voice almost made Carver's ears ring.

Rivard spoke, his voice was a little nasal. "Apologies, High Cleric. I may have said some things that provoked Carver. I'm sorry."

Carver didn't believe the contrition in his tone, but then, the act of humility hadn't been for him.

The high cleric stopped pacing and straightened his spine, his bald head catching the sunlight that poured through the window as he twisted to face them. "Well, I'm relieved to hear you're sorry. But that doesn't excuse your behavior today—and it certainly doesn't do anything to touch General Vincetti's violent outburst." He looked between them. "The animosity between you is potent. I want to know why. Daersen and Westmont are not enemies."

"Carver and I have a personal history," Rivard said.

Hearing Rivard broach the topic in such a measured tone—as if he were only pointing out the weather—made the back of Carver's neck heat.

"A personal history," the high cleric echoed, his eyes sharpening. "What kind of history?"

"There has been some . . . unpleasantness between us," Rivard said. Carver shot him a look, but the other man hurried to say, "I would prefer not to go into details at this time." He eyed Carver. "For the sake of the empire, I can make peace with you."

Zacharias turned to Carver. "And you?"

Never.

That's what he wanted to say. But it wouldn't get him out of this room any faster, so he spoke through gritted teeth, directing his words to the high cleric. "I won't hit him again."

The high cleric's eyebrows pulled together. "Lord Quinn, go clean yourself up. You and I will meet again another time to finish this discussion."

Rivard tipped his head, then left. As the door thudded behind him, the high cleric's attention was fully on Carver.

Carver met the man's stare without blinking.

"Would you like to tell me about your history with Rivard?"

"No."

The high cleric's eyes narrowed. He settled in his chair, opened one of the desk drawers, and drew out a letter.

Curiosity tugged at Carver, despite his dark mood.

Then the high cleric cleared his throat and began reading. "'You have asked for my thoughts on General Carver Vincetti. Carver is an impressive man. His devotion to both his family and the empire is admirable, and his military service is beyond reproach.'"

Carver's body had tightened. "Who wrote this?"

"Cleric Varner." Zacharias arched one heavy brow. "Did you really think I wouldn't make the effort to correspond with each of your local clerics? I needed to know exactly who was going to stay in my temple."

Irritation rose, but so did a spark of intrigue. Those letters would contain useful information about the Empire's Chosen. He may need to borrow them.

Zacharias continued to read aloud. "'Because you specifically asked, I must inform you that his attention to religion is not, in fact, very religious.'"

Carver's mouth twitched. Cleric Varner's wit was one of the things he liked best about the man. Of course, he wasn't exactly pleased Varner had replied to the high cleric's letter, but he supposed he couldn't expect Varner to ignore his religious superior.

"'General Vincetti recently returned from the front lines of Harvari,'" Zacharias read. "'He served the empire honorably, and the men under his command praised his leadership. He has my utmost confidence in every respect.'" He looked up from the letter. "That's all he says."

Carver said nothing. It seemed the safer course.

Zacharias dropped the letter onto the desk and steepled his fingers in front of his mouth. "Out of all the clerics who responded to my questions, Varner was the least detailed. Why do you think that is?"

"I've never been regular with my confessions. Perhaps that's it."

The high cleric's brow furrowed. "I've counseled many a broken soldier, Carver. I know one when I see one."

Carver's gut clenched. The high cleric's tone, his words—the fact that he'd used Carver's name instead of his title. All of it made him tense. His hands fisted on his knees, and he forced himself to speak evenly. "I'm fine."

"Are you? Or will your control snap again when someone looks at you in a way you don't like?" The high cleric leaned back in his chair. "I am going to be frank. I had doubts when I learned you were coming here. Your return from Harvari was recent enough to warrant these doubts; I've seen plenty of soldiers struggle to adjust back to normalcy. Throwing you into an arranged marriage that is vital to the empire, while also isolating you for a year in a remote place that might only make you feel trapped . . ." Zacharias shook his head. "I expressed my concerns, but the emperor insisted you could handle this—that another man from Westmont didn't need to be brought in. So let me say this: I will not tolerate any more violence or trouble from you. Is that understood?"

Carver forced his stiff mouth to move. "Yes."

"Good." His head tipped to the side. "Perhaps you shouldn't be allowed on the training field again. It may have incited the violence inside you."

The thought of not being able to step back into the one place that promised him peace here loosened his tongue. "If Rivard keeps his word and doesn't provoke me, there will be no further problems."

Zacharias studied him for a long moment. Then, "You're a general. A leader. You know what it's like to feel responsibility for those under your charge. You also understand the necessity of obeying a commander. Following orders. Leaders see what mere soldiers can't. They know things soldiers don't." He paused, giving the air a weighty moment. "While you're here, you're a soldier. I'm your commander. Can you respect that?"

Every nerve grated, but he said, "Of course."

"Good. Because the success of Esperance has been laid on my shoulders, and I'm not going to let you ruin this."

Carver forced his teeth to unclench. "There will be no further problems," he repeated.

"I'm pleased to hear it." Zacharias folded his hands atop the desk. "Would you like to talk about what you experienced in Harvari?"

"No." The finality in his voice echoed in the room.

"And you're sure you don't want to talk about you're history with Rivard?"

"Yes."

The man's lips pursed. He began to re-fold Cleric Varner's letter. "The emperor has a clear fondness for you. I would hate to see you disappoint him with any repeats of today." He gave Carver a pointed look. "The peace is more important than any personal disputes. Do you understand?"

His throat tightened. "Yes."

Zacharias nodded once. "I'm glad we could reach an understanding." He gestured to the door. "I'll see you at dinner."

The dismissal was clear, and Carver didn't hesitate to stand. He exited the office and strode down the hall, his frustration living in each step he took.

He didn't stop walking for a long time.

11

AMRYN

VOICES ROSE AND FELL, UNDULATING with conversation and bursts of high, flirtatious laughter. The clink of glass and the click of heels on stone punctuated the din. The sounds weren't all that different from the empathic feelings Amryn felt as she stood outside the open door. Nerves fluttered above swells of amusement, excitement, and homesickness. Hunger wove its way throughout; for dinner, and—for some—an intense desire to be alone with their new spouse. Amryn's cheeks burned in the dim hallway, and she fought to focus on other emotions. There was irritation. Frustration. Grief pierced high and sharp, and Amryn recognized the strong emotion as Cora's. The more time Amryn spent with a person, the more accustomed to their emotions she would become.

She hung outside the doorway, shielded in the shadows. She was reluctant to join the others. She was exhausted after suffering the barrage of so many diverse and relentless emotions. It was entirely different from her life in Ferradin, which she spent mostly secluded. The castle staff had thought she was excessively private, and some even speculated she was often ill. But the truth was much simpler—as an empath, it was draining to be around others. Not to mention, it was exhausting to constantly worry that she would do something to out herself.

Of course, she was also reluctant to enter the room because she was late, and she hated when people stared. And the thought of facing a room full of couples while alone was *not* pleasant.

She had been ready to go down to dinner for at least half an hour, but she'd been waiting for Carver. Who hadn't shown up in their suite, even though Ahmi had assured her all the men were back from their time at the training yard.

Ahmi had helped her dress in a sapphire blue dress with thin sleeves that were tight to the wrist, then belled out to drape over her hands. The waist was fitted and the skirt fell to the floor, rippling like water when she moved. Her long red locks were gathered over one shoulder and secured with a simple tie low against the side of her neck. A simple silver necklace— a gift from her uncle—completed the outfit.

The only thing she was missing was her new husband.

When she could no longer stand to feel Ahmi's sour mixture of worry and pity, Amryn had simply walked herself down to dinner. She didn't know where Carver was, nor did she care. She certainly wasn't going to feel slighted by his disappearance.

Reminding herself of that resolve, she took a deep breath in the dimly lit hall, and then she swept into the room.

Everyone stood in twos, the couples hanging onto each other's arms or at least standing close. Conversations abounded, and everyone sipped amber liquid from short glasses. Carver, she noted, was not there.

"Ah!" Marriset's voice rang out. "There you are, Amryn.

You've finally deigned to join us?"

Amryn stiffened at the now-familiar wave of spite that came from the other woman. After their agonizingly long afternoon together, she was thoroughly out of patience for Marriset and her false smiles.

Jayveh and Argent both twisted, and Argent grinned at her. "Amryn! Where by all the Divinities is Carver? He didn't leave you to walk alone, did he?"

"I'm not sure where he is." Amryn joined their circle, even though it included Marriset and her husband, Darrin. Stealing a glance across the room, she saw Tam and Rivard talking with Samuel and Sadia. Her eyes lingered on Rivard; his nose was swollen and bruised. Ivan and Cora stood slightly apart from the others, sipping drinks.

Argent frowned, and something like guilt and worry squirmed through him. "Perhaps he's still meeting with the high cleric."

Amryn blinked. "He had a meeting with the high cleric?"

Marriset's fingernails tapped her glass—a subtle way to draw their eyes. Her smile appeared innocent enough, but her pleasure at gaining their attention was only too clear. "You didn't know?" She rubbed a hand over her husband's arm. "Darrin told me all about the fight."

Darrin cleared his throat and shifted his weight, though he didn't pull his arm away from Marriset. "That makes it seem more dramatic than it was."

Jayveh looked sharply at Argent, strands of diamond earrings swaying near her long neck. "What fight?"

"Nothing to be alarmed about," Argent hurried to assure her. "Carver and Rivard got carried away in the training yard. It's nothing, really. They both went to see the high cleric."

Marriset chuckled. "Rivard's nose is terribly bruised. But

then, it shouldn't surprise us that Carver won the fight. He is the emperor's favorite general, after all. And Westmont is known for raising the best soldiers. Didn't you go there to train, Your Highness?"

"I did," Argent said. "So did Rivard. We all met there." His distaste with Rivard was clear to Amryn's empathic sense, though the others didn't seem to see anything past his diplomatic tone.

Amryn was more focused on her own emotions, however. Surprise, that Carver had attacked Rivard. Something like irritation that Marriset had known about the fight before her. She should probably feel uneasy at the fact that Carver had beaten someone, but when Amryn glimpsed Rivard's purpled and swollen nose from across the room, she only felt thin satisfaction. After the way he'd been treating Tam, he deserved it.

Jayveh turned to Amryn. "We should get you a drink."

Since it would take her away from Marriset, Amryn readily agreed.

Jayveh moved to step away, but Argent swept her hand up to his mouth and pressed a kiss to the back of it. "I'll miss you," he said.

Jayveh smiled, joy and love sparking inside her. "I'm not even leaving the room."

"You're leaving my side, though."

Her expression softened. She rose on her toes and pressed a kiss to his cheek. "I'll return soon," she promised.

"If you don't, I'll come find you."

The air between them was charged with their flirtation and mutual attraction. The depth of Argent's feelings for Jayveh, and the overall kindness inside him . . . Amryn hadn't expected any of that from the heir to the empirical throne.

Jayveh took Amryn's arm and led her away. Behind them,

they could hear Marriset clear her throat. "Darrin, didn't you want to ask Argent about the revised farm tax in Vadir? I thought your proposal was rather fascinating . . ."

The moment they were far enough away, Jayveh ducked her head toward Amryn. "A drink is the only way we'll make it through the night without strangling her."

A small smile tugged at Amryn's lips. Jayveh's annoyance was as sharp as her own when it came to Marriset. It was an easy thing to bond over, though she had to admit, she'd enjoyed Jayveh's company today. The princess had a no-nonsense attitude, and usually spoke exactly what she felt—which was refreshing. But she was also kind, and that rare combination of honesty and compassion made Jayveh much less exhausting to be around than the others.

While Amryn still didn't know what the rebels would ask of her, she knew she should take this opportunity to befriend the future empress of Craethen. And, since Jayveh made it so easy, Amryn's reply was nearly effortless. "You handled her expertly at tea."

"Thank you. I tried to be diplomatic, but . . . Well, if I were slightly less civilized, I may have followed Carver's example and broken her nose." They reached the sideboard, and the princess poured two fingers of the brandy and offered the glass to Amryn. "How are you feeling about Carver?" Jayveh asked.

Wary. Apprehensive. Confused. Nothing she was going to say aloud. "I'm not sure."

Jayveh's head tipped to the side. "How does he feel about you?"

Mildly surprised. Cautious. Curious. Amryn tightened her hold on the glass. "How should I know?"

"I thought it might be obvious." She gestured with her chin.

"Marriset and Darrin try to appear like a power couple, but they're both disappointed in their match; Marriset wanted Argent, and Darrin probably wanted Tam, since Vadir has been trying to negotiate better trade routes with Kalmar for years. Sadia and Samuel are actually quite pleased with each other—notice how they can't stop touching and smiling at each other?"

Amryn followed Jayveh's gaze, and she did indeed catch sight of stolen touches and endearing glances between Sadia and Samuel.

Jayveh's voice lowered a little further. "Cora and Ivan are an interesting match, though. She's so quiet and young, and he's . . ." She didn't finish, but she didn't really have to.

Ivan was the largest man in the room. He was tall with broad shoulders. His expression rode the line between bored and brooding, and his long blond hair slightly shielded ice-blue eyes that seemed to miss nothing.

"They're both quiet," Amryn said. "So I suppose they have that in common."

"That's true enough." Jayveh's eyes drifted to the last couple in the room—Rivard and Tam. "He seems a bit grim, but that's probably more about his broken nose than his marriage. Truthfully, he seems nearly as listless about Tam as she is about him."

Amryn eyed the princess. "You certainly notice a lot."

The princess snorted. "As if you don't. I can tell you're a quiet observer, like me. Did I miss anything?"

Amryn shrugged. "I'm not very good at reading people."

"Hmm." Jayveh took a sip, then grinned. "Carver's eyes rarely wandered from you at breakfast, or during the tour. I think that's telling, don't you?"

"He's not the first to stare at my flaming red hair."

Jayveh opened her mouth, but before she could pursue the topic, the dinner bell rang.

High Cleric Zacharias walked in from the dining hall, beaming at them. "It's so good to see you all. I can't wait to hear your impressions after your first day at Esperance. Come!" He waved them forward, and Jayveh left Amryn so she and Argent could exit the room first, arm in arm.

Amryn hung back, watching as the other couples fell in line.

High Cleric Zacharias spotted her and crossed the floor. "Lady Vincetti, where is your husband?"

Her heart hammered, having a cleric stand so close to her. Any bit of levity she'd felt while talking to Jayveh had vanished. "I'm not sure," she said, finally answering him. "He must have been delayed somewhere."

The high cleric frowned, which pulled at the wrinkles carved into his face. "Well, allow me to escort you, my child." He extended an elbow, and ice shot through Amryn's veins.

The high cleric had surely gotten his rank through years of service to the church. Years of oppressing others. Years of standing by—or even standing witness—as empaths were slaughtered by the Order of Knights.

How many cries for mercy had this man personally ignored? Hundreds?

"Lady Vincetti?" Zacharias lifted his elbow a little higher. "Shall we?"

Her ears rang and her pulse pounded. She couldn't take his arm. She couldn't—

She felt Carver's presence a second before he strode into the room. Amryn tried not to gasp at the dark bruising along his jaw. His eyes swept the scene, narrowing on the high cleric's extended arm. He cleared his throat, and Zacharias turned.

"Ah, General Vincetti. Good of you to finally arrive. Where were you?"

"I couldn't find the right jacket." Carver held out a hand to Amryn. "Shall we?"

She couldn't keep from staring at the stark discoloration on his bronze skin. For some reason she'd assumed that, since he'd won the fight, he'd be unharmed. It was strange—and a little alarming—how much it bothered her to see him hurt.

"Amryn?" Carver prompted, his voice a little lower than before.

His hand was still extended.

Perhaps it shouldn't feel any different than when the high cleric had offered his arm, but it did. While both men had blood on their hands, she didn't know for certain that Carver had helped kill empaths. And that made all the difference in this moment.

She put her hand in his.

His fingers flexed around hers, and then they walked into the dining room.

It was larger than the breakfast room they'd eaten in this morning, and it was decorated lavishly. Candelabras were spaced along the dark wood table, and cushioned high-back chairs were tucked in close. Servants lined the room, waiting for the couples to be seated so they could serve the food. Rich aromas of flat bread dusted in seeds, baked vegetables, and rice with pale gravy and shredded poultry permeated the air. Amryn's stomach growled. She hadn't eaten much during tea, and she was ravenous.

The other couples were already seated, leaving two open chairs at the end of the table. Carver only released her to pull back her chair, and then he settled beside her.

"Where were you?" she asked in a whisper.

He glanced at her, and that faint white scar on his chin caught her attention. "I went for a walk and lost track of time." The skin around his eyes tightened. "Did the high cleric say anything to you? You looked upset."

She pursed her lips, her eyes dipping to his bruised jaw. "Apparently I wasn't the only one to get upset today. What happened with Rivard?"

Carver's expression closed off. "Nothing."

Her curiosity was fierce, but it was clear Carver wouldn't answer her questions, and now really wasn't the time to press.

The high cleric stood at the head of the table, palms pressed together, and everyone quieted as he said the blessing of plenty.

Then dinner began.

Amryn was exhausted. Dinner was a long affair, filled with conversation, high emotions, and strange foods. Carver hadn't spoken another word to her, and she had ignored him, too. Cora sat across the table from her, and the younger woman felt the same misery Amryn did.

She was grateful when a tray of fruit was brought out for dessert. That meant it was almost time to retire for the night.

She was ready to be away from people.

Unfortunately, the night wasn't over. The high cleric insisted they all move to the nearest sitting room so they could play Servaht. Small tables were set up to accommodate all the players, since only four could play at a time. The high cleric directed them to their places, then explained that each game's winner would progress up to the head table, while the loser would move down. Clearly, he wanted them to mingle and get to know each other—and he intended to do the same, since he'd set up an extra table. He recruited some clerics to play with them, and a few other clerics took seats in the corners of the room. Amryn wasn't sure why they lingered; they just talked amongst themselves and watched as the high cleric directed everyone to their seats.

Servaht was a game of luck more than strategy, and Amryn wasn't very lucky. The only positive was that Carver's cards were unerringly good, and he was able to bluff well. So while they started at the same table, he quickly advanced to play with the other winners, until the space of the whole room separated them.

Amryn currently played with Samuel, Darrin, and Cora. Samuel shuffled the deck, and cards were drawn. After the requisite four turns, in which they could choose to keep their cards or exchange for new ones, Cora spread out a winning set.

Darrin groaned. "You're a lucky woman."

Cora felt a sharp pang at his words, and her lips pressed together.

Darrin seemed to remember that Cora's brother had been killed in front of her yesterday. Unease filtered from him, and he cleared his throat.

Samuel shuffled the cards and Darrin chatted with him.

Cora's pain and grief was overwhelming. Amryn reached for her without thought, setting a hand on her arm.

The younger woman glanced over at her, surprise sparking from her.

"I'm sorry for your loss," Amryn said softly. "If you ever need to talk . . . let me know."

Cora's eyes watered. Her emotions were chaotic, but her words were sincere as she whispered, "Thank you."

When the current game concluded, the winners and losers at each table rose and shuffled as needed. Cora was the winner at their table, so she moved up, and a scowling Rivard took her place.

His boot bumped Amryn's foot under the table. He muttered an apology and slouched in the chair. His dark mood was a mixture of things, and it wasn't easy for Amryn to sort through. He was upset at losing the game of cards, but that was superficial. His nose radiated pain. His pride was deeply wounded. His anger sharpened when the sound of Argent and Carver laughing drifted from the winning table, and his irritation flashed when he saw Tam join them.

He shot a look at Amryn. "Are you going to deal?"

She grabbed the deck and took her turn to shuffle and deal the cards.

Darrin looked across the table at Rivard. "Did you have someone look at your nose?"

"Yes." He scowled. "It isn't broken—just cracked."

Darrin winced. "The year's off to a hard start for you."

"The Divinities are testing me." Rivard waved his glass in the air and a servant hurried over to top it off with more brandy.

Amryn could already feel the haze of his drunkenness, and she forced her empathic sense to ease back from him. If she narrowed in on someone too much, their emotions could impact her own. Ignoring Rivard wasn't easy, though. His emotions nearly shouted his anger, disappointment, and jealousy.

His mood didn't improve as he lost the first two rounds. He threw back the rest of his brandy and lifted his glass for more.

"Perhaps you've had enough," Amryn said.

He shot her a look. "Excuse me?"

She knew the brandy was only honing his anger, and he

kept looking meanly at Tam. Amryn didn't want her to have to deal with his anger once they were alone in their suite. So, she said more firmly, "I think you've drunk enough."

His features sharpened into a glare. "Your opinion means nothing to me."

Darrin and Sadia both stiffened with embarrassment, but Amryn ignored them. She shrugged. "Your loss." She laid out her cards—a clear winning hand. She smiled thinly at Rivard. "Literally."

Darrin chuckled.

Rivard threw down his cards, cursing.

Darrin swept the cards up, pushing them into a pile to shuffle. "Don't be a poor loser."

Rivard's gaze narrowed on Amryn, but he said nothing more.

Amryn couldn't stop her smile when, minutes later, she won again.

Rivard glowered as she stood and moved up to the next table, passing Jayveh as she went. As they brushed by each other, Jayveh whispered, "Good luck with Marriset."

That stole the smile from Amryn's face. She sat in Jayveh's vacated seat, which put Marriset on her left. The woman was shuffling the deck.

High Cleric Zacharias was also seated at the table, and a female cleric was just leaving, advancing to the top table to take Argent's place.

Argent sat across from Amryn, though his eyes trailed his wife as she took her seat by Rivard at the other table.

The high cleric smiled, and Amryn could feel his self-satisfaction. "Perhaps we'll have to play a different game tomorrow night. One that keeps the couples together a bit more."

Marriset began to deal. "I think this is fun. Though I'm

pleased to have you finally lose, Your Highness."

"Hmm?" Argent glanced at her.

Marriset eyes fairly twinkled. "I'm grateful I can finally play you."

Argent seemed wholly oblivious to her flirtation. He merely sent her a small smile and the game began. Amryn let the others carry the conversation. And, since Argent kept stealing glances at Jayveh, it was mostly left to High Cleric Zacharias and Marriset to talk. As the cleric droned on about Esperance's gardens, Marriset's looks at Argent became more lingering. And definitely hungry.

Perhaps it was the brandy she'd drunk, or she was feeling the effects of Rivard's growing intoxication, but Amryn had little patience for Marriset's fixation on Argent. Especially after Jayveh had been so kind to her.

Impulsively, she bumped Marriset's glass of brandy into her lap.

Marriset flew to her feet with a gasp. "My dress!"

"I'm so sorry," Amryn said, setting her cards down. "Shall I find a napkin?"

Marriset's glare was pure ice. She stomped away without another word, and Darrin leapt up from his table to follow her, ruining that game as well.

Rivard's annoyance was sharp, though Amryn couldn't muster the energy to care. The high cleric frowned, but he didn't call Marriset or Darrin back. Instead, he rose to find a couple more clerics to take their places.

"You should be careful," Argent told her quietly. His words sounded grave, but mirth tickled the air between them. "She could make quite the enemy."

"I think Marriset wants to eat you," Amryn informed him.

He choked on a laugh. "What?"

"I've seen that look in a person's eye before. Like they're staring down a fresh-baked pie."

Argent's mouth twitched. "If she starts licking her lips, I assure you I'll run."

"She'll chase you."

"She won't get me." He cocked his head. "Can I ask you something?"

Amryn tried to sober up, but a low buzzing remained in her head. She couldn't afford to be questioned in this state.

Saints, he was still waiting for her answer. "Sure."

"I couldn't help but notice you and Carver didn't say a word to each other during dinner. Is something wrong?"

"No."

Argent's mouth pressed into a line. "Well, in case you were worried about the fight between Carver and Rivard, I wanted you to know that—despite his occupation—Carver isn't prone to violence. He was provoked, and I'm afraid if his usually good temperament has a weakness, it's Rivard. I don't want you to feel uneasy around him. Carver is the best man I know."

His friendship with Carver was a tangible thing, as was his belief in his words. But Amryn knew she would never feel completely at ease around Carver. She could never relax fully around anyone. No empath could afford such a thing, let alone one who was now part of the Rising.

The high cleric returned, along with a young male cleric who was eager to join the game.

After a couple more rounds, Tam excused herself from the room. Rivard left a little while later. Since others were leaving without repercussions, Amryn finished the round and quietly excused herself, too. As she stood from the table, she caught

Carver's eye from across the room. Cards were spread in his hands, and he didn't make a move to follow her as she hurried for the door.

She stepped into the corridor, which was darker than the sitting room. Movement from the corner of her eye made her turn, and her body locked up as she spotted Rivard peel away from the shadowed part of the wall.

As he stepped into the light of the nearest glowing lamp, she had to fight the urge to step back.

He stopped a couple paces away from her, and his voice was low as he said, "Make a fool of me again, and you'll regret it."

Amryn's pulse skittered, but self-preservation bled away under the blunt edge of his intoxication, which she felt full-force now that they were relatively alone. She lifted her chin. "It doesn't seem like you need help to play the fool."

Rivard's expression hardened. He took a menacing step forward, and Amryn tensed.

She felt someone step up behind her, and without looking she knew it was Carver.

Rivard froze.

"Do you *really* want me to hit you again today?" Carver asked, his voice dripping with threat.

Rivard's hands curled at his sides. "Keep your wife in line, and we won't have a problem."

"Never speak to her again, and maybe we can avoid problems." Carver's words were low and deep, and the anger pouring off him tightened Amryn's skin like the searing heat of a fire.

Rivard gave them both a silent glare, then spun and stalked down the hall.

Amryn's heart continued to stutter in her chest, and Carver

didn't look away from Rivard's retreat until he'd disappeared around a corner. Then Carver's full focus shifted to her, and their gazes locked.

His blue eyes burned. "Did he harm you in any way?"

"No," she said, feeling a little breathless under that direct stare.

"What did he say to you?"

"Nothing. Truly. I think he was just drunk and upset from losing at cards." And having his nose broken, though she didn't say that.

Carver's hard expression didn't alter. "For my sanity, I'm going to ask you to stay away from him."

"I didn't seek him out."

"Good. Don't. And if he ever threatens you again, taunt him all you want—after you've informed me, so I can break his jaw."

A low chuckle broke free.

He frowned. "What?"

"Just something Argent said."

"What did he say?"

"That you're not prone to violence. I don't really believe it."

He stared at her a moment, then rubbed the back of his neck. "I guess I still haven't managed to make a good impression, have I?"

"No. You're either stabbing people over dinner, breaking noses while I'm at tea, or threatening to break jaws. What am I to expect next?"

He cocked his head, studying her face. "I'm wondering the same thing."

The flush she felt had nothing to do with the lingering effects of Rivard's intoxication, and everything to do with how closely Carver was standing.

She cleared her throat. "You quit the game?"

"You left," he said. "I wanted to escort you back to the room."

"Oh." Her cheeks remained too warm under his gaze. Saints, maybe *she'd* sipped too much brandy tonight, because she found herself saying, "You didn't care about escorting me to dinner."

Carver's expression softened. "I'm sorry. I truly lost track of time. I won't let it happen again." He offered his arm. "Shall we?"

Slowly, she curled a hand around his bent elbow. The instant she touched him, she felt Carver's throb of attraction.

It only amplified her own, and that was completely disconcerting.

He walked her to the suite in silence, and when they entered their apartment, Amryn instantly pulled away from him. Her heart pounded, and she balled her tingling fingers into a fist. "Goodnight," she said, purposefully not looking at him as she stepped toward the hall that led to the bedroom.

"Amryn, wait." His voice was pitched low; deep and slightly rough.

She turned to face him, and in the dim glow of the lanterns the servants had lit, her breath caught at the sight of him. At the way he looked at her.

She had studied him intently at the altar, but now, standing alone together in their suite . . . it was like seeing him for the first time. The dark hair that fell over a deeply tanned brow. Those piercing blue eyes set under thick eyebrows. The high cheekbones and angular jaw that looked sculpted by the Divinities themselves. The cords of muscle that ran along his neck, and the exposed column of his throat. The line of his mouth.

Despite his reputation, and the fact that he was her enemy . . . Carver Vincetti was undeniably the most captivating and handsome man she'd ever seen.

Of course, that only made him more dangerous.

Her breathing was too shallow as she forced herself to meet his eye. "Yes?"

He didn't answer right away, and she tensed. She felt his gaze like a physical touch as it swept over her hair. The curve of her cheek. Her lips.

Her stomach dropped. She could feel his desire, and she wasn't sure what he was going to do about it. This morning, he'd told her they wouldn't share a bed. But with the way he was looking at her . . .

Carver reached into his pocket and withdrew a ring of iron keys. "These are for you. I requested extra copies, so you can have a set."

He held them out, and Amryn took the ring automatically. The cold metal bit into her palm. "Thank you."

He dipped his chin. "There's a key for each door in the suite. I think it would be best if you keep things locked, especially when I'm not around."

She nodded, squeezing the keys in her hand. She hadn't expected this from him. It was a measure of control that he'd relinquished; it made the apartment a little less confining. "Thank you," she said again, her voice a mere whisper.

"You're welcome." He took a step back. "Goodnight."

She echoed the same, then moved for the bedroom. As she twisted the lock on the door and prepared for bed, she could hear Carver moving; washing in the bathing chamber, then shuffling around the sitting room as he arranged his bed on the settee. But more than the small sounds, she could *feel* him.

The brandy he'd indulged in at dinner blurred his emotions, making his exhaustion and frustration bleed together. However, through it all, that heady sense of attraction remained locked in place.

As did her own.

It took a long time for Amryn to fall asleep.

12

CARVER

CARVER'S SHOULDERS PRESSED against the hard back of his chair, his eyes sweeping over the faces around him. They'd gathered in the east tower for their first meeting as the new Craethen Council, and they'd taken seats around a large round table that dominated the room. Chancellor Trevill had yet to join them, so the meeting hadn't officially begun.

It had been one week since their marriages, and Carver had hardly felt able to breathe. High Cleric Zacharias had kept the newly wedded couples busy with his meticulously cultivated schedule, which included teas, religious lectures, and games designed to help them get to know each other. They rarely had a free moment, which meant Carver was on constant alert. He studied the men and women around him, watching for any signs that someone might be an enemy to the empire. His only respite—other than his morning meditations—were the few times the men had been granted an hour or two on the training field. When he was holding a sword—even a practice one— the buzzing in his head quieted. The restlessness that twitched throughout his body stilled.

He itched to be out there right now. Saints, the afternoon couldn't come soon enough.

He stretched his stiff neck, barely holding back a grunt. Sleeping on that cursed settee wasn't helping his irritability. The thing was hard as stone, and far too narrow for his wide shoulders. He wasn't getting enough sleep, though he couldn't blame that all on the sleeping arrangements. Since Harvari, he rarely got a solid night's rest. Either insomnia snared him as memories replayed in his mind, or he'd jerk awake drenched in sweat, gasping against a nightmare. His lack of sleep these days came from a different source, though. Most notably, from the woman who sat beside him.

Amryn was a distraction he hadn't anticipated. Whenever she was near, his eyes seemed incapable of looking anywhere else. Her scent filled his nose, even when she wasn't with him. It was there every morning he dressed in the washroom—in the soap on the counter and in the brush that rested beside his comb. It permeated the air of their sitting room, swirling around him every night as he tried to sleep.

They'd only had a handful of conversations over the past few days, since the high cleric kept them so busy, but already her voice whispered in his mind. He was attuned to her to an almost obsessive degree. Whenever she entered a room—even if she was still out of his view—he knew it. And in those moments, every thought in his head seemed to be snatched away. Even now, sitting silently beside him, she stole his attention. Which was bloody inconvenient, since he was supposed to be paying attention to everyone in the room, and not just her.

A yawn pulled at his jaw, making it crack. At least his lack of sleep last night had been for good reason. He'd been up half the night sneaking into the high cleric's office and going over those letters about each of the Empire's Chosen. He hadn't dared remove them from the room, so he'd read them by the silver moonlight that streamed through the window. He didn't bother with making copies, as that would be too time-consuming. Instead, he strained to read and assimilate every word that the local clerics had written about each of those selected to come to Esperance.

He couldn't find a letter about Argent, so he started with Jayveh.

According to her cleric in Xerra, Jayveh attended services with her uncle and her brothers, and she never spoke out against the empire—even after her father's throne had been taken from him. She was involved in several charities in Xerra. All of this, Carver had already known.

Rivard attended chapel religiously with his family. That was no surprise, since his bloodline was riddled with men and women who had dedicated their lives to the religion. Many had even been knighted by the church. The Order of Knights carried out a variety of duties for clerics; historically, they had been defenders, assassins, and empath hunters. Rivard's cleric had only positive things to say about him, though he added it was "regrettable that Lord Quinn did not have the necessary skillset to join his older brothers in becoming knighted". It was noted that "despite some troubles in his past", all sins had been paid for. According to reports, Rivard visited his mother's grave weekly, and he was a gentle soul.

Tam's mother was apparently very ill—practically on her deathbed. It was a hard sacrifice for Tam to come to Esperance, but the cleric was certain she would do her duty; she honored her father too much to disobey. She came from a large family, she never spoke ill of anyone, and she devoutly attended all services and prayers that the church held. Her days were usually spent with her family, drawing, or designing dresses. Her tutors claimed she was smart enough to attend any university in the empire, though her father preferred to keep her home.

Samuel—who he knew vaguely from years ago—was reportedly one of the smartest students at Wendahl's most prestigious academy. He studied everything from mathematics and biology to history and religious lore. He was an academic in every sense of the word. Samuel was, as his cleric put it, "a gifted young man with a thirst for knowledge and a mind open enough to explore religion, even if he is not always devout in his worship." Samuel had never spoken against the empire or the church—or the rebels, it was noted.

Sadia reportedly grew up in the castle library—which made her an ideal match for Samuel, really—and she was reportedly a joy within her cousin's court. She was often quiet, but she was kind. She wasn't extremely religious, but she observed all the holidays. She had started several charities in Cael, including one that taught children of lower classes to read. Sadia could often be found tutoring many of the children herself. She was friendly to everyone, and freely gave her time and attention to anyone who asked. The cleric could think of no faults to share—only praise.

Darrin, due to his myriad of illnesses in his youth, had never travelled beyond the borders of Vadir. This was noted by the cleric, who made a point of saying this shouldn't reflect poorly on his patriotism. He preferred days spent indoors, counseling with his father on the running of the kingdom. He wanted Vadir's farms to flourish. He had been engaged once, about a year ago, but his betrothed had died in a carriage accident a month after the announcement was made. He would make a well-loved king one day.

Marriset had started a fund for orphaned children in Palar when she was only ten years old, and her charitable pursuits had only grown with her. The cleric had known her since childhood, and he recalled fondly that she'd always wanted to live in the capital city of Craethen where "everything in the empire" happened. She was deeply involved in every event on the island she called home. She was the daughter of a highly respected lord and lady in Palar's ruling circle. It was noted that she had a tendency to be blunt, and that she *may* resent the isolation of her island upbringing. "She will undoubtedly make every effort to fit in with the others," the cleric said.

Ivan was not religious. The cleric stated that no one in Ivan's family—save the king and queen—had embraced the church. He was a quiet man, and his older brother had been killed during a rally against new taxes that got out of hand. Despite this, the cleric had never heard Ivan speak against the empire. He hadn't joined the war effort, though, even after the emperor had asked specifically for the Wolves—an elite warrior force in Sibet, of which Ivan was a member—to travel to Harvari. That could be viewed as a treasonous leaning. Carver had made a mental note to bring up the war around Ivan to gauge his reaction.

Cora had an anxious personality, and, apparently, it had always been so. She was generally fine if she took her powders, but sometimes she could be overwhelmed by her surroundings. She preferred peace and quiet, and she hated confrontations. Her mother was the king's sister, which made her a close relation to the ruler of Hafsin. Cora was noted to be religious, though her brothers were not. The cleric had even mentioned that Cora's oldest brother, Kian, had been vocal about his sister's appointment to Esperance. The letter allowed Carver to see Kian in a different light: an older brother, trying to protect his little sister. It didn't make the man's actions any less treasonous, but Carver had little sisters; he understood the need to protect. As he refolded the letter, he resolved to check in on Cora.

Finally, Carver picked up the last letter—the one he'd been anticipating the most.

Amryn had been born and raised in Ferradin, though the cleric who wrote the letter hadn't known her until some tragedy years ago had placed her in her Uncle Rix's care. King Torin viewed her as a ward, which meant she was highly elevated in his court—which was, undoubtedly, why she'd been chosen to come to Esperance. However, despite her station, Amryn rarely attended any social events or parties. She spent most of her days privately, often with books, or practicing music. She attended chapel with Rix weekly, though the cleric noted that many in Ferradin did so without truly feeling devotion to the Divinities; as the newest country to enter the empire and the church, it often took a full generation before people felt they could quit the religion without fearing some form of reprisal. At twenty, Amryn was old enough to have already been married, but according to the cleric, she hadn't seemed interested in such a thing.

The information the cleric had shared only made Carver more curious about Amryn. What tragedy had she faced? It had presumably stolen her parents, but how? And how young had she been when she'd lost them? She was important in Torin's court, but she was anti-social—why? And did that have something to do with why she hadn't married before now? Even smaller details, like the fact that she had musical talent, grabbed his attention.

Overall, the letters had been helpful, but they also made Carver's thoughts churn. He needed more time. If he had a bloody moment that wasn't already arranged in a careful schedule, he might find the opportunity to actually have a conversation with Amryn. Until that happened, he wouldn't get any answers. The same went for the others—he needed time to talk with them. Feel them out.

The clip of boots on stone announced Chancellor Trevill's entrance into the room, and Carver shook off his thoughts.

"Apologies for my tardiness," Trevill said, his voice echoing in the large chamber. "My meeting with the emperor ran long."

"How is the emperor?" Darrin asked.

"Recovering well," Trevill said, moving to take the empty chair on Argent's left. "He will be leaving for the capital in another week or so."

"Will we get to see him first?" Sadia asked.

"We should have a dinner with him before he goes," Marriset said. "I'd be happy to talk to the cooks about making a grand feast!"

Trevill shook his head. "That is a kind offer, but unnecessary. The emperor doesn't want to intrude or interfere in any way."

It could have been Carver's imagination—or his ridiculous attunement to Amryn—but he thought he saw her shoulders loosen at that.

Trevill lifted his chin, and his voice projected clearly. "This is the first meeting of the Craethen Council. This is a new political structure for the empire, and I hope you all realize what a privilege it is to be a part of something so historic. Now, as you've already been told, the council will be a voice of the people. Each kingdom in the empire will have a say, and a vote, before the emperor passes laws or instigates new policies. When the council is in session, you will reside in the capital. If the time comes that one of you are no longer able to perform your duties as a council member—whether due to taking the throne in your kingdom, illness, or any other reason—you will work with your local monarch to select your replacement for this council. They must be from your native kingdom, and be deemed worthy of this political responsibility."

There were nods all around the table. This was information they'd all heard previously.

Trevill placed his hands on the table. "As I'm sure you all know, the emperor already has an advisory staff, of which I'm a lead member. The chancellors have always counselled the emperor, but since you will be instrumental in shaping the empire's future, we will also advise you." He nodded toward Argent. "Our prince is currently holding the Craethen seat on the council, but he will relinquish his spot once this year is done. The same is true for Princess Jayveh and Xerra's seat. This is the emperor's will, as they will have separate responsibilities within the government, and the point of this council is to be a voice of the people.

"During this next year, we will debate laws that are currently being considered, and discuss issues that concern the empire as a whole, as well as individual kingdoms. You will be assigned readings and attend lectures that cover a variety of subjects, taught by me and clerics who pursued other professions before their religious oaths were taken."

He glanced around at them, his bearded face set. "I know this responsibility may feel overwhelming. Frankly, if you don't feel a little anxiety, I don't think you grasp the gravity of your role. But I'll be here to help you find your footing, and you will be able to lean on each other for support. Now, are there any questions?"

Silence reigned.

Trevill leaned back in his chair. "Very well. Then let us begin by discussing the implications of an increased highway tax."

Carver nudged Samuel's elbow up. "Don't let your arm fall. You need to be ready to parry the next blow, or strike your own."

Samuel's face was flushed, his forehead beaded with sweat. "How are you not breathing hard?"

Carver grinned. "Practice." He lifted his wooden sword. "You go on the offensive this time."

Samuel nodded and swung, not paying enough attention to his footwork, but Carver was pleased at the strength behind the blows; he was gaining confidence in his abilities.

Carver met the blows, slowly retreating. Dirt slid underfoot, scratching out a melody to accompany the crack of the leaded blades. Across the yard, Argent was practicing his archery alongside Rivard, and Ivan was dueling Darrin—and clearly playing with him, though Darrin didn't realize how easily Ivan could win.

All of them had an excess of energy, after another morning full of meetings. It had been three days since their first council meeting; they'd just finished their second, and when Trevill had finally released them, the women had been led to their tearoom and the men had been shown to the field.

Samuel swung low, and Carver jumped back. "Remember, that sort of swing leaves your upper body open—you're practically begging me to chop off your head."

"Right. Sorry." Samuel tossed back the hair on his forehead, sword dragging toward the ground. "I got carried away. I read about an expert swordsman who could sweep the legs out from under his opponent."

Carver almost smiled. "An exciting thought, but it wouldn't ever happen to an experienced fighter. Not on a level battlefield, anyway. Let's try again, but this time I'll attack you."

Samuel nodded, raising his sword to a defensive position.

Carver struck fairly rapidly, hoping to teach him a little more endurance, as well as show him how instincts could come into play. He was still going strong when a feminine voice called out, "Do you mind if we join you?"

Carver spun, blinking slowly as he saw the women step onto the dirt field, Jayveh in the lead.

"We hate to interrupt," the princess continued, "but tea was about to turn violent from boredom. We could use a distraction."

Argent lowered his bow, his grin wide. "We could use a beautiful distraction ourselves."

Jayveh smiled as she stepped up to the prince. "Teach me?" she asked, gesturing to the bow. Argent was only too quick to pass the weapon over, explaining the best way to hold it. Marriset inserted herself between Darrin and Rivard, vying for both of their attentions. Samuel mumbled an excuse and darted to Sadia's side so he could show her the blade he held.

Carver's eyes were drawn to Amryn, who stood just inside

the dirt circle, her hands clasped before her. Tam and Cora stood near her. Tam looked as solemn as always, and he knew now it might have something to do with her mother's illness. The shadow of sadness in Cora's eyes was in evidence, as usual, but she seemed more relaxed standing next to Amryn than she had since Carver had known her.

Amryn looked decidedly uncomfortable as she eyed the nearby stores of mock weapons.

Carver advanced on the small group. "Would you ladies like to learn a few basics?" he asked.

Cora shook her head.

"I'll just watch," Tam said, eyeing him almost warily.

He turned to Amryn. "Would you like to spar?"

Her eyebrows drew together. "I've never touched a sword in my life."

Carver tipped the blade up until it bumped her clasped hands.

Her fingers twitched and she frowned at him.

Carver shrugged, lifting the weapon and making a show of examining it. "Technically you still haven't touched a sword. I know it might be hard to tell with an untrained eye, but this is made entirely of wood."

Amryn's mouth pinched, but Carver could have sworn her green eyes glittered. "You don't say," she deadpanned.

He liked her humor, though she didn't show it enough. When they were in a group setting, she rarely spoke. Even though that aligned with what her cleric had written about her, Carver wanted to coax her out of her shell.

He rolled his wrist, spinning the blade. "Come on. It won't hurt you to try."

Amryn lifted one brow. "No, but it might hurt you."

He chuckled, but stepped forward to help her select a practice sword with an ideal weight for her unpracticed hand, before leading her to a quiet corner of the field.

Amryn did a few practice swings, her long braid swaying behind her and her skirt rippling in the humid breeze. "I don't think I'm dressed appropriately for this."

"You look fine." She looked pretty, really. The green and white gown was simple, but Carver couldn't help but notice how it accentuated her narrow waist and flared at her hips. He cleared his throat. "How was tea?"

She cocked an eyebrow. "Jayveh stopped things before they could get too interesting. I was about to pull Marriset's hair out."

"Do I need to defend your honor?"

"No. She's just . . ." She shook her head. "It doesn't matter." She hefted the sword. "When do we start hitting each other with these?"

A smile tugged his lips. "We'll get to that part. First we need to make sure you have balance, or you'll buckle under any strong hit." Carver had taught countless soldiers how to fight and hone their skills. He had even helped train his brothers and sisters. But he knew the moment he stepped up behind Amryn and set his hand at her waist that this would be nothing like those other lessons. His blood warmed and he felt her stiffen in response—but she didn't pull away.

Carver's voice was a little deeper when he spoke. "You need to keep your feet apart and your knees slightly bent. You can't be rigid in a fight. Be flexible, ready to move as you need to."

She jerked out a nod, and he caught a whiff of her soap. That clean scent of citrus and mint was becoming one of his favorites.

He forced himself to take a step back, his hand falling away from her. He showed her the basic positions and angles to hold her sword, and though he avoided touching her again, he was painfully attuned to her. Every breath, every time she gritted her teeth or darted a look at him. The rest of the yard vanished, leaving only them.

It was exactly what he'd wanted, but he didn't even know what question to ask her first. They were still virtually strangers, even though the letter from her cleric had given him some information. They'd known each other for ten days.

It somehow felt longer than that.

Amryn poked his chest with the tip of her sword. "Now that you've taught me how to hold it, do we get to hit each other?"

"Have you always been this violent?" he asked.

Her head listed to the side. "No. You must bring it out in me." She lifted her sword. "So. Can we start hitting each other?"

Carver grinned. "Absolutely."

She echoed his smile, and they began to exchange blows. She made several mistakes, but she took correction well. She never made the same mistake twice, and there was real power behind her blows. She wanted to win.

A ridiculous goal, but just as endearing as her earlier awkwardness.

After they'd exchanged several more blows, Amryn stepped back, tossing her long braid over her shoulder. Her breaths were deep and full, her face red from exertion. "When did you begin sword fighting?"

He lifted one shoulder. "I've always done it."

"Do all Westmont children start right out of the cradle, or just you?"

"Not all, but my family does." He leaned toward her. "Between you and me, I think my father gave my sisters a dagger *before* they left the cradle."

Amryn cracked a smile. "They can beat you, then?"

"Absolutely. All they have to do is pretend to cry, and I let my guard down. Happens every time."

Amusement sparked in her eyes. "Maybe you shouldn't fall for their tears."

"I can't resist a lady's tears. Completely helpless against them. It's embarrassing, really."

Amryn shook her head at him. "How many sisters do you have?"

"Three. One older, two younger."

"So they outnumber you."

"Only when they ambush me. In a fair fight, they'll take on my brothers, too."

Her brow wrinkled. "How many brothers do you have?"

"Three."

Amryn's eyes bugged. "There are *seven* of you?"

"I also have one brother through marriage, and a niece and nephew." Carver said. "Plus four grandparents, two parents, a rather crazy great aunt, and a handful of other aunts and uncles that are a little more stable, as well as a couple dozen cousins. Really, it's a good thing you have a year to memorize the Vincetti family tree."

"Saints." She shook her head a little. "What are the names of your siblings?"

"Loreena is my older sister. She's married to Leo, one of my father's top strategists. Bethi, their oldest, is four, and Jerome is two."

"Am I to assume you're their most doting uncle?"

"Of course! Now, after me comes Berron; he's twenty-two." He couldn't think any more about his brother without ruining the mood, so he hurried on. "Elowen is nineteen, and the biggest flirt in Westmont—possibly all of Craethen. Being her older brother is a bloody nightmare. Keene is sixteen, and a prankster; he makes more trouble than the rest of us combined. Then there's twelve-year-old Wren. She loves to read in trees to avoid interruptions and, yes, she has fallen asleep in the branches numerous times—it drives my mother mad. And then there's ten-year-old Fowler; he loves to make people laugh, and if his dog loves you, Fowler will love you." His mouth twitched, seeing Amryn's wide eyes. "I'll quiz you sometime," he told her.

She muttered a curse. "I'll never remember them all."

He chuckled. "What about you? Do you have any siblings?"

"No." Amryn set the tip of her sword into the dirt. "How did your parents ever keep up with you?"

"I have no idea. But they wanted a full house."

"Well, they certainly got that. Especially with four boys!"

"In our defense, the girls were just as unruly. But despite some occasional comments, my parents adore the chaos." There was a slight pause, and he gentled his tone. "Your uncle brought you here. Are your parents . . .?"

Her shoulders tensed, and any trace of a smile vanished. "They're dead," she said flatly. "They died a long time ago."

"I'm sorry." And he was. Sorry for whatever loss she'd suffered, and for shattering the lighter mood they'd established.

Amryn brought up her sword, slanting it in a defensive pose. "Shall we try again?"

It was a very deliberate change in subject, and he decided not to press her. So he nodded, raised his sword, and continued their practice. And though the tension between them gradually relaxed, it never fully went away.

13

AMRYN

AMRYN WINCED AGAINST HER pillow. The soft cotton felt like rough bark against her sunburnt cheek. Yesterday, when Jayveh had suggested they join the men in the training yard, there hadn't been time for Amryn to return to the room and apply the protective lotion Ahmi had given her after her first sunburn.

At the time, she hadn't thought she'd be outside for long, but sparring with Carver had proved to be a surprisingly pleasant distraction. And she was always so hot and flushed in this climate, she'd hardly realized the sun had been burning her until it was too late. It had hurt last night when she'd bathed, and Ahmi had gently spread some aloe on her skin.

By all the Saints, it hurt even more this morning.

Her face and neck were on fire. The fresh dawn light that bled around the closed curtains proved it was early morning. She couldn't wait for Ahmi to come; she needed the relief of that cooling aloe now.

She pushed out of bed, only to discover soreness in her arms, legs, and back. It was a good thing she'd enjoyed the sparring, because she was certainly paying the price for it today.

She stood, lifting the blue wrap on the end of her bed and gingerly shrugging it on over her white nightgown. As she padded barefoot to the door, she strained her ears for sounds beyond her room, but she didn't hear movement. It was possible Carver was still asleep in the sitting room, though he was more likely in the middle of his meditation. She'd stumbled in on his morning exercises a couple of times now. Though, to be fair, he was generally such an early riser that he was usually finished by the time she came out and rang for Ahmi.

She unlocked the bedroom door and pushed into the hall, walking on cool stone toward the wash room. When she reached the open door, she stopped short.

Carver stood in profile, shirtless as he peered into the mirror and carefully dragged a long razor over his jaw. His bronzed skin, so much darker than her own, was on proud display. His arms were corded with muscles that jumped and rolled as he guided the razor across his skin, his gaze never wandering from the glass before him. Broad shoulders shifted as he leaned in, and she could see the curve of his spine, and the dip of his lower back.

She also saw scars. Some were nothing more than narrow white marks, clearly long-healed. Others were newer. Pink, and puckered. Some even looked like stripes. Were those . . . whip marks?

She must have inhaled too sharply, because Carver's eyes snapped to hers in the mirror. He lowered the razor and turned to face her. It took considerable effort not to stare at his bare chest and the lined ridges of his abdomen, but somehow she kept her eyes on his face.

Mostly.

White cream still streaked the lower half of his face, since he hadn't finished his shave, and his blue eyes were intent on her. "Amryn." His voice was rougher than usual—probably still heavy from sleep. He cleared his throat. "Did I wake you?"

"No." Her own throat felt dry, and if her cheeks weren't already sunburned, they'd surely be flaming with her embarrassment. She clutched at her robe and took a quick step back. "I'm sorry, I didn't mean to interrupt. I didn't hear you. I can come back later—"

"It's fine," he cut into her rambling. "You just startled me." His fingers tightened on the razor's handle. "Did you, uh, need the room?"

His flash of embarrassment as he glanced toward the chamber pot only made her own flare.

She shook her head. "No, I . . . I just wanted to retrieve something Ahmi brought for my sunburn."

"Oh." His wave of relief might have made her laugh, under other circumstances. He shifted back from the counter, and she noticed his feet were bare beneath the black cuffs of his pants.

Saints only knew why that detail made this whole moment feel more intimate.

He gestured to the counter with his razor. "I'm not sure which one it is . . ."

She followed his gaze to the array of bottles that sat on the countertop. As much as she wanted to simply run away from this whole situation, her skin *was* burning. So she forced herself to step into the washroom, even though it put her closer to him. If only she could be as nonchalant and confident as she'd felt yesterday on that training field with him.

She found the aloe with a little searching, and then she sidestepped toward the door. "Sorry again for the intrusion."

"It's fine, really." He gestured to the looking glass. "Do you need the mirror?"

"There's one in the bedroom."

His eyebrows tugged together as his gaze narrowed on her neck. "That's quite the burn. Do you need help applying the salve?"

"I . . ." It would be so easy to say no.

But this truly would go easier with help. And though she didn't have her orders from the Rising yet, she knew the rebels wouldn't want her to miss an opportunity to get closer to Carver.

She lifted the ointment. "If you're sure?"

"Of course. Can I finish shaving, first? I'm nearly done."

She nodded and stepped back into the doorway, allowing him the space to finish.

Other than their breaths, the low rasp of the blade against his skin was the only sound. He angled his chin in the mirror, moving the blade deftly but with precise strokes. Each movement was controlled and practiced, and watching him was strangely fascinating.

When he finished, he rinsed the razor in the shallow basin on the counter and dragged a towel over his face, wiping away any residual cream. Then he faced her and held out a hand.

She passed him the jar, and her pulse jumped when their fingers brushed.

As he twisted the jar open, she slipped into the space in front of him, so she could stand in the light coming in from the small window. She turned her back to him and gathered her loose braid over one shoulder.

Her voice seemed especially loud in the silence. "If you'd rather just do the back of my neck, I can do the rest."

In the mirror, she caught the corner of his mouth lifting. "I really don't mind. I have younger siblings, remember? I've been putting aloe on sunburns my whole life."

The images that leapt to mind made something low in her belly curl. Carver, kneeling before a child and tending their sunburn. Dabbing blood from a scraped knee. Drying tears.

Her pulse skittered, and she lowered her head, partly to give him better access to her neck, but mostly to avoid seeing him in the glass.

He stepped closer, and she could feel the heat that radiated from his larger body. Even though he didn't touch her, she was wholly aware of the fact that he stood directly behind her, bare to the waist.

His warm breath teased the nape of her neck before she felt the cool salve of the aloe mixture. Every hair on her body lifted as he brushed the salve carefully over her burned skin. She could feel the rough callouses on the pads of his fingers, but his touch was infinitely gentle.

Ahmi had applied this salve last night, but it had felt *nothing* like this.

"Sorry," he murmured. His voice was so low and deep, it resonated throughout her entire body.

Her fingers tightened on the end of her braid, which she still held. "Sorry?"

"I had no idea you were getting sunburned yesterday. If I'd realized, I wouldn't have kept you so long in the yard."

She forced herself to speak past the tightness in her throat. "Unfortunately, sunburns are common for me. My pale skin can burn in Ferradin, even on a cloudy day."

His short laugh brought a sharp exhale against her neck. With the ointment covering her skin, the sensation was heightened, making her shiver.

His fingers lifted, only to return a moment later with more aloe. His touch started just below her ear and slid down the side of her neck, to the edge of her nightgown's wide collar. Her skin tingled.

She peeked into the mirror just as his eyes flicked up, and their gazes locked.

The air was charged, and nothing in her experience had prepared her for a moment like this. The surge of attraction they both felt made her lungs tighten. Her toes curled against the stone floor.

His throat rolled as he swallowed. He eased back a half-step, still keeping her stare in the mirror. "Can you turn?"

She should say no. She should take the salve from him, thank him for his help, and leave to do the rest herself. Getting close to him for the rebels was one thing, but this . . .

This was something else entirely.

Her body moved without her giving the order. She twisted to face him, her lower back now pressed against the hard edge of the counter. She tilted her chin up. She couldn't meet his gaze, so she stared at his jaw as he leaned in, the crisp smell of the aloe mixing with the spicy sandalwood scent that was purely him.

The brush of his fingertips against the curve of her cheek made her knees weak. She gripped the counter's edge behind her, silently ordering herself to stop reacting to a stupid, medicinal touch, but her body didn't seem interested in listening. While his smooth touch drifted over her cheeks, offering relief to the burn on her skin, it only strengthened the burn low in her belly.

Feeling the heat and intensity of *his* emotions did *not* help.

As he angled his head for a better view of the side of her face, she caught sight of the small scar on his chin that she'd noticed at the altar. Out of all the scars on his body, it would be the easiest to ask about. But despite the strange intimacy of the moment, she didn't feel like she could.

His fingers skimmed along her jaw, leaving a tingling trail. Then his fingertips dipped to her throat.

Her breath caught.

His fingers stilled, then curled away.

She nearly leaned in to follow his retreating hand, but he was only scooping up more of the ointment to apply to her throat.

A tremble skated through her entire body at his gentle touch.

When he finally shifted back, she could feel the pulse of his reluctance.

Strange, how it echoed her own.

She had to crane her neck to meet his eyes. "Thank you, Carver."

His throat flexed as he swallowed. "You're welcome."

The moment felt weighted, and neither of them moved.

A distant knock on the main suite door made her jump. She straightened sharply, and Carver took a deliberate step back, the jar of ointment dangling from his long fingers.

"Thank you," she whispered again, because she didn't know what else to say. Then she ducked her head and fled to the safety of the bedroom.

Carver left with Argent soon after the prince had come knocking. Today was the first time they'd any free time; the high cleric was busy tending to matters of Esperance and couldn't oversee their usual morning activities. Amryn planned to take full advantage.

She ate the breakfast Ahmi had carried in on a tray, enjoying the simple pleasure of eating a meal alone. Then she found a book and curled up in a chair in the suite's sitting room.

Concentrating on the words proved nearly impossible. All she could think of was Carver's touch, and the unexpected way her body had reacted. After nearly half an hour spent on the same page, she gave up.

Pushing out of the cushioned chair, Amryn dropped the book and went to get a drink of water.

The sight of a letter on the floor near the door stopped her cold.

The envelope had a crimson dot of wax, and it had clearly been slid under the main suite door; it hadn't been there when she first sat down with the book.

Pulse jumping, Amryn retrieved the letter. Flipping it over, she saw it was addressed to *Lady Vincetti*, with no indication of who had sent it.

She cracked the wax seal and unfolded the stiff paper.

Lady Vincetti,

Good news! As you requested, I checked Esperance's library, and we do indeed have a copy of Zerrif's Voyage. *It is the unabridged version, which I knew was of particular interest to you. It even includes his visit to the snowy mountains of Sibet!*

It would be best not to remove the book from the library, but you may come view it at any time.

Do let me know if I can be of further assistance.

It was unsigned, as if she should know exactly who had sent it—as if they'd been engaged in a conversation about an obscure book she'd never heard of.

This was from the Rising.

A thrill went through her, followed quickly by a spill of nerves. She folded the note and shoved it into her pocket, cutting a glance over the room. Of course, she was still alone—there was no one to play witness. Even so, her heart beat a little too fast.

The message was clear enough: she was supposed to find that book in the library. Perhaps there, she would find her orders.

She'd been to the library only once since their initial tour, but she was able to re-trace her steps with little difficulty. A few of the guards and servants she passed asked if she was lost or needed anything, but she was able to quickly put them at ease and continue on her way.

When she reached the vast library, the comforting scents of leather, dust, and wood surrounded her. She'd always considered the library in Torin's castle to be impressive, but the collection in Esperance was easily ten times as expansive. The entrance to the large room was an open study area, dotted with square tables and chairs—some of which were occupied by clerics—and tucked in the corners of the study area were cushioned chairs clustered together. Every bit of wall space was overtaken by towering, dark wooden bookshelves, with a balcony that ringed the entire room and gave one access to even more shelves. Beyond the study area were rows upon rows of bookshelves, filled to bursting with volumes of every size. Different collections were housed in separate sections— novels, histories, sciences, religious texts, ancient scrolls—

each had their place. But despite the organization, the shelves still felt like a maze.

As Amryn walked quietly through the open study area, she felt more than one pair of eyes track her. When she reached the bookshelves, she hesitated.

She had no idea where she'd find *Zerrif's Voyage*. She didn't even know what sort of book it was. Fiction, or a detailed travel log?

"Can I assist you?"

She turned and found an older male cleric standing in the aisle to her left. He had a small book cart in front of him, and he looked to be in the process of returning books to their shelves.

"I hope so." She moved toward him. "I wanted to find a copy of *Zerrif's Voyage*, if you have it."

His brow furrowed. "Yes, I think we do. It's not a very popular book, though. Too long. And, truth be told, Zerrif's often seen as laughable by scholars." He lowered his voice a bit conspiratorially. "He's overly dramatic."

"Oh. I was told by my uncle that it would be enjoyable."

The old man chuckled. "Perhaps he thought to tease you." He stepped away from the cart, gesturing forward with a slightly gnarled hand. "It will be this way."

"I don't want to interrupt your work."

"You're not, dear girl. My calling is to take care of the books in this library, and a large part of that is finding the right books for readers. Come." He beckoned for her to follow, and she easily fell into step with him as they walked down the aisle.

"Thank you," she said. "I truly appreciate it."

"No trouble at all. Working among these books is my greatest joy." He sent her a small wink. "Don't tell my superiors I said that. I'd probably lose my clericship if they thought I enjoyed books more than praying to the Divinities."

The corner of her mouth lifted. "Your secret is safe with me."

His eyes twinkled. "I thought I sensed a fellow soul in you." He pressed a hand to his chest. "I'm Cleric Felinus."

"Amryn Lu—I mean, Vincetti."

"A pleasure to meet you, Lady Vincetti."

"Please, just call me Amryn." Her new name was ill-fitting, and made her think too much about her husband.

"Where are you from?" he asked.

"Ferradin."

"Ahh, I've longed to travel there. I'm from Palar originally, and that's where I took my oaths as a much younger man."

"How long have you been a cleric?"

"Oh, Saints if I know. At least twenty years, now." He guided them deeper into the library until they came to a stop at one of the shelves. Felinus had to stretch up on his toes in order to reach a thick, leather bound volume and drag it off the shelf.

She reached for the book, and he relinquished it with a grunt. "A very long-winded man, that Zerrif," he huffed out.

Amryn had to agree; the weight was considerable.

"Would you like me to find a servant to take it to your room?" the older man asked.

A line from the Rising's message raced through her mind: *It would be best not to remove the book from the library.*

"Is there a quiet place I can read it here?" she asked.

"Of course." Felinus pointed down the aisle. "There's a table around the corner."

"That would be wonderful. Thank you."

"Just let me know if you need anything else, my dear."

While Felinus ambled back toward his book cart, Amryn toted *Zerrif's Voyage* around the corner and to the table he'd indicated. There was no one around, and not even a whisper of sound. She was close enough to a window that she didn't need the aid of the nearby lamp, so she didn't bother lighting it. She settled at the table, lifted the leather cover, and began flipping through pages.

About midway through the book, she found a mention of Sibet. After she turned a couple more pages, she found a loose piece of paper—a handwritten note.

She leaned in to scan the words.

Messages will be left in this book. Return it to the shelf when you are done, and destroy all messages before you leave. You will know there's a new message if you see a pin in the bottom left corner of the painting of the late High Cleric Sahrind. If you must get a message to me, leave it in The Ode of Saint Feyjinn. *I will find it.*

Make arrangements to volunteer in the museum. Gain access to the storerooms and locate the empirical seals. Do not remove them. Press them in wax so we can make replicas. Caution is imperative. Take your time, and alert me once copies have been made.

Use your husband's connections to befriend those whom it would benefit us to monitor.

Together, We Will Rise.

The message was cryptic enough that, if it had been accidentally discovered, it could not be traced directly back to her. But for her, it was pointed.

The Rising knew she was married to Carver Vincetti, and she was to use him to get close to Argent and Jayveh. She also had her mission, which made her heart race.

Her part in the rebellion had truly begun.

14

CARVER

CARVER STOOD WITH ARGENT AND Jayveh in their sitting room, re-reading the letter Jayveh had handed him.

The message was from the rebels, and had been left for Jayveh to find after Argent had left to visit his grandfather; something he did first thing every morning.

The note had been slipped under the main suite door, so Jayveh hadn't seen who had delivered it. It was sealed with a single drop of crimson wax, which gave them no further clues.

Princess Jayveh,

I'm pleased to inform you that, as per our conversation the other day, I have located the painting you inquired about. The Cliffs of Ovair is located in the south wing of the gallery, and it is indeed exquisite. I hope you enjoy your study of it.

Do let me know if I can be of further assistance.

Carver finally looked up. "I'm assuming you already went to the painting."

Argent nodded and handed over a smaller piece of folded paper. "This was pinned to the back of the frame."

Carver took it, though his frown was deep. "You should have sent for me immediately."

"You couldn't have come with us," Argent said. "What if someone saw you?"

Jayveh snorted. "You shouldn't have come with me, either."

Carver wholeheartedly agreed.

Argent wrapped an arm around his bride. "I wasn't going to let you go alone. What if it was some sort of trap?"

"You think everything is a trap." Jayveh shook her head. "At least he pretended to become very fascinated with a painting on the opposite wall. While he and the guards looked the other way, I was able to retrieve the note. If a rebel was somehow watching, they wouldn't have thought anything amiss."

Hopefully.

Carver unfolded the second note, which was cramped with small lettering.

Messages will be left with this painting. You will know a message is waiting for you if you see a blue flower petal in the partially closed palm of Grant's statue of the emperor. Messages will be few, due to your unique situation. Your husband does seem thoroughly enamored, though. Use that to your advantage, and work to ensnare him completely.

Propose immediately to the high cleric that everyone should volunteer within Esperance, at a place of their choosing. You must work in the library. In the historical section, there are valuable archives. Gain access to them and locate maps of every military stronghold in the empire. Do not remove them. Memorize them. You have a year.

Together, We Will Rise.

"What do you think?" Argent asked, as soon as Carver looked up.

He frowned. "It's proof the rebels are active here and going after information." He pursed his lips. "They might have more violent plans that don't involve Jayveh, so we can't just assume this is all they're doing in Esperance."

"In other words," Argent said dryly, "you think they might try to kill me this year?"

"It would be a perfect time to do so. You're trapped here like the rest of us and . . ." His eyes dipped to the note. "*Thoroughly enamored.*"

The corner of the prince's mouth lifted as he glanced at Jayveh. "Guilty."

Her lips twitched, but worry hung in her eyes. "Perhaps we could position a guard near that statue. That way we'll know who lingers around it, and maybe even catch them placing a petal."

"I'm not sure that will work," Argent said. "The statue is in the main gallery, but not in plain sight. A guard's presence in that area would be suspicious, and possibly make them think you betrayed them."

Of course Argent had already investigated the location of the statue as well. Carver barely bit back a sigh. "What did I tell you about leaving this investigation to me?"

"I'm not stepping back," Argent said firmly. "Not when my wife's involved."

There was a beat of strained silence, then Jayveh said, "What if it isn't a guard? Maybe Rivard can clear some of the clerics, and they could be positioned discretely around the gallery on some kind of rotation. They can take note of anyone who repeatedly visits the area of the statue."

Argent was already nodding. "I'll talk to Rivard. It may take some time to ascertain loyalties, but it's a good idea."

Carver handed the notes back to Jayveh. "In the meantime, I think you should begin doing as instructed. It's obvious from the wording that they don't expect you to have a lot of mobility, being married to Argent." That was her, *unique* situation, he imagined.

Unless that was a coded message for her alone; the Rising's way of stating that they knew messages would be tracked closely, because she was a double agent.

He kept that to himself.

"I can propose the volunteer work to the high cleric today," Jayveh said.

"Good. We should all pay special attention to those who seem eager—especially those who have particular places in mind they'd like to volunteer. That might lead us to other rebels who received instructions similar to yours."

"And I should search out the stronghold maps," Jayveh said. "To fully play my part."

"You'll have me or a guard with you at all times," Argent insisted. "I don't want you alone in some remote corner of the library where you could be ambushed."

Jayveh knocked her hip against his. "There you go again with your paranoia about everything being a trap."

"If the Rising learns you've turned on them, or if they simply don't have a use for you anymore, you could become as much of a target as Argent," Carver pointed out. "As future empress, your death would be considered a terrible blow to the empire."

Jayveh paled slightly, and Argent's jaw hardened as he tucked her even closer to his side.

But even if his words frightened them, Carver wouldn't take them back. Not when they were true.

Jayveh may be loyal to the empire, or she may be a rebel. Either way, she was a pawn. And in the end, pawns were nothing more than sacrificial pieces.

After leaving Argent and Jayveh to what remained of their free morning, Carver returned to his suite in search of Amryn. He tried to ignore the flip in his stomach as he opened the main door and stepped into the sitting room, but anticipation hummed through his veins.

What had passed between them before Argent's interruption had been . . . unexpected. Something as mundane as tending her sunburn had become much more. His fingers still tingled from touching her skin. Her burn had scalded his fingertips, but he'd be lying if he said that was the only reason for the heat he'd felt in that moment.

Images had lodged in his brain that he knew instinctively he'd never be free of. The delicate curve of her neck as she'd captured her braid and pulled it aside. The intensity in her sea-green eyes as she'd met his gaze in the mirror. The way his fingers had brushed just under the curve of her parted lips. He could still hear the tentative edge in her voice as she'd accepted his offer of help. The whisper of every exhale. The way her breath had hitched when he touched her—especially the delicate skin at her throat.

His skin tightened even now, just remembering it. She was so soft. Fragile, yet no less fierce than her fiery curls. She was a mystery, and he was anxious to see her again. To know if the air between them would still be charged. If she would still be vulnerable with him, and share her thoughts. Because he needed to know if he could trust her. At least, that's what he told himself. Truthfully, he just found himself increasingly interested in getting to know *her*.

It didn't take long to ascertain that she wasn't in their suite. He didn't know where she would choose to spend her morning, and she'd left no note. A book lay abandoned on one of the cushioned chairs in the sitting room, so perhaps she'd gotten bored and decided to wander the grounds? He somehow doubted that, considering her sunburn.

Intent on finding her, Carver left the apartment and made his way to the nearest staircase. He assumed one of the guards or servants would know where she was, but before he reached someone he could ask, he spotted Ivan.

He'd had brief interactions with all of the Empire's Chosen by now, but Ivan had been among the most reticent. Carver needed to get to know him if he was going to determine his loyalty. So, with a pang of regret he'd examine later, he pushed aside all thoughts of Amryn and focused on Ivan.

"Good morning," he called out.

Ivan's cool blue eyes regarded his approach without any change in his features. "Good morning." His heavy Sibeten accent was perhaps the most pronounced among them all; it was as rugged as he was. His blonde hair brushed his cheekbones, and his broad form was hulking, even though he was the one standing at the base of the stairs. He wore a thin white shirt that stretched over bulging arms, and he was drenched in sweat.

Carver kept a small smile in place. Friendly, but not as open as the smiles he'd exchanged with Samuel or Darrin. He thought the warrior in Ivan might respond better if he glimpsed a bit of the general.

He tipped his head toward Ivan's appearance. "You've been out in the training yard?"

"*Neeyev.* I went for a run." Ivan swiped the back of his hand over his brow. "I must learn my endurance in this inhospitable climate."

"You know, the frozen lands of Sibet are considered inhospitable by most."

Ivan arched a brow. "Not by Sibetens."

The corner of Carver's mouth twitched. His humor was surprising. Maybe he'd misread the serious-looking man.

That wasn't exactly an encouraging thought, was it?

He reached the base of the stairs and the two faced each other in the long corridor, which was lined with towering columns and tall windows. "If you truly wish to test your endurance," Carver said, "perhaps we should spar."

"Is the Butcher of Westmont so afraid of fighting a Sibeten Wolf that he first must tire his opponent?"

Carver shrugged. "A general must be strategic."

Ivan snorted, but humor glowed in his eyes—as did challenge. "Very well, I accept."

Carver dipped his chin and they fell into step together down the hall. "Are you enjoying your morning?"

"*Yenn.* And I'll like it even more when I beat you on the field." He shot Carver a look. "What of you?"

"I like having a little freedom," Carver said, choosing his words intentionally. "The high cleric's schedule is . . . time-consuming."

Ivan grunted. "The high cleric likes to hear himself speak."

"I think you're right," Carver said. "And we're literally a

trapped audience. I don't know how I'm going to survive the man's sermons for a year."

Ivan made a sound in his throat that could have been agreement, but he didn't verbally respond. He may have simply been done talking, but it could also have to do with the two clerics walking past them—the male and female certainly shot them some looks that made it clear they'd overheard Carver's statement.

With Carver's luck, they'd tell Zacharias, and he'd be in for yet another lecture from the high cleric.

Not wanting to lose the conversation completely, Carver changed the subject. "Where is your wife this morning?"

"I am not her *souvrin*," Ivan said, his gaze trained ahead. "She is free to go as she wills."

Carver heard the unspoken undercurrent to those words. "How are things between you?"

Ivan shot him a look.

Carver lifted a hand. "I don't mean to pry. It's just . . . well, nothing about this experience has been what I expected."

A muscle in Ivan's jaw ticked as he once again focused on the corridor that stretched before them. The only sounds were their boots against stone. Then, "Cora is of a delicate constitution and easily startled. She has many fears and anxieties, and I do not know how to . . ." His words drifted, and the muscles in his shoulders bunched. "I have found that she is uncomfortable any time we are alone, so I try never to be alone with her." He looked at Carver. "Is your wife afraid of you?"

The question caught him off guard, and he wasn't sure how to answer. "I think she's cautious," he finally said.

Ivan nodded once, the motion clipped. "That is fair."

It really was. His name alone chilled the blood of enemy

soldiers. That was a good thing, his father had told him. *Let your reputation grow far beyond who you really are. Let it be vicious and bloodthirsty. Because if the mere mention of your name can give armies pause, then a battle may be averted, and countless lives on both sides could be saved.*

It had never bothered him that people called him the Butcher. It didn't matter if his friends or family heard it, because he knew they wouldn't look at him any differently—they knew him.

Amryn didn't. And it bothered him that she might think of him as *the Butcher.*

It didn't help that—after returning from Harvari—he could barely stand to hear the nickname. Probably because it felt too true.

Carver cleared his throat. "I fought beside Wolves in Harvari."

Ivan's head tilted slightly to the side as he looked toward Carver.

Saints, that topic change had been too abrupt.

"It was difficult to let them go," Ivan said. "To know they would die so far from home." He rubbed at his arm, and it was only then Carver remembered he had been injured during the wedding feast.

"They saved many lives," Carver said. "Entire villages were defended with only a handful of Wolves left to guard them."

"You wonder why I did not go with them," Ivan said bluntly.

"Yes," Carver said, just as directly.

They both stopped in the middle of the empty corridor, and Ivan met his stare. "I did not abandon my Pack," he said, his voice low and rough.

"The emperor called for the best Wolves, but you didn't come."

He bristled. "I am no coward."

"Then why didn't you come?"

"I did not stay behind by choice. My father—my king—commanded me to remain at home."

"Why?"

Ivan took a step forward, and Carver's body stiffened in alert.

But the Sibeten didn't strike him. He only glowered. "My mother had just buried one son. She could not have survived burying another, so he assigned me a task at home." He leaned back, fully glaring at Carver now. "You tell me what is easier, General. Bleeding alongside your men, or watching them march away, knowing that none of them are likely to return?"

Carver held his stare, his skin feeling too tight as he said, "I know the pain of both."

Ivan blinked. But before he could form a response, a terrible shriek rent the air.

Carver's hand instinctively dropped to his belt, but, of course, he had no weapons. He and Ivan turned together and sprinted toward the screaming, which continued at a hysterical pitch and rang shrilly against the stone walls. It seemed to be coming from one of the many sitting rooms at the end of the hall; a fact that was confirmed by the cluster of clerics, servants, and guards gathered near the doorway.

Trepidation shot through Carver as he and Ivan shouldered their way through the crowd.

Standing just outside the doorway of the sitting room was a maid. The young woman was no longer screaming, though she was crying as a female cleric gripped her arms and shook her. "Mathe, what is it? What's wrong?"

The woman's eyes were wild, and the terror on her face made Carver's gut fall.

"In th-there," the maid pointed toward the sitting room, her hand shaking as much as her voice. "On the—floor. Opened the door, and—she—she's—*dead*!"

His blood turned to ice.

Amryn.

Her name slammed into his mind without cause or warning. Fear blasted him, and he shoved around the maid, ignoring the shout of a guard for him to stay out of the room. He felt Ivan follow him.

The sitting room was a small space, clearly designed for more intimate gatherings. The settee on the left was the largest thing in the room, so that's where his gaze cut.

Two small, slippered feet poked out from behind the settee, the hem of a blue skirt draped over them.

Carver's lungs stopped working. He didn't know what dress Amryn had worn today, but she had a blue dress.

Please, no . . .

His ears roared as he lurched forward, Ivan beside him.

When he rounded the settee, his eyes shot to the woman's face.

Black hair—not red.

Dusky skin—not pale.

Lifeless brown eyes—not fathomless sea-green.

Relief cut through him, and he knew that was wrong. Because while this wasn't Amryn, it was—

"Cora," Ivan whispered, stunned. He was frozen for the space of a heartbeat, then he darted forward, only to drop to his knees beside his wife's head. His long fingers grazed her neck, searching for a pulse.

Even without checking for life, Carver knew Cora was dead. The braided rug beneath her was drenched in blood and the hilt of a knife stuck out of her unmoving chest.

Clutched in her hand was a piece of paper.

Ivan spotted it as soon as Carver did. He pried it from Cora's fingers before Carver could tell him not to disturb the scene.

He read the note over Ivan's shoulder, and the words rippled a chill down his spine.

Retribution has come for you.

15

AFTER BURNING THE RISING'S NOTE using one of the library's lamps, Amryn returned *Zerrif's Voyage* to the shelf and made her way to the library's exit. She'd barely stepped into the hallway when rapid footsteps made her head turn.

Carver and Ahmi both strode toward her, and Amryn frowned as she felt Ahmi's edge of fear. The maid's pale face revealed nothing. Carver's expression was set in stone, though Amryn felt a pulse of relief once he spotted her.

It was a relief she certainly didn't feel. She felt caught. Trapped. And with every step closer, Carver's presence felt more threatening.

He couldn't know about the Rising's note. There was no way. And yet, her heart thundered in her chest.

Carver drew to a stop before her. "Are you all right?"

Surprised by the intensity in his demand, she glanced at Ahmi. "I'm fine. What's happened?"

Her maid visibly swallowed, but it was Carver who answered. "There's been an attack. We've all been summoned by the high cleric."

Her blood chilled. "An attack? Is everyone all right?"

Ahmi's sharp intake of breath was answer enough. Her waves of sadness, shock, pain, and fear only solidified Amryn's sinking suspicion.

She met Carver's unwavering gaze. "Who?" she breathed.

"Cora."

Denial whipped through her, but she knew Carver wasn't lying. She just couldn't accept the fact that Cora—the youngest bride among them—was dead. That poor girl . . . She was quiet, but she had a gentle soul and a kind heart. Amryn hadn't known her long enough to truly befriend her, but she felt a horrible pang knowing she was dead. The terror she must have felt . . . Amryn pressed a hand to her stomach.

Carver stepped closer and cupped her elbow. He looked to Ahmi. "Will you go ahead and tell the high cleric we're coming?"

"Of course," Ahmi murmured. She hurried away, leaving them alone in the hall.

Carver's thumb brushed against her sleeve. "Do you need to sit?"

"No." She lifted her gaze to his. "How . . .?"

"She was stabbed. A maid found her body in one of the small sitting rooms."

Her gut twisted at the gruesome image her mind conjured.

"We don't know who did it," Carver said, his voice grim. "But it was a fresh kill. She'd been dead maybe an hour by the time the maid found her."

"You saw her?"

His nod was stilted. "I was with Ivan when her body was found."

Amryn's eyes pinched closed. The swell of emotion in her

own chest was exacerbated by what Carver felt. "How is he?"

"I think he's in shock. And he's angry."

The flatness in his voice had her peeking up at him. "You're angry, too."

His jaw locked. "She didn't deserve that."

No, she didn't. Cora had been timid. Shy. Grieving her brother, and anxious about being away from home and married to a stranger—especially an intimidating one like Ivan. Despite attempts to befriend her, Cora had still been closed off from the rest of the brides.

Carver's voice was heavier as he continued. "Ahmi didn't know where you were. No one did. We've been looking for a half hour."

"I'm sorry."

"You didn't know." His hold on her tightened infinitesimally. "Until we find Cora's killer, I need you to promise me that you won't go anywhere alone."

She looked into his penetrating blue eyes, knowing that was a promise she could not keep. But still she lied and said, "I promise."

He seemed to realize he was still holding her arm, because he suddenly pulled away. "Do you need another moment before we join the others?"

She didn't want to go anywhere near the tumultuous emotions everyone was sure to be feeling, but dragging her feet wouldn't help anything. So she shook her head, and they began walking side by side. There was space between them, but not enough to keep from accidental brushes; her shoulder against his upper arm, his knuckles against her forearm.

Those brief moments of contact were surprisingly comforting, but even before they entered the large receiving room of Esperance, emotions punched through Amryn, stealing any sense of calm.

Fear. Rage. Shock. Sadness.

Amryn wasn't sure why, but the absence of grief in the room hit her the strongest. None of them knew Cora enough to feel the full depth of her loss, and that seemed a crime. Even her husband had only known her a week.

Carver's hand settled at the small of Amryn's back as he guided her across the floor. The large receiving room had once been an ancient throne room. It jutted out from the main temple, which allowed for windows to stretch along both walls, all the way to the end of the room. Stairs led up to a dais, where High Cleric Zacharias stood with Chancellor Trevill, their heads ducked toward each other as they each took turns speaking quietly and rapidly.

Argent was climbing the stairs to join them, and Ivan followed just behind him.

Amryn was still learning to distinguish everyone's emotions, especially in a crowd, but she could feel Ivan's fury.

"Amryn!" Jayveh rushed over and grasped Amryn's hand. "I was so worried when no one could find you!"

The wash of her relief was wholly sincere, and Amryn squeezed the princess's fingers. "Is everyone else accounted for?"

Jayveh's head bobbed, but before she could speak, the high cleric's voice boomed, calling for quiet.

Once he was sure he had the room's attention, he said, "I know this is difficult and you all have questions, but I need you to remain calm."

"Remain calm?" Darrin bit out. "Cora was *murdered* and you want us to *remain calm*?"

Marriset clung to her husband's arm, and she visibly trembled as she said, "Any one of us might be next!"

"I can't believe she was killed." Sadia burst into tears, and Samuel put his arm around her.

The high cleric lifted his hands. "We are increasing the guards and conducting a search of the grounds. Obviously, there will be an investigation—"

"By who?" Ivan interrupted. "Your worthless guards?"

The high cleric's expression tightened as he shot the other man a look. "I know you're upset, but please step down from the—"

"*Neeyev.*" Ivan took a menacing step toward the high cleric, but Argent caught his arm and held him back. That didn't stop Ivan's glare, or the accusing finger he thrust toward the high cleric. "*Solicht var is haveroff!*" he spat.

Amryn stole a look at Carver to see how he'd reacted to Ivan's use of Sibeten. While old languages could still be taught, everyone in the empire spoke Craethen. It was the required language, and usually no one dared speak an old tongue in any official setting.

Carver's face revealed nothing, however, and his emotions were once again strangely muted.

She didn't know how he did that.

The high cleric's face went red. "Now, see here—"

"This is *your* fault," Ivan growled at him. "She should have been safe here! How could you let this happen?"

Chancellor Trevill stepped forward, putting himself between Ivan and the high cleric. "Easy. There is no use in—"

"Where were you?" the high cleric demanded of Ivan, over-riding Trevill. "What have you been doing this morning?"

Ivan's fury darkened, making Amryn's stomach twist. "Are you truly accusing me of this?"

"You were perhaps the last person to see your wife alive," Zacharias said.

"Enough!" Argent's voice filled the room, silencing everyone on the dais and everyone standing near it. He turned to the high cleric. "You will increase the guards, and you will continue to search every part of Esperance."

The high cleric bristled. "Of course. The emperor placed me in charge, and I will see that Cora's killer is found."

Beside Amryn, Carver felt a flash of irritation.

Argent's annoyance was less pronounced, but it was still clear that he didn't appreciate the high cleric's unsubtle attempt to re-establish his authority. His lips parted, but before he could speak, someone new entered the room.

Amryn turned with the others to see Emperor Lorcan, surrounded by guards, slowly cross the floor toward them. His movements were labored, and the guards that hovered protectively around him only made him seem frailer. Sorrow billowed out from him, along with pain from his still-healing wound. He didn't move for the dais, but instead came to a stop near Carver.

Amryn had never been so close to the emperor, and every hair on her body lifted in response to his proximity.

Everyone bowed deeply—Amryn included.

The emperor gestured for them to rise, weariness dragging his shoulders down as he said, "I am deeply grieved by Cora's death. It is an atrocity that never should have happened, especially on such hallowed ground." His gaze drifted to Ivan. "I offer you my condolences, as well as an assurance that her death will be avenged."

Ivan said nothing—his face could have been carved from stone.

He switched his focus to Trevill. "I want you to conduct

the investigation."

The high cleric made a pinched sound in his throat. "Emperor, I thought that I would—"

"Your responsibilities are already many," Emperor Lorcan interrupted. "Chancellor Trevill has experience in leading investigations, and I know he can balance his duties with the council while searching out the killer. And, as he operates independently of the church, I believe that makes him the obvious choice. Zacharias, you will assist him as needed."

The high cleric clearly didn't like this, but he nodded.

Trevill bowed, accepting his role.

Emperor Lorcan looked over the rest of the room. "All of you will cooperate with Trevill's investigation."

It was their turn to nod.

There was a brief moment of silence, then Jayveh asked, "What about Cora? Her funeral . . . her family?"

The emperor's face softened. His sadness was still there, but his affection for Jayveh was obvious as he looked at her. "Her funeral will be held as soon as the high cleric can make arrangements. When I leave Esperance, I will convey news of Cora's death to her family. They deserve to know."

Trevill's voice was quiet. "What about the council? The Cael seat will be empty."

The emperor sighed. "It would take months to get a replacement here, and at that point, I fear the newcomer would have missed too much. The Cael seat will be filled after the council's time in Esperance is finished; Argent and Jayveh will be switching out at that time, so there will be multiple new faces."

"Cora is not replaceable," Ivan said. His voice was a little less combative, now that the emperor was among them, but it was still hard.

Compassion rippled from Emperor Lorcan. "Of course she is not. We all mourn her loss."

Amryn stared at the emperor. Like at the wedding feast, she was struck by how worn he looked. How . . . common. He was just an old man. And yet, he was responsible for so much death. So much oppression. He was the reason empaths were hunted. He was the reason Ferradin was not an independent kingdom. He was the reason Torin's family had been slaughtered, and he was the reason Amryn was here; alone, isolated, and afraid.

He had ordered Cora's brother's execution a week ago, and now he stood here, sorry that she was dead.

Amryn would never understand a man like that.

High Cleric Zacharias shifted his weight. "Your Eminence, I wonder if you and I might discuss your decision not to find a replacement for Cora. I understand your reasoning, insofar as the council is concerned, but the fact remains that these marriages are integral to the peace we're trying to build here. If Ivan has no wife . . ."

"I understand the implications of my decision to not bring another bride from Cael to Esperance. I will contemplate how best to proceed after the year is over." The emperor looked at Ivan. "I may yet arrange a marriage between Sibet and Cael, but for now, I ask you to focus on strengthening friendships with the other kingdoms of the empire."

"I can assist in finding Cora's killer," Ivan said. "As a Wolf, I have all the necessary skills to—"

"I appreciate your desire to help," the emperor said. "But your focus should be elsewhere. Leave the investigation to Chancellor Trevill."

Ivan's eyes were dark, but he did not argue.

The emperor looked back toward the dais, his voice a little deeper as he said, "Trevill, find the truth. Zacharias . . . keep the rest of them safe."

The high cleric must have heard the undercurrent of threat, because he swallowed hard before he bowed his head. "It will be done, Your Eminence."

Amryn's eyes opened, her senses on alert as she came suddenly awake. It was the middle of the night, and she was surrounded by darkness, but something had woken her. Straining her ears, she soon heard Carver's soft pacing in the other room.

She wasn't sure how that muted sound could have woken her—then she felt the stab of his pain.

It had been two days since Cora's death. Her funeral had been held this morning, and she'd been buried in Esperance's cemetery. Through it all, Amryn had felt nearly every emotion from Carver, from anger to sadness. But this pain was different. Sharper. Deeper.

This wasn't about Cora.

The fact that he was pacing—not to mention the overall mood she sensed from him—made it clear that his pain wasn't physical. He didn't need assistance. And yet, she found herself sitting up, pushing aside the blankets, and lifting her simple robe. She slipped her arms inside the wide sleeves and padded her way to the door.

Carver was in the sitting room, pacing near the balcony. The full moon gilded everything in silver, giving ample light for her to see that he was shirtless. Saints, why did she always catch him this way? It made her stomach flip and her cheeks warm, and it was a struggle to keep from staring. Especially when curiosity pulled her gaze toward his many and varied scars.

Carver's attention snapped to her, and his movement ceased. "Is something wrong?" he asked, his voice low.

She shook her head. "I heard you pacing."

"Oh." He shoved a hand through his hair. "Sorry."

"It's fine." She was surprised by her desire to move closer to him. Refusing to cave to such a thing, she kept her feet firmly planted. "Are you all right?"

"Fine." It was clearly a lie, and he must have realized she wasn't convinced, because he exhaled slowly. "I often have trouble sleeping."

He didn't expound, and she didn't pry. She didn't have to be an empath to sense his reluctance to talk about what was troubling him.

Instead, she said, "I'm sorry if I disturbed you."

The corner of his lips twitched. "Clearly, I'm the one who disturbed *you*."

His burst of humor was fleeting, but her interruption had dulled the edge of his pain; possibly enough that she'd be able to ignore it if she returned to the bedroom, but she hated to feel any person hurting—no matter who it was.

Still, they hardly knew each other, and she didn't know if he'd want her to stay—or if she truly wanted to.

Her bare feet shifted against the cool stone floor, indecision tugging at her. "I can leave you to your thoughts," she offered.

"Please don't," he said softly. "My thoughts are rarely good company these days."

She never would have expected that raw vulnerability

from Carver; she couldn't leave him now.

She moved for the settee, which put her closer to him, but still maintained some distance. She'd decided it was best to never get too close to Carver; whenever she did, her body betrayed her.

She settled on the end of the settee at an angle, so she could easily view him over the cushioned back. "I used to have trouble sleeping," she said. "After I lost my mother."

"I'm sorry." He leaned back against one of the balcony columns, his gaze never leaving hers. "How old were you when she died?"

"Seven."

His emotions—already tumultuous—became more so. Sadness, compassion, pity—they all prodded her. "I'm sorry," he repeated.

Her fingers picked at the edge of her wrapper, anxious for something to do as she remained otherwise still. She never talked of her mother.

Ever.

She edged her thoughts away from the actual loss of her; that horrible feeling of her death. "I missed her during the day, of course, but it was in the darkness of night that I mourned her. I . . . I hated the dark. And the quilt on top of me would become stifling. I'd have to shove it off. I'd pace. And I'd hate the fact that all around me, everything was still as everyone else slept peacefully. It made me feel more alone."

Carver said nothing, just watched her, but his shoulders looked heavy, as if they were supporting the column he leaned against, and not the other way around.

"One night, Rix—my uncle—found me pacing in my room. He was surprised to find me awake, but not crying from a nightmare." That's how he'd usually found her, in those early months after losing her mother. How many nights had he heard her screams, stumbled into her room, and gathered her into his arms?

She forced those memories away and focused back on Carver. "I don't think he really knew what to do with me. He got me a glass of warm milk, he tucked me into bed, but I still couldn't sleep. So, he told me stories. Silly ones. Fantastical ones. Stories from his childhood that included Torin and my mother."

"He distracted you."

She nodded. "He'd sit with me for hours, even though he had a schedule full of important meetings the next day."

"Did it work?"

She smiled faintly. "Yes. Somehow, even though I knew what he was doing . . . it worked every time. He would tell me stories, and I'd tell my own, and eventually I'd tire and fall asleep."

"I'm glad you had him," Carver murmured.

"So am I."

In the following pause, he looked over his shoulder toward the jungle that loomed outside the netted balcony doors. He slowly spun the silver ring on his forefinger, the motion clearly unconscious.

"I never used to have trouble sleeping," he admitted. "It's been more recent. Since I returned from Harvari." He didn't say anything else.

Amryn drew her feet up onto the settee and hugged her knees to her chest. "When I was nine, I thought I found the fairy realm."

He twisted back to her, and in the glow of the moon she

could see his eyebrows tug together. "What?"

"In Ferradin, every child hears stories of how the fairy realm can touch ours. And if you're very lucky, you might be able to find one of the pathways that join our worlds."

A thread of amusement rippled from him. "And you thought you found this pathway?"

"I was sure of it. I'd been playing in one of the palace gardens, and I fell through a hedge."

A huffing laugh escaped him. "It's lucky you weren't on one of those infernal mountains you love, or you might have fallen to your death."

She rolled her eyes. "Mountains are lovely. Now, can I finish my story?"

He lifted both hands. "Please do."

"As I was saying, I fell through a hedge, and I knew instantly that I'd entered the fairy world. Right in front of me, in this grassy, forgotten space, I found tiny little chairs and a small table made of weathered wood."

Curiosity rose in Carver's eyes, and she felt his stirring of surprise.

She tucked her shoulder into the corner of the settee, the cushioned arm pressing into her lower back as she viewed him a bit smugly. "I see I have your attention."

"You always have my attention." The soft words—so quiet she barely heard them—made her stomach flutter, and warmth spread through her body. He wasn't even touching her, but he had a physical effect on her. Something about that was alarming.

She mentally shook herself and continued her story. "There were four chairs lying around the table. They'd been painted once, but everything was chipped and long faded, and weeds had done their best to overgrow the entire setting, but they were there. Like a long-abandoned fairy tea party.

"I wanted to run and tell everyone what I'd found, but I also didn't want to leave without seeing a fairy—just in case I wasn't able to find my way back. So, I plucked the weeds and righted the chairs, and I even found some berries nearby to place on the table, as a sort of offering. But the fairies didn't come.

"Evening set in, and even though I was tucked between hedges, I started to get cold. I was hungry, too, so I ate the berries—and immediately got sick."

Carver's eyebrows slammed down. "This had better have a happy ending."

"Clearly, I'm all right."

"Maybe. But you were a child trapped in a hedge, delusional, and now sick, and night was coming on. Didn't you have a nursemaid? And where was your uncle?"

"Oh, he was searching for me, along with half the castle. Torin was the one who eventually found me. He heard my vomiting."

The king of Ferradin had poked his head through the hedge, taken one look at her, and instantly gathered her into his arms—even though she retched all over his new tunic.

"He wanted to take me back to the castle at once, but I started crying because I hadn't seen any fairies yet, and I didn't want to leave the fairy realm. I made him swear he'd bring me back later, and he promised he would. When I asked him how he'd find it again, he said, '*That will be easy enough. This was your mother's favorite hideaway.*' And that's when I realized the table and chairs had been hers. I later learned that she'd begged Rix to craft them for the fairies. She'd left them there as a child and yet, somehow, years later, I found them." She smiled a little. "It felt very much like fairy magic."

The corner of Carver's mouth rose. "That's a nice thought. And a good story."

"It is. Less so for Torin, of course. I kept throwing up on him as he carried me back to the castle. His clothes were ruined."

Carver chuckled. "Hopefully you learned not to eat unknown berries."

"You can't tell me you never ate anything questionable as a child."

He shrugged. "I ate a stick."

She blinked. "You ate a *stick*?"

"It's not exactly something I'm proud of, but yes. I ate a stick."

A laugh burst out of her. "Why by all the Saints would you do that?"

His smile stretched. "Loreena told me I couldn't, so I did it to prove her wrong. It was utterly disgusting, and I don't recommend it."

"You ate a *stick*, just to spite your sister?"

"Yes." He pushed away from the column and moved to sit on the other end of the settee. "To be fair, it was more of a twig, but it still tasted horrible."

"You actually ate it?" she asked, her voice rippling with suppressed laughter.

"Yes. Every bark-ridden bit of it."

She shook her head. "You eating a stick is far more embarrassing than me eating foul berries. At least most berries are *supposed* to be eaten."

"You haven't even heard the most embarrassing part yet." His dimple flashed as he smiled. "I was thirteen."

Her eyes rounded. "Seriously? A thirteen-year-old should

have more sense than that!"

"Have you *known* any thirteen-year-old boys?"

She chuckled, he smiled, and while they talked, the moon continued its quiet journey across the sky.

16

CARVER

WHILE CARVER SILENTLY PREPARED to sneak out of Esperance under the cover of darkness, he couldn't help but think of the previous night he'd spent talking to Amryn. As much as he needed to see Ford, he wished he could stay in this sitting room and talk with Amryn until late into the night again. Something had changed between them, though he was hard-pressed to define what it was. She'd stayed with him. Distracted him. And when she'd begun to nod off, he hadn't hesitated to take her hand and lead her back to the bedroom.

He hadn't entered her space—he *did* view the room as hers— but when her head had tipped back and their eyes had met, and she'd whispered *goodnight* . . .

Saints, his heart started pounding again just thinking of it.

Which wasn't exactly helpful, since he needed to focus on sneaking out of this temple and past the increased guard.

He eased his way onto the balcony, moving as quietly and fluidly as a ghost. He wore his darkest clothing, including a knitted hood over his head, leaving only his eyes visible. The

heat was stifling, even in the middle of the night, but he needed to be invisible.

Though he hadn't yet snuck out of Esperance, he'd carefully plotted his route and done a practice run as far as the
compound's wall. It was now a routine matter to swing over
the balcony's railing and find grooves in the temple's carved,
ancient stone.

Fingerholds and toeholds were all he needed to scale his
way to the ground. His breaths were muffled by the hood, but
loud in his ears. Loud enough, it nearly drowned out the echoing sounds of the jungle, as alive at night as it was during the
day.

He landed in a crouch near the foliage that butted the side
of the temple. He strained all of his senses, but when he picked
up no signs of movement, he slipped into the shadowy garden.

Carver had always excelled in matters of stealth, even as
a boy. He'd learned to scale walls just so he could smuggle toads
into his sisters' rooms. Their screams had awakened the whole
castle, and his father had lectured him, of course. But then
he'd also turned Carver over to the spymaster of Westmont
for further training. If he hadn't chosen to become a soldier,
he might have been a spy.

He was a soldier at heart, and the role of a general suited
him well. But he'd always love the thrill and challenge that came
from slipping unnoticed through the shadows, and past patrolling guards—it was exhilarating.

He found the towering cluster of trees at the back of the
garden and moved to kneel near the sprawling roots.

They weren't allowed to have weapons in Esperance—a
fact that he hated—but his father had helped him smuggle
in a few daggers, which he'd hidden in strategic places. One

of which was here, a placement he'd decided when he'd solidified this route as his best option for sneaking out of Esperance.

Between the twisting roots he found the stones he'd laid atop the wrapped dagger. As soon as his fingers curled around the hilt, he breathed a little easier.

He scaled the wall, using the vines and trees that grew along the ancient stone. In moments, he was dropping to the ground on the other side. The ground was wet beneath his boots from an earlier rain, but that didn't slow him down as he followed the nearly overgrown path that would lead him to Ford.

As he moved in the darkness, he remained alert. Jungles were dangerous places that demanded respect. Night birds made their calls and insects hummed. The thick foliage rustled when animals brushed past, but none were large enough to worry him. Vines draped between towering branches, and some of them moved and coiled. Snakes. They were large and definitely a threat, but they didn't seem to mind him.

As soon as Carver was far enough away from Esperance to be free of any patrols, he tugged the knitted hood off and ran his fingers through his mussed hair. The smell of fresh rain and wet earth mingled with the musky scents of the jungle and the creatures who called it home. It smelled just like Harvari.

His body tensed, and he had to force himself to relax. To breathe.

He wasn't in Harvari. He wasn't fighting for his life. He wasn't watching his men die.

He wasn't a prisoner.

He ground his teeth so hard his jaw cracked. *Those* were thoughts he refused to dwell on.

But others snared him.

Ever since finding Cora's body, he'd been haunted by memories he'd tried to leave behind. Women and children sprawled out in poses of death. Burying them. Mourning them even though they were strangers, because they were innocent. They hadn't deserved to have their homes turned into a battleground, just because their leaders wanted war.

He needed another of Amryn's stories. He needed the distraction of her; her grounding presence, her comforting voice.

The fact that he wanted her was undeniable—and a bit terrifying.

His walk through the jungle lasted nearly two hours. The distance was enough to ensure Ford's location wouldn't be scouted out by one of Esperance's guards, but not so far that Carver couldn't reach him for these meetings.

The cabin was one of many Carver had glimpsed tonight, but this one had a lamp glowing behind the window. These small, scattered houses had been built for soldiers who required accommodations away from the main temple, so having Ford hole up in one wasn't really a misuse of the place. Not that the high cleric would see it that way, since he thought they'd all been cleared out.

Carver climbed the wooden steps that protested underfoot and crossed the narrow porch. He knocked on the door—two times, a pause, then three.

Silence greeted him. Then a floorboard creaked inside, and the door swung open.

Ford's grin was all Carver managed to take in before his friend grabbed him in a hard embrace. "About time you showed up," he griped. "I know we said two weeks, but I was starting to talk to myself!"

Carver grunted, his ribs straining against Ford's crushing

grip. "You've always talked to yourself."

Ford released him with a clap to the shoulder and a chuckle. "Maybe. But now I'm talking to monkeys, and that's definitely new."

They stepped inside and Carver blinked quickly as his eyes adjusted to the low-burning lamp. There wasn't much to the cabin. One room, a bed with rumpled blankets in the corner, a table with four chairs, and a small stove for cooking. The table was covered in art supplies, and canvases littered the room. Oil paintings of the jungle, animals, and even some of Westmont and the sea. Ford had been busy.

"It helps pass the time," his friend said by way of explanation as he moved to clear off two chairs for them. "And I didn't know when you'd manage to come tonight, so I wanted to keep busy."

Carver's eyes caught on a painting of a dark-skinned little boy with closely shorn hair. He was grinning, his brown eyes too big for his head. He held a dagger in one hand and a whittled figurine of a horse in the other.

The image was a punch to Carver's gut. His fingers twitched at his sides, feeling the memory of the wood in his hands. He remembered how the grin on his own face had felt as he'd handed the carving to the boy. The sound of the boy's excited chatter, speaking a language Carver had not yet fully learned, still rang in his memory.

He'd buried that boy a week later. He'd pressed the blood-soaked figurine into his small, folded hands, and then he'd wrapped him in cloth and covered him with dirt.

"It helps," Ford said quietly. "The dreams aren't so harsh after I've painted their faces."

Carver's throat clenched. "I'm glad," he said, his voice too tight.

Ford was twenty-four, one year younger than Carver. They had met as teenagers, and Ford had served as one of Carver's scouts in Harvari. They'd saved each other's lives on the battlefield more times than either of them bothered to track. Ford's steadiness, humor, and loyalty had gotten them both through Harvari, but that didn't mean he hadn't been stained by the war, too. Their scars were different, but they both had them. Ford had clearly found an outlet for his demons, and while Carver was happy for him, he definitely didn't want to talk about the war tonight.

Ford must have sensed that, because he turned his attention back to moving the paintings, including the one of the Harvarian boy.

Carver breathed a little easier once the boy's face was gone.

After the table was cleared, they settled into the chairs, sitting across from each other. Ford was from the northernmost part of Westmont. He had brown hair that curled over his ears, bronze skin, and a slender build that made him perfect for his job of infiltrating dangerous places. Whenever sneaking wasn't appropriate, he used his good looks and charm to get the information he needed. He also relied on humor to loosen tense air.

He smiled slowly at Carver. "Your father stopped by after the wedding. He told me about your wife. Red hair and all."

Carver rolled his eyes. "Did he tell you about the attack at the feast?"

"Yes, but let's focus on the important things first." His friend leaned in, his eyes dancing. "I won the bet. She's got flaming red hair."

"You're an idiot."

"I'm a *winning* idiot."

"That really doesn't sound like a good thing."

Ford shrugged. "So, what is she like? Is she a rebel?"

"I don't know. But she has . . . surprised me." That was the most succinct way of putting it.

Ford lifted one eyebrow. "There's a story there."

Several, actually. But he redirected Ford's attention to where it needed to be. "One of the brides was murdered three days ago."

Ford blinked. Then his eyes narrowed. "Who?"

"Cora, of Hafsin." He relayed the details, and Ford listened raptly.

When he finished, Ford shook his head. "The message that was left behind . . . *Retribution has come for you;* that's got to be from the rebels."

"Most likely," Carver agreed. "But I don't want to blind myself to other possibilities."

"Do you have other theories, then?"

"Cora could have been a rebel. She might have done something her contact didn't like, and that note could be a warning for other rebels."

Ford leaned back in his chair. "From your father's description of Cora, she was young and timid—even nervous. Would she really make a good rebel?"

"No," Carver admitted. "Which could be another reason why they killed her. Or they killed her because they didn't like the way her brother attacked the emperor. It could have been a punishment for his actions."

"Why would the rebels be upset about an assassination attempt?"

"Maybe if it upset a larger plan." He went on to explain the message Jayveh had received from the rebels.

Ford's brow furrowed. "They basically gave her a year to memorize the strongholds of Craethen, which means they're playing a longer game."

"Unless they suspect she's playing double agent, and they want to throw us off."

"True. But if we assume they believe she's loyal to the Rising, and if we also assume they have multiple contacts and they all have different jobs, then it's very possible no one has the full plan."

"Except for the person writing the messages."

Ford tipped his head in agreement. "You should collect samples of handwriting."

"That's a good idea." Since no one would be writing letters, he might need to ask Argent to influence either Trevill or the high cleric into creating some exercise for the couples that required writing.

Then again, the lead rebel in Esperance could be a cleric, guard, or servant, and they couldn't very well collect every person's handwriting. Hundreds of staff lived at Esperance, and any of them could be involved.

"If the rebels are playing a long game," Ford said, cutting into Carver's thoughts, "then it's possible they aren't planning anything violent in Esperance at all. Which would mean someone else might have killed Cora. She was married to Ivan, right? We both know Sibeten Wolves are a little crazy. He could have killed her."

"I'm not sure what he'd gain from her death." And Ivan had been angry about her murder. That could be an act, of course. Carver *had* found him at the base of the stairs; he could have just come from killing Cora. The sitting room she'd been found in was just down the hall.

"Any other crazy happenings I should know about?" Ford asked.

"Not really." Except maybe the fact he'd broken Rivard's nose, but there was no need to mention that. "Get this report sent off to my father and ask him to investigate Cora. I want to know if her family has any secrets, or if there's any history between her family and Ivan's—or any of the others here at Esperance."

"Anything else?"

Carver hesitated only briefly before he said, "Ask him to learn what he can of Amryn's parents and how they died."

Ford eyed him. "You can't just ask her?"

"She's private, and I don't want to pry. But I want to know if their deaths were in any way associated with the empire."

Concern pinched Ford's face. "You're really worried she's a rebel, aren't you?"

"I can't afford to take any chances." His head tipped to the side. "I assume you haven't heard anything from my father since he left?"

"No. I doubt he'll send any word until he's back at West-mont."

Carver nodded and pushed to his feet. "I should start back so I can return before dawn."

Ford lifted an eyebrow. "You just don't want to stay and tell me about your wife and what it's like to be married."

That was true, but he didn't have to admit it. He lifted the knitted hood off the table. "Be sure to tell the monkeys hello for me."

"Ha. As if they'd care about a jester like you."

A smile tugged at Carver's lips, but as he met Ford's eye, he grew serious. "Be careful out here."

Ford's features settled, chasing away all signs of mirth. "I'm not the one surrounded by potential enemies, Carve. And I'm certainly not married to one."

That was a fair point.

Ford rose from his chair.

Outside, the wooden steps creaked.

Carver and Ford froze. Then they were both moving; Carver drew his knife while Ford did the same as they crept silently toward the door.

There was an urgent knock; three hits, a slight pause, then three hits again.

Ford's brow grew lined as he hurried to open the door. "Hugo, what—"

"I'm sorry," the young man interrupted. Hugo had served alongside Ford as a scout in Carver's army in Harvari, and he'd agreed to become one of Ford's messengers here in Esperance for the next year. The usually calm man looked harried; his face was flushed and his eyes widened as he saw Carver. He offered a quick salute. "General, I—I didn't expect you."

"What's happened?" Carver asked. "Is it word from my father?"

"No, it's far worse than that." Hugo looked to Ford. "I was heading back to the village after our meeting tonight, and I decided to take a shortcut. I found something just off the trail—scorched bones. *Human* bones."

A chill skated down Carver's spine. "Where?"

Hugo's expression was grim. "About an hour's walk from here."

Carver glanced out the window, trying to gauge the night sky. If they ran . . . He turned to Hugo. "Show us."

Carver spotted the scorched bones before Ford lit the lamp he had brought to the scene. As Hugo had described, it was right off the trail. It wasn't a main road to the nearest village, or to Esperance—but it connected both places, and that seemed significant.

The skulls had been separated from their bodies, and all the bones had been gathered into a pile on the muddy ground. The earth surrounding the pile had been scorched, but the fire hadn't spread to the surrounding foliage.

Whoever had started the fire had remained to watch while the bodies burned.

The frequent jungle rains had washed away nearly all traces of blood, and the footprints stuck in the mud were indistinct. Still, Ford was scanning them intently, tracking the entire area with his skilled gaze.

Hugo crouched near Carver, both of them studying the bones. Without touching the macabre pile, Carver could see four skulls. He was sure there were a few more.

"Maybe they're locals," Hugo said, though he didn't sound confident. "This could have nothing to do with what's happening at Esperance."

Carver eyed Ford, who was still exploring the small clearing. "What do you see?"

"It's difficult to tell," his friend murmured, studying the foliage on the edge of the clearing. "Some of the breaks here could have been from animals passing through, but . . ." He fingered a spot on a tree trunk and frowned. "This notch is from a blade." He continued to explore the area while Carver tried to rein in his impatience.

Ford was good at what he did, but he did it in his own time.

Carver didn't want to disturb the bones before Ford had a chance to study them, so he pushed to his feet and waited.

After several long minutes, Ford finished his assessment and twisted to face Carver and Hugo, the glow of the lamp casting strange shadows over his serious face. "My best guess? These people were ambushed on the road and dragged over here." He nodded to the edge of the clearing. "They were killed against that tree—beheaded. Not only do we see the skulls detached, but there are multiple notches at varying heights on the trunk, and some dried blood remains in the deeper marks where the rain couldn't reach. The fact I can see any blood at all, not to mention any residual footprints, suggests that this attack is relatively recent—possibly within the last couple of weeks."

About the time everyone was arriving at Esperance.

Ford continued. "While beheading is something the nomadic peoples of southern Xerra practice, I don't think this was the work of locals—or that these people were locals themselves. One reason being, the locals avoid Esperance; no settlement is built too close to the compound, and Esperance is self-sufficient—they don't have need for deliveries of any kind, so why would locals have been here?"

Those were fair deductions. Carver frowned toward the bones. "They could have been some of the soldiers the high cleric evicted from the temple."

"Who would have ambushed them?" Ford questioned. "And why?"

"Nothing was left behind," Hugo pointed out. "There's not a coin or jewel on any of these bodies, and no signs of supplies—not even a basic pack with food or clothing. Maybe the attackers were thieves."

"Why only attack this group, though?" Ford asked. "Why not attack one of the entourages of the Empire's Chosen? They represent some of the wealthiest people in the empire. The rewards would have been far greater."

"Thieves *would* have attacked one of the Empire's Chosen," Carver said. "And we would have heard about it, or we would have been short one of the delegations. So the attackers weren't simple thieves."

Ford was scanning the pile of bones again. "No, but they did steal. Hugo's right, these people should have at least had basic supplies. And there's nothing left but bones."

"*Burned* bones," Carver said quietly. "Someone was trying to hide the identities of the dead."

The knot that had been tightening in his gut since arriving here clenched. He met Ford's gaze.

His friend looked unusually solemn as he whispered, "I don't think Cora was the first murder victim here."

Hugo's brows pulled together. "What are you thinking?"

Ford twisted back toward the road. "There are tracks in the road—wagons have used this route. Possibly a carriage. And when we count those skulls, I think we might find seven to eight people were murdered."

Just the right number for a couple of servants, some guards, an escort . . . and one of the Empire's Chosen.

Hugo breathed a prayer and touched his heart, a sign of reverence to the Divinities.

Carver muttered a curse. If they were right . . . "Someone in Esperance isn't who they claim to be."

There was an imposter living among them.

Ford's eyes narrowed. "How could a stranger fool everyone?"

"We don't all know each other," Carver said. "Not even the emperor knows all of us personally. Or what we look like."

Ford swore. "This is insane. You really think someone ambushed one of the delegations on their way into Esperance, killed the entire party, and replaced them with guards and an escort? That an imposter *married* one of the Empire's Chosen?"

It *did* seem ludicrous. And yet . . .

Carver pinched his eyes closed, his mind racing. "You need to ask my father who he knew personally at the weddings. I'll ask the emperor, Argent, Jayveh, and Rivard." Between them all, they might account for each of the newlyweds and dispel this entire idea of an imposter. At the very least, they would narrow down their list of suspects.

He looked to Ford. "I also need to know if any of the escorts don't make it back to their homes." If someone reported them missing, that could tell them which kingdom these murdered souls had come from.

"We might not hear anything for a long time," Ford warned. "Especially if they came from one of the more northern kingdoms."

"That doesn't matter. Just ask my father to verify all the escorts are accounted for."

Ford nodded. Then, "If there *is* an imposter, do you think they killed Cora?"

Carver's jaw firmed. "Maybe. Especially if she discovered their secret."

17

AMRYN

THE FEMALE CLERIC GRUNTED as she heaved the wooden crate onto the scuffed table. "Here you are, Lady Vincetti."

"You just want me to catalogue them?" Amryn clarified.

Cleric Jane nodded and waved toward a leather bound book on the table. "You can follow the example of the other entries in there. And if you're not sure how to identify an item, you can just leave it in the box. If you have any other questions, just come to my office."

After the museum caretaker walked away, Amryn was alone in the museum archive. There were no windows in this part of Esperance, since she was in the heart of the temple, so she relied purely on the lamps around the room and on the table for light.

It was easier than Amryn had thought it would be to start volunteering in Esperance's museum. A few days after Cora's funeral, the high cleric had announced over breakfast that from now on, everyone would dedicate time each week to volunteer in some endeavor at Esperance. "It may help you heal during this time of mourning," the high cleric explained. "Acts of service can be an exceptionally powerful balm."

Everyone seemed eager—perhaps because the high cleric's schedule was so regimented, and volunteering meant a break from some other lesson or task Zacharias appointed.

Jayveh elected to spend a few hours a week in the library, which Argent, Samuel, and Sadia all echoed a desire to do. Tam volunteered to work in the gardens, while Marriset offered to help the clerics in their charitable efforts, which included making clothes, blankets, and bandages for their soldiers in Harvari. Darrin and Rivard both volunteered to work in the museum, and Amryn added her interest in working there as well. Luckily, the museum had many wings, including the art gallery, religious artifacts, and other historical objects, so she didn't think they would actually run into each other. Ivan volunteered to help repair some of the outbuildings within the compound's walls; Amryn could feel his need to do something physical, and outside the main temple. Carver had volunteered to join him.

Carver had seemed preoccupied lately. They hadn't spent much time together since that night he'd been unable to sleep, and she'd tried to distract him. That had been nearly two weeks ago.

Saints, she'd been married for one month now. *That* was a strange thought.

Though isolated in Esperance, time still passed. Nothing new had been learned about Cora's murder, despite Trevill's ongoing investigation. The topic of Cora's death came up in some form nearly every day—often during lunch, which Amryn generally took with the other women in their dedicated sitting room.

"I just don't feel safe," Sadia confessed one day. "Even with the increased guards."

"A guard could have been the one to kill her," Tam pointed out. "No one else in Esperance is allowed to have weapons."

"Someone could have smuggled weapons in," Marriset argued.

Jayveh usually managed to steer the conversation to other things, but the feeling of turbulent unease remained in the room, and Amryn's own thoughts didn't help.

She'd nearly written a message for her rebel contact so many times since Cora's death. But how could she ask a faceless, nameless stranger if the Rising had killed Cora?

Just thinking the words made her doubt her suspicion. Why would the rebels kill Cora? She wasn't a key player here in Esperance. If they were going to kill someone, it would be Argent or Jayveh.

Or Carver.

She didn't care to admit how much that thought bothered her. Carver wasn't a friend. He wasn't anything more than her husband—a man she hadn't chosen, and one who was her enemy in nearly every way.

The thought of any death made her feel a little sick; it was part of being an empath. That's all it was.

Forcing her distracting thoughts aside, Amryn focused on the job at hand. This was her second time volunteering here. The first time she'd reported to the museum caretaker, the female cleric had seemed unsure of what to have her do. She'd settled on having her dust some of the displays, which was not exactly what Amryn had had in mind. But today, the cleric had walked her back to the archives to help with inventorying new items. She needed to do this well so she'd be allowed back, and hopefully—eventually—gain access to the storerooms that housed the seals she needed to copy.

She pulled the ledger closer and followed a wide ribbon that had been laid in the pages as a bookmark, about halfway through the book. Four columns of various widths were on the page, and clearly labeled at the top: date of entry, description of item, kingdom of origin, and initials of the one who made the notations.

Scanning the last page, she saw that it had been months since the last entry, and that in the description of the item—in this case, a marble bust of an old king in Palar—the condition of the item was also noted: *Missing part of the nose, and clearly suffering damage from being left too long in the harsh sea air.*

The crate the female cleric had brought out was large and inscribed with the words: *From Daersen; donated from Murdon Savin's private collection at the time of his death.*

A peek into the crate showed the items were eclectic. Velvet boxes of various sizes, weathered books with broken spines, miniature paintings, and what looked to be part of a granite hand were just some of the things Amryn spotted.

She lifted one of the top velvet boxes, which easily fit in the palm of her hand, and pried open the lid—and instantly dropped it.

It hit the table with a dull *smack*, and the iron ring nestled in the satin bed of the box stared up at her.

It was decorated with scrollwork and other embellishments, but nothing could disguise the horrific centerpiece. At the top of the ring, the metal flattened, giving a foundation to a crystalized dome. Inside the dome, a fragment of human bone was trapped.

Amryn's heart thudded as she stared at the ugly ring. She had only seen one once before—on the hand that had killed her mother.

Well, *one* of the hands.

They were worn by the Knights of the Church; men and women who were specifically trained to hunt empaths, among other things. Some whispered the piece of bone they all wore in their rings—which was the bone of an empath—helped guide them to other empaths. Bone seeking bone; like seeking like. Amryn didn't know if she believed in the superstition, but it certainly revealed their viciousness and cruelty.

Inside the lid of the box was inscribed:

For Murdon Savin
Ordained member of the Order of Knights

Amryn slid back a step, every hair on her body standing up as she viewed the crate with new eyes. These were the belongings of a knight.

Her fingers itched and she rubbed her palms against her skirt. She didn't want to touch any of it. Evil clung to her skin, and she hadn't even touched the actual bone ring.

She was grateful she didn't have the ability some empaths did—to touch an object and sense the emotions that lingered from anyone who had ever made contact with it. Just being near that ring, even without truly sensing its malevolence, made her shudder.

It took a concerted effort to make herself snap the lid back into place. It took even more effort to remain in this room, not that she could afford to leave. The rebels needed her to complete her mission. Every person the empire had ever killed or harmed needed her.

So, Amryn forced herself to take a seat at the table, drag the book closer, and make her first entry.

Once she'd documented the bone ring, she pulled out the next item. It was a small framed landscape, a setting sun that glowed red in the sky, casting a field into shades of orange and purple. According to the label on the back, it was an original by Murdon Savin.

The inventory continued, and she tried to be as removed from the items as possible. To not think of anything other than what each item was. A tarnished silver brooch. A jeweled letter opener.

Then she came across a pocket-sized book. When she lifted the stained cover and glimpsed handwriting, she thought she'd found Murdon Savin's journal. But the writing on the inside cover quickly dispelled that assumption.

Taken from Saul Von. May shed light on the search for bloodstones.

Amryn's brow furrowed. Saul Von was a name everyone in the empire knew. He was an empath who had killed the emperor's wife, which had sparked the emperor's hatred of empaths so many years ago. The church had been quick to label all empaths as unnatural, evil creatures who were not even human. They claimed that empaths could use their magic to read minds and force all sorts of atrocities on the rest of humanity.

Saul Von's last act had been to help assassinate Argent's parents. Argent had nearly died in the attack, too, but his guards had managed to save the young prince. The Knights had succeeded in capturing Von, and they'd executed him, but the hunt for empaths had only grown more aggressive.

Amryn had never heard Saul Von described in a positive way; he was hated by most empaths for igniting the emperor's wrath, and he was certainly despised by citizens of the empire for orchestrating the murder of three members of the empirical family.

Curiosity had Amryn thumbing to the first page of the small journal, and she began to read.

My name is Saul Von, and this will be the record of my quest to find the five bloodstones. I must locate them before anyone else, and I must find a way to destroy them, or all of us are doomed.

Amryn had never heard of bloodstones before. Were they something out of empath lore? Murdon Savin had obviously been searching for them as well, so maybe they were something the Order of Knights or the Church believed in?

She turned the page, but she didn't get any answers. Von had drawn a map of some kind, but without any labels or reference points, it was nothing more than lines on yellowed paper. The next page only contained numbers—some kind of code?—and the next simply held three large words: *IN THE EMPIRE?*

The distant sound of a door opening made Amryn jerk. While heavy footsteps approached, she shoved the small journal into her pocket. The lump was obvious, so she quickly folded part of her skirt over her lap, hoping to conceal it.

She expected a cleric, but it was Rivard who strode into view.

His nose was no longer swollen or bruised, but his mood had remained sour. He caught sight of her, and his steps slowed. "I didn't realize you would be back here."

"I'm cataloguing items for the clerics."

Rivard took in the crate and items scattered on the table. In the silence, Amryn's heart pounded. Von's journal felt disproportionately heavy in her pocket, and she didn't know why she'd taken it. She shouldn't risk stealing something from the museum—especially *this* item. She heard Rix's voice in her head, reprimanding her. He'd raised her to never show undue interest in empaths. It was yet another way to protect herself. Yet here she was, pocketing the journal of the most infamous empath to ever live.

Rivard stepped forward, pausing at the end of the table. His knuckles rapped softly against the dented wood as he scanned the room. "I was told Cleric Jane was back here."

"She was, but she went back to her office a while ago."

Rivard grunted. But he didn't leave to find the museum caretaker. Instead, his attention dropped back to the items strewn on the table. When his gaze fell on the small velvet box that held the bone ring, a furrow grew between his thick eyebrows. He plucked up the box and lifted the lid. His eyes narrowed. "What's this doing here?"

He spoke lowly enough that she wasn't sure if he was asking her, or just musing aloud. The macabre nature of the ring stole her breath, but she forced herself not to cringe away from it, just as she forced herself to speak in the most off-hand way she could manage. "It was in the crate Cleric Jane gave me to sort through. She said they get all manner of artifacts, and they sometimes gather dust for years before they're documented."

Rivard touched the crystal that topped the ring, though he didn't remove it from the box. "This is a very important relic of the Order of Knights," he said. "It never should have been so callously set aside. They're usually handed down through families, if other generations are knighted." He glanced up at her. "My father is a knight, and so are my older brothers."

A chill rippled down her spine. "Really?"

"Yes." His focus remained fixed on the bone embedded under the crystal. "It's a family calling, really. Though not everyone passes the trials." He straightened suddenly and snapped the lid closed. "Do you know who owned this ring?"

"Murdon Savin, I would guess," she said, gesturing to the name written on the crate.

"Really?" Surprise twisted through the air and lifted his tone. "He was a legend among the Order. Became a bit of a recluse before he died, though." He took a step back, the velvet ring box held in one fist. "I'll take this to Cleric Jane. She'll make sure it's held safely until it can be returned to the Knights."

Amryn didn't give a verbal answer. As she watched him turn and walk away, she knew she should just be relieved he was going.

Instead, she stood and called out, "Rivard?"

He stopped and twisted back to face her. "Yes, Amryn?"

Saints, she didn't like her name on his lips. Or the way his eyes grew colder the longer she looked at him. Clearly, he wasn't a knight. But knowing that he came from a family of knights made him even more vile to her, regardless of the other things she knew about him—or had been hinted about him.

She cleared her throat. "Tam has seemed especially quiet the past few days."

Confusion wafted from him. "Your point?"

"I hope you haven't done anything to distress her."

His expression tightened, and she felt a wall of defensiveness hit her. "Are you insinuating that I've done something to hurt my wife?"

"I'm only saying I hope you haven't."

"Cora was murdered," Rivard said bluntly. "That, if anything, is what's causing Tam's distress."

"If you hurt her, I'll find out. And you will regret it."

The air turned icy. Rivard's upper lip curled slightly. "You know, you and Carver make a good match. You're both insufferably arrogant, and you think you're morally superior to everyone else. Tam is *my* wife, which means she's *my* concern—not yours."

"She's my friend. And even if she wasn't, I'd still look out for her."

Rivard took a step toward her, but Amryn only steeled her spine.

His voice was low and dark. "Whatever she's told you is a lie. I haven't hurt her."

"She hasn't told me anything specific, but I have eyes."

A malicious edge joined his defensiveness. "Keep your nose out of my business."

"If you want to avoid another broken nose, take care not to hurt her in any way."

Rivard bristled, but before he could offer a retort, Cleric Jane walked in. "Ah, Rivard. I was told you were looking for me?"

Amryn took advantage of the interruption and returned to the table, letting their conversation drift over her as they walked away. Strange, how much better she felt once Rivard was gone—the gruesome bone ring along with him. Her chest felt warmer after standing up for Tam and, for a moment, she forgot the heaviness of the stolen journal in her pocket.

18

CARVER

CARVER STOOD ON THE BALCONY in his shared apartment with Amryn and studied the list Argent, Rivard, Jayveh and the emperor had helped him make after discovering those scorched bones. He hoped staring at the list yet again would spark some new thought.

There were two columns of names; the first listed the people they knew personally before coming to Esperance: Argent, Jayveh, Carver, Rivard, Marriset, Samuel, and poor Cora.

The second column were those they did *not* know personally: Darrin, Ivan, Sadia, Tam, and Amryn.

If Carver's suspicions were right, one of the names on that list had been taken on by an imposter. Ford's count of the skulls supported the idea that an entire delegation—including one of the Empire's Chosen—had walked into Esperance without anyone suspecting the lie.

Carver knew his instincts were right. Now he just needed to figure out *who* was lying about their identity.

For the most part, Carver trusted the names in the first

column; Jayveh had vouched for Cora, who she'd met once years ago. Carver, Argent, and Rivard had all met Samuel years ago, and the emperor was certain Samuel's father had not been an imposter when he'd spoken briefly to him at the wedding feast. Argent had been a child when he last saw Marriset, and the emperor hadn't seen her any more recently, so Carver was also hesitant to eliminate her as a suspect just yet. Looks could be emulated. Personalities, pretended.

Argent trusted Carver's instincts, and had promised to help in any way he could. The emperor had been less sure about Carver's hunch.

"You've made a great deal of assumptions without much evidence," the emperor told him when Carver had made his report. "And the sheer magnitude of such a thing . . . It would be a very difficult thing to accomplish. Fooling everyone at the wedding, and now . . ." He shook his head. "Investigate this, but do not become so focused on this possibility of an imposter that you lose sight of all else."

It was good advice, and Carver was trying to follow it. But the idea of a pretender walking among them nagged at him.

The emperor had finally healed enough to travel, so he'd left Esperance days ago. In many ways, that was a relief. Though he'd been isolated in his suite and under heavy guard, the emperor would make a tempting target for the Rising.

Thank the Saints there had been no attempts made against him.

Far behind him, the door to the suite opened. Carver shoved the list into his pocket and twisted to see Amryn walk into the sitting room. Her eyes found him, and he felt a spark of surprise—and an undeniable thrill—when she moved to join him at the stone railing. It had been days since they'd had any real opportunity to talk, and he found he'd missed her.

"How was your morning of volunteering?" she asked.

"Fine." He'd spent it repairing a leaky roof in one of the servant huts, and he'd enjoyed his time working in the sun. "How was the museum?"

"It was interesting. Cleric Jane had me catalogue some old artifacts today."

"Better than dusting," he noted.

She chuckled. "Definitely." She twisted to face him, her hip resting against the railing. "Can I ask you a question?"

"Of course."

She bit her lower lip. "What is your history with Rivard?"

The unexpected question froze him.

Amryn must have seen him tense, because the color in her cheeks rose and she was quick to say, "You don't have to answer, I was just curious."

His eyes narrowed. "Did you see him today?"

"Our paths crossed briefly."

He didn't like that. At all.

When the high cleric and Jayveh had presented the volunteer opportunities to the couples, Carver had already decided to do whatever Ivan did. He needed to learn more about the Sibeten prince—something that had become even more important since learning about the imposter among them.

But when Amryn had chosen to work in the museum—where Argent had asked Rivard to go so he could keep an eye on Darrin—Carver hadn't been thrilled. He knew the museum was large, and they wouldn't necessarily be working together. But the thought of Rivard being around Amryn made his skin crawl. Especially since he'd been rude and threatening to her after their night of cards. It didn't matter that Rivard had been drunk at the time. As Carver well knew, Rivard wrecked anything he touched.

"He really doesn't like you," Amryn said, pulling Carver from his thoughts.

He met her searching gaze. "No, he doesn't. But the feeling is mutual."

"Why?"

Carver folded his arms over his chest as he leaned back against the side of the balcony, the hard stone digging into his lower back as he faced her. "We were friends, once. I trusted him. Allowed him into my family. And he destroyed my brother's life."

Concern swam in her pale green eyes, but she didn't ask any questions. She just waited.

Slowly, he exhaled. "I first met Rivard when I was ten. He was nine. Like most noble sons in the empire, he came to Westmont for a couple of months each year to train. Argent and I both befriended him. Like Argent, Rivard spent time with my family. While he stayed in Westmont, my mother insisted he join us for family meals, and he joked and laughed with my brothers and sisters. He was part of the family because he was my friend."

He shook his head. "Rivard's father is a high-ranking member of the Order of Knights. His older brothers are all part of the Order, too. But when Rivard undertook the trials to become a knight, he failed. There were no second chances, and that failure shattered him. Becoming a knight was all he'd dreamed of. It was all his family wanted. And when that didn't happen . . . I knew his family didn't make it easy on him. What I *didn't* know was that he was coping with his failure with the use of *sonne*, a Daersen drug."

Amryn was silent as she watched him, and Carver was grateful she wasn't asking questions. Wasn't forcing him to reveal anything, or change the pace of his story. It gave him time to grapple with the memories. The anger.

The guilt.

His fingers dug into his arms. "This was five years ago. I had just gotten a promotion, and I knew my success would be hard on Rivard. But I also knew that staying with his family wasn't helping his melancholy, so I invited him to spend the summer in Westmont. I wanted to help him, but I was also extremely busy with my new duties, and I didn't have as much time for him as I thought I would. I was relieved when I saw Rivard and Berron spending time together. I didn't think anything of it, and I didn't notice the subtle changes in my brother. The growing secretiveness. The sneaking out. The lies he told. How many meals he missed. I didn't notice any of it until it was too late."

He met and held Amryn's gaze. "Two years after that summer visit, we learned the truth. That Rivard gave Berron *sonne*, and my brother quickly became addicted to it. Before Rivard left Westmont, he introduced Berron to dealers in the city, and when Berron couldn't afford more of the drug, he stole from us—from me, my parents, even my grandparents. When we noticed the missing coin and began to speculate about the thief, Berron tried to steal *sonne* from the dealers. They caught him." His throat was dry, but he forced himself to continue. "Men like them rarely kill the rats that bite them; that would be one less rat for them to feed off of. One less buyer for *sonne*. But punishment had to be meted out as a warning to others, and the son of High General Vincetti made a powerful example. They cut off his right hand and took one of his eyes."

Amryn sucked in a pained breath.

Carver's teeth clenched. "When we found him, Berron was so addicted to *sonne* that he screamed more about his need for the drug than he did about what they'd done to him. When my mother tried to sit with him on his sickbed, to comfort him, he struck her."

The sound of Berron's fist cracking against their mother's cheekbone had never dulled in Carver's ears. The shock and hurt that contorted her face as she'd stumbled back was forever in his mind. The pained growl in his father's throat as he'd caught his wife in his arms. The hatred and desperation in Berron's single, red-rimmed eye as he tried to hit his mother again, screaming for her to get him more *sonne*.

That monster hadn't been his brother. In that moment, he was someone else entirely.

Carver blinked and forced himself to focus on Amryn. She was standing as still as ever, the pain and sorrow in her eyes speaking volumes, even though she was silent. "Rivard did that to him," Carver said, his voice a little hoarse. "He knew how dangerous *sonne* was, but he still gave it to him. He introduced Berron to those dealers so he could get a cut of the profits, and he didn't care what it would do to Berron. To my family. He knew how far gone Berron was, but he said nothing. Did nothing." He swallowed. "The next time I saw Rivard, I confronted him. He told me none of it was his fault, and that Berron's weakness wasn't his guilt to carry. And I just . . . I kept hitting him until I was dragged away."

"You blame yourself," Amryn said softly.

A muscle ticked in his jaw. "Yes. But I blame Rivard, too."

"Do you blame Berron?"

Yes.

But how could he verbalize that without sounding like a

monster? "I should have noticed," he said instead. "For two years he was suffering, and I was so preoccupied with my own life, I didn't notice. I should have seen that he needed help. I should have known."

"You can't blame yourself. What Rivard did was a huge betrayal, and completely wrong, but he made those choices. And when Rivard gave Berron *sonne*, your brother would have been . . ."

"Seventeen."

Amryn's expression softened, her eyes sad. "He was young. But Berron made his choices, too. He wasn't a child."

"He was my little brother, though." Carver let his arms fall, elbows jutting back as he grasped the railing on either side of him. "I became a general soon after we learned of Berron's addiction. And it was only a few months later that I was called to Harvari. Before I left, I sought Berron out. He'd become reclusive after everything that had happened, and he rarely left his room. I knew I needed to tell him goodbye, though. That I loved him. That I didn't think less of him for what had happened, and I didn't blame him. And he looked right at me and said, *I blame you. I hate you.*"

Berron's voice had been clear. There was no *sonne* in his body, no way Carver could tell himself that Berron didn't mean the words. It had been two and a half years since that day, but the animosity in those words hadn't faded in his mind.

"I'm sorry," Amryn said. "It's a terrible truth that the people closest to us are the ones with the greatest ability to hurt us."

Her words were too heavy to not be gained from experience. Since her parents were dead, he wasn't sure how to tactfully ask if they'd been the ones to hurt her, or if it had been someone else. She had no siblings, and he doubted it was her uncle, since she spoke so highly of Rix.

"I've never really talked about this with anyone," he said.

He thought the admission might coax her to be vulnerable in return, but she only watched him, waiting for more.

He didn't know what it was about this woman that made him open up, but he found himself telling her something else he hadn't shared with anyone. "Six months ago, when I returned from Harvari, I expected Berron to take the words back. I expected that he would have healed in those two years I was away, but . . . he didn't." Berron hadn't visited him once during Carver's recovery. He'd nearly died from his injuries, and his brother couldn't even be bothered to walk down the hall to see him. *That* was how much Berron still hated him.

Carver hadn't bothered telling Berron goodbye when he'd left for Esperance.

"I'm sorry," Amryn said again.

"So am I."

An especially shrill birdcall cut through the tense air, interrupting the moment.

Carver shoved a hand through his hair. "Did Rivard say anything to you that needs my retaliation?"

"No." The pink in her cheeks darkened, but he knew it wasn't in embarrassment because she was smiling a little. "I may have been the one to threaten him this time."

Carver's eyebrows lifted. "Do tell."

"I don't like the way he's been treating Tam." She must have seen the sudden darkening of his expression, because she lifted a staying hand. "I haven't seen any blatant abuse, and Tam hasn't said anything specific. I just wanted to make it clear to him that, if I learned he hurt her in any way, there would be consequences."

The corner of his mouth lifted. Amryn may appear small and delicate, but she had an inner strength that continued to impress him. "Good."

Her smile widened, but she shook her head. "I think you're rubbing off on me."

"How so?"

"Before I met you, I was never this confrontational. And I never resorted to threats or any sort of violence."

His head tilted to the side. "I don't know if I believe you. You seemed awfully eager to hit me the day we sparred."

She rolled her eyes. "That's exactly what I'm talking about. That's very *not* me."

"So who are you really, Amryn?"

The question seemed to catch her off guard. Her gaze lowered and she set a hand on the railing beside her, her thumb following a groove in the worn stone. "How is one supposed to answer that?"

"However you want to," he said with a shrug, hoping to convey nonchalance when he badly wanted an answer.

Her gaze dropped to watch her thumb's tracing. "I'm an orphan from Ferradin. A girl who grew up in a castle even though she never felt like she belonged there. I've never had close friends, and I'm not always comfortable around people. But I try to do the right thing." Her head lifted, and their eyes met. "What about you, Carver? Who are you?"

The railing he leaned against suddenly felt harder. She'd asked a bloody good question. After Harvari, he really wasn't sure.

He didn't have to fumble out an answer, though, because the main door to their suite banged open without warning.

Carver snapped to his full height and shifted in front of

Amryn. He felt her edge around him to watch several guards and the high cleric stride into the sitting room.

"Search everywhere," the high cleric ordered.

"What's going on?" Carver demanded.

The guards ignored him as they scattered throughout the apartment. Some disappeared down the short hall to the bedroom while others remained in the sitting room and began to riffle through the items and furniture.

From the corner of his eye, Carver saw Amryn stiffen.

Carver stalked toward the high cleric. "What's the meaning of this?"

Zacharias's eyes narrowed. "Do you have anything you'd like to confess, General?"

"I think my irritation is obvious enough," Carver said flatly. "But I can declare it, if you'd prefer."

"Don't try to be clever." The high cleric glanced to Amryn, who had trailed Carver into the room. "Lady Vincetti, have you seen any of the general's weapons?"

"Weapons?" Carver echoed before Amryn could speak. "You think I smuggled weapons here?"

"Yes. Weapons you used to kill Cora."

The accusation made his gut drop and his head spin.

A crash came from the bedroom and Amryn jerked beside him.

For some reason, her apprehension grounded him. He squared his shoulders as he faced the high cleric. "I had nothing to do with Cora's death. And you have no right to come in and question me. The emperor put Trevill in charge of the investigation."

"Trevill is on his way," Zacharias said, looking far too pleased with himself. "He asked me to gather some guards, and meet him here for your interrogation."

"What proof do you have?" he demanded.

Before Zacharias could answer, Chancellor Trevill prowled through the open door of the suite. Anger pinched his face as he approached. "Zacharias, you overstep. I will lead this investigation."

The high cleric waved this away. "I was merely getting started. You asked for my help."

"I asked you to gather guards—not start the search without me." Trevill turned his attention to Carver. "If you could please follow me to my office, I have some questions to ask you."

A loud thud came from the bedroom, making Amryn startle again.

Carver dug in his heels. "I'm not leaving Amryn here alone."

He couldn't quite make out her expression, but he could feel her gaze burn into him, and it suddenly occurred to him that she might be more nervous about being near *him*.

Before anyone could respond, yet another person strode into the room. This time, it was Argent, with Jayveh and their bodyguards behind him.

Argent's eyes bounced between Zacharias, Trevill, Carver, and the guards who were tearing apart the suite. "Do I dare even ask?"

The high cleric shoved a finger at Carver. "We believe *he* killed Cora."

Argent's eyes flew wide. Then he coughed on a weak laugh. "That's insane."

Zacharias's face flushed, while Trevill sighed and said, "I simply said Carver should be questioned."

"I already gave my account of that morning," Carver said,

his patience wearing thin. Especially because Amryn had taken a step away from him, and that space felt like a widening gulf.

"Yes," Trevill said. "But you failed to mention that you may have had a grudge against Ivan."

"*What?*"

"Ivan was called to go to Harvari, but he never went," Trevill said. "I learned this after consulting with the high cleric, who also shared a letter written by your own cleric that said you were deeply affected by the war."

"What does that have to do with anything?" Carver snapped.

It was the high cleric who answered. "You may resent the fact that Ivan didn't suffer as you did. Or—perhaps more likely—you might look upon him as a traitor deserving of punishment. A punishment you decided to mete out by killing his wife. *Retribution has come for you,*" he quoted sharply. "Did you leave that message for Ivan to find?"

Carver couldn't believe this. The sheer insanity of it made him want to laugh, but he couldn't manage it.

"You *did* lose your temper and attack Rivard," Trevill said.

He barely swallowed a curse. "I did. But I didn't kill Cora."

"You obviously have some issues with your temper," Zacharias pressed. "Now, we must search your rooms to determine if you have weapons."

"Carver didn't kill Cora," Argent said firmly. He turned to Trevill. "If you have questions you must ask, then ask them. But do so carefully. You're accusing a decorated general in the empirical army, and my life-long friend."

"I realize that, Your Highness," Trevill said, deferring at once to the prince. "And I do not make this accusation lightly. I simply want answers."

"Fine," Argent said. "But the hostile manner of this interrogation cannot continue. You're upsetting Amryn."

Carver glanced toward his wife, who indeed looked a bit sick. The guards were still searching the room, and her fingers danced near her pocket, her nerves obvious.

Jayveh instantly stepped forward and threaded her arm through Amryn's. "I'll take her to our rooms," she said.

Trevill nodded, accepting this.

The high cleric looked less than thrilled. He was used to having the run of Esperance, but in this scenario, he had little power; the emperor had put Trevill in charge of the investigation, and Argent was still the empirical prince—no matter the high cleric's speeches about leaving all titles behind while in these walls.

Amryn resisted Jayveh's gentle pull. Her eyes flicked to Carver, but just as quickly cut away. "I can stay, if it will help."

Carver wasn't sure if she wanted to help *him*, or Trevill.

The chancellor shook his head. "I may have questions for you later, but it would be best if you left with the princess."

Amryn pursed her lips, but this time she didn't resist Jayveh's pull toward the door. She did glance back at Carver once, her green eyes nearly impossible to read.

As soon as they left—a bodyguard following them—another thud sounded from the bedroom.

Carver ground his teeth. "You don't need to break her things. I don't have anything in there."

"Ah, yes," the high cleric said at once, as if seizing on Carver's words. "You bring up another relevant fact—you don't share a bed with your wife. I learned this when I questioned the servants who clean your suite. You've been sleeping on the settee."

Argent's eyes narrowed. Trevill looked uncomfortable.

Carver just felt anger. "You're spying on me?"

"I'm keeping track of *all* of you, as the emperor instructed me to do. So tell us: why don't you sleep with your wife?"

His question made the back of Carver's neck itch, and he hated that every eye in the room leapt to him. "That's none of your business."

"It is, in fact. My duty is to make sure these marriages succeed, and that everyone at Esperance complies with the emperor's will. The fact that you aren't being a true husband tells me a great deal about you, and your disregard for orders."

"This is absurd." Argent took a step forward. "Carver's commitment to this peace, let alone the empire, cannot be questioned. He's a blasted war hero." He looked between Trevill and Zacharias. "I know you want to be done with this—declare a murderer, and move on—but I assure you, Carver *did not* kill Cora."

"I *do* want to find Cora's murderer," Trevill said, his voice low but firm. "I want to be done with this investigation so we can all move on. But I won't let that determination blind me to the truth. So, please let me ask my questions, so we can clear Carver, if he is indeed innocent."

Argent crossed his arms, but didn't relax his stance. "Very well. But I'm not going anywhere."

Carver appreciated his friend's defense, but he wasn't exactly worried. He hadn't killed Cora, for one thing. And their search would render nothing incriminating, because he'd hidden his dagger back under the tree in the garden after his visit to Ford. Not to mention, their presented motives—at least so far—were ridiculous.

"Carver, where were you the morning Cora was killed?" Trevill asked.

"I was here. As I already told you when you first asked me."

"Can anyone vouch for that?"

"Amryn can."

The high cleric opened his mouth—probably to say something that would make Carver want to punch him in the teeth—but Trevill cut him off. "You were with her all morning?" he pressed.

"No," Carver said. "I visited Argent and Jayveh."

"A strong alibi to secure," the high cleric noted. "But you could have killed Cora before going to visit them."

"Yet I didn't."

"How did you cross paths with Ivan?" Trevill asked. He seemed to be ignoring the high cleric entirely, which wasn't a bad strategy.

Carver forced himself to take a breath. "After I left Argent and Jayveh, I returned to my suite to find Amryn gone. I went looking for her, and I met Ivan on the stairs. He told me he was returning from a run."

"So, he was on his way up to his rooms while you were headed down?" Trevill clarified.

"Yes."

"But you convinced him to change course?"

"Yes. I felt like sparring, and he decided to join me."

"Or perhaps you simply wanted to be with him when Cora's body was discovered," the high cleric inserted.

Carver's eyes narrowed. "For the last time, I didn't kill her."

Trevill settled his weight back on his heels. "According to the timeline I've established, the last person to see Cora alive was her maid. Ivan had already gone on his run before the maid left. Cora had no plans to leave her room, at least that's what she told her maid. It is my estimation that Cora must have left her rooms just prior to your visit with Prince Argent."

"I was with Amryn from the time she woke up until the moment Argent knocked on my door," Carver said.

"You could have snuck out before Amryn woke," the high cleric said.

"That wouldn't fit the timeline of Cora's death, though." Trevill's expression was grim. "I'm sorry, Carver. I had hoped to be less dramatic about all of this. But with no real leads, and after conferring with the high cleric and learning of the potential grudge you might bear toward Ivan, I needed to follow up with you."

"I understand." He didn't like being a suspect, but he understood Trevill's need to find the murderer. Just as he understood how desperate the high cleric must be feeling. If the peace at Esperance failed, he would be the one the emperor held accountable.

Carver still thought the man was insufferable.

Argent tapped his booted toes against the floor, his arms still folded. "High Cleric, call off this search, or I will."

Zacharias's mouth firmed into a harsh line. He signaled to the guards, and they began to right the furniture they'd upset.

Carver focused on Trevill. "If you have questions for Amryn, I want to be in the room. If that's not possible, Argent will be present."

"That can be arranged," the chancellor said. "And I assure you, something like this won't happen again." He looked pointedly at the bald man standing beside him. "Will it, Zacharias?"

The sour expression on the high cleric's face was severe as he said, "No, it will not."

19

AMRYN

"I CAN'T BELIEVE THEY'D THINK Carver killed Cora," Jayveh said as she and Amryn walked the cobbled path of one of Esperance's gardens. The princess's bodyguard trailed behind them, saying nothing. He hadn't protested when Jayveh had insisted they go for a walk instead of retreating to the princess's room, but he did watch them closely.

Amryn had been fairly quiet since leaving Carver. The room's chaotic emotions had clashed violently against her. Not to mention she'd been sweating profusely since the high cleric had burst into the apartment.

Von's journal was still in her pocket.

For a terrifying moment, she'd thought it had been found missing, or that somehow the high cleric had figured out she was an empath.

The fact that he thought Carver was a murderer had come as a relief. Then a shock.

That was a feeling worth analyzing. After all, he was the Butcher. Saints knew he'd killed before. And yet, she couldn't imagine him murdering Cora. It didn't match the Carver she'd been getting to know.

"It's utterly ridiculous," Jayveh continued. "He would never do something like that."

Amryn glanced toward the princess. She meant every word. Conviction thrummed the air around her, and her eyes flashed with righteous anger.

"Carver and I haven't always gotten along," Jayveh said. "But he'd never hurt a woman. Certainly not murder one in cold blood."

Amryn's nature was to usually remain silent around those she didn't know well, because there was always a risk she might say something that would give away her deadly secret. Truthfully, it was a miracle that she seemed able to talk so easily to Carver.

A miracle, or a curse that would get her killed.

But Jayveh seemed intent on becoming her friend, and the rebels had asked her to get close to the princess. Besides, she *was* curious to know more about Carver.

"You mentioned that you grew up with Argent," Amryn said slowly. "Did you know Carver as a child, too?"

"I met them both when I was six years old. Argent was nine, and Carver was probably ten. But I wouldn't say I grew up with them." She exhaled slowly before continuing. "As you know, my father used to be the king of Xerra. That meant we spent a couple of months every year at the capital, in the empirical palace."

Amryn nodded. She knew that the kings and queens of the kingdoms had to go to the palace whenever the emperor summoned them. Torin usually asked Rix to come with him, which meant Amryn was especially lonely, cooped up in her room most of the time they were gone.

"Those visits were endlessly boring for me," Jayveh said. "Especially because my older brothers didn't like it when I tried to play with them. They didn't want me tagging along after them. But then I met Argent and Carver, and those visits to the capital became something I looked forward to. Argent and Carver were older than me, but not as old as my brothers, and they were kind and played with me."

Melancholy slipped over Jayveh, rearranging her features as she continued more slowly. "Everyone knows my father's crown was taken by the emperor, but few know why. That was an unexpected kindness the emperor gave our family." She glanced at her bodyguard, but he'd drifted back, giving them some semblance of privacy.

Jayveh still lowered her voice. "During one of our visits to the palace, when I was nine, my older brothers attempted to assassinate Argent."

Shock blasted Amryn. "*What?*"

Jayveh's sorrow was mixed with pain, regret, and a muted echo of old anger. "Argent was only eleven years old. My oldest brother, Yeffah, was sixteen, and Aven was fourteen." She shook her head. "I knew Yeffah had been arguing with our parents a lot before we went to the capital, but I had no idea what those fights were about. I didn't know what he and Aven planned. None of us knew, until it happened. They failed, obviously, but the damage was done. The emperor had no choice, really. He had to take my father's crown, and he gave it to my uncle. Aven was imprisoned. And Yeffah . . ." She swallowed hard. "Yeffah died in the attempt."

Amryn reeled from Jayveh's story. The details were horrific enough, but the emotions Jayveh felt—even after all these years—were still heavy.

"I didn't see Argent again after that," Jayveh said, her voice soft. "Not until about two months before coming here."

The admission surprised Amryn. "Why did the emperor match you with Argent?" How could he trust Jayveh after her brothers had tried to kill the prince? After he'd taken her father's crown and imprisoned her surviving brother?

"He didn't," Jayveh said simply. "*Argent* chose me, and the emperor agreed to the match." She glanced at Amryn. "We weren't supposed to share that, since the emperor arranged all the other marriages from the people each kingdom chose."

"I won't tell anyone," Amryn said.

Jayveh nodded once, then continued her story. "I hadn't heard from Argent in over ten years, but . . . our paths crossed before coming to Esperance, and we reconnected." Heat, attraction, desire, love—it all wound together, and Jayveh cracked a smile. "I think I always loved him, even when I was only six years old."

Amryn shook her head. "It's amazing that you could both overcome so much."

"Trust is a choice. And so is love." Jayveh eyed her. "Carver has changed over the years, far more than Argent has. But even as a child, he was fiercely loyal, and I know he's a good man. Maybe a little lost right now, but you're safe with him. He's not a murderer."

Amryn was grateful for Jayveh's attempts to comfort her. The princess had been nothing but kind to her, and to the others here in Esperance—well, perhaps she'd been a little curt with Marriset, but that woman would try the patience of a saint.

But even though Jayveh had played the part of a friend,

she was married to Argent, the future emperor of Craethen. More than that, she was undeniably in love with him. The fact that she didn't despise the emperor after everything he'd done to her family made it clear that Jayveh was loyal to the empire. That made her an enemy, no matter how much Amryn wished that wasn't the case.

"I would appreciate it if you wouldn't share this story," Jayveh said, breaking into Amryn's thoughts. "My parents died years ago, but I have two younger brothers to protect. They don't know the full story, and I don't want them to have to carry it. At least not yet."

"I won't say anything," Amryn said, though she wasn't sure if it was a promise she could actually keep.

Jayveh smiled. "Thank you, Amryn. It's been a long time since I had a friend."

"I find that hard to believe." She was far too friendly to be as reclusive as Amryn.

A shadow crossed her face. "I suppose growing up with your uncle must have been very different from growing up with mine." Her lips pressed into a thin line, and Amryn felt her spike of resentment. "My uncle is a cruel man. When my parents died and he had dominion over me and my brothers . . . well, my life changed drastically."

She really didn't have to say anything else. There was a particular pain that survivors of abuse felt. It was edged with shame, and the agony ran deep. "I'm so sorry, Jayveh."

"It's in the past," the princess said, raising her face to the sun. "He no longer has any power over me."

Amryn tugged her needle and thread through the soft material of the small blanket on her lap.

It had been a week since the high cleric had accused Carver of murder, and speculation was buzzing in Esperance. And Carver's name wasn't the only one whispered. Servants, guards, clerics—even the Empire's Chosen had their suspicions.

"I wonder if it was Ivan," Sadia whispered. "Is that terrible of me to think?"

"It's possible," Marriset said, bent over her own sewing. They were gathered in their shared sitting room, making blankets for Esperance's charitable efforts. Marriset volunteered with the clerics who ran the project, and she had volunteered all of the ladies to help today.

She'd made a grand show of her charity work, and the emotions twisting from her—not to mention the looks she shot Jayveh—made it clear that her intention was to usurp the princess's control of the room.

Jayveh hadn't risen to Marriset's games. She'd only picked up a half-finished blanket and gotten to work.

Amryn had to smother a smile when she felt Marriset's bitter disappointment.

Tam glanced up from her work. "Ivan has been rather quiet since his initial outburst." She darted a look to Amryn. "What do you think? Could it be him?"

"I don't know," she said, disliking the weight of all their eyes on her. "What reason would he have had to kill her?"

Marriset shrugged one shoulder. "Perhaps she looked at him the wrong way. Who knows? My father always said Sibetens are little more than cold-blooded brutes."

Sadia frowned. "Doesn't Palar have an old feud with Sibet?"

Marriset's eyebrows lifted. "You mean the fact that they

used to raid our island, steal our goods, and abduct women to become their slave-wives?"

"That was before the empire," Jayveh said. "We shouldn't let old prejudices have a place here."

Marriset's irritation prickled the air, but she straightened her spine and focused once more on her sewing.

Sadia glanced over at Jayveh. "Argent must get updates on Chancellor Trevill's investigation. Can you share what he's found?"

"I don't know all the details, but I do know that Trevill is looking at all possibilities. Including people outside of the couples."

"That's probably why the high cleric is in such a bad mood," Sadia mused. "He doesn't want it to be one of Esperance's staff."

Marriset blew out a heavy breath. "Can we please talk about something else?"

For once, Amryn agreed with her—though probably for different reasons. Marriset's petulance about being pushed out of the conversation was obvious, while Amryn simply didn't want to dwell on Cora's death.

She still hadn't received any sort of message from the rebels, which only made her more nervous that killing Cora had indeed been part of the Rising's plan. That disturbed her in many ways. If they had callously killed such a harmless young woman, what would they plan to do to someone like Argent, Jayveh, or Carver? Worse, would the Rising ask her to play a part in their fates?

The needle jabbed Amryn's thumb, and she sucked in a breath.

"Are you all right?" Jayveh asked her.

"Fine," she said at once, though her throat was dry and her thumb throbbed.

Jayveh's concern lingered for a moment, and it only made Amryn's guilt flare hotter. The princess was fast becoming a friend, and Argent had defied all her expectations as well. The future emperor was kind, funny, and wholly in love with his wife. Not at all the evil man she'd expected.

And then there was Carver.

He wasn't anything like the man she'd anticipated. The general. The Butcher. Instead, he'd been attentive, thoughtful, and even vulnerable. He made her laugh. He brought out a lighter, more playful side of her that she hadn't been since her mother's death. He had given her the full use of the bedroom, and had kept his word and not touched her. He was surprisingly protective. Even after the high cleric had barged in and accused Carver of being a killer, Carver had been more worried about Amryn. When Amryn had returned from her walk with Jayveh, Carver's intense gaze had locked with hers, and he'd asked, "Are you all right?"

As if *she'd* been the one the high cleric had come after so hotly.

Carver was an enigma. He was a war hero, but he didn't glory in war. In fact, she knew he was haunted by it. And instead of letting him suffer alone in the middle of the night as the emperor's favored general no doubt deserved, she'd gone to him a few times now and offered him comfort in the form of distraction. Those talks they'd shared, the stories of their childhoods . . . it was making him more human. Which only left her more confused.

How could she comfort a man, *and* conspire with the Rising—a group who would most likely try to kill him before the year was out? How could she *not* help the Rising, when Carver represented the empire who had taken so much from her, and so many other innocents?

How could she be growing feelings for a man who would kill her if he knew what she was?

Her thoughts and emotions were impossible to untangle. But sometimes, when Amryn caught Carver staring at her, she wondered if he was slowly unraveling her.

"Amryn, do be careful not to bleed on the blanket."

Marriset's voice jerked Amryn from her thoughts, and she realized the others in the room had noticed her pause.

Her cheeks warmed, but she met Marriset's condescending stare. "It's fine."

"Well, we only have so much fabric, so do try to be careful." Marriset tossed her long brown hair over one shoulder and returned to her sewing with a rather imperious air. "It's a shame these weren't dyed in Palar. We have the best dyes. Just because these blankets are destined for the poor doesn't mean they shouldn't have the best."

Tam snorted beside Amryn, and under her breath she muttered, "Only she could be insulting while engaged in charity."

Marriset shot a curious glance their way, which only proved she hadn't heard Tam's words.

Sadia—who must have heard, or at least guessed that Tam's words weren't favorable toward Marriset—was quick to ask about Palar dyes, which distracted the other woman.

"You shouldn't provoke her," Jayveh whispered.

Tam—who was seated on Amryn's other side—quirked one dark eyebrow. "She's trying to steal Argent from you, you know."

Jayveh ghosted a smile. "Oh, I know. But she's doomed to fail."

"I think she knows it now," Amryn said quietly. "She seems extra peevish today."

"She'd have to be blind and dumb not to notice how little attention he pays her," Tam said. "Did you see the way he shrugged her off last night after dinner?"

Jayveh's smile widened "He does seem to be immune, doesn't he?"

Amryn was just grateful that Tam was talking with them. She'd still been quite solitary, but she was warming up to her and Jayveh. Her grief at being parted from her sick mother seemed to have drifted from the forefront of her emotions, which Amryn was grateful for. That weight had been painful for both of them.

Tam cracked a smile as she asked, "I wonder what Darrin thinks of her flirting?"

From what Amryn could tell, Darrin didn't seem to care. He noticed his wife's dogged pursual of Argent, but there was no sting of jealousy. Only a hum of satisfaction. Like he knew Marriset was his, no matter what she tried to do or who she tried to snare.

The door to the sitting room opened, and servants bustled in with steaming tea and trays of food. This gave a natural break from sewing, and Amryn was happy enough to fold the blanket aside. She was far too distracted to be trusted with a needle today.

Jayveh took pity on Sadia and re-entered the conversation with Marriset while the three of them drank their tea.

Amryn poured her cup and paced toward the tall windows at the back of the room. It felt good to stand, and she wanted a view of the gardens below while she sipped her tea. The hot liquid was a comforting spiral all the way down to her belly, and it relaxed muscles she hadn't even realized were tensed.

A ripple of discomfort hit her. Not her own—Sadia's.

She twisted to look at her, and she caught sight of the woman's slight frown.

A prickle of unease teased the air as Jayveh lowered her cup of tea, her brow furrowed as she placed a hand on her flat belly. "Does anyone—"

Marriset gasped as she doubled over, her teacup and saucer falling to bounce against the rug. Tea splashed everywhere, and Marriset's eyes flew wide. "Poison," she rasped, a hand going to her throat.

Fear punched Amryn, and then she felt it. A strange pinch in her stomach. Then a stab.

Tam coughed and dropped her cup of tea, clutching her throat.

The room spun.

Amryn locked her knees, but she still swayed. Her grip on the teacup spasmed when she felt a surge of panic, fear and pain. Things she herself felt, but so did everyone else in the room, which only made them more disarming.

Jayveh staggered to her feet, dropping her teacup as she gripped the arm of her chair, her gaze on the closed door. "Help," she tried to call out, but her voice was hoarse, and there was no real volume.

Marriset shoved up from her chair but immediately fell to her knees, gagging.

Sadia and Tam similarly collapsed.

Amryn stumbled. Her cup shattered on the stone floor, splashing hot tea across her legs and feet. She barely felt it as another gut-wrenching spear of agony ripped through her middle.

Tears sparked her eyes, and pain seared her throat.

They'd been poisoned. They were dying, and she could feel it.

She felt all of it.

She felt herself falling, and she tried to grab the back of the couch, but she missed it. Her knees cracked against the floor, narrowly missing the shattered remains of her teacup.

There was a muted thud—someone weakly hitting the door. "Help," Jayveh cracked out.

Amryn crawled around the couch, dragging her body each painful inch. She saw Jayveh grasp the door handle, but it didn't budge.

Locked. They were locked in.

Jayveh slumped against the door, her cries so strangled they were hardly there anymore.

Amryn tried to crawl to the door, but every clawed movement only made the agony in her gut worse.

Her throat was frayed by flames, and she watched as first Sadia, then Marriset, then Tam curled up on the floor, surrendering to the agony.

Jayveh fell onto her side.

Then it was Amryn's turn.

Her body stopped working. Her cheek scraped against the rough carpet and she blinked at the closed door, her vision hazing. Her fingers twitched, but she couldn't lift her hand. She couldn't lift her head, couldn't utter a word or a cry, even when a slip of paper was pushed beneath the door.

Someone was there.

Someone was on the other side of that door, and they were ignoring the tortured, groaning breaths of the dying women.

That was Amryn's last coherent thought. All she could do

was lie there and experience the pain and terror of this death five times over.

20

CARVER

CARVER PICKED AT THE FOOD ON his plate, but he wasn't hungry. Talking with Darrin was making his head ache. The man was dull, shallow, and conceited. He had to comment on everything, and he always had to demonstrate how he knew more than anyone else in the room. He would have felt bad for Marriset, except they seemed well-matched.

What Carver really wanted was to spend more time with Amryn.

When he'd come to Esperance, he knew he'd gain a wife. He hadn't dreamed of actually developing feelings for her, though. It was a complication he didn't need, considering everything. He needed to focus. And *not* on the way the light caught in Amryn's fiery hair, or the way her smiles warmed her sea-green eyes.

Approaching footsteps pounded in the hall outside.

Carver and Ivan were the first to stand, and Argent and the others were only a beat behind them.

A servant ran into the room, his twisted face flushed and

his eyes wild as he gasped for breath. "Ladies—poisoned—tea room!"

There was a half-second of total incomprehension, then Carver was running. He darted around the servant, who was doubled over and struggling to say more.

Carver didn't need to hear any more.

Amryn had been poisoned.

He couldn't run fast enough.

He bolted down the hall, Ivan at his heels, the others close behind. As Carver ran, his palms itched for a weapon. Not that there was anything a sword could do against poison.

The blood in his veins flashed hot with adrenaline. He tried to find the mental bridge to stand on—to be separate from the emotions churning his insides—but the calming exercise failed. If Amryn died . . .

The tea room was one floor below their dining room, and when Carver reached the stairs he grabbed the bannister and swung down several steps at a time. He landed hard and nearly stumbled, but he managed to leap down the rest of the stair-case.

After far too long—even though it had only been mere min-utes—he reached the women's sitting room.

Clerics and servants swarmed the space, along with a physi-cian and his apprentices. High Cleric Zacharias stood near a cluster of guards, and his expression was thunderous as he spoke rapidly with them. The ladies were stretched out on couches and the floor. Carver's eyes cut over everything until he found Amryn.

She was on the carpeted floor, and her maid—Ahmi—was supporting her head as she coaxed her to drink from a small cup pressed to her lips. Amryn's hands shook at her sides, and she struggled to swallow. Her eyes were red, with tears slowly leaking from them.

She was alive. Relief nearly took him out at the knees.

Ivan strode around him, marching toward the high cleric. Argent shot past him as well, his focus on finding Jayveh, while the other men searched for their wives. From what Carver could see at a quick glance, every woman was still breathing.

That was a small consolation, considering someone had just tried to kill them.

Carver crossed to Amryn's side and sank into a crouch on the rug beside her.

He folded one hand around hers without thought. "Are you all right?"

Tears welled in her eyes, but she jerked out a nod.

He tightened his grip on her hand. "Are you in pain?"

"Speaking is difficult for her," Ahmi told him gently. "The poison burned her throat."

Carver's heart lurched. "She'll recover?"

"Yes," Ahmi said. "The physician said all the ladies will, in time. The damage seems to be temporary, nothing permanent."

"Carver," Amryn croaked, the sound ragged, thin, and pained.

He leaned over her, the knuckles of his free hand instinctively brushing her cheek. "I'm here," he told her, trying to make his rough voice sound comforting. "You're going to be fine."

Amryn clenched his hand. "There was . . . a note."

His brows slammed down. "What?"

"Under . . . the door." She rasped a breath, flinching as she swallowed. "Couldn't see. High Cleric . . . took it."

"It's all right," he tried to soothe her. "I'll find out what it says, but I'll stay with you for now."

She shook her head. "Go."

He wanted to growl, but arguing with her when she was in pain seemed wrong. He looked to Ahmi. "Stay with her."

The woman nodded.

Carver released Amryn and pushed to his feet. The high cleric still stood in the center of the room. He was clearly fighting to keep his voice low as he squared off with Ivan. The Wolf's bulk was enough to intimidate anyone, but the comparison between him and the aging, bald cleric was especially stark.

Argent was kneeling beside Jayveh, who was laid out on the settee nearest to the high cleric. The prince seemed torn between paying attention to his wife, the physician who stood nearby, and the high cleric.

Carver stalked up to them, easily interrupting Zacharias's defensive words toward Ivan. "Where is it?"

The high cleric's eyes narrowed. "Where's what?"

"The note."

Argent's head whipped up. "What note?"

"It reveals nothing of importance," Zacharias said, his nose in the air.

Ivan's body stiffened. "A note was left and you weren't going to share that?"

The high cleric bristled. "I would have done so, just not here. It won't do any good to further upset the ladies."

"The ladies were almost killed," Carver snapped. "I don't see how a message from their would-be killer could cause them much more distress." He stretched out a hand, his stare intent.

Zacharias's scowl was deep, but he drew a folded piece of paper from his pocket and handed it over.

Carver flipped it open, his eyes scanning the scrawled words.

We killed your future when we killed your wives. Without them, there can be no children. No peace.
No empire.

"The handwriting is different," Ivan said, reading over Carver's shoulder. "This isn't Cora's killer."

Unless the killer had disguised his handwriting.

Argent held out his hand, and Carver surrendered the note to him.

Zacharias huffed. "It's merely an attempt to demoralize us, Your Highness."

"The attempted murder of five of the most important women in Esperance is more than demoralizing," Argent bit out, his eyes livid as he looked up from the note.

Footsteps sounded at the door and Chancellor Trevill rushed in. He staggered briefly as he took in the scene, and then his darting eyes settled on the knot of people in the middle of the room. He hurried over to join them.

"A guard told me the women were poisoned," he said. "What happened?"

"It was the tea," the physician said grimly. "*Kazzah*, to be more precise. It's a local poison that causes agonizing death. Usually. From what I can determine, it wasn't a strong enough dose to actually kill them."

"Is there any way to determine if that was intentional on the part of the poisoner?" Trevill asked.

"Unfortunately, no," the physician said.

"I think the message leaves little doubt that the goal was

their deaths," Ivan said, his tone dark.

"The door," Jayveh rasped, struggling to form words.

Argent bent closer to her. "Easy, my love. You don't need to speak."

Her lips pursed, and she shook her head. "Door was . . . locked. No one . . . came."

Argent's brow furrowed. Then he shot a look at the high cleric. "Why were there no guards outside this room?"

"I—I don't know. There should have been, but it's possible they stepped away for a brief time."

Argent's expression grew thunderous. "When you complained about my wife's bodyguards being in the way of your men, you assured me that Esperance guards would be sufficient to defend any room she was in. And now you tell me that they may have left her for a *brief time*?"

Zacharias's jaw worked. "This is a temple, Your Highness. While the guards are attentive, we've never had such things happen—"

"Cora was *murdered*," Argent growled. "We still haven't found her killer, yet you allow your guards to act like they're guarding nothing more than an empty chapel?"

The high cleric flipped a hand toward Trevill. "*He's* the one who hasn't found Cora's killer yet!"

Argent didn't give Trevill a chance to respond. "You want the credit for the peace, Zacharias; you can shoulder the disasters as well."

The high cleric's face flushed from the reprimand, but he said nothing as Trevill asked to read the message.

When the chancellor finished, he was frowning. "This message is longer than the last and in a different, messier hand. I'm not sure it's the same person."

"But it could be." Argent looked to him. "I want you to investigate this as well, Trevill. Talk to the servants, the guards—everyone. Ensure something like this cannot happen again."

"Of course, Your Highness." Trevill eyed the high cleric. "If you'll stop impeding my investigation and let me talk to everyone I need to, that would be appreciated."

Zacharias's eyebrows smashed together. "If you'll stop accusing clerics of killing Cora—"

"I'm not the one who rushes to make accusations," Trevill snapped. "I'm simply asking questions."

"A cleric would never do this! Neither would my guards, nor my servants."

"This tea was prepared in *your* kitchen, carried in by *your* servants, and this room was supposed to be guarded by *your* men," Trevill said. "Whether you like it or not, I will be questioning them all."

"Enough," Argent broke in before Zacharias could offer a retort. He then turned to the physician. "Can the women be moved to their rooms?"

"Yes, I think they're all stable enough. They won't be able to walk that distance, though. I can call for servants to help carry—"

"No need." Argent instantly scooped Jayveh up, one arm at her back and the other beneath her knees. She wrapped her arms around him and ducked her head against the curve of his neck. Argent tightened his hold on her. "Dinner will be taken privately tonight," he said to Zacharias, each word a clear command. "And I want guards outside the rooms of every woman."

The high cleric stiffly bowed his head.

Argent barely acknowledged the man as he strode for the

door, ignoring the servants who rushed forward and offered to carry Jayveh.

Carver returned to Amryn.

Ahmi was still with her, a comforting hand on her shoulder. Amryn's eyes were closed when he approached, but they fluttered open the moment he knelt over her. "Would you like to go to our rooms?" he asked.

She nodded with a wince.

Carver slid his arms beneath her and pulled her against his chest. Her cheek pressed against his shoulder, and her arm felt weak as it curled around his neck. Ahmi trailed him as he walked out of the room.

Amryn said nothing as he carried her. His boots clipped against the floor as he made his way to the staircase, and his arms locked more tightly around her as he ascended the steps. Small tremors wracked her body, and each one cut him like a knife.

When they finally reached their suite, he shifted her weight in his arms so he could grab his keys.

"I've got it," Ahmi said, rushing forward with her own key. She unlocked the door and pushed it open.

Carver's focus was solely on Amryn. The flutter of each thin breath. The soft brush of those long curls against his arm. The warmth that seeped from her body and into his.

Heat curled low in his gut, and he had to shove those thoughts away. It didn't matter how well she fit against him, or the perfect weight of her in his arms, and it certainly wasn't a good idea to acknowledge how soft she was, pressed against his chest.

His hold on her tightened as Ahmi led the way into the bedroom. Carver moved right for the four poster bed and laid Amryn on top of the quilt, gently easing her head onto the pillow. As he pulled away, his empty arms fell to hang at his sides.

Ahmi turned to him. "I'm going to fetch some soothing tea for her throat and more medicine from the physician, in case she needs it later. She'll be tired from what was already given to her, but will you stay with her? Or I could send for another maid to—"

"No. I'll stay with her." He couldn't imagine leaving.

The maid nodded, then hurried from the room.

The only sound was their breathing—his low and deep, hers soft and wavering. Afternoon sunlight streamed through the window, and Amryn's eyelids drooped. Her lips parted, but all that escaped was a scratchy rasp.

Carver bent toward her. He didn't analyze why he wrapped his hand around hers—again. "Do you need anything?"

The movement was slight, but she shook her head.

He squeezed her hand. "You should rest. I'll wake you when the physician comes."

A tear slipped out from the corner of her eye. "Stay," she croaked.

The waver of fear in her voice filled him with anger, but his movements were gentle as he shifted to sit on the edge of the bed, his body turned toward her. "I'm not going anywhere," he whispered.

21

AMRYN

AMRYN LOWERED HERSELF INTO the library chair, eyeing the large book she'd just dropped on the table. She knew a message waited for her within the pages of *Zerrif's Voyage*. She'd seen the pin in the painting yesterday—which was the sign her rebel contact had said would be used to alert her to a new message—but she hadn't had an opportunity to slip away and view it until now.

Things in Esperance had been tense the last several days. While all the women had mostly recovered from the physical effects of the poisoned tea, no one could relax. Trevill's investigation had found nothing about the origins of the poison, or who could have been responsible. The only thing that seemed sure was that another strike was imminent. Argent had ordered an increased guard on all the ladies. Amryn had managed to leave hers at the library entrance.

Carver had not been so easy to shake.

Her stomach dipped, her mind conjuring up images of him. His burning gaze as he'd stalked toward her in the tea room. The strong yet gentle way he'd carried her to their room. The way his eyes had held hers as he'd taken her hand, and stayed with her.

Over the next few days, he'd only left her occasionally—usually when Ahmi came to attend her. He'd even fallen asleep on the edge of the bed that first night, just so he could be near if she needed anything. She'd been so exhausted and weakened by the poison and the drugging effects of the medicine, she'd barely acknowledged the fact that Carver was sleeping in the room with her.

When she woke the next morning, she became *very* aware of him.

Early morning light filtered through the window when she stirred and found him sprawled out on the bed beside her. He was still sleeping, and she couldn't look away. He was on his back, with one arm thrown over his head and the other resting against his side. He'd slept on top of the quilt, and his shirt had tugged up to reveal a swath of bronze skin, broken by a myriad of thin lines of scarring. Those marks didn't detract from the muscled ridges of his abdomen, which tempted her fingertips, though she fought the impulse to touch him. His breaths were low and even, heavy in sleep, and his face was more relaxed than she'd ever seen it. Dark hair fell over his brow and the hard lines of his jaw were covered in a shadow of scruff. The silver band on his forefinger winked in the sunlight, and for the first time, she wondered about the ring. It was the only piece of jewelry he wore. She wondered what it meant to him—who had given it to him. She'd never asked. Just like she'd never asked about the pale scar on his chin, or the countless other marks that covered his body.

When his breath had caught and he stirred, she'd closed her

eyes. A coward, not wanting to be caught staring.

But even though he woke, he didn't move. And as the silent moment stretched, she realized *he* was staring at *her*.

Tingles broke out over her skin, lifting the hair on her arms and starting a flutter in her stomach. She could feel his gaze like a caress, his emotions edged with undeniable attraction. Unwanted heat bloomed in her cheeks, and she silently cursed the fact that her fair skin would do nothing to hide a blush.

She stubbornly kept her eyes closed, even though he had to know she was awake. He didn't say anything or tease her, like she might have expected from him. Instead, he shifted on the bed, making the mattress dip as he left it. He padded on bare feet to the door, then quietly eased from the room.

He hadn't been gone long, giving her just enough time to gather her composure. He hadn't mentioned the awkward moment when he returned with a glass of water. He also hadn't slept in the bed again, and she wasn't sure how she felt about that.

Today was their first day back to a somewhat normal routine, and the hawk-like stare Carver had given her when the women and men had separated for lessons was, well . . .

Her cheeks warmed and she mentally shook herself. She shouldn't want to be back in her room with him seated beside her, talking in that strong, level voice as he told her story after story about his siblings and their growing-up antics—anything to distract her from the pain, and then the boredom. She shouldn't crave his undivided attention as he asked her about her life in Ferradin, and she definitely shouldn't still thrill at the way he'd looked at her when she told him about her music—as if by revealing the fact she played the cello, she'd given him something of infinite importance.

She needed to focus on her mission. Which was why she was here, finally coming to claim the message the rebels had left her.

She'd just come from her lesson with the other women, where a female cleric had spent the last couple of hours telling them the important role they would all play in the empire, as women on the first Craethen Council. She told them they needed to emulate many of the female saints in the church, if they wished to succeed. It was a mixture of history and lecturing that was hard to pay attention to.

Especially when her thoughts kept returning to Carver.

After the lecture, they had a little time before they needed to go to the afternoon council meeting Trevill mediated, so Amryn had slipped away from the others to visit the library.

And she needed to focus, because she didn't have much time.

As she riffled through the pages, searching for the message the rebels had left for her, she almost wished she wouldn't find it. That errant thought alarmed her, because so many people were counting on her—Rix, Torin, the Rising, and all those who suffered under the emperor's rule. She couldn't afford to become distracted, or doubt herself—or get caught up in the way Carver made her feel.

A piece of folded parchment lifted with a turned page, and even though she'd known it would be there, Amryn's heart kicked in her chest. She lifted the note free and opened it.

The Rising had nothing to do with poisoning the tea, or Cora's death. Someone else is at work here. Learn what details you can about the investigation—anything Argent, Jayveh, or Carver might know. Relay your findings to me. Be careful.

She folded the note and pushed it into her pocket, her thoughts racing. The fact that her rebel contact was desperate to know anything Amryn could learn about the investigation made her think the Rising truly wasn't behind Cora's death, or the poisoning. It also didn't make any sense for the Rising to poison all the women, when Amryn was on their side.

"Back to that one, are you?"

Amryn jumped, her hands tightening on the book.

The cleric she'd first met in the library—Felinus—was standing there, and his eyes twinkled with humor. "Sorry to startle you."

"That's all right. I was lost in my thoughts."

He nodded toward the book. "Zerrif has never had such a staunch admirer."

Amryn forced a smile, though her pulse still skipped at his unexpected appearance. "I'm intrigued by his stories."

Felinus huffed a laugh. "Well, that's not something I've heard before. If you're so fond of him, you can take that tome to your room. It won't be missed, I assure you."

"Thank you, but no."

"Ah. Worried you couldn't carry it up the stairs?"

That caught a laugh from her still-tender throat. "No, it's just . . . I like reading in here. It's peaceful."

"It is that." The cleric folded his arms, which made his brown robe billow. His gaze swept the towering shelves around them. "There is an unrivaled peace in a library. Surrounded by words, but enfolded in silence. Knowing that stories lie dormant on the shelves, but a little time with you and they would come alive." He quirked a smile. "There's a reason I wanted to work in the largest library in Craethen."

"You could have been a poet."

"You flatter me." His expression shifted, and concern wafted from him. "Are you feeling recovered?"

"Yes, thank you."

"I'm glad." He took a small step back. "I can leave you to your studies; I simply wanted to check in with you."

"That's very kind of you."

"It's my pleasure, Lady Vincetti." He gestured toward Zer-rif's book. "If you ever tire of that and wish for something else to read, let me know. This library holds many wonders, and I'd be happy to share them with you."

"Thank you."

Felinus bobbed his shaved head, bid her farewell, and walked away. She watched him disappear around a tall shelf of books, a small smile lifting her lips. Her empathic sense found Felinus to be a warm individual, though she got the impression that he was generally quiet. It made her all the more pleased that he seemed to feel comfortable around her.

She turned her attention back to the open book on the table. She thumbed the pages as she slowly closed the book. She knew she shouldn't be late to the council meeting, but she didn't feel like moving quickly. As the fanned pages settled, she caught scattered words and phrases.

Bloodstones flashed out at her, and she stilled.

She'd made it through most of Saul Von's journal, though the notes were chaotic and hard to follow. And while it was a diary dedicated to his search for the five bloodstones, nowhere was there an explanation of what bloodstones actually *were*.

Amryn skipped to the beginning of the paragraph in Zer-rif's book that had caught her eye.

There isn't much known about the origins of bloodstones, which, of course, only makes them more fascinating. Stories about them are vague and seemingly impossible to verify. Bloodstones are so rare, most consider them to be myth—if they're even acknowledged at all. The majority of empaths I have questioned about the bloodstones scoff at their very existence. Only a few seem to believe they actually exist. My curiosity led me to the isle of Palar, where a bloodstone was rumored to be, but alas, I never found it. Perhaps they are rumor only. And perhaps that is best. One of the empaths I met in Palar exhibited fear as I asked my questions, and his final words remain with me— a warning not fully explained. A caution that makes me wonder if the bloodstones should, in fact, be relegated to mere legend: "The price some men pay for power is nearly as terrible as the fact that evil men are often the only ones who gain it."

Amryn's brow furrowed. She skimmed the following paragraph, and the next, but there was nothing more about bloodstones. She also didn't find any mention of them before that paragraph, either. The whole topic seemed to be an aside from the rest of Zerrif's thoughts, which centered around his visit to Palar.

Feeling as if she'd only gained more questions, Amryn closed the book. She'd delayed too long, and she'd need to hurry if she didn't want to be missed. She could dwell on the mysterious bloodstones later.

She dragged the massive book to the edge of the table and hauled it into her arms. The weight made her grunt as she carried it down the aisle and found the clear spot on the shelf. It was above her head, but she managed to perch the tip of the book on the edge of the shelf, then she pushed out her fingers, straining on tiptoe to put it back.

A curse bit out behind her and she twisted. The heavy book

dipped down, but a large hand caught the spine.

Carver stood nearly on top of her, and his sudden closeness stole her breath. She had known he was tall, and his shoulders were broad, but in this moment, caged in by him, she realized just how large he was. His hand was braced above hers, holding the book aloft as he gazed down at her. The emotions coming from him were familiar. Residual fear and concern were prominent, as they had been since the tea poisoning. But there was also elation.

He was happy to see her.

Heat warmed her cheeks and she dropped her hand, trusting Carver to keep the book from smashing down on her. She pressed back against the shelf, facing him fully. He was nearly trapping her with his body.

She found she didn't want to escape.

Carver's eyebrows lifted. "You didn't cheat death only to be crushed by a bloody book."

"You're the one who nearly made me drop it. And you shouldn't curse—we're in a temple."

He pushed the book into place and his arm lowered to another shelf, bracketing her against the books. He leaned his head in, his voice lowering conspiratorially. "I cursed because that book was going to fall on your head."

"No, it wasn't."

"Yes, it was. I had the better vantage. Trust me."

Trust me. Those words shouldn't have awakened longing, but she wished in that moment she could trust him. But that was impossible.

She lifted her chin, catching his stare. "I got it down just fine."

"Yes, well, natural laws make that easier, don't you think?"

Amryn's mouth twitched.

Carver's eyes drifted over her face, and his perusal made her pulse skip. His emotions warmed and deepened. "You shouldn't have left your guard at the door," he said, his voice more serious than before.

"It was only for a moment."

The intensity rolling off him tightened her belly. "You need to be careful, Amryn. The danger is real. Especially for you. Whoever poisoned that tea made it clear you and the other women are targets."

We killed your future when we killed your wives.

Carver had told her what the would-be assassin's note had said, and she fought a shiver.

The lines on his face deepened. "How are you feeling?"

Had he asked her a moment ago, she could have answered blithely. Now, she fought to slow her pulse. "Fine." She swallowed, and her throat was so dry, she fought a grimace.

Concern flared in Carver, a second before his fingers brushed her throat.

Her heart tripped.

"I'm sorry," he whispered, the calloused pads of his fingers warming her skin.

She barely registered his words. He hadn't touched her like this since he'd applied the salve to her sunburn. Her body came alive in an alarming way, and she found herself staring at his mouth, which hovered so close to hers. What would it feel like to kiss him?

The sudden thought made her knees weak.

Attraction flared, and she realized Carver was now focused on *her* mouth. His desire mixed with her own, creating a heady mix that held her immobile.

Carver's chin lowered. "Amryn—"

"Not exactly what the clerics had in mind when they built these shelves, I'd imagine," Argent called from the end of the row, his amusement strong.

Heat slammed Amryn's face and she ducked her head, but not before she saw that Argent wasn't alone. Samuel and Darrin were with him, all of them looking on.

While Argent was quite pleased to have found them in this position, Samuel felt discomfort, and he was quick to shift his gaze. Darrin looked on with lewd interest, which only made Amryn's cheeks burn hotter.

Carver's arm dropped and he took a small step back, but his hand touched Amryn's arm, a quiet reassurance, as if *he* were the empath and could feel her flash of embarrassment. "I can't think of a better use for a bookshelf," he tossed back, taking the brunt of their attention.

Argent chuckled. "I don't think I can argue that. But perhaps you can save this for later? I don't think Trevill will appreciate us being late." He sent Amryn a wink, then clapped a hand on Darrin's shoulder, moving them all along.

Carver looked down at her, even as he eased back a step. "Sorry about that. Sometimes Argent can't seem to help himself."

"It's fine," she said. "What were you going to say?"

He bit his lower lip, which only brought her attention back to his mouth. "It can wait," he finally said. "Shall we?" He offered his arm, and Amryn slowly took it.

Curiosity hummed inside her, but she didn't press him as they walked through the maze of shelves.

"Can I ask you something?" Amryn asked.

"Of course."

"Have you heard anything about Trevill's investigation?"

"No." He glanced down at her. "Why do you ask?"

She shrugged, not quite able to meet his gaze. "I just didn't know if maybe Argent received separate reports from the rest of us."

"If Trevill learns anything, I'm sure we'll all be told."

That wasn't exactly a denial, was it?

"So Argent *does* know more than the rest of us?" she pressed.

"He *is* the empirical prince." Carver surprised her when he laid a hand over hers, which pressed her palm more firmly against his arm. "If I learn anything concrete, I'll share it with you. All right?"

She nodded, distracted by the comforting weight of his calloused hand against hers.

It wasn't long before they entered the council chamber, and Carver pulled out her chair, then sat beside her.

Chancellor Trevill waited until everyone took their seats, then he began. "I thought today it might be beneficial to debate a current event—the war in Harvari."

Carver tensed, but it was his sudden spike of dread that nearly stole Amryn's breath. He quickly clamped down his emotions, once again going strangely muted. She could barely feel anything from him, and the abruptness of that shift made her shiver.

"I know we'll have some strong opinions here," Trevill continued, and his gaze cut to Carver. "After all, we have a decorated war hero among us, not to mention the prince of the empire. But that's why I chose this topic. It will be important for you all to learn how to share unique viewpoints on potentially controversial topics, and find common ground—especially with your spouse. For this reason, I would like to divide the couples for this debate." Trevill gestured. "Jayveh, Carver, Rivard, Sadia, and Marriset—please sit on the left side of the table. The rest of you, please be seated on the right side."

It didn't take long for all of them to find their new seats.

The emotions in the room were many and varied, and it was hard to pinpoint them all. Samuel was anticipating the debate, but then he always seemed to enjoy these council meetings. Ivan—who landed in a chair next to Amryn—felt a mixture of restlessness and annoyance. Marriset felt a flutter of excitement when she took a seat beside Carver, though he didn't even look at her—his eyes were on Amryn. Sitting across the table from him, she avoided his gaze.

Her anxiety mounted. These council meetings had tackled a variety of issues, from tax rates, to how best to send aid to kingdoms in need. She knew this debate would be different. The war in Harvari was a stark reminder that the empire took what it wanted, regardless of who got hurt. It was a reminder that Carver was the emperor's favored general. That he led armies and conquered cities.

And moments ago, she had wanted to kiss him.

"Now," Trevill said, calling their attention. "Those seated on the left will argue for the war, and those on the right will be against it."

That was one mercy, at least—Amryn wouldn't have to say anything positive about the empire's war.

Trevill flipped over a sheet of paper that had been lying on the table, his eyes scanning the page as he said, "Let's begin by addressing the emperor's reasons for going to war."

"Harvari posed a threat," Rivard said bluntly. "They wanted war with Craethen, and we made the tactical choice to invade first to keep the war on their land."

"They also posed a threat to many of their own people," Marriset added. "A faction within Harvari had begun to kill Harvarians who didn't agree with them."

"Some of those targeted pleaded for the emperor's help," Jayveh said. "Going to war to defend them was a compassionate move."

"And yet," Ivan said coolly, "how many innocents died in this *compassionate* fight?" He shook his head. "The war is unnecessary, brutal, a drain of life and resources on both sides, and impossible to actually win."

"The necessity of war was already established," Rivard fired back. "And all wars are brutal. But how can you argue that it's impossible to win? Craethen has already all but won the fight."

"By slaughtering anyone who refuses to be conquered?" Ivan challenged.

"This fight wasn't about conquering Harvari," Carver said, his tone level, his expression as unreadable as his emotions. "It was about guarding the empire's southern border, and protecting those in Harvari who needed it."

Ivan leaned forward, his arm brushing Amryn's. "How many of those villages did you go in to protect, only to abandon them when it became strategic to leave?"

Carver's face was so hard it could have been etched in stone. "You wouldn't know, because you weren't there."

Ivan's mood turned infinitely darker.

Trevill cleared his throat. "There's no need to get overly personal."

Marriset nodded absently, but the interested way she looked at Carver made Amryn feel an out-of-place surge of jealousy.

"I think we should remain with the facts," Trevill continued.

"Now, does anyone else want to state any other motivations or criticisms?"

There was a short silence, then Argent spoke. "Many have argued that the threat Harvari posed to the empire was minimal, and that our response was disproportionate." While his tone was diplomatic, Amryn could feel his discomfort as he looked toward his friend.

A muscle in Carver's cheek jumped, but it was Rivard who said, "It's better to hit hard once, rather than render a hundred ineffectual blows. That's something they teach in Westmont."

Darrin set a hand on the table. "I think it should also be stated that the war has had a severe financial cost. The fact that our taxes were increased to fund a war in another country isn't exactly making anyone feel better about things."

"That's a good point," Samuel said. "Especially when the war has dragged on longer than anticipated."

"Now, that's hardly fair," Marriset said. "It's impossible for anyone to accurately guess how long a war will take."

"Estimations were made, though," Samuel countered. "The emperor said the war would be won in a matter of months." He gestured to Carver. "How long were you personally in Harvari?"

His voice was neutral. "Two years."

Samuel nodded. "Two *years*. And the war is still being wrapped up, even though the main fighting is over."

"People may criticize how long the war has lasted," Rivard said. "But is that really strong grounds for arguing the fight wasn't worth it?"

Tam—who had been as silent as Amryn—suddenly spoke. "It's not the strongest grounds, but it's still a valid criticism."

Rivard's mouth pinched as he stared at his wife.

Tam didn't flinch, nor did she look away.

"The fight took longer because the enemy was more pervasive than expected," Carver said flatly. "Many people in Harvari didn't want us there, but most were grateful. Especially when the extremists came to their villages and burned them."

"They burned them because you were there," Ivan said.

"Sometimes," Carver allowed. "But mostly the extremists just wanted everyone in Harvari to unite with them, or die. They wanted every tribe, village, and city to align with their views."

"How is the empire any different?" Ivan demanded. "You expect me to believe that the empire cares about defending the individuality and rights of another kingdom, even though it conquered all of our kingdoms?"

Amryn was surprised Ivan would so openly criticize the empire, even if he had the thin excuse of it being part of the debate.

Carver also felt a flash of surprise, but that settled quickly into a hum of satisfaction. "If you want to debate the ethics of the empire, I'm happy to do so," he told Ivan. "Without the structure and peace the empire brings to all of us, we would be as war-torn as Harvari."

"But we would be free."

"Would we?" Carver asked. "We know how many battles were fought among us before the empire was formed. Maybe none of you have had to dig graves for children that didn't survive the horrors of war, but I have. And I thank the Divinities that I've never had to bury children in Westmont, or anywhere else in our kingdoms due to senseless war."

Ivan's voice was quiet. "How many children did you kill

in Harvari, General? How many children died there because of you?"

The sudden silence bristled with tension. Amryn's fingers knotted in her skirt, and her head ached as her empathic sense was bombarded with all the conflicting emotions in the room.

Carver didn't say anything. No protest or denial. His expression was hard, and even though he fought to control his emotions, Amryn felt his sickening guilt.

Something deep inside her shriveled.

"Enough." Argent stood. "I think we should dismiss for the day."

Trevill bowed his head. "Of course."

Ivan was the first to shove back from the table. He strode to the nearest door and wrenched it open before disappearing down the hall.

More slowly, others found their feet and made their way from the room. Argent hurried around the table to reach Carver, and he spoke quietly enough that his voice didn't carry.

Beside them, Jayveh cast a worried look toward Amryn.

Saints, she needed to get control of her expression. She gave the princess a small smile that was meant to be reassuring, but when she stood, her legs trembled a little.

Tam moved to stand beside her. "Are you all right?"

"I'm fine," she lied.

Tam clearly didn't believe her. She touched her arm. "I promised to help in the gardens, but perhaps we could go on a walk later?"

"I'd like that."

Tam nodded, then swept away.

Even though Amryn had made no plans to volunteer in the museum archives today, she could use the solitude. So she hurried out of the exit that led toward the museum.

She hadn't made it far down the empty hall before footsteps rang out behind her.

"Amryn, wait."

Her fingernails dug into her palms, but she twisted to face Carver. "Yes?"

A furrow grew between his dark brows. "Where are you going?"

"The museum. I promised to help this afternoon."

He rubbed a hand over the back of his neck. His unease rippled out and made her skin itch. "Are you sure you're up for that? You're still recovering."

"I'm fine."

"I could come with you."

"No, that isn't necessary."

"I don't mind."

"No thank you."

She couldn't quite read what flickered in his eyes. It was too quick, and his emotions were still clamped down tight. He took a single step forward, his voice lowered even though they were alone in the corridor. "You didn't say anything in there. Not a single word."

"I didn't have anything to say."

His eyes narrowed. "Somehow I doubt that."

She looked away, her heart thumping in her chest. "I really need to go, Carver."

"You don't have any opinions on the war, or a single question for me?"

She said nothing.

After a long moment, he let out a short, hard laugh. "And here I thought we were past this."

Her eyes darted to him. "Past what?"

"The silences. I thought we were making progress and getting to know each other, but you're as much a mystery as the day I met you. And you don't seem to care about figuring me out—you've already made your assumptions." He took a step back. "I'll find a guard to escort you."

As he turned on his heel, she couldn't help herself. "Why do they call you the Butcher?"

He froze. Pulses of despair and fury hit her, a tangled mess that made her lungs catch.

He looked over his shoulder at her, his expression hard as he said, "I think you can figure that out."

His footsteps echoed her hammering pulse as he strode away.

22

CARVER

CARVER SIPPED HIS WINE, HIS spine stiff as he sat at the long dinner table. Amryn was beside him, but they hadn't spoken to each other since the incident in the hall after the failed council meeting.

What truly bothered him wasn't the things Ivan had said, or what anyone else in that room thought. It was the way Amryn had looked at him. Judged him. Dismissed him. When he'd followed her into the hall, his intent had been to reassure her. And when she'd viewed him so coldly . . .

His hands tightened on the stem of his glass, and he took another deep swallow.

Self-loathing, disgust, horror—fear. It was all a part of him, and this afternoon had dragged everything to the surface. His defensiveness was the only weapon he had, but it had proved a feeble shield today. It was hard to justify death, and harder still to come to terms with the fact that he was perhaps the most hated man in Harvari. But if the war was necessary—if he'd done the right thing by fighting and bleeding there—

then he wasn't the monster he felt like. The men he'd lost, the villages that had burned—it would have been a worthwhile sacrifice, if the end result was for the greater good. If he had been captured, tortured, and nearly killed for a reason . . .

It was the only thing that kept him sane. He had to believe the cost was worth it.

He threw back his head and emptied his glass, and he didn't stop the servant who rushed to refill it.

Beside him, Argent frowned. "Are you all right?" he whispered. His concern was as palpable as it had been when he'd intercepted Carver after the council meeting. And just like then, it only made him feel more raw and exposed.

"I'm fine." He tipped the fresh glass up to his lips and drank.

The high cleric came to his feet at the head of the table. "I'd like your attention, please." He waited until every eye was lifted before he clasped his hands in front of him, his bald head shining in the candlelight that burned from the large chandelier overhead and the towering candles on the table. "I know there have been some unforeseen struggles here in Esperance, and I believe we could all use the healing touch of the All-Seeing Divinities. And so, I have planned an important excursion. As you all know, many troubled souls come to Esperance to heal their spirits and their minds. It is, at least in part, why Emperor Lorcan chose Esperance to be the ground on which this new peace was made. Your marriages are what will strengthen the bonds between kingdoms, and the council you form will forever change the way the empire is ruled. I believe this makes you the perfect candidates for the Walk of Kavaraugh."

"Kavaraugh was one of the founders of the church," Samuel said.

"Correct," High Cleric Zacharias said. "After he was sainted, he came to Esperance to live out the rest of his days. He also began a tradition when he made his final walk to the top of a nearby mountain peak, called Zawri. When an offering is carried to Zawri's summit and left with a heart of forgiveness, then the Divinities will bless you with a cleansed soul. Many have made the trek over the years—especially in preparation for the Feast of Remembrance. And, as you're all no doubt aware, that holiday is only a few weeks away. I think it would be a beneficial experience for all of you to climb Zawri, and since we're not leaving the general area of Esperance, I do not see this as breaking the emperor's decree of remaining isolated."

He paused briefly, but no one argued. He continued: "We will all travel to the foot of the mountain and make camp, and then begin our hike at first light. Each couple will hike together. You will never be truly alone, however. Guards will be nearby, and you won't be spaced too far apart on the path from each other. The walk itself takes less than a day, and then we will return to the temple." He looked around at them all, his eyes lingering on Ivan. "I know this may sound like it won't help, but I've made the walk myself several times. It is a powerful experience."

"What sort of offering is expected?" Rivard asked.

"Anything will do, but people often take a piece of jewelry, or even something they've made. Some of the soldiers who make the walk leave a weapon, and I've seen mothers who mourn their children bury locks of their hair."

"It seems like a beautiful tradition," Sadia said.

"It is. And I think all of you will be stronger for it." The high cleric turned to Trevill, who sat nearby. "You are, of course, welcome to participate as well."

The chancellor tipped his head. "Thank you for the invitation, but I have plenty of things to do here."

"Is it safe to be in the jungle overnight?" Darrin asked, his brow furrowed.

"With precautions and an experienced group, yes," Zacharias assured him. "You will have nothing to fear, I assure you."

Except maybe the fact that one of the couples might have an imposter with them.

"When do we leave?" Jayveh asked.

"It will take several days to make the necessary arrangements," the high cleric said. "You'll all have plenty of time to prepare."

The questions continued, and Carver glanced toward Amryn. Of course, she was silent; she rarely spoke in group settings, but this silence was different. He felt it stretching between them, and he didn't like it. He just didn't know how to clear the air, so he took another swallow of wine.

When dinner concluded and everyone moved into the adjacent room for their ritual of conversation, drinking, or games, Carver fell back, allowing Amryn to cross the sitting room to join Tam and Jayveh.

Argent came to walk beside him, his voice low as he asked, "What happened between you and Amryn?"

"Who said anything happened?"

Argent gave him a look. "Please. You two aren't even looking at each other."

Carver slid his thumb over the smooth glass in his hand, unable to hold his friend's stare. "She was reminded of who I am. That's all."

The prince's eyes narrowed, but before he could reply, Jayveh strode over to them. "Tam, Amryn, and I are going up to Tam's room to visit." Her eyes slid to Carver. "I'll be sure Amryn is escorted back to your room with a guard when we're done."

The point that he was *not* to come looking for her was clearly made, so he did nothing but nod.

Argent leaned in and dropped a kiss on Jayveh's cheek. "Enjoy."

"You, too." She gave a last pointed look toward Carver, then swept back to join Amryn and Tam.

Amryn didn't look back once as they left.

Argent exhaled slowly. "Those things Ivan said today . . . the things *I* said . . ."

"Don't. It's fine."

"Clearly it's not." Argent set a hand on Carver's shoulder. "We can talk, too, Carve."

"Talking is the last thing I want to do right now."

Argent's lips pressed into a line. "All right. But I'm here for you. You know that, right?"

He did. But how could he verbalize how he felt when he wasn't even sure *what* he felt?

The sitting room was spread out with chairs and settees arranged in such a way that multiple corners could be utilized for semi-private conversations. The high cleric stood in the far corner with Trevill and a couple of other clerics who had joined them. Rivard was speaking to Ivan, Darrin, and Marriset in another corner.

Argent was almost instantly pulled into a conversation with Samuel and Sadia, and Carver moved to find his own corner. On the way, he passed a side table with decanters and glasses. He eyed the brandy, but kept walking.

He sat on the edge of a cushioned chair and tossed back the last of his wine, then set the long-stemmed glass aside. It clicked lightly against the polished wood table.

He thought about leaving. Clearly, he wasn't in a mood to socialize or investigate. His head ached. He'd had too much wine, yet not enough to dispel the darkening cloud that hovered over him.

He closed his eyes and pinched the bridge of his nose. He didn't know how long he remained that way before there was a whisper of movement in front of him.

"I think you deserve this."

He opened his eyes and lifted his head to find Marriset standing in front of him, a glass of brandy in her hand. She held it out to him, the corner of her mouth lifting. "The clerics are distracted and your wife isn't here, so there's no one to judge."

He stared up at her. Marriset was beautiful, with long brown hair that fell in shiny waves, and perfectly sculpted features. Her lips were painted a deep red that complimented her olive skin. Yet all he could think when he looked at her was that she wasn't Amryn. But he hadn't cleared her from his suspect list, and he should take advantage of the fact that she'd approached him.

He took the offered glass.

Their fingers brushed. Hers were cool, and he felt nothing more than that.

She perched on the edge of the chair angled beside his, their knees so close they almost touched. "The debate today was quite intense."

"It was." He took a sip of the amber liquid and swallowed the welcome burn.

She leaned toward him, setting a hand lightly on his forearm. Beneath her fingers, his muscles bunched.

"I'm sorry if anything Ivan said upset you," she said. "I hope you know that not all of us agree with what he had to say. You're a hero, Carver. And anyone who thinks otherwise isn't worth your attention."

"Thank you." His voice was a little dull. To cover it, he took another drink.

Marriset withdrew her hand and crossed one leg over the other. Her foot gently bumped his shin as she picked at her red skirt, adjusting it primly over her knee. Her eyes shined as she caught him watching. "It didn't escape my notice that Amryn seemed a bit bothered by the debate."

He made a sound in his throat that could have been agreement. And maybe it was, because she clearly *had* been bothered.

Marriset shook her head. "She does seem to be a quiet sort. Not one for any type of confrontation." She paused, clearly waiting for a response.

He thumbed the edge of his glass. "I think her issue wasn't with the debate, so much as with me."

"Oh?" Her interest made the back of his neck itch. She was the type of woman he normally avoided, but she was seeking some sort of connection with him; probably since she'd realized by now that Argent would not be swayed from Jayveh, but she still craved power. He'd noticed the way she had focused on him during the debate, and he should have anticipated her attention.

Having drunk too much tonight might prove helpful after all. It would help dull the voice that told him not to return her flirtations.

He bit his lower lip, his eyes locking on hers. "She hasn't exactly been fond of me." He hated that that wasn't entirely a lie.

"Really?" Her dark eyes widened. "You've seemed so happy with each other. I would have guessed you make the strongest match, next to Argent and Jayveh."

"No one could really be happier than them."

She chuckled. "True. It's a little nauseating, isn't it?"

"Yes." He shifted in the chair, twisting slightly more toward her as he lowered his chin and his voice. "He's my friend, but I can't help but wonder why he's even here. Obviously his match wasn't a blind one, like ours."

"It does seem to put the rest of us at a disadvantage of sorts."

"Are you content with your match?" he asked.

Her head tilted to the side as she viewed him. "Are you content with yours?"

He didn't let himself blink. "No."

The corner of her mouth lifted. "Neither am I. But perhaps there are some things we can do to improve our situation."

The words surprised him, but maybe they shouldn't have. Marriset had never been anything other than direct. His gut felt strangely hollow as he returned her smile and whispered, "Perhaps we can."

She reached out and took the glass from his hand and raised it in a salute before she took a long sip. As she lowered the glass, her tongue swept her full red lips. "I'm glad we had this talk, Carver."

"I hope it's not the last."

"Oh, it won't be." She passed the glass back to him and stood. "Will you join me for a walk tomorrow in the gardens before breakfast?"

The drink felt heavier in his hand, knowing her mouth had been on it. "It would be my pleasure."

Marriset's eyes glowed and her hips swayed as she walked away from him.

The strong smell of her perfume lingered, burning his nostrils.

He glanced toward Argent, who was looking at him. The severe frown on his face made it clear he knew what Carver had been doing with Marriset—and that he disapproved.

You would stoop to this? his eyes seemed to ask.

Yes, Carver thought back at him. *For you, for the empire—for the safety of everyone here . . . yes.*

Besides, what would it matter? Amryn already hated him. And he hated himself.

He set the brandy aside and stood. As he strode from the room, he caught Marriset's gaze. She was standing beside her husband, her arm looped through Darrin's, but her eyes were locked on Carver as she smiled.

Carver pressed his hand over Marriset's, pinning it to his arm as they walked the garden paths. Marriset was close enough to him that her chest deliberately brushed his arm as they moved.

They had taken a few different walks in the garden now; stolen moments, away from anyone who might see or judge.

Carver hated every second of the time they spent together. He hated feeling her touch. These past few days had been a unique torture, made all the worse by the fact that Amryn was still avoiding him. And the fact that, while Marriset talked a lot, her flirtations so far hadn't led to any real information.

"That's fascinating," he lied, responding to her latest comment—about flowers and their meanings, of all things.

"We live in a complicated world," she said. "Things often have deeper meanings. That's why it's helpful to have people around us that can make things feel simpler." She nodded toward a bright red flower. "If only that were a rose. Would you have any guess as to what that particular flower might mean, if I gave one to you?"

That you want to stick me with a thorn? "I have no idea."

Her long lashes fluttered as she gazed up at him. "I'll give you a hint. Roses symbolize passion."

The urge to roll his eyes or fling her off his arm was strong, but that wouldn't help him learn more about her. So he merely raised an eyebrow. "I think Darrin might mind."

"You're not afraid of Darrin."

"No."

"And I'm not afraid of your wife, so what's the harm?" Marriset didn't wait for an answer. She drew back her shoulders and peered up at him, her brown eyes direct. "Besides, what they don't know can't hurt them. And if you and I decide to seek some happiness where we can . . ." Her tone was suggestive, her expression even more so. "I don't know about you," she whispered, her voice a little husky now. "But I've lost sleep thinking about what this could be between us."

"I haven't slept much, either," he admitted. Of course, that had had nothing to do with Marriset, and everything to do with the fact that his wife wasn't really speaking to him.

Marriset's mouth curved, revealing her pleasure at his words.

They'd been walking together since dawn, and he'd gained nothing except a headache and a souring guilt in his stomach.

But as they rounded a hedge on their slow walk back toward the temple for breakfast, Marriset tugged him to a stop beside a trickling stone fountain.

"I've been thinking a lot about my future," she said, still holding his arm. "And you strike me as the sort of man who also makes plans."

He tipped his head.

Encouraged, she spoke in a low rush. "Your friendship with Argent is as valuable as your reputation as the emperor's favored general. And one day, you will inherit Westmont's throne from your father. Not to mention, you have a seat on the council. If we were to make an alliance, I would benefit from your position, and you would benefit from mine; I have great influence in Palar, and together we would have two votes on every council matter—four, if we persuade our spouses to our agendas. We could be two of the most powerful people in the empire."

He leaned toward her, dropping his chin so their eyes were level. "And what exactly would we do with this power?"

"Anything we wanted." Her palm glided up his arm and she shifted to stand fully in front of him, their chests brushing. "You can't be happy with her," she whispered. "I know men like you. You need more than a timid waif."

Amryn wasn't timid. She was strong, kind, thoughtful, observant, beautiful—

"I could see to your needs," Marriset breathed. Her hand crested his shoulder and moved to the nape of his neck. As she pulled his head down, she rose up on her toes.

Everything inside him shriveled as her lips brushed the corner of his mouth. "Make me your mistress, Carver. You won't regret it."

Her lips felt wrong against his skin. Her hands on him, her body pressed against his—it was all wrong. And when her mouth skated to his jaw and her tongue flicked across his skin, he stiffened.

She read something else entirely in his reaction. She pulled back with a grin. "Well? What do you think?"

He lifted a hand to her cheek—mostly as a way of holding her back. "I admit, an affair would be diverting," he murmured.

"More than a simple affair. I'm not one to propose a tryst that ends in a year. You could appoint me as an ambassador in Westmont, and Darrin would have to let me go. That would give us many opportunities to see each other."

"Hmm." He leaned down, dropping his lips to her ear. "Yet we still have our spouses to consider."

"We will need to be discreet, of course. I don't imagine anyone else would understand, or be supportive of our . . . alliance. But I don't see our spouses as a problem. Do you?"

"No." Amryn's face flashed in his mind, but he shoved her away as he leaned in and laid his mouth on Marriset's neck, just under her ear.

She relaxed against him, and he forced himself to hold his ground. He needed her to fully believe him. To be comfortable with him. But her skin was oddly cold beneath his lips, despite the morning sunlight.

As intimately as they stood right now, he had felt so much more when Amryn simply looked at him from across a room.

Marriset slid her hands up into his hair, keeping his mouth against her skin. "We would be stronger than any of the other rulers in Craethen, second only to the emperor himself."

Carver's nose skimmed her neck as he tried to bury his flash of excitement. Was she really so drunk on her own seduction that she would tip her hand so soon? He curled an arm around her lower back, tugging her more firmly against him. "And then what?"

She chuckled, her exhales teasing his skin. "Isn't that enough?"

He didn't have a chance to coax any more out of her.

Footsteps scraped the cobbled path, but it wasn't enough warning before three people rounded the bend.

His focus snapped to Amryn first.

Her red hair was gathered with a simple ribbon and the curls cascaded over one shoulder. She wore a green dress today, the color of sage. It nearly matched her eyes. Eyes that dug their way over him and Marriset, trying to find where he ended and she began.

It was a difficult task.

Shock bled across her face, making her look more pale than ever. Hurt followed close behind.

Jayveh stood beside Amryn, her eyes round with shock. Tam stood on the princess's other side, and the disapproval in her expression was scathing.

Carver straightened, tugging Marriset's hands out of his hair.

Marriset twisted around, and she gave a little laugh. "Oh. Hello." She made a show of fixing her perfectly coiffed hair, and she put a little more of a pant into her breath. "A lovely day, isn't it?"

Tam arched one brow. "That's one word for it."

Carver looked to Amryn. Disgust had risen in her eyes, along with anger.

Her lip curled. "If you'll excuse me," she said, clearly speaking to Jayveh and Tam. "I'll find my own way back."

"Seen enough, have you?" Marriset asked, her voice sickly sweet.

Carver barely hid his grimace, but Amryn met Marriset's mocking head-on. She even adopted the same prim tone as she lifted her chin. "Yes. I didn't realize the garden would be infested by snakes."

Tam coughed, though it sounded more like a swallowed laugh.

Amryn turned on her heel, brushing past the bodyguards who had drifted up behind them, and disappeared around the hedge.

Carver wanted to dart after her, but he stayed where he was. And when Marriset slid her hand into his, he didn't pull away. Not even when Jayveh's face fell with disappointment, and Tam's eyes narrowed.

Carver had shouldered loathing before. This was nothing new.

Except he didn't think he would ever forget the pain that had cut over Amryn's face as she'd walked away.

23

AMRYN

AMRYN SHOVED THE BOOK ONTO the shelf in front of her, her arm heavy with a stack of other books waiting to be shelved. Her focus was on the task Cleric Jane, the museum caretaker, had given her of returning these reference books to the library. She definitely wasn't focusing on what she'd seen in the garden this morning, or on the surprisingly deep stab of hurt and betrayal she'd felt.

Yet, all she could see when she closed her eyes was Carver's face buried in Marriset's neck, and her hands knotted in his dark hair. And all she could feel was the flood of excitement they'd both felt. Right before Carver's eyes had locked on her, and he'd felt a rush of incriminating guilt.

She slammed another book into place. The extra force helped hide the fact that her hands shook.

"You didn't care for the ending?"

She glanced over her shoulder.

Cleric Felinus stood behind her, a stack of books in his arms. He nodded to the one she'd just shelved.

Her hold on the books tightened. "I haven't read them. Cleric Jane just asked me to return them."

Concern billowed gently, but he kept his tone light. "And yet they managed to offend you?"

"No."

"Ah." Cleric Felinus drifted to her side, the hem of his robe skating across the stone floor. "If I may ask . . . *who* offended you, then?"

Amryn bit her lower lip. She didn't even want to say his name.

"*Ah*," Felinus said again, more knowingly this time. Compassion and pity mingled, making her throat dry.

"It's nothing." She pushed another book onto the shelf, but didn't manage to feel any lighter.

"I've found that sometimes the most vexing things are *nothing*." The bald cleric lifted one of his books and shelved it, not looking at her as he continued. "I'm sure you have many friends here, but if you ever need to talk about anything—or *nothing*, as the case may be—I am available."

"Thank you," she said. And she meant it. Felinus had uncomplicated emotions and a calming presence, and she was touched by his quiet friendship. But the last thing she wanted to do was talk about Carver.

Jayveh and Tam had followed her from the garden, and they'd hugged her and offered to cry with her or help break his jaw. But Amryn didn't want any of that. She just wanted to get away from him, and forget that she'd ever—even for a moment—felt something for him.

Amryn and Felinus continued to place books on the shelves adjacent to each other, though after a moment of silence he said, "I think you've inspired me."

She looked over at him. "How so?"

"After seeing your devotion to Zerrif, I think I need to re-look at his book, as well as other histories I once dismissed as dry. While it may be true that not every person who put ink to page had a story to tell, I'd like to be the sort of person who gave their words a chance." He eyed her. "We expect writers to give us everything, but sometimes it's up to the reader to look a little deeper. And if you don't . . . well, you might miss something wonderful."

She twisted toward him. "Are you trying to tell me that I need to judge less?"

The corner of his mouth lifted. "There you go, looking deeper."

She scoffed and turned back to the shelf. "Some people don't *have* anything deeper. Sometimes, they're exactly who you thought they were."

"I thought we were talking about books, not people?"

She rolled her eyes. "Your metaphor was heavy-handed."

He chuckled as he placed his last book, but when he turned to face her, he was serious. "What you have all been asked to do here . . . it is no easy task. And while I have never been good with reading people, I am adept when it comes to reading books. The best characters always have layers and flaws. It's what makes them real. It would be a shame if we had more compassion and understanding for a fictional character than we do for those closest to us."

Amryn slid the last book into place, not quite meeting his gaze as she said, "Fictional characters don't have the ability to hurt us."

"The best ones certainly do. But I'm sorry if you've been hurt, Amryn."

She remained where she was, and Felinus didn't seem in any rush to leave their sheltered spot between the towering bookshelves. Perhaps it was their isolation, but she found herself whispering, "I don't know what I'm supposed to do."

With Carver. With the rebels. With her growing friendship with Jayveh, and even Argent.

"To live is to face the unknown. It is the joy and the challenge we all must meet. But I know you're equal to the task."

Amryn's eyes stung. Felinus's kindness, his confidence in her . . . it felt like having Rix with her, comforting her. She blinked back the moisture before tears could form. "Thank you."

Felinus's smile was gentle. "You are most welcome. And if you'd like, you can remain here. I can send a message to Cleric Jane."

She shook her head. "I should return." There were many items to put away, and she hoped Jane would let her into the archives today, so she could look for the empirical seals.

She and Felinus walked together through the shelves, and perhaps it was because of the comfortable air between them, but she dared ask, "I was reading in *Zerrif's Voyage*, and I came across something I didn't understand."

"That doesn't surprise me. Zerrif wasn't one to describe things plainly."

"It was just in a paragraph as he described his visit to Palar, but . . . he mentioned something called a bloodstone."

Felinus shot her a look. "He said that?"

"Yes." Her heart tripped at his rush of emotions. There were many, including disbelief and curiosity. But the strongest emotion surprised her: fear.

Felinus glanced around them, but of course they were still

alone. Even so, he lowered his voice. "Bloodstones are a very rare bit of lore. I didn't know Zerrif wrote of them."

"What are they, exactly?"

The lines in his forehead deepened. "There isn't much known about them. Younger clerics have probably never heard of them at all, and even among the older ones you'd be hard-pressed to find someone who actually believed in them. Bloodstones are mere fables."

His reaction—that pulse of anxiety—did not feel like a mere fable.

Amryn frowned. "All fables come from somewhere. Where did the bloodstones come from?"

"Empaths."

Her breath caught.

He tipped his head. "Exactly. Which is another reason so little is known about them."

Most empaths had been hunted down and killed, so any lore or knowledge they'd had as a collective was lost.

Felinus took a slow breath. "In truth, I know very little about the subject. But I can tell you that the bloodstones were first talked about around the time the empire was created. The church learned of a rumor; that empaths had a way to access unparalleled power. Obviously, this alarmed the church—and the emperor. The Order of Knights was ordered to track down the bloodstones, but no real evidence of them was ever found. And as the empaths continued to die . . . well, to be perfectly blunt, the church decided that the bloodstones couldn't exist."

It made a horrible sort of sense; if the empaths had been able to access a weapon, they would have used it to save themselves.

"Bloodstones have been officially dismissed by the church,"

Felinus said. "Which is why they're no longer even whisper-ed about."

"But I still don't understand what a bloodstone *is*."

He shrugged. "I don't know that anyone really understands them. No rumor was ever perfectly clear. The lore merely stated that there were five bloodstones, and that with them, the empaths could wield enough power to kill thousands—to break the very earth we stand upon."

His dread and fear tangled, making her gut twist. "You're afraid of them."

"I fear the *idea* of them, absolutely." His mouth tightened. "It could have been a rumor the empaths started as a way to dissuade an attack, and that could be the end of it. All I know is that bloodstones have never been proven to exist, and I find a great deal of comfort in that."

Amryn wasn't so sure. Her thoughts turned to Von's jour-nal. He was the most infamous empath to ever live, and he had clearly believed in the bloodstones. And the knight who had eventually killed him also believed in them—why else had he kept Von's journal?

Felinus cleared his throat. "This is a dreary topic. One best left behind, I think." He gave her a pointed look, and she gave him a nod.

Back in the shadowy backrooms of the museum, Amryn had a hard time shaking off the tension from her conversation with Felinus. The only good thing about talking about the mysterious bloodstones was that she forgot about Carver for a while.

Of course, the moment Cleric Jane handed her a number-ed crate and asked her to shelve it in the appropriate place in the archives, she was reminded of the rebels and her mission, which inevitably brought Carver to mind.

At least she'd finally been given access to the archives. She trekked alone in the vast room, the crate heavy in her hands as she walked past the many shelves. There were no windows, and lamps were infrequent—just enough to avoid bumping into anything. She had to squint at the passing shelves so she could make out the numbers etched into the wood. There was a place for everything, and at this point she shouldn't be sur-prised that Esperance housed so many relics and riches that not all of them could be displayed in the main part of the mu-seum. Instead of distributing the wealth back to the kingdoms, it sat on shelves in the darkness. That was very like the empire.

She'd taken several trips back and forth from the archives. Each time, she'd taken slow steps and tried to read as many of the tags as she could. She didn't know where the seals would be stored—or in what—but they had to be inside this cavern-ous room somewhere.

Finally, on one of her trips out of the archive, she spotted a wooden box sitting on the end of a shelf. The marker on the box read: *Item 254 – Empirical Seals.*

Her heart kicked in her chest, and she stepped closer. The dust-covered box was a faded green, and a quick inspection showed that it was locked. She would need to learn lock-picking if she hoped to reach them without anyone ever learning she'd disturbed them. She also needed wax, for copying the seals, and she'd have to find a good place to hide them—

She sensed him before she saw him.

Carver.

Her stomach dropped and she whirled, coming face-to-face with him as he rounded a corner.

His emotions were tightly clamped, making it hard to read him. But the shadows cast by the distant lamp made his expression dark and hard. "Amryn."

She shifted slightly, using her body to shield the seals from his view, in case he bothered to read the inscription on the box. "What are you doing here?"

His thick eyebrows pulled together as he drew to a stop in front of her. "You weren't at breakfast."

His face, lost in the curve of Marriset's neck. His mouth on her skin. Her fingers wrapped in his hair—

"I had no appetite."

He tensed. His gaze was unrelenting and unapologetic, though she swore she felt a thread of regret from him.

Saints, if the Butcher felt any regret, it was probably only that he'd been caught.

She folded her arms over her chest. "What are you doing here?"

"I wanted to speak with you, and Cleric Jane said you'd be back here."

"I don't want to speak with you."

His chin lowered, and her pulse sped up as he took a step closer. "We need to talk."

His voice—deep and rough—vibrated through her entire body.

Her fingers dug into her arms, and she hoped the bite of pain would distract her body from the fact that Carver was standing right there, overpowering everything with his broad shoulders and intense presence.

"If you need someone to talk to, perhaps you should find

Marriset."

His eyes narrowed. "I don't want Marriset."

There was a flutter low in her stomach, and she hated that. "I think you made it very clear that you want her. Frankly, I don't care."

One eyebrow quirked. "You don't?"

"Of course not."

He took another step forward, and she couldn't help but feel like cornered prey as he studied her face. "You're jealous."

Her spine stiffened. "I am not."

"You are." That fact seemed to surprise him. And she absolutely hated his flash of excitement.

She dropped her crossed arms, and stepped forward, not stopping until she'd invaded his space.

He didn't retreat, but she could feel his sudden tension.

Her smile came out a little sharp. "If you want to make a fool of yourself by panting after Marriset, be my guest. But don't expect me to care."

His gaze darkened. "Amryn—"

"No," she overrode him. "Our marriage has never been real. We both know that. So do whatever you want with Marriset. Just leave me out of it." She stepped around him, but his hand banded around her wrist.

She twisted back to face him, her pulse pounding. "Let go of me."

His hold flexed—not bruising, but not releasing. His jaw worked, and his emotions churned as he fought to find words. "I didn't mean to hurt you," he finally said.

She stared up at him, her shoulders stiff and her heart aching. "To be hurt, I'd have to care." She jerked her hand free

of his grip and spun on her heel.
    This time, he didn't come after her.

24

CARVER

CARVER STOOD ON THE EDGE OF camp, the multicolored tents behind him and the emerald and onyx jungle before him. The sun was falling behind the distant mountains, casting the world in shadow. Behind him, servants chatted and laughed as they tended the cooking fires.

He had no idea where Amryn was.

He had glimpsed her during the day as they made their trek to the base of Zawri, but they'd both been avoiding each other since his failed attempt to apologize in the museum archives a few days ago.

He knew she was angry and hurt. It was obvious in the tensed way she held herself, and he regretted that. But he hadn't been able to find the words to apologize, and he couldn't very well explain what he was doing with Marriset.

Especially when he'd found the first piece of evidence that Amryn might be a rebel.

When he'd found her in the archives, she'd been startled. He'd assumed his presence alone was reason enough, but then she'd deliberately shifted to block his view of something on the shelf. So, when she strode away, he forced himself to stay, even though he'd burned to go after her.

"To be hurt, I'd have to care."

Those words still rang in his ears, even days later. But that hurt had been overshadowed when he'd stepped closer to inspect the shelf.

His throat had run dry.

The empirical seals. She'd been looking at them, he was sure of it. And he hated everything about that, because that was the sort of thing the rebels would have an interest in. Just as the Rising had asked Jayveh to memorize the blueprints of every stronghold, they might have asked Amryn to steal the seals, which could be used for forgeries; false reports and messages, and other conspiracies that could damage the empire and destroy lives.

He hadn't shared this in his report to Ford last night, and he didn't know why.

Saints, that was a lie. He hadn't told anyone because he didn't *want* it to be true. He didn't want Amryn to be part of the Rising.

All day as they'd walked to this campsite, he'd turned things over and over in his mind. Maybe Amryn, like Jayveh, had joined under some kind of threat? But that hardly made sense. Jayveh's uncle, the king of Xerra, was a terrible man who'd threatened her younger brothers if she didn't help the rebels. Amryn was fond of both her uncle and King Torin. There was no one to blackmail her.

And even if there had been, she could have found a way to come forward, as Jayveh had done.

So, no, blackmail didn't seem likely.

It struck him then that he had all but dropped Jayveh as a suspect. He wasn't sure if she'd convinced him she wasn't a double agent, or if he'd just become distracted.

As for Marriset, he was mostly convinced at this point that she was just power-hungry. Her greed was too personal to be tied to an organized rebellion. Besides, her ambitions were not to tear down the empire, but to use anything—and any-one—to her advantage.

It was actually a depressing thought. It meant he'd hurt Amryn for nothing.

Then again, he'd hurt her just by existing. Their first rift hadn't come from Marriset, but from the moment she remem-bered who he was: General Vincetti, the Butcher.

Footsteps sounded behind him, and he was surprised to see Ivan. "May I join you?" he asked.

Carver nodded. He'd been watching Ivan closely ever since they'd hotly debated the war in Harvari, but the Sibeten hadn't said or done anything else inflammatory.

Ivan came to stand beside him, also gazing out into the dar-kening jungle. They stood in silence for a long time before Ivan said, "I do not believe you killed Cora."

He didn't know what he'd expected from Ivan, but it wasn't this. "I didn't," he affirmed.

The large man grunted. "Trevill gives me reports, but he does not tell me everything."

"He probably doesn't want you to jeopardize his investi-gation."

Ivan's icy eyes fixed on Carver. "I do not think he is look-ing in the right place."

"What makes you think that?"

The man's jaw tightened. "He dismissed all of us, and he's

now looking exclusively at the clerics, guards, and servants. But what reason did any of them have to kill her?"

"You think one of us had reason?"

"None of us knew Cora well, yet we spent more time with her than any servant or cleric. She was shy and quiet—what could she have done to offend anyone enough to provoke her murder?"

"Perhaps someone was offended by the violence her brother enacted at the wedding feast," Carver said. An overzealous cleric might have thought more punishment was necessary for violating the sacredness of the temple. "If it was a cleric, it would explain the note."

Retribution has come for you.

Ivan's frown deepened. "I have considered this, but it does not make sense. First of all, Cora wasn't to blame for the violence. That was her brother's doing, and it grieved her greatly. Second, if a cleric was angry enough to kill, how did they have the patience to wait for weeks to do it?" He shook his head. "This was a calculated murder. Not one of anger or passion. The note left with her body indicates that as well."

Carver nodded. "That makes sense."

"And a servant or guard seems unlikely. As I already said, they would have had few interactions with her. And while Cora was reserved, she was never rude. It just doesn't make sense."

"You think it was one of us, then."

"Don't you?"

Well, yes, as a matter of fact. Especially if Cora's killer was an imposter who had murdered and lied their way into Esperance.

"I assume if you're talking to me about this," Carver said slowly, "you want my opinion."

"Despite our personal differences, you are a decorated general. And since I have determined that you did not kill her, I could use your strategic viewpoint. Who do you think killed her?"

"I don't know. But I don't think that's the question we should be asking."

Ivan cocked his head, silently asking for an explanation.

Carver lifted one shoulder. "*Why* was she killed?"

Ivan's brow furrowed. "To send a message."

"To who?"

His frown deepened. "Maybe the emperor, or the high cleric. A message that this attempt to make peace was doomed to fail."

"All right, but why choose her? If this was a message for the emperor—a way to undermine the peace—it would have been stronger to have picked someone with deeper ties to the emperor."

Ivan shifted his weight, his eyes distant as his thoughts clearly raced. "Argent. Jayveh." His gaze cut to Carver. "Or you."

"Exactly."

Ivan considered this. "All of you would be harder to get to. Argent and Jayveh had guards from the beginning, and you . . ."

"Intimidate people."

Ivan huffed. "Not how I would phrase it, but *yenn.* So why bother with one of you, if they could get to Cora?"

Carver ghosted a smile, but it was fleeting. "Even if the killer didn't dare strike me or Argent, Jayveh would have made more sense than Cora. Obviously Cora was lured to that sitting room. The killer could have done the same to Jayveh."

"But it would have been riskier."

"Committing murder in an isolated temple was already risky. A little more of a threat shouldn't have stood in the way of a stronger message. So, why Cora?"

Ivan crossed his arms over his wide chest. "Do you have an answer?"

"Not really. But I think Cora was targeted specifically. It wasn't random, as you said earlier. She was deliberately lured from her room, killed, and left with a message."

"Cora isn't from a notable or wealthy kingdom. As far as I've been able to tell, no one here had any grudges against her, or her kingdom. She was arguably the least threatening of all of us."

"Unless she was dangerous to the killer," Carver pointed out. "What if she learned something about the killer? Identified them as a threat?" It could have been the imposter—like he'd suspected before—or someone else entirely.

Ivan's brows slammed down. "A threat to who?"

"All of us. The peace. The empire. What if Argent was the target all along? Or Jayveh, or even me, but Cora figured it out first and the killer had to silence her."

Ivan considered this. "It would explain why Cora—arguably the least dangerous of all of us—was targeted first. She uncovered a plot to destabilize the peace, and she had to be killed." He looked to Carver. "It's an interesting theory, but how would we prove it?"

A good question.

"Did Cora ever mention anything to you about the others here?" Carver asked. "Did anyone give her a bad feeling?"

Ivan's eyes clouded. "We did not speak much. But I do not recall her saying anything negative about anyone."

"And did she know anyone before coming here?"

"I don't know. I don't think so." He eyed Carver. "Could this be the Rising?"

The direct question took him off guard. "I don't see how," he hedged. "Esperance has been sealed off from the rest of the empire."

"Yes, but what if they have someone inside the temple. Do you think that is possible?"

Considering the fact Ivan was an ideal candidate for the Rising, Carver wasn't about to share anything he knew about the rebels infiltrating Esperance. He couldn't risk showing his hand to a rebel.

"No," he said, holding Ivan's stare. "I don't think it's possible. The high cleric's security was checked by the emperor."

Ivan glanced away, his expression unreadable. "Clearly, the security here isn't infallible. Cora was murdered, and the other women were poisoned."

It was hard to argue his point. Especially because Carver felt the same.

There was a short silence, then Carver asked, "Do you have any suspects?"

"*Neeyev*. But I'll find her killer, and I will avenge her."

"Your devotion to her is admirable."

A muscle jumped in his cheek. "She was little more than a frightened child. She didn't deserve this fate. Having to leave her home and come here, her marriage to me—her death was just another thing she didn't deserve. And even though I could not protect her, I *can* kill the one responsible for cutting her life short."

"Her death wasn't your fault," Carver said.

"It wasn't," Ivan agreed. "That weight falls on the shoulders of her killer, as well as the man who ordered us all here."

He strode away without a backward glance, leaving his vehement words to hang in the air behind him.

Carver walked up the dirt trail, sweat dampening his clothes and slicking his brow. The weight of the pack on his back pulled at his shoulders, and the humidity of the jungle was oppressive. He carried a silver coin, which would have to do for his offering to the Divinities, because he wasn't sure what else he had to give.

Amryn walked behind him, silent as she'd been since they had set out alone from the main camp.

The high cleric had sent guards ahead of them, and there were servants waiting at the summit with an afternoon meal. The couples had been sent out at slightly staggered times, and along two different paths that led to the peak. Ivan had been paired with a cleric.

Carver had insisted on being put on the same path as Argent, and after the prince had added his insistence, High Cleric Zacharias had acquiesced.

The hike up to Zawri's peak would take half the day, and as long as they didn't lag, they'd be back at camp before dark. The pack he carried had food and water for him and Amryn, but nothing else. He didn't even have a knife, because he couldn't risk being caught with a weapon he'd smuggled into Esperance. The high cleric was convinced that the soldiers spread across the mountain would be sufficient to guard against any jungle predators.

His conversation with Ivan last night continued to turn over in his mind. The bitter note they'd ended on was a stark reminder that Ivan had no love for the emperor. But the points he'd brought up about Cora's death were worth considering. He'd wondered if Cora had been killed because she may have discovered the imposter. But what if she'd discovered something to do with the rebels instead?

Either way, Carver doubted the murderer was done.

He hadn't had long to think on things, though. Soon after Ivan had left him, it was time for dinner. He and Amryn sat together, and Marriset and Darrin had sat across from them. While they ate, Marriset had sent him a few secretive smiles—and Amryn had noticed.

She'd excused herself, claiming a headache. By the time he'd joined her in their tent, she was already asleep—or pretending to sleep. Her back was to him, and her bedroll was tugged as far away from his as the limited space allowed.

They hadn't spoken a word to each other all morning, and he didn't relish being alone with her for the day.

Especially if this bloody silence continued.

He peeked over his shoulder at her. "Let me know if you need a break."

Her cheeks were flushed from the heat or the exertion of the hike, or both. With her fair skin, he'd learned it didn't take much to show a blush. Her riotous red curls had been roped into a single braid that trailed down her back, and the azure-colored dress she wore had a hem that fell just below her knees, with black leggings that covered her calves and disappeared into her ankle boots. It made hiking easier for her, but he was definitely distracted by the view.

She didn't respond, or even look at him, but he knew she'd heard.

Though he'd endured her silence for days, her choice not

to acknowledge him now hurt more. Or perhaps his thoughts were what hurt him, and a conversation with her—even if it was a fight—would at least give his mind something else to focus on.

"You look overheated. Maybe you should take a drink."

"I don't need water."

The, *"or anything else from you"*, was strongly implied.

Carver stopped and twisted around to face her. "You don't need to be stubborn."

She kept walking, her eyes on the trail rather than on him. "You don't need to pretend to worry about me."

"I'm not pretending."

She drew even with him and paused, finally meeting his gaze. "Don't worry about me. I'm not the one with a fear of falling off mountains."

He blinked. Her voice was edged with a threat, and that was the last thing he'd expected from her. Under other circumstances, he may have laughed. Now, he just stared at her. "But you're afraid of the jungle."

She grunted. "What a sorry pair we make." She resumed walking, and the path was just wide enough here that he moved to walk at her side.

All around them, the jungle hummed with life. Colorful birds squawked at them and small brown and gray monkeys chirped and swung on vines, following them overhead. Lizards zipped off the path ahead of them, and though Carver didn't see any snakes, he knew they were in the underbrush and in the trees.

He thought it would be best not to tell Amryn that.

"I'm surprised you didn't insist on doing this hike with Marriset."

He glanced over at her. "Why would I have done that?"

She rolled her eyes. "As if I need to point out *why*," she muttered.

"I thought you didn't care."

"I don't." She kicked at a small stone in the path, and it skittered across the packed dirt.

He gentled his tone. "It was never my intention to hurt you."

"Don't worry. Your intentions were glaringly obvious." Her hands fisted at her sides. "To be honest, you didn't strike me as the sort of man to share. Is it every other night with you and Darrin?"

He shot her a look. "I haven't been with her. Not like that."

She snorted. "How naïve do you think I am?"

"I'm telling you the truth."

"You want to tell me the truth? Fine." She stopped walking and they faced each other, a mere pace between them. He could see the flush in her cheeks, the barely leashed hurt in her accusing eyes. "Where were you our last night at Esperance? I woke in the middle of the night and you weren't in the apartment."

He'd been with Ford, but he couldn't admit that. "I wasn't with Marriset."

"Then where were you?"

"I couldn't sleep. I went for a walk."

"You're lying." She started walking again, and her tone was tighter than before. "Perhaps we could set up a rotation and I can entertain Darrin. We wouldn't want him to miss his wife too much."

The mere thought of Darrin touching Amryn made Carver's blood heat. "Stay away from him."

Her chin tipped up in challenge. "Or what?"

It was that red hair, he decided. He'd grown up on stories about legendary harpies who had flaming red hair and tore men asunder, and Ford had warned him that redheads of Ferradin had notorious tempers.

He just hadn't expected his own to be so easily riled by her.

He smiled, and it wasn't a nice one. "If Darrin touches you, I'll kill him."

She folded her arms with a huff. "That's one way to get her all to yourself."

Frustration made his skin itch. "How do I convince you that I haven't done anything with Marriset?"

"You *won't* be able to convince me. I've seen it for myself." Her sharp tone couldn't mask the hurt in her voice.

Guilt settled in his gut, dulling the heat of his temper.

Amryn's eyes narrowed, as if she didn't like the softening in his expression.

"I'm sorry," he said. "I truly never meant to hurt you."

She stiffened. "Carver Vincetti, let me make one thing clear. I couldn't care less who you crawl into bed with. As long as it's not me, we'll never have a problem."

25

AMRYN

SHE AND CARVER HADN'T SPOKEN since their fight. They were halfway up Zawri, and though Amryn's calves ached, she didn't stop walking. The sooner they reached the top of the mountain, the sooner they might see other people, so she could have a break from Carver.

The jungle was alive around them. Was it too cruel to hope it swallowed Marriset?

Probably.

She wished it anyway.

The humidity was oppressive, the heat sweltering. She wanted to dive into one of Ferradin's northern lakes. Perhaps that would cool her burning hurt and flaming anger, too.

One of the problems with being an empath was the fact that she could feel the pain she inflicted. When she'd snapped at Carver, she'd felt his cut of hurt. That made it hard to feel like she'd actually won their earlier spat.

The fact that she could feel his frustration, shame, and regret was also difficult to bear. She just wanted to be angry with him. She especially hated feeling his guilt, because it only confirmed everything she already knew.

He'd touched Marriset. He'd been touched *by* her. The thought of him holding her, kissing her . . . It brought out a possessive, painful rage that confused and unsettled her.

She didn't want Carver. *She didn't.* But she also didn't want Marriset to have him.

"I'm sorry. I never meant to hurt you."

She hated his words. The apology was just another confirmation of his infidelity, and the soft way he'd spoken them, like he truly cared about her feelings . . . It made everything he'd done with Marriset feel even more cruel. If he cared about Amryn at all, why had he turned to Marriset in the first place?

In the distance, dark clouds gathered. She knew Carver was tracking them, too, because his wariness was magnifying her own.

The clouds rolled closer, sweeping across the sky until they blotted out the sun. Thunder rumbled, and the first raindrops splashed down on them.

"We need to find cover," Carver said.

"The high cleric said it would be dangerous to leave the path."

"This path is going to be washed out once the rain starts pouring. Unless you want to be washed off the mountain, we need to get off it."

She looked up toward Zawri's peak, but Carver shook his head.

"We won't make it. We need shelter." He peered into the trees on their left, then their right. "This way," he decided, leading the way off the path.

Amryn considered staying where she was, but digging in her heels didn't really make sense. As irritated as she was with

Carver, he had more experience with tropical storms than she did. So, she followed him, carefully picking her way through the thick foliage.

The coming storm charged the air. As Amryn strained to pick up any dangers, she became aware of a low vibration that brushed against her empathic sense. She didn't know how else to describe it, except maybe a weak hum. Feeling it, she frowned. She had no idea what it was, but she was soon distracted as the wind kicked up.

Her short skirt whipped around her knees, and she was grateful for the protection of the leggings, even though she'd been cursing them earlier for being stifling.

Without warning, the drizzling rain turned into a downpour. She crossed her arms over her chest, hugging herself as the water pounded down. It was loud as it slapped against the leaves, and only the most strident bird calls could be heard over the sound.

She was drenched by the time Carver indicated their impromptu shelter. At the base of a large tree, several bushes with wide fronds offered meager protection. She settled her back against the trunk, shivering as she pushed wet curls off her face.

Carver settled beside her, so close that their shoulders brushed.

She jerked away.

His frustration spiked, but he didn't say anything. Instead, he started digging around in the pack.

Amryn peeked over his arm, trying to see what was inside. "I don't suppose there's a tent, or a lamp, or change of clothes?"

"No. Just food and water." He handed her one of the canteens, and she took it carefully so their fingers wouldn't brush.

While she sipped the tepid water, he bit off a piece of hard jerky.

"How long do you think this will last?"

He shrugged. "In Harvari, storms like this could last for days."

That was not encouraging.

She passed him the canteen, and he offered her some jerky.

Eating only took so long, though, even when she chewed slowly. After Carver set aside the pack, there was nothing else to do but wait out the storm.

Amryn wrapped her arms around her knees, pulling them tight to her chest. Rainwater dropped from the fronds all around them, and her clothes were plastered to her body. Wind whipped through the trees, making the foliage around them shudder.

"Do you think the others found shelter?" she asked.

"I'm sure they did." He draped an arm over one bent knee, his other leg stretched out in front of him. His eyes roved the area around them, alert and focused.

The tension between them hummed.

Amryn was surprised when Carver felt a sudden burst of amusement.

When he chuckled, she eyed him. "What?"

He flashed a small smile. "I don't think the high cleric will be very happy with the Divinities for sending this storm."

She snorted. "He's probably frantically trying to decide how to explain to the emperor how he lost all of us."

"Without actually taking any blame."

She shook her head. "I don't know how he became a high cleric."

"One of the great mysteries of our time."

Something out there squawked, and Amryn jumped.

He glanced at her. "It's just a bird."

Her cheeks warmed, but she didn't acknowledge his reassurance. "If I get eaten out here . . ."

"Don't worry. Any animal would take one look at your hair, think you were on fire, and eat me instead."

"Good."

The corner of his mouth quirked up, revealing his dimple. His jaw was covered in dark stubble. He hadn't bothered to shave before leaving camp. It made him look rugged, and the dark blue shirt he wore brought out his bronzed skin. The sleeves were rolled up, baring his forearms, and she wasn't sure why the muscles and tendons there were so distracting.

She had to pull her gaze away. Her cheeks were a little too warm as she asked, "What offering did you bring?"

"A coin."

"Ah. Hoping to buy forgiveness for your sins?"

He swallowed. "I don't think there are enough coins in the world for that."

His sobering answer was wholly unexpected; she wasn't sure how to respond.

In her short silence, he asked, "What about you?"

"I brought a rock."

One eyebrow lifted. "A rock?"

Her spine stiffened as defensiveness rose. "It's a pretty rock." She'd grabbed it off the ground that morning, and it seemed as good as anything to leave on top of a mountain. Especially when it was a symbolic ritual that stemmed from a religion that thought she should be dead.

Carver didn't press her for more details, and she was grateful—because she didn't have a safe answer for him.

There was a long silence, and his emotions shifted.

"I have no interest in Marriset." His words were muted because of the battering rainfall.

Amryn said nothing. The sincerity coming from him was at odds with his actions—and his prickle of guilt.

The silence stretched, and Carver's shoulders slowly tensed. Finally, he looked over at her, and his aquamarine eyes locked on hers. "I didn't like how she'd been throwing herself at Argent. I didn't know why she persisted, even when he showed no interest. I thought she might be a danger to him. So, when she took an interest in me, I reciprocated her flirtations as a way to determine her threat level. That's all it ever was."

His words were calm, his tone penitent. And while she sensed truth, there was something else. Something he wasn't telling her.

"I'm sorry you were hurt in the process," he continued. "That was never my intention. But I needed to protect Argent."

"Why should I believe you?"

His eyebrows tugged together. "I guess you don't have any reason to. But it's the truth."

"Is it?" She angled toward him, her pulse skittering when her knee brushed his leg. "If protecting Argent was your only goal, why not just tell me that?"

"I tried to talk to you in the museum archives, but you wouldn't let me finish."

"That's a feeble excuse. You could have said something at any time."

His jaw hardened, and he looked away. Within the space of a few breaths, his emotions were carefully clamped.

"How do you *do* that?" she muttered.

He frowned. "Do what?"

Her gut dropped. "Nothing," she hurried to say.

There was a long pause. Then, "I handled all of this poorly, and I'm sorry for that. What I did with Marriset was wrong. Flirting with her—no matter the reason—was disloyal to you. I'm not looking for forgiveness, I just . . . I wanted you to know why, and know that I'm truly sorry."

His remorse was undeniable, even with his muted emotions.

She just didn't know what to say to him, so she remained quiet.

Carver didn't say anything else, either.

Thunder cracked and boomed, and the storm raged on.

Amryn woke with a start. She was curled on the hard ground beside the large tree, and rain was still falling.

It hadn't let up all day, so after eating and drinking a little bit more at nightfall, they'd both fallen asleep.

She guessed it must be the middle of the night, and at first she didn't know what had woken her.

Then terror and agony stabbed her, and her breath caught.

Carver was lying nearby, and though he was asleep, there was nothing restful about his pose. His hands were fists, digging into the dark soil, and his shadowed expression was tight and twisted with pain. He was trapped in a nightmare, and the helplessness and despair he felt were gut-wrenching. The raw panic that clawed him made her flinch. His breaths came too fast, and a low whimper tugged at her heart.

It didn't matter that things between them were still strained. No one deserved to suffer like this.

She crawled toward him. "Carver?"

A soft groan was his only reply.

She set a hand on his shoulder, and his eyes snapped open.

In seconds he had her pinned on the ground, her back hitting so hard it knocked the breath from her lungs. Pain shot across her shoulders, but it was the strangling grip he had on her wrists that made her squirm.

His knees dug into her hips as he straddled her and pinned her hands to the ground. He was trembling, and though she couldn't see well in the darkness, she could feel his eyes boring into her.

She didn't think he actually saw her.

His hold on her wrists spasmed, grinding her bones together.

Tears sparked in her eyes and her heart pounded. "It's me," she gasped, a quaver in her voice. "Carver, it's me."

His hold didn't loosen, and his body remained tense on top of hers. Dark hair hung around his face, which was still obscured by darkness. His full weight wasn't on her, but she still struggled to breathe.

"Carver . . ."

His fingers convulsed around her wrists. Confusion. Bafflement. Shame.

He shuddered and released her, then recoiled until his back hit the tree. "I'm sorry," he rasped. He thrust a hand through his hair and curved in on himself. "I'm so sorry."

Slowly, Amryn sat up, her fingers shaking a little as they ran over her bruised wrists. She shifted slightly away from him, her throat dry as she whispered, "You were having a nightmare."

He scrubbed both hands over his face, his groan nearly lost in a distant roll of thunder. "Saints, I . . ." His shoulders stiffened, and his hands dropped so he could look at her. "Did I hurt you?"

"No."

His emotions were chaotic—still half-locked in his horrific dream, yet also adjusting to the fact that he had attacked her. He eased forward on his knees, his palms open. "I just want to check, all right? I need to make sure you're not hurt."

It was only then she realized she was still clutching one of her wrists. She relaxed her hold. "I'm fine."

He'd reached her, and his fingers brushed against her knuckles. "Please?"

His plea was soft in the darkness. Something about it cracked something inside of her. Slowly, she peeled back her hand and Carver leaned in, his fingertips brushing over her tender skin.

His careful touch raised every hair on her body, and her breath caught.

Carver stilled, his eyes flicking up to hers.

The intimacy of the moment—his hand paused against her wrist, their breaths mingling in the dark—was startling. It felt like they were the only ones on this mountain.

His gaze tracked to her mouth, and his lips parted.

Her own tingled.

A sudden tremor rocked him, and Carver pulled back. His fingers brushed across her palm as he withdrew. "I'm sorry," he repeated.

Amryn swallowed tightly, her nerves gradually settling as she gained a little space from him. Not much, but every bit counted, especially around him.

They sat together in the dark. Rain fell, frogs croaked, and insects buzzed. Slowly, their breathing steadied.

"Do you want to talk about it?" she asked.

"No."

She could feel his resoluteness. A boulder in a river, unmovable. He wouldn't change his mind.

He was frayed, and so was she. This was more extreme than any of the nights he was up pacing and she distracted him with stories from her childhood.

This nightmare had left him shredded, vulnerable, and haunted.

She owed him nothing. But she couldn't bear for him to sit in silence, shrouded by darkness. Not after the torture he'd just endured.

"My mother was murdered," she whispered.

Carver stopped breathing.

Her stomach twisted, and she didn't know why she was telling him this. His nightmare had been ugly—he didn't need *more* ugliness.

But she couldn't stop now.

"I was there," she said. "I saw it happen."

"Amryn . . ." Horror, sorrow, and a fierce desire to protect swam around her.

"I'd come to her bed that night, after a bad dream. She let me sleep beside her." Her fingernails dug into her palms. "Men burst into the bedroom without warning. They dragged her from the bed."

She could still hear her mother's screams. Her pleas for mercy. Her begging Amryn to run, to look away.

She'd been frozen.

"They stabbed her. So many times, and . . . all I could do was sit on that bed and scream. I didn't help her. I just watched her die."

"You were a child," Carver said, his voice edged with a fury she knew wasn't directed at her. "There was nothing you could have done. Saints, you never should have had to witness that. I'm sorry."

"They tried to kill me, too."

He stiffened.

She absently rubbed her arms. "After they killed her, they grabbed me. I can still feel their hands on me, dragging me from the bed."

She didn't realize he'd taken her hand, to stop her nervous motion, until he squeezed her fingers. It was a silent reminder that she wasn't alone. That she was *here*, not *there*.

That she was safe.

Her eyes peeled open. Even though his expression was shadowed by the filtered moonlight, she could feel that he was wholly attuned to her, and despite all sanity . . . in this moment, she felt completely safe with Carver Vincetti.

"What stopped them?" he asked.

A face materialized in her mind. One she'd tried so hard to forget, but never could. "Someone saved me. He took me to my uncle. He . . . made sure I was safe."

"Were the murderers caught?"

"Yes." Not by the law, because no law in Craethen would condemn them. The knights had killed an empath; they'd done nothing wrong.

No, they'd been condemned by something else entirely.

The knights had been distracted when her savior tore into the room. When he saw the dead body on the floor, and Amryn in their hands . . . The knights hadn't realized they were going to die. They'd laughed, mocking him as he squared off in front of them.

He hadn't stopped until they were in pieces. The carnage had painted every surface in the bedroom—including *her*.

When their killer had crouched in front of her, covered in blood, he'd smiled. There was something horribly wrong about that smile. "You're safe now," he whispered. "See? Look at them."

She didn't want to look. But her eyes wouldn't close. Everything about that night was burned into her mind. The horrific sounds; the screaming, tearing, stabbing—and then nothing but the slow drip of blood hitting the wooden floor. The feel of blood on her skin, in her hair. The sight of a hand lying close to her, long fingers curled in remembered pain, that horrible bone ring streaked with blood. The rest of the man's body was gone—strewn about the room. And the smells . . .

Tiras touched her cheek, the blood on both of them mingling. "They can't hurt you now," he said, not even breathing hard. "They're nothing now, Ryn. I made them nothing."

She couldn't stop shaking.

She'd learned that night that monsters were everywhere. Even in the beloved face staring back at her.

"Was it your father?"

Carver's question ripped her from her memories. "What?" she asked, the word sounding breathless.

"Did your father save you?"

A chill skated over her skin. "No."

Pity pricked the air between them. "Was he already gone, then?"

Her stomach churned. "Yes."

Ferrin Lukis hadn't died, like Carver assumed. No, he'd betrayed his family for a purse of gold, and he'd run away. He knew the Order would come, and he knew exactly what the knights would do. In the end, Ferrin hadn't cared about his family. The father Amryn had loved and cherished all her life . . . he'd thrown her away. He'd violated his wife's trust and betrayed them all.

Carver could do the same. *Would* do the same, if he learned about her abilities.

It was a harsh reminder, but something she couldn't afford to forget.

She drew back, tugging her hand free from his. Self-consciousness made her cheeks heat, and she was grateful he could not see her well in the dark. "We all have nightmares," she said quietly. "I guess I just wanted you to know that you aren't alone."

He didn't say anything as she settled back on the ground, her back to him as she curled up in her wet clothes.

As her eyes closed once more, he said softly, "Thank you."

26

CARVER

AMRYN HAD WANDERED AHEAD of him as they picked their way down the muddy mountain path. She hadn't said much this morning as they'd eaten a little food, and she'd only nodded when he suggested they forget about making it to the summit and instead return to the camp and regroup with everyone.

The silence between them wasn't like yesterday. The air had shifted. It wasn't peace, exactly. Maybe a truce.

He couldn't stop thinking about what she'd shared last night. The scene she'd painted of her mother's murder was horrific. The image of Amryn—a little girl with flaming red hair—screaming on the bed as she watched her mother die . . . it fractured something in his chest. He'd fought so hard to protect everyone in the empire. He'd gone to war to save his siblings from violence. He wanted to save every child.

He wanted to save her.

Impossible, because he couldn't save her from what she'd already suffered. But maybe he could save her from the Rising, if she truly was a rebel.

Carver rubbed the back of his tensed neck. He eyed Amryn as she walked ahead, carefully stepping over some fallen fronds and branches—debris left from the storm.

No one had ever been with him in the aftermath of a nightmare. He'd kept his family at a careful distance since his return from Harvari, and while Ford sometimes talked about what they'd experienced, it was always brief and understated.

But Amryn hadn't forced him to talk about it. She didn't question the cold sweat that coated his shaking body, or even the fact that he'd tackled her. Instead, she'd shared her own nightmare. Just as she had calmed his insomnia in Esperance by sharing stories that had given him precious glimpses of her, last night she had comforted him with the knowledge that he wasn't alone in suffering. Even though she had no idea what he'd suffered. Even though he'd hurt her with his Marriset scheme.

Even though he was *the Butcher.*

Amryn slowed her step.

He was ridiculously attuned to her, so he noticed at once. She peered into the thick jungle foliage on their left, her brow furrowed.

He followed her gaze. "What is it?" he asked, his voice pitched low.

Her eyes darted to him, then back into the trees. "I think someone is out there." Her whisper was soft, but edged with anxiety.

His eyes narrowed on the trees. "What did you see?"

"Nothing, I just . . ." Her spine stiffened. "Someone is out there."

The hairs on his arms lifted. As much as he searched, he saw nothing hiding in the thick foliage. But his instincts screamed, and his palm itched for a weapon. "Maybe it's the guards."

Amryn's head shook slightly. "It's not the guards."

"How do you know? What do you hear?"

She glanced at him, and the dread in her sea-green eyes made his heart lurch. "We need to get off this path. *Now*."

"Why?"

She surprised him by snagging his wrist. He couldn't remember the last time she'd touched him. Saints, had she *ever* initiated the contact between them? "Just trust me. We need to hide."

He nearly dug in his heels, but everything about this felt . . . wrong. Eerie. And trusting Amryn was strangely intuitive, despite everything. So he allowed her to pull him into the trees on their right, and the path quickly disappeared behind them.

Amryn didn't release him, though dragging him was unnecessary. He knocked a frond away from his face, curiosity raging. "How do you know someone is out there?"

"It's not just someone," she said, her breaths coming out faster as they hurried through the underbrush. "There's a group of them."

She'd avoided his question. Twice, now. "How do you know it's not the guards or one of the other couples?"

She darted a look over her shoulder, but didn't stop moving. "I guess I don't know. But something isn't right."

On that, they agreed. He could only think of one reason for Amryn to know so surely about a threat: if it was the rebels, and she knew of their plan.

She stumbled, and her fingers strangled his wrist.

He flipped his hand and grabbed her forearm, steadying her.

She twisted toward him, making her messy braid swing. The fear on her dirt-streaked face was unmistakable. "They're following us," she breathed.

Carver strained his ears, and his pulse ratcheted when he heard movement behind them. Distant and quiet, but deliberate. Not an animal. And not just one man—several.

Every part of his focus went to the coming threat. He could interrogate Amryn about her impossible knowledge later.

"How many?" he asked quietly.

"I don't know. Maybe three or four." Her panic was palpable, putting a tang in the air that he remembered all too well. His muscles relaxed, easing into a trained battle state.

He released her, shrugged the pack off his back, and handed it to her.

She took it without a word and pushed her arms through the straps, her nerves obvious as her body trembled.

He tried to keep his voice even and calming. "I need you to keep going. Double back to the road as soon as it feels safe. I'll find you." She'd only divide his attention if she stayed for the coming fight; mostly because he'd need to keep her safe, and partially because she might be the one who *actually* tried to kill him.

He bent, reaching for the nearest stick he could use as a club. Thankfully, the storm had created several good options. When he straightened, he saw Amryn hadn't moved.

She gripped the straps of the pack with tense fingers and her freckles appeared all the more stark as she paled. "You can't overpower a group of men. You don't even have a weapon."

He hefted the makeshift club he'd chosen.

Her eyebrows slammed down. "You can't be serious."

That was something Ford or Argent would say. The corner of his mouth actually twitched. "I'm completely serious. Now, go."

She was visibly torn. Her stance shifted as she wavered, her gaze flicking from him to the trees behind her, and then back toward the path they'd left behind. Then she focused back on him. "I don't know who they are, but they're dangerous."

She was worried about him. That warmed him, though he figured now wasn't the time to really dwell on why. "I'll be careful." She didn't look wholly convinced, so he added, "I've fought in the jungle. I know some tricks."

The enemy was nearing; he could hear the rustle of leaves and underbrush. This time when Carver motioned for Amryn to go, she did.

The moment she was out of sight, Carver moved for the nearest tree and scanned the crooked limbs, quickly finding what he was looking for.

By the time the four men crept into view, he was in position in the branches. The men wore dark clothing, but not uniforms. They all carried knives, and the one in the lead was focused on the disturbed foliage, tracking their prey. His eyes darted forward, catching the path Amryn had taken.

Carver held his breath and waited until two of the men were directly beneath him. Then he kicked the large green snake from his coiled perch, and the thing hissed and thrashed as it fell. It landed on the shoulders of the two men with a thud that took them both to the ground.

Their screams pierced the air—pain and alarm. The monstrous snake wrapped around the torso of one man, even as it bit the other's nearest arm. Carver barely registered the flash of fangs or blades as the two men attacked the twisting body of the creature.

His focus was on the other two men, who'd staggered back in shock.

Carver jumped from the tree, his boots clipping the shoulder of their tracker. The impact vibrated up his legs, though he managed to keep hold of the club in his hand. He was the first to roll to his feet.

The man he'd knocked down sprang up a moment later. His knife was gone and one hand gripped his upper arm. He stumbled back from Carver, and the fear that etched his expression made it perfectly clear he knew who Carver was.

The fourth man, however, was over his shock, and he charged Carver from behind.

Carver spun, and the club slammed into the man's swinging arm. There was a terrible crack, and he howled and dropped his blade.

The tracker—now recovered—grabbed his knife, and pressed his advantage.

The gruesome sounds coming from the bushes nearby were a horrible backdrop as Carver ducked, sidestepped, and swung his club. Bones snapped as the snake constricted more and more tightly around the two men, who were now only gasping as they cried for help.

Carver kicked the tracker's knee, and the man collapsed. He grabbed up his knife just in time to parry a swipe from the other attacker. The man fought with only one arm, since the other hung limply at his side.

It didn't take long for Carver to disarm him, and then he stood over both fallen men, his chest rising and falling quickly. "Tell me who you are or you'll join your friends," he growled.

The man with the broken arm looked downright terrified. Sweat dotted his brow as he kept looking toward the nearby bushes. The writhing body of the snake and the men it strang-led could just be seen through the thick leaves.

Even though the tracker gripped his dislocated knee with white-knuckled fingers, he only looked furious. "Where's the girl?" he demanded.

Carver let a little more of the Butcher shine through as he gave a sharp smile. "Where you'll never find her. Now, who are you, and why did you attack us?"

The tracker's lip curled in a sneer. "You *will* die, General. Where we didn't succeed, someone else will."

"You came all the way to a remote mountain in the jungle to kill me? I'm flattered." Carver kicked the man's injured knee. The tortured scream tore at festering wounds inside him, but there was no place for hesitation here. "Who are you?" he snarled.

The tracker's lips were mashed together, preventing fur-ther screams.

It was the other man who spoke, his voice shaking. "Even if you beat us, you've lost. Four men were sent for you, but eight men went for the prince."

Carver's stomach dropped. *Argent.*

He didn't let fear invade his expression. He wouldn't let anything break the hard façade he wore. "Who. Are. You?"

His eyes were on the weakest link, but he still saw move-ment from the edge of his vision as the tracker's hand flashed for his boot.

"No!" Carver moved to stop him, but the man had already buried the small knife in the side of his friend's neck.

The man fell back, gripping the knife in his neck before he shuddered and died.

Carver tackled the tracker, pinning his wrists to the ground beside his head. "Your death won't be so easy," he promised darkly.

The tracker smiled then, and it was cold and wrong. "No, I don't expect it will be. But I won't break."

"Everyone breaks," Carver snapped.

"You didn't."

His heart stopped.

The man's smile curved higher. "Yes, I know all about you, General. There's a reason I volunteered to kill you."

"Why?"

The man's terrible smile faded, and he lowered his voice. "My little brother was captured in Harvari, too. Tortured, just like you. Only he wasn't rescued by the empire. His life wasn't valued as highly as yours." Hatred sparked in his eyes, shattering the coldness there until his dark eyes burned. "Even if I don't get to kill you myself, I *will* see you in hell. Because together, we will rise!"

It was the sudden darting of his eyes that gave him away.

Carver released him and rolled, spinning to face the man who'd crept up behind him. He was limping and bleeding, his body sagging. One of the men who'd fought the snake.

He'd thrown his dagger before he'd registered Carver moving.

Instead of hitting Carver's back, the knife went into the tracker's chest.

The man gasped as the blade tore into a lung, and Carver leapt to his feet to square off against the newest threat.

But he crumpled before Carver could touch him, and it was only then Carver spotted the blood that stained his stomach. His breath gurgled as he stared up at Carver, the life already leaving his eyes. "We . . . will . . . rise."

Carver stood in the jungle, a stitch in his side and various cuts and bruises aching across his body. The snake was dead, and so was everyone else. He was the only one standing, and the pounding in his head was making his ears roar.

We will rise.

Rebels.

This had been an assassination attempt—he and Argent were targets. They may even be targeting others.

The attacks had been delayed by the unexpected storm, but this mountain was crawling with rebels.

He needed to find Argent.

He had to find Amryn, too.

He was frozen.

"I know all about you, General."

Something about those words snatched him back to another time. Another place.

"General... That seems too formal after what we've been through. After all, my blades are covered in your blood..."

That voice.

It was seared into Carver's mind; burning his ears, running through his blood, making every breath raw. It brought back every nightmare—every memory—that scarred more deeply than any groove carved into his flesh.

He couldn't breathe. His lungs were locked in a vice. His knuckles screamed as he gripped the dagger too tightly.

Captured. Tortured. *Agony.*

The bridge. He needed the bridge. He couldn't be dragged into the past by his demons. He needed a clear head. He needed to breathe without feeling raw. He needed to focus. Not on the nightmare behind him, but the one currently staring him in the face.

Rebels were on the mountain, hunting Argent.

Amryn was alone.

He needed to move.

Forcing himself into motion, Carver made a quick perusal of the bodies and pocketed every knife he found.

When he straightened, his body instinctively turned in the direction Amryn had disappeared. Hesitation gripped him. Calling out to her didn't feel safe; while he'd eliminated this threat, there were other rebels on Zawri. And though he could follow her, he wasn't a skilled tracker, and she'd had a decent head start. He'd also told her to double back to the road, which meant she could already be there. Out in the open. Unprotected.

He shouldn't waste time following her when he could head her off on the path.

Decision made, Carver moved for the road they'd abandoned. He hadn't gone far when the back of his neck prickled a second before he heard a voice calling out.

"Carver!"

The voice was too deep to be Amryn, and far enough away that it probably came from the path.

When he heard the shout again, he recognized Argent.

He cursed and bolted, uncaring of the branches and leaves that lashed him as he ran. When he broke through the trees and skidded to a stop on the muddy road, he had to duck the sword that swung for his neck.

"Stop!" Argent roared.

The bodyguard that had nearly taken Carver's head blanched. "General Vincetti! Sorry."

The man was clearly on high alert, and he wasn't the only one. A quick count showed that Argent was down by two guards, and the prince himself looked a little worse for wear. He held a sword at the ready, and there was a haphazard bandage wrapped around his upper arm. He'd set himself in front of Jayveh, but since she peeked around him, Carver could see she clutched a knife. Their group was muddy and bedraggled, but at least the prince and princess were still breathing.

"Are you all right?" Argent demanded.

"Fine. You?"

"Yes." His friend's eyes narrowed. "Where's Amryn?"

"I told her to run when we were attacked. She should be doubling back to the road."

Jayveh's dark eyes were frantic. "We haven't seen her."

"She would have found a place further downhill." Carver looked to Argent. "I'm going to assume you didn't take any prisoners?"

"No. The last man we cornered slit his own throat."

Carver grunted. "Mine killed each other."

Jayveh muttered a prayer while Argent's jaw tightened. "The Rising?" the prince asked.

Carver nodded curtly. "One of mine specifically named you as a target, and I was one as well, but . . ."

"We can't assume no one else will be targeted," Argent said, finishing Carver's thoughts. He motioned for everyone to keep moving down the path, and Carver was grateful; he needed to find Amryn.

"Are we sure this was the Rising?" Jayveh asked.

"Yes," Carver and Argent said together.

Jayveh's lips pressed into a line, and Carver could see her thoughts racing. Of course, with guards around, she didn't dare voice her concerns.

If the rebels had planned to assassinate her, they must not believe she was really on their side. It seemed as if her time as a double agent was over—if they'd ever actually believed in her loyalty at all.

"None of us knew about this outing until Zacharias announced it," Argent said. His voice was pitched low, but he still chose his words carefully. "Coordinating an attack while we were vulnerable and exposed . . . it had to have been done by someone in Esperance, and they must have had contacts just outside the borders."

"Or possibly inside them." The rebels Carver had killed hadn't looked like guards from Esperance, but they may have been servants. Perhaps the high cleric could identify them. He'd need to bring guards back here to gather the bodies.

Of course, it was also possible that these men hadn't come from Esperance, but had still managed to be close. Just like Ford was living in an abandoned cabin, perhaps rebels were scattered across the jungle.

He needed to warn Ford.

They continued down the mountain in silence, alert and watching the trees around them for any threat. Sweat gathered along his spine and bled through his shirt. His heart pounded, and around every bend in the path he expected to see a flash of fiery hair. But there was no sign of Amryn, and panic began to squeeze his lungs.

Had they passed her, somehow? Or was she moving faster, and still just ahead of them?

Footsteps sounded around the next bend of the trail, and Carver motioned for their party to divide to either side of the road, creating an ambush.

He kept to Argent's side, who hovered protectively beside Jayveh.

They waited, poised to fight. But when the group moved

into view, they relaxed.

The uniformed Esperance guards looked just as relieved to find them. "Your Highness, thank the Divinities you're all right." The middle-aged man in the lead stepped forward, leather armor creaking. "The high cleric sent us up the mountain as soon as dawn broke, to make sure you were all unscathed by the storm, but there are enemies around."

"We're aware," Argent said. "Have you found anyone else?"

"No, you're the first."

Dread rose in Carver's gut. "You haven't seen Amryn?"

The man frowned. "No. Is Lady Vincetti missing?"

His throat dried. "Yes."

If she was on the road ahead of them, the guards would have encountered her. Which meant she was either on the road behind them, or she'd never made it out of the jungle.

"We need to find her," Jayveh said. "*Now.*"

"We will," Argent assured her. "But you need to get off this mountain." He turned to his bodyguards. "Escort the princess to safety."

Jayveh looked like she was about to argue, but Argent leaned in and kissed her. It was surprisingly gentle, though fast. When he pulled back, his gaze was serious. "I promise, I'll find her. But I need you safe."

Carver opened his mouth to tell the prince he should also get to safety, but a high, feminine scream rent the air. His blood froze, and his head snapped in the direction it had come from.

Amryn.

He plunged into the trees on his right, his heart pounding as another shriek ripped through the sweltering jungle.

27

AMRYN

AMRYN WASN'T BREATHING AS she ducked into a cave. Holding her breath probably wasn't necessary, as the rush of the nearby waterfall was probably enough to mask any sound she might make. But she could feel the emotions of the men hunting her, and she had no doubts about what they would do if they caught her.

She didn't know who they were, but there were two of them, and their low-burning fury was a deep and terrifying thing. So was their frustration.

She didn't know if they'd broken off from the men who'd originally stalked her and Carver, or if this was a different group, but that didn't really matter. The fact that they were following her made them threatening enough.

Saints, she couldn't believe she'd exposed her secret to Carver like that. She hadn't told him she was an empath, but she'd admitted to sensing a danger that was impossible to have gleaned any other way. She hadn't thought about the consequences when she'd sensed the danger, though. The murderous intent of those men had been impossible to ignore, and if she hadn't said anything, they both might be dead, and then there would be no point in keeping her secret.

She didn't look forward to the questioning that Carver's sharp gaze had promised was coming later.

If they both survived this, of course.

She'd moved far enough away from Carver that she'd only heard muted shouts, and then everything had gone silent. She could only hope he was still alive. He was General Vincetti, after all. He didn't just order his men to battle, he marched with them.

He had to be alive. She wasn't going to examine too closely why she felt that so emphatically.

Amryn had done exactly what Carver said. She'd moved as quickly and as silently as she could through the jungle. At first, she'd only been intent on putting distance between her and the fight. But after all the sounds vanished and it was just her heavy breaths and pounding heart, she'd paused.

She had no idea where she was. The jungle was so disorienting, she didn't even know if she'd be able to find her way back to the path.

As she'd stood there considering—and panicking—she'd picked up on a low hum.

It was the strange vibration she'd felt yesterday, right before the storm had struck. After all that had happened, she'd forgotten about the anomaly. But now, she latched onto it. She had no idea what it was. It felt nothing like any other emotion she'd ever detected, but it felt almost . . . comforting.

A giant spider skittered near her foot and she barely swallowed a scream as she leaped back.

She needed to keep moving.

Another look around gave no indicators of which way she should go. But that hum . . .

She started walking in that direction, and soon she realized she was following the downward slope of the mountain. That seemed like as good a direction as any, so she kept going.

As she walked, she kept her empathic sense sharp. She made slight corrections to her course whenever she felt the hum fading. Even if she didn't fully understand it, the strange hum made her feel less alone. Less afraid.

Then she sensed the men behind her, doggedly tracking her. She moved faster, keeping just ahead of them.

She had no idea how much time had passed—adrenaline had blurred that—but she guessed it had been close to an hour since she'd separated from Carver. Her lungs burned and her legs ached. Sweat slicked her skin and curls stuck to her face and neck. She was exhausted. She needed to rest. She needed to hide.

The hum was stronger now, resonating deep inside her.

When she'd spotted the cave, she'd hurried inside.

Now that she was here, she was beginning to second-guess her hiding place. Was it too obvious? Would the hunters spot it and instantly know she was here?

They drew closer. Their emotions grew more distinct. More overwhelming.

And then—miraculously—they began to fade.

She didn't breathe deeply until their presence ebbed and then vanished completely.

She'd lost them.

She pinched her eyes closed and sagged against the cave wall, silently thanking Ferradin's gods that she was safe. Her fingers closed around the small pocket sewn into her dress that hid her mother's old prayer coin.

The pack dug into her shoulders as Amryn stood there, legs trembling. Her emotions were all over the place, but as they calmed, she could feel the cold fear curling in her gut—for Carver, and for herself.

She had no idea how far from the path she'd wandered in her effort to evade those men. And while she could continue to follow the downward slope of the mountain, she wasn't sure how long it would take to reach the bottom without a cleared path.

Spending the night out here—alone—was an absolutely terrifying thought.

But before she set out again, she wanted more distance between her and those men. And she needed food.

She took off the pack and sank to the floor of the cave. The rock was cool and a little slick from the mist of the nearby waterfall. It soothed her overheated skin as she riffled inside the pack and found some nuts, dried fruit, and the last piece of jerky. She washed it down with the warm canteen water.

As her heartbeat finally settled, she began to notice little things. Like the frogs that croaked and jumped along the near-by river's edge, the lizards darting over the rocks, and the calls of the birds. They'd probably been making those sounds the whole time she'd been chased, but she'd been too panicked to notice. Too focused on the hum.

The hum that had settled a little, but now pulsed once.

Her scalp prickled, but it wasn't a *bad* feeling. It wasn't an emotion at all, really. It wasn't coming from a person. It was something else. And it was coming from the deep shadows of the cave.

Amryn placed the canteen into the pack and pulled the

drawstring closed, then folded over the top flap. Pushing to her feet, she crept deeper into the cave.

The sunlight didn't illuminate the thickest shadows, but she had enough light to cautiously edge deeper, until she found stones stacked into a deliberate mound. The stack wasn't high—maybe a couple of hand-spans—and the diameter was the same, the whole thing shaped like a dome. It had obviously been made by man, and she couldn't imagine what it was supposed to be. It was too small for a monument—not to mention hidden in a cave—and it couldn't have buried anything larger than a fist.

But there was something there. She could feel it.

Curiosity had her kneeling beside the pile, and after a slight hesitation, she began to pull aside the rocks. The grate of shifting stones was the only sound, until finally she reached the bottom.

And there—ringed by stones—was a small drawstring pouch. The cloth was decayed, hinting at an old age. Amryn gingerly handled it and eased it open.

A dull, black gemstone set in tarnished silver landed gently on her palm. An attached chain coiled into her hand as well, and it was just as age-blackened as the rest of the amulet. There were no smaller gems or precious stones set around the black one on the pendant.

In appearance, there was nothing remarkable about the amulet. But the low vibration she felt clearly emanated from it, and everything about that was unsettling.

She'd never picked up any sort of feeling from an object before; and she'd never picked up anything at that distance. So, even though there was nothing alarming about what she felt, the mere fact that she felt *anything* gave her pause, even though it wasn't malevolent.

Amryn didn't know a lot about empaths, but she knew there were variations. Some people could feel the emotions of animals, for instance—which was something she couldn't do. Others had a sensitivity for objects, and could often glean something about where they had been, or who had last touched them. She'd never demonstrated that ability before, and she wasn't picking up on any other items, even though she tried to *feel* the pack she'd left behind.

Nothing.

But the amulet in her hand continued its dull hum.

A ripple of emotions tugged her attention away from the strange necklace. A man—only one this time—was creeping back toward her location, and he was focused. Ready to kill.

Amryn shoved the old amulet into her pocket and moved back to the pack, scooping it up as quietly as she could and fitting it over her shoulders. As much as she wanted to remain in the shelter of the cave, this time the hunter was being more careful. She couldn't risk him spotting the cave and trapping her here.

She wasn't exactly sure which direction the path was, but she could feel the general direction of her hunter.

She went the opposite way.

Amryn's fear was strangling. A second man had joined the first. Now, she felt the presence of a third.

It was late afternoon and thunder rumbled distantly, threatening another storm. She was exhausted, blisters covered her feet, and she knew she had to rest before her body simply dropped. She'd run out of water hours ago, and her empty stomach ached. She was thoroughly lost, and the hunters were closing in. The game of cat and mouse she'd been playing with them was one she knew she'd lose eventually.

That left only one option.

She ducked behind the thick trunk of a tree and dropped her pack. She bent, her fingers scraping over moist earth, brushing past clutches of grass until she found a large rock with some jagged grooves that would make it easy to grip. She straightened, her back pressed to the trunk behind her.

Her body shook from more than just adrenaline or exhaustion. Knowing she would feel flashes of any pain she delivered made her stomach pitch with dread. If she managed to kill one of them, she would probably double over and be violently sick, leaving her vulnerable to one of the other attackers.

The rock was a heavy weight in her hand, but she didn't drop it. She couldn't. She would fight for her life, even if she was doomed to lose.

Thunder boomed. As the three men drew closer, their emotions became more distinct.

Focus. Determination. Rage.

Anger. Frustration. Need.

Cool fury. Desperation. *Protect.*

Sensing that last desire, Amryn's hold on the rock flexed. Confusion sparked along with a flash of lightning. That third presence didn't feel the same as the others. He wasn't driven with a desire to kill, but a need to *protect*. A desperation to not be too late . . .

It wasn't Carver. She knew his essence well enough that she would have known him instantly. No, this was someone else. Someone new.

When she felt his sudden elation, she tensed—just before she felt a life go out.

Her hollow stomach clenched, and she fought a gag.

The next death happened near enough to her that she heard the gasp, and the body hitting the ground.

Only the third man remained, and his footsteps slowed as he approached her position.

"Hello?" a deep voice called out. "Can you hear me?"

Amryn didn't make a sound.

"I know you're close," he continued, still moving forward. "I'm not going to hurt you. The men hunting you are dead. You're safe."

It was possible he was a guard from Esperance, but she wasn't sure. All she knew was that he was dangerous. She could feel his lethal edge, even if he wasn't currently threatening her.

He'd openly admitted to killing two people, and nothing in his even tone showed remorse.

"Look, I'm only trying to help," he said. "I spotted those men a while back, and when I realized they were tracking you, I knew you needed help." His footsteps paused. "I swear, I just want to help you get to safety. I can take you back to the trail and escort you off this mountain."

Amryn pried into the man's emotions, searching for anything that would prove him to be an enemy. All she felt was sincerity. He was dangerous, yes, and determination still lived inside him—but not as forcefully as before, when he'd been stalking her hunters. He didn't know who she was, but he genuinely wanted to help her.

In the distance, thunder rolled. "A storm is coming," the man said. "We need to make it as far as we can before we're forced to find shelter."

Saints, she didn't want to be caught out here—alone—with another storm coming. And she felt absolutely no threat from this man. Still . . .

"Who are you?" she asked, still gripping the rock.

"Ford Gallo," he answered promptly. Something in his manner had softened as soon as he heard her voice, and his protective instincts flared. Perhaps he hadn't known she was a woman?

"Your name tells me nothing," she said. "What are you doing on this mountain?"

"Would you believe me if I said I just fancied a climb?"

The humor in his reply was a surprise—as was the strange calm it brought to her racing heart.

Slowly, she peeled away from the tree.

Ford Gallo stood in the cloudy light of the stormy afternoon. His bronze skin was streaked with dirt, and his dark hair was an unruly mess. He looked to be in his early twenties. He was handsome, and a little shorter and more slender than she'd expected. He felt a flash of relief at the sight of her, and his gaze gentled as he took in her appearance. When he noticed the stone clutched in her hand, amusement rippled and the side of his mouth kicked up. "I do hope you don't intend to brain me with that."

She tightened her hold on her makeshift weapon. "Are you a guard from Esperance?"

"No."

"Are you a cleric?"

He snorted. "Definitely not." His hands sank into his pockets, probably in an effort to look non-threatening. All it did was bring her attention to his belted knives. "What's your name?" he asked again.

She pursed her lips, but she saw no reason to lie. "Amryn."

Surprise lit through him and registered on his face. "You're Carver's wife."

Her knuckles creaked around the rock. "How do you know that?"

Immediately, his gaze shuttered. He regretted what he'd said. "I hear things."

Amryn's eyes narrowed. "How? We're in a remote jungle, and you're not supposed to be anywhere near Esperance—no one is."

Unease feathered inside him, but he was careful to school his features into a neutral expression. "I'm an ex-soldier. I came to Esperance for some peace and quiet. The high cleric threatened to throw me out because they were sealing the temple by order of the emperor." He lifted a single shoulder. "I figured no one would know if I stayed in one of the cabins in the jungle." Truth rang in his words, but she could sense his nervousness.

He was lying, at least partially. But even if some of his words were a deception, Amryn could feel that he didn't mean her any harm. He truly wanted to help her. "How do you know Carver?" she asked.

"I served with him once, a long time ago. I don't know him well."

"Yet you know he's here and married to me."

"Yes." He didn't expound on that.

And, frankly, when thunder rumbled more loudly than before, she decided it might not matter why Ford was here, or how he knew she was married to Carver. That storm was rolling in fast.

Ford eyed her. "Are you all right?"

The question caught her off guard. Then she glanced down at herself. Her clothes were smeared with mud, and her face and hair were no better. She met his concerned gaze. "I'm fine."

Ford nodded once. He gestured to the left. "There's a path just a little ways down there. It will lead us straight to the camp."

"How do you know about the camp?"

"How about I give you answers while we walk? I'm sure Carver is tearing the jungle apart to find you."

Heat curled low in her belly at his words, and the absolute *knowing* Ford felt. She knew he was right. She may not understand Carver, but he would be looking for her—and he wouldn't stop until she was found.

She set her shoulders. "All right, I'll come with you. But I'm keeping the rock."

Ford's eyes danced. "I'm pretty sure I like you."

28

CARVER

CARVER RACED THROUGH THE jungle, chasing that chilling scream until he burst into a clearing. There was a small pond, but it was the bodies on the edge of the water that snared his attention.

Darrin lay there, unmoving. Another man Carver didn't recognize was also on the ground, and Marriset cowered nearby, clutching her side.

Her dress was drenched in blood.

Carver darted for her, falling to his knees to inspect her wound.

She was shaking, and it took real effort to pry her fingers away so he could see the damage. It was a deep slice—a dodged strike for her gut that would have been fatal.

Marriset's eyes were partially glazed and tears splashed down her cheeks. "I'm dying," she gasped.

He pressed her hands back over the wound, his own fingers slick with her blood. "You're going to be all right." He had no needle and thread here, but they could staunch the flow of blood and carry her down to the camp's physician.

Marriset blinked at him, and it was almost like she was see-ing him for the first time. "C-Carver?"

"You'll be all right," he repeated, even as he tore his sleeves to make a bandage. He wrapped her waist tightly, knotting the makeshift bandage over the wound to increase the pressure.

Argent came to stand beside him. "Darrin's dead. It looks like he managed to stab his killer before he died."

"He almost killed me," Marriset choked. "He almost killed me after he killed Darrin, but then he fell."

Argent and Carver shared a look. Argent, Jayveh, and Car-ver hadn't been the only targets, then. Or the rebels had simply decided to kill anyone from Esperance.

Carver tried to stand, but Marriset snagged his wrist. "Don't leave me," she begged, terror stamped across her face.

He wrapped his hand over hers, squeezing once. "It's all right. The guards are going to take you to the camp."

Her gaze was frantic. "Where are you going?"

"Amryn is missing. I'm going to find her."

Marriset's lower lip trembled. "If she's out there alone . . ."

"I'll find her," he repeated. He pushed to his feet, sliding out of Marriset's grasp. He turned to Argent. "You should go with them to the camp."

"No." The prince turned to the guards. "Two of you will take Marriset down the mountain, the other three of you will come with us."

Carver thought about protesting, but that would just take time. And as thunder rumbled in the distance, he knew that time wasn't something they had to waste.

They left Darrin's body. Someone would have to come back for it later, but for the moment, they didn't have the manpower to move it. Carver led the way back to the main path, with Argent at his side and the guards trailing behind.

The prince's voice was low as he said, "That's everyone on our path accounted for, except for Amryn. Ivan, Samuel, Sadia, Rivard, and Tam were on the other side of the mountain. Do you think they would have been attacked, too?"

"I don't know." It all depended on who the rebel informant was. If the high cleric had shared with guards or clerics beforehand who would be on which path, it was possible the attacks would be focused here. But if the rebel informant was someone else and hadn't known, attacks could be happening all over the mountain.

"Cora and Darrin," Argent murmured. "Saints, we can't lose anyone else."

The words hung ominously around them, like a taunt to the Divinities.

Carver walked faster.

The storm was all but upon them. Wind snagged their clothes and hair and made the trees around them shudder. Lightning streaked the sky, and thunder cracked.

They hadn't found Amryn.

They'd backtracked up the path and come back to the scene of Carver's battle with the rebels. One of the Esperance guards had some training as a tracker, but what Carver wouldn't give for Ford's skills right now.

While the Esperance guard scouted the area, searching for Amryn's trail, Carver took a moment to re-inspect the bodies of the rebels.

Argent followed him.

"We'll find her," he said.

Carver's jaw clenched as he crouched beside one of the bodies. "I should have had her hide nearby instead of run deeper into the jungle."

"You didn't know how this fight was going to go." Argent glanced toward the large dead snake. "It does seem like you had to improvise."

That was true enough. But by telling her to run, he'd lost her. The jungle had innumerable dangers, even aside from the Rising. Amryn might be safe from them because she was potentially one of them, but that didn't comfort him. The rebels were ruthless. They might kill her anyway; they'd killed each other easily enough.

Argent's voice was quieter than before. "You care about her."

Carver shot him a look. "Of course I care."

The prince shook his dark head. "No, it's more than that. You're falling in love with her."

The mere idea made his blood run cold. "No I'm not."

Argent cocked an eyebrow. "You're in denial, then. That can be one of the stages."

"I think you're confusing this with grief."

"Maybe *you* are."

"You're not even making sense."

"Love rarely does. Have you kissed her yet?"

"No."

But, Saints, he'd wanted to.

He stood, facing Argent with focus and a pulse that refused to slow down. His voice was a whisper, since he was very aware of the guards scattered around them. "She might be a rebel."

"So? Jayveh's brothers tried to kill me once."

"That's different."

"Is it?" Argent leaned closer. "Maybe you're too close to see it, but Amryn is perfect for you."

"Other than the fact that she might be trying to kill me." He indicated the bodies beside them. "She knew they were coming. She told me they were following us. It's why we left the road."

Argent frowned as he processed that. Then he surprised Carver by shrugging. "If she'd wanted you dead, she wouldn't have warned you about the threat."

That gave him pause.

Argent sighed. "I don't know her mind. But I do know that she's been a good friend to Jayveh, and I've seen her kindness toward others. She has a good heart. And the way she looks at you makes it clear she has feelings for you, too."

"You've noticed how she looks at me?"

"A blind man could have seen it. You're just so distracted by searching every shadow for a threat that you missed her falling for you."

Carver's heart thrilled, but he rolled his eyes. "You're a romantic fool."

"And you're terribly rude to your prince." Argent crossed his arms over his chest. "This Marriset scheme of yours . . . I know you're trying to determine if she's a threat, and I'm grateful for your help. But it's hurting Amryn. Jayveh told me if you break her heart, I have to duel you."

He huffed a laugh. "You'd lose."

"Probably. So don't let it come to that."

Carver gazed into the darkness, his shoulders suddenly heavy. "I don't think I have the power to break her heart. She never gave it to me."

"And what about you?" Argent asked. "Did you give your heart to her?"

He snorted, trying to breathe past the sudden pang in his chest. "No."

The red-haired harpy had stolen it.

Their tracker joined them, and his expression wasn't encouraging. "I found her trail, but this storm is going to wash out everything. We don't have enough men to properly search for her. We should mark what we can of her trail, and then return to the camp for more men."

"No," Carver said.

Argent set a hand on his shoulder. "You know stumbling around out here isn't going to help her. We'll find her much more quickly if we get reinforcements. You showed her how to weather a storm out here; she'll be all right."

Tactically, all of that made sense. But every part of Carver rebelled against leaving. Amryn was brave and resourceful, but she was terrified of the jungle. He hated the thought of her out here, alone and afraid.

He gritted his teeth. The sooner they recruited help, the sooner they'd find her. "Let's go," he said, already moving.

29

AMRYN

AMRYN AND FORD TOOK WHAT shelter they could as the storm raged. Her stomach still gnawed hungrily, but he'd shared the rations he had.

They hadn't spoken much in the beginning, since they'd been trying to cover as much ground as possible before the storm truly lashed out. Now, sitting side by side under dripping leaves, Amryn eyed him.

He had a handsome profile, and his brown hair looked even darker now that it was wet. His deeply tanned skin was similar in tone to Carver's, making her wonder if Ford was from Westmont as well. Though she hadn't known him long, she already knew his alert eyes were never without a spark of humor for long.

"You and Carver have the same strategy for surviving a jungle storm," she told him.

"We learned in Harvari." Ford nodded to the fist-sized rock sitting beside her. "You finally dropped it."

"It's still close enough to grab."

A smile ghosted across his lips. "Saints, you're perfect for Carver."

The splash of amusement and genuine happiness made her strangely uncomfortable. She swiped a wet curl off her temple. "So, are you finally going to tell me what you're doing here?"

"I already did."

"You really didn't." He'd said he was a soldier, and that she believed. But the way he pretended to know Carver only in passing, as his general, was clearly false. The friendship he had with Carver was tangible. It made it hard for her to believe that his living nearby was a coincidence. "Does Carver know you're here in Esperance?"

"No."

A lie. She could feel it.

Ford continued without prompting. "I followed him here to protect him."

That was at least partially true.

"I would really appreciate it if you didn't tell anyone about me," Ford added. "The high cleric would kick me out, and after all that's been happening, I think Carver—all of you—are in more danger than anyone guessed."

All true.

Amryn shifted her weight. "What were you doing on Zawri? And don't tell me you just chose today for a hike."

Ford smiled, but his expression quickly grew serious. "I happened to stumble across some of those men creeping up the mountain. It was too late for me to warn anyone, so I followed them. Truthfully, I was looking to save Argent. But then I found your tracks, and I knew someone wandering out here alone wasn't a good sign. You know the rest."

Argent. Not *Prince* Argent.

Another friend.

Ford became more of a puzzle by the minute.

Amryn crossed her arms over her chest. "Do you know who those men were?"

"Do you?" he asked, turning the question back on her.

"No."

He searched her face as he said, "I think they were members of the Rising."

Her stomach tightened. She fought to keep her sudden tension off her face. "Why do you think that?"

"It makes sense. If anyone would want Esperance to fail, it would be them."

She'd known the rebels had a plan to destroy the empire. She'd also guessed that killing Argent, Jayveh, and Carver would possibly be in those plans. But this attack had been brutal, and done without telling her. Saints, they'd been hunting *her*, too. Maybe they hadn't known who she was when they were tracking her, but they should have. Though, to be fair, that wasn't even what concerned her most at the moment. She'd felt the darkness in them. The all-consuming hatred. Their desire to kill.

The Rising hadn't felt entirely real to her until this moment. It had been hidden notes and quiet missions. It hadn't been *this*. The thought that she might be helping men like that made her ill.

What had she expected from the Rising? They wanted to tear down the empire. She'd known that would mean death for many.

But she hadn't known Argent and Jayveh then. She hadn't known Carver.

Ford was still watching her.

Amryn tried to clamp down on her rioting thoughts. "The rebels would make sense."

He nodded once, still gazing at her. "How did you get separated from Carver?"

She told him—leaving out the part where she'd sensed the attackers sneaking up on them—and Ford listened raptly. Shadows darkened his eyes by the time she finished. "Carver will have gone back to the road looking for you. When he doesn't find you, he'll probably recruit help at the camp. This storm will have slowed him, though."

"I had the pack," she said. "He won't have food or water."

"He'll be fine." There was no doubt in Ford's voice, which she appreciated. She was also grateful that he didn't point out that Carver might not have walked away from the attack.

Amryn peeked out at the rain. "I hate that we're stuck here."

"I'm not *that* poor of company, am I?"

"I really don't know. You're a stranger."

He blinked at her. "How are we still strangers? I saved your life. We exchanged names and pleasantries. We've been together for hours, *and* you put down the rock."

She glanced over at him. "I have a feeling you get on Carver's nerves."

The corner of his mouth lifted. "I do."

A smile tugged at her own mouth. Ford might be keeping things from her, but she was undeniably comfortable around him. Even if it was a little reluctant on her part. "How long have you been living in this jungle?"

"Interrogating me, Lady Vincetti?"

"Only making conversation."

"Hm." He scratched his shoulder. "I arrived soon before the temple was closed to outsiders."

"And have you had any contact with Carver since your arrival?"

"No. I already told you, he doesn't know I'm here."

Before she could press him further, there was a short cry.

Ford and Amryn both stiffened.

That hadn't been an animal.

While Ford drew a knife, she probed the area with her empathic sense. She'd been so tuned into Ford, she hadn't noticed anything around them, but someone was out there. And they were in a great deal of pain.

"Stay here," Ford said, already slipping out into the pounding rain. Gone was the light, mirthful man he'd been. This was the first time she'd actually seen the soldier, and a shiver tracked down her spine.

It took a moment to realize she knew who was hurt out there. She'd learned the feel of everyone she frequently encountered at Esperance by now.

Ivan.

She ducked out into the rain, desperate to stop Ford before he could ambush Ivan.

She reached Ford just as Ivan came into view.

The Sibeten man was limping. He had used his shirt to create bandages on his thigh and forearm, and he was pressing the rest of the bunched up cloth to his side. His other hand fisted a dagger. His blond hair hung limply around his face, and he—like them—was totally drenched.

"Ivan," Amryn gasped.

His eyes flickered to her, but went right back to Ford. His wide shoulders tensed, and the dangerous edge that lifted his emotions cut into his hard face. "Get away from her."

Ford shot her a look. "Did I not tell you to stay? I think I told you to stay."

"That's Ivan," she snapped. "He's one of us."

"He's also holding a knife," Ford pointed out.

Ivan's brows slammed down. "So are you."

Amryn sensed no malice from Ivan. Only pain, and a steely resolve to protect her.

She hurried toward him, ignoring Ford's curse. "Ivan, are you all right?"

"*Yenn,*" he grunted.

She didn't believe him for an instant. "Have you seen any of the others?"

"Tam and Rivard. I found them after I was ambushed, and escorted them most of the way back to camp. Then I came back to look for the others. I have not found Samuel or Sadia." He studied her. "Are you all right?"

She nodded. "I got separated from Carver when we were ambushed, but Ford found me."

"Ford?" Ivan's eyes narrowed. "Are you an Esperance guard?"

"Yes."

Ford lied quickly, but he wasn't particularly good at it.

Ivan cocked his head to the side. "Where is your uniform?"

"I'm off rotation. Came up here for a nice bit of fresh air. Nature heals, or so they say." He looked to Amryn, and actually pouted. "You didn't threaten *him* with a rock."

Amryn might have retorted, but Ivan's legs gave out.

She caught his shoulders, and even though she staggered under his weight, she kept him from slamming face-first onto the jungle floor. "Ivan?"

He blinked, his eyes a little hazy as he tried to focus on her. "I think I may not be all right," he whispered dully.

Ford darted forward to help lower him to the ground.

"Saints," he bit out. "Look at his leg."

Amryn did, and her stomach rolled. Blood soaked the rough bandage and his entire leg.

"He's losing too much blood." Ford grabbed Amryn's hand and pressed it against the bleeding leg wound. "We need to close this," he said. "I think I have needle and thread in my pack."

Panic fluttered in her chest as Ford bolted, leaving her alone with Ivan.

He was dying. She could feel it.

"I'm glad you're safe," Ivan said, his quiet voice a faint echo of what it usually was. "I needed to make sure all of you were safe. No one else . . . should die here . . ."

His agony ripped through her. Mostly physical, but there was another pain there, coated in guilt.

"Couldn't save her," he cracked out, sweat beading on his forehead. "Didn't even know she was in danger . . ."

Blood slid between her fingers, but Amryn only tightened her hold on the wound.

Ivan intimidated her, but he didn't deserve this. He didn't deserve to die here, blaming himself for Cora's death.

None of them deserved to die.

Her spine stiffened. She bent her head, her fingers digging into Ivan's leg as she did something she hadn't dared to try in years. Not since the day she'd hugged her mother's body and sobbed for her to come back.

Unlike that day, there was still life in Ivan.

She latched onto his pain, then she pulled it into herself.

Her breath caught as agony ripped up her leg, but she didn't stop. She dragged more of his pain inside herself. Her body shook. Something deep inside her burned.

She ignored Ivan's other wounds. They were minor compared to the damage in his leg, and she couldn't risk healing too many of his injuries.

She couldn't risk anyone discovering what she could do.

She didn't understand her healing ability. Her mother—who could also use her empathic gift to heal others—had taught her a little, but she'd warned Amryn to never use it. It was too obvious of a gift. It could expose her as an empath—a powerful one—which would get her killed.

She wasn't thinking about that as she fought to save Ivan. Because if she did nothing, he would die, and she couldn't have his death on her conscience.

As she took on his pain, some of the tension left his body. His torn skin and muscle was knitting back together from the inside out. If she kept going, she could heal him completely—there wouldn't even be a scar. She couldn't do that for him, though. Not without risking discovery.

Saints, she was already risking too much. But she refused to stop now.

The pain was excruciating. As it passed into her, her magic burned away the damage. She felt the pain, but she didn't have to bear the injury. Still, healing came with a cost. According to her mother, she could take on too much, and the draw upon her energy would be too great. Her body would fail, and she would die.

Her mother's caution rang in her ears when Ivan's heart started to beat more strongly, and Amryn's stuttered. Her vision hazed.

She needed to stop. The fatal damage in Ivan's wound had been healed.

Somewhere, in the back of her awareness, something hummed. Beckoned.

She ignored that and released her healing hold. Her lungs strained, and she couldn't stop her gasp of pain.

Ivan blinked up at her, his eyes growing sharper. Confusion wafted from him. "What . . .?"

She pulled back her shaking hands, which were covered in blood. Fatigue dragged at her shoulders, and her breathing was thready.

The last thing she heard was Ford's frantic shout as she went down.

30

CARVER

CARVER SHOVED BLADES INTO HIS belt, which he'd demanded from one of the Esperance guards. He was finally in dry
clothing, but frustration throbbed inside him.

Amryn had been missing since morning, and it was full
dark out there now.

He and Argent had followed Amryn's trail until the rain
had washed out every sign. They'd found shelter and stayed
until the worst of the storm had passed, and then they'd had
to make their way back to the camp at the foot of the mountain. They needed reinforcements if they were going to conduct a thorough search of Zawri.

Leaving the mountain had felt like leaving Amryn. Carver had hated every step. He'd hoped that, somehow, Amryn
would be safe at the camp.

She wasn't. Not only that, Ivan was also missing.

Standing in the main tent of the camp, Carver tried to ignore the heated argument happening behind him as he secured his weapons.

"It's too dark," the high cleric said. "There's no point in sending out a search party now."

"We'll bring lanterns," Argent said. "We can't leave Amryn and Ivan out there overnight. Ivan went back out there to find Samuel and Sadia, but they came back without him. The Saints only know what might have happened to him."

"And if another storm strikes?" Zacharias challenged. "Or some animal attacks? I cannot endanger any of you further. You must all remain in the camp."

"We've already been endangered. Darrin is *dead*." Argent's tone deepened. "I know you worry about your standing with my grandfather, Zacharias. But we need to find Amryn and Ivan. I think that should be a personal priority of yours."

The high cleric flushed. "You can't blame me. This was—it was a deliberate attack! And the storms were an act of the Divinities."

"Yes. But I *can* blame you if you keep trying to stop us. And, trust me, I *will*."

Zacharias threw his hands up. "I'm not trying to *stop* you, I'm trying to *protect* you! There's no point going out there tonight, especially when doing so limits the guards here. We can't leave the camp undefended. What if those attackers are still out there?"

"You'll be fine," Argent said. "Give swords to Rivard and Samuel, and stay here. In the morning, head back to Esperance."

"Your Highness, I can't let you go out there. Your life is worth too much, and you were injured this morning!"

Argent drew up to his full height. "This isn't a debate, Zacharias. We're conducting a search for Amryn and Ivan, and I'm going. There is no discussion."

That got Carver's attention. He twisted to face his friend. "You're not going back out there."

Argent's voice was edged with steel. "I'm the bloody crown prince of the Craethen Empire. You do not command me. I'm coming with you."

"This is all pointless anyway," the high cleric muttered. "They're probably dead."

Carver stiffened. "You'd better pray they aren't, Cleric."

Zacharias threw up his hands. "Of course I pray for them. But they've been missing all day, and we know the dangers out there. I'm merely being realistic."

"Are you sure that's all you are?"

The bald man drew back. "What is *that* supposed to imply?"

"Carver," Argent bit out warningly.

He ignored his friend, his gaze pinning the high cleric where he stood. "This excursion was your idea. Who's to say you didn't plan the attack as well?"

Zacharias spluttered, his face going from white to red. "How dare you accuse me of this? I'm the high cleric!"

"No," Carver snapped. "You're a pain in my—"

Jayveh pushed into the tent, ignorant of the tension as she hefted two packs. "One for each of you," she said, handing one to Carver and the other to Argent. "There are bandages, fresh clothes, food, and water—anything she or Ivan might need."

"Thank you, love." Argent pressed a kiss to her forehead, then shrugged on the pack. "How is Marriset?"

"In shock, I think. But her wound has been treated, and Sadia and Tam are both with her."

"In the morning, you're all going to head back to Esperance," he told her.

"Only so I can bring reinforcements back to help you," she

countered.

Argent huffed. "We'll try to hurry so you don't have to."

She hugged him briefly. "Thank you for not telling me I have to stay back there."

"You wouldn't have listened."

"True." She turned to face Carver. "She's going to be all right."

She couldn't know that, but she spoke with such resolve, Carver found himself nodding. Then he turned to Argent. "If you're coming, we've got to start moving."

They'd wasted enough time. Amryn was out there, and—

The tent flap pushed open and Amryn and Ivan limped inside.

They were drenched. Amryn's arm was around Ivan's back and her whole body was tucked under his shoulder, as if she were steadying him. It didn't look like the huge Sibeten was actually allowing her to take much of his weight, though. Both of them were covered in mud. Ivan had no shirt, and he had his arm around Amryn—which were ridiculous things to fixate on when *she was alive and standing right in front of him.*

Argent darted forward and took the burden of steadying Ivan. Bandages were wrapped around various parts of his body, but Amryn looked unscathed. Exhaustion cut lines in her mud-streaked face, and her braid was a tangled mess of soaking red curls. Her clothes were dirty, torn, and wet, and her sea-green eyes were weary.

But she was *here*.

That fact thawed Carver's frozen body.

He strode forward, not caring that they had an audience. He registered the surprise that flickered across Amryn's face, but then she was locked in his embrace. His lungs felt too tight as her smaller body pressed perfectly against his. Her wet clothes instantly dampened his, but he didn't care. She was alive, and she was in his arms. Relief nearly took him out at the knees. All he could do was bury his face in the curve of her neck and breathe in her citrus and mint scent.

Amryn didn't move. She was rigid. Saints, he'd overstepped. She was still rightfully angry about Marriset. She didn't want him—

Her arms wrapped around his middle, and her cheek settled against his chest. *She* was holding *him.*

No one else in the tent existed.

His heart swelled and he held her tighter.

Then he realized she might be hurt, even if she didn't have bandages, and he instantly pulled back.

She swayed at the sudden loss of him, and he grasped her shoulders to steady her.

He was far too thrilled to note that her hands had settled to grip his waist.

He made a cursory scan of her body, then cupped her face in both hands and tipped her head back, searching every visible inch of her pale face. The freckles on her cheeks were smudged with dirt, and there were some shallow cuts marring her skin. There was even a bruise on her cheekbone. He thumbed the edge of it, his throat too tight for words.

"I'm all right," she whispered. Hearing the soft caress of her voice sent another wave of relief through him. Her cheeks pinkened slightly under his stare. "I, ah, fell."

"You fainted," Ivan said.

Carver's heart stopped. "*What?*"

Amryn sighed, her head still framed in his palms. "I'm fine. I just don't do well with blood, and Ivan was bleeding out."

Her eyes widened. "Saints, he needs a physician."

"Argent and I will take him," Jayveh said from beside them. The princess set a hand on Amryn's arm, her eyes watering even as she smiled. "I've been so worried about you."

Moisture shone in Amryn's eyes, and then she shifted, giving Carver no choice but to drop his hold so she could embrace her friend.

His hands felt empty as he watched them.

The princess groaned as she squeezed Amryn. "Are you sure you're fine?"

"I'm sure. Just don't make me tend any injuries again."

Carver remembered the way Amryn had reacted to the violence at the wedding feast; he'd felt bad for the servant who'd had to scrub his boots clean. He hadn't made the connection before, but now that he knew she'd witnessed her mother's murder, he wondered if that's where her aversion to blood came from.

He probably should have stepped back to give the two women more space, but he couldn't make himself move away from Amryn.

Argent seemed to notice his need, because he cleared his throat. "Jayveh, let's get Ivan to the physician." As the princess pulled back from Amryn, Argent looked to the High Cleric. "Tell the guards to shore up the camp's defenses, and prepare to leave at dawn."

Zacharias bowed his head, already giving orders to the nearby guards as he strode for the wide flap of the tent door.

In moments, Carver and Amryn were alone. Lanterns glowed in the tent, softening her expression as she looked at him.

"Are *you* all right?" she asked.

He didn't have a voice to answer her, and he couldn't stop

his fingers from lifting to touch her again. Her round cheek. The soft skin of her jaw. His eyes drifted down to her mouth.

A slight tremble ran through Amryn and her lips parted, but she didn't pull away. His heart pounded in his chest, his pulse racing as the pad of one thumb whispered over her lower lip.

Her breath caught on a sharp inhale.

Tension filled the small space between them, a thread stretched to the breaking point.

Something had shifted inside him. Maybe it had been shifting for a while. But this woman had him. Completely. Forget the suspicions, fears, and consequences. He might not understand everything about her, but in this moment, it didn't matter.

She had given him comfort when he didn't deserve it. She had given him beauty in every smile, when all he'd seen for too long was horror. She had trusted him with her darkest memories when he was drowning in his own.

Amryn Lukis was the light he hadn't known he needed.

She peered up at him, her pulse fluttering in her neck.

Carver gently tilted her chin up as he bent his head, leaning in.

Before their lips touched, she stiffened and jerked away.

Hurt slashed him a second before she sneezed. Violently. Three times.

When she finally looked up, her eyes watered. "Sorry." A blush darkened her cheeks.

Saints, he didn't care. The need to kiss her burned through his tightening body. His pulse raced. He'd been married to his wife for two blasted months. She'd been a temptation the entire time—even when he hadn't wanted to admit it.

And she had never looked more beautiful to him than she

did right now.

Her tongue darted over her lips, her eyes almost panicked as she slid back a step. "I . . . I should get out of these clothes."

If she'd said anything else, he might have pressed into her space and just bloody kissed her. But she was soaked and cold, and taking care of her was a job he'd done poorly at. That needed to change. *Now.*

He bent to snatch up the pack Jayveh had brought earlier. "There are dry clothes in here. Let's get you warm."

Her blush deepened, and something low in his gut clenched. Saints give him strength . . .

He ordered his body to *bloody stop* and shouldered the pack.

A shiver wracked her. He took her hand, thinking nothing of it until his palm starting tingling warmly.

He led the way out of the tent, taking her to their own. He was grateful when they didn't encounter anyone.

He released her hand once they were inside. He set the pack on her bedroll and found the lamp, making quick work to light it.

He twisted to face her. "I'll get you food and water. Do you need anything else?"

"No." She hesitated. "When we entered the camp, one of the guards mentioned Darrin was killed. Is anyone else . . .?"

"No. Everyone else is accounted for, now."

"Good." Her voice was quiet, and he could tell by the way she bit her lip that she had something else she wanted to say.

It took all his self-control not to smooth a thumb over that lip and save it from her teeth. "What else do you want to ask me?"

She eyed him. "How is Marriset?"

"She was wounded, but she'll be all right. Jayveh said she's in shock, but that's to be expected."

Her brow furrowed. "You haven't visited her?"

"No." He thought his tone made it quite clear that he didn't plan to visit her, either.

Amryn's throat flexed as she swallowed. "Oh."

He took a step back. "Change into something dry. I'll be right back."

He left her, though he motioned for an Esperance guard to watch the tent. He gathered rations quickly from the cooking tent, stacking a plate with figs, fried eggs, bacon, and scones. Then he filled a canteen and hurried back to the tent.

He slipped inside, just in time to see a flash of pale skin as Amryn dropped the hem of the baggy shirt into place.

His pulse pounded. Blazing Saints, that brief glimpse of her lower back was going to torment him.

Amryn turned to face him, rolling the sleeves of the shirt back from her hands. Everything was too big, since she was wearing a man's shirt and pants; she'd already rolled the cuffs of the pants, but there was nothing to be done about the length of the shirt that hung nearly to her knees. She clutched the throat of the shirt, though the collar still fell wide, exposing part of one white shoulder.

"If Jayveh thought I could hike in this, she's overestimating my abilities."

Divinities take him, if she'd had to walk down a mountain in this, he wouldn't have been the only man to stare.

The mere thought of *anyone* but him ever seeing her like this made him want to throw a blanket around her.

Amryn's stomach grumbled, and that snapped him out of his possessive haze. He waited until she sat on her bedroll before he handed her the food.

She attacked it hungrily, pausing only to drink gulps of water.

"Take it slowly," he cautioned as he sank onto his bedroll, facing her.

She nodded, but didn't really slow down until the plate was nearly empty. Only then did she look up at him. "Are you really all right?"

"I am now."

Her cheeks colored. "I was worried about you."

That warmed him more than it should have. "I'm fine. I was coming to find you."

"I know."

A shallow laugh rushed out of him. "You did?"

"Yes." She stared at him, and he swore she was looking into his soul. "You promised you'd find me."

The words were simple, but their impact was anything but. His heart squeezed. What was bloody wrong with him? "I'm sorry I didn't find you sooner."

"That's all right." She popped a fig into her mouth and chewed. "I suppose it's good to know I can survive on my own."

"And rescue Ivan."

The corner of her mouth rose and her eyes sparked with quiet pride. "That, too."

"How did you find him?"

Amryn rubbed the side of her neck, her braid still a haphazard mess. "It's kind of a long story."

"I want to hear it."

She exhaled. Then she met his gaze and said three words he'd never expected to hear: "I met Ford."

31

AMRYN

CARVER STARED. HIS EXPRESSION was blank, but his emotions were not. Disbelief. Surprise. Panic.

At least he wasn't feeling that knee-weakening desire anymore. *That* had been completely unexpected, and after everything that had happened today, she didn't have the energy to process the fact that Carver Vincetti had almost kissed her. Or that she'd *wanted* to kiss him. Saints, they *would have kissed,* if she hadn't drawn away. Because, even after that embarrassing sneeze, his desire hadn't waned.

Amryn tried to focus on the issue at hand—the fact that she'd stunned him into silence with her revelation. "You don't need to bother denying you know him, or that you had no idea he's staying in one of the cabins here. Ford's not the best liar."

Carver pulled back a little, but he remained sitting cross-legged across from her. They were close enough that their knees almost touched. She could have reached out and grabbed his hand.

She didn't. Instead, she took a sip of water and waited. She'd considered keeping her encounter with Ford a secret from Carver, but it really wouldn't gain her anything; she assumed Ford would tell him everything once they met next. Because, obviously, they had meetings. Why else would Ford be here?

Carver eyed her, his aquamarine eyes unreadable. "Ford found you?"

She nodded. "He saved my life."

Anxiety thrummed from him, and the skin around his eyes tightened. "I would like to hear more about that, please." He spoke calmly, but his worry was obvious.

Her compulsion to comfort him was inexplicable. It had always seemed to be that way with him. "I'm fine," she reminded gently.

His expression didn't change.

She expelled a breath, then lengthened her spine as she began to tell him everything that had happened. When she got to the part about hiding in the cave, she was very aware of the tarnished amulet that hummed softly in the corner of the tent, still tucked in the pocket of her wet dress.

She decided not to mention the necklace to Carver. Not because she felt guilty for taking it—though she sort of did— but mostly because she couldn't exactly explain that she *felt* something from an inanimate object. That could lead to questions about her empathic ability, and after the warning she'd given in the jungle about their attackers, she shouldn't give him anything else he could hang her with.

She told him of how she'd left the cave, only to be stalked through the jungle until Ford had saved her from her would-be killers. She then explained how they'd eventually found Ivan—or rather, how he'd stumbled across them.

"Then we waited for the worst of the storm to pass and

made it the rest of the way down the mountain. Ford left us just outside the camp. He said he was going to meet up with his patrol, but I don't think Ivan believed him about being an Esperance guard." She tilted her head as she eyed him. "So, I assume Ford is nearby so you can get messages in and out of Esperance?"

"Yes."

"I'm assuming Argent knows?"

"Yes. So does the emperor. The high cleric doesn't. It really needs to stay that way."

"But, why would the emperor allow messages between you and Ford? He was the one who ordered our isolation."

"The heir to the empire cannot afford to be completely isolated."

Lie. The waver of apprehension gave Carver away.

He didn't want her asking about this, and with all the thoughts churning in her mind, this wasn't something she needed to press.

The Rising was dangerous. They'd targeted all of them on Zawri. They'd killed Darrin. They would have killed Ivan, if she hadn't healed him.

They'd tried to kill *all* of them.

It was possible the men who had hunted her would have stopped once they'd seen who she was, but that didn't bring her much comfort.

When she'd come to Esperance, she'd been determined to help the Rising destroy the empire. She hadn't questioned their methods. She hadn't worried about the costs. She'd focused on her mission—her non-violent part—and dismissed everything else. But now she *knew* the people the rebels wanted to kill.

Argent was no longer just the heir to the empire. He was

a friend to her; kindhearted, and a wholly enamored husband to the woman who had quickly become Amryn's best friend. Argent did not represent the continuation of a dark empire; he had become Amryn's hope for a future where the empire could change.

If the rebels killed him, that future would be lost.

The dread Carver was feeling tore her from her thoughts, and instantly made her tense. His expression was far too serious. "Amryn—"

He stopped when a yawn chose that moment to crack her jaw.

She blinked rapidly. "Sorry."

"No, don't apologize. You need sleep." She felt an odd flicker of relief from him as he grabbed her empty plate and pushed to his feet. "We can talk later."

She had a feeling it wasn't going to be a conversation either of them enjoyed.

Her own dread rose in a wave, and her voice was quiet as she said, "All right."

Darrin was buried near Cora in Esperance's cemetery. His funeral had been solemn, and Amryn felt mostly numbness from Marriset as she stood at the foot of her husband's grave. There was no deep grief. No gut-wrenching despair. Just . . . nothing.

Everyone mourned differently, and Amryn imagined the new widow was still in shock. They'd only been back from Zawri for four days.

Trevill and the high cleric had worked together in an effort to identify the rebel bodies that had been recovered from

Zawri. None of the staff or guards in Esperance had recognized them, which indicated the rebels must have been hiding nearby in the jungle. Trevill had yet to figure out who might have told the rebels about the excursion to Zawri, and he wasn't the only one who burned with curiosity.

Carver, who stood beside Amryn during Darrin's burial, also had questions. He hadn't asked them yet, though. The conversation he dreaded having with Amryn hung in the air between them. She knew it was only a matter of time before he asked how she'd known about the attackers before it was physically possible to do so, but she was grateful for every day he delayed in broaching the subject.

She'd left a message for the rebels the day they'd returned to Esperance. Her note had been short, and tucked into the pages of *The Ode of Saint Feyjinn*. She'd asked for an in-person meeting, but hadn't received an answer yet.

A part of her wondered if she ever would.

When the burial was concluded, the high cleric moved to talk to Marriset while the rest of them dispersed.

Jayveh wandered over and linked her arm in Amryn's. "Walk with me?"

The princess didn't really leave her much choice, as she guided her toward the nearest garden entrance.

Amryn glanced back at Carver, but he was talking to Argent.

Jayveh used her other arm to snag Tam away from Rivard, who took one look at the princess and decided not to protest.

The three women entered the garden with two bodyguards trailing behind them.

"I feel like we should do something for Marriset," Jayveh said. "I just don't know what."

"Sadia's been spending a lot of time with her," Amryn said.

"I think that's what Marriset needs. Time, and to not be alone."

Jayveh eyed her. "I know she was horrible to you."

Tam made a sound in her throat. "No less horrible than Carver."

Amryn's gut tightened. "I know. But that's all over."

The princess pulled them to a stop, her excitement flashing. "Really?"

Amryn's cheeks flooded with heat as the women stared at her. "Yes."

Jayveh grinned.

Tam felt shock. "You've forgiven him?"

"Yes."

Amryn didn't know quite when that had happened. Maybe when Carver had explained that he'd only gotten close to Marriset to protect Argent? Or when she'd comforted him after his nightmare? Or maybe it had been in the moment he'd embraced her in the tent, with no hesitation, and she'd felt his burning relief that she was all right.

It didn't really matter, she supposed. She knew now that he'd never felt true desire for Marriset. Amryn knew that for a fact, because desire is what she felt emanating from him every time he looked at *her*.

Tam's disbelief was overshadowed by Jayveh's elation. The princess tugged Amryn close for a quick hug. "I'm so happy for you two! I *knew* something was different between you. At first I thought he was just being overly protective, but now . . ." She pulled away and her eyes danced. "It makes perfect sense. He's in love with you."

Amryn nearly choked. "He's not."

He was attracted to her, and he'd nearly kissed her. But he wasn't *in love* with her.

Jayveh shook her head. "I can't wait to see the moment you realize you're wrong." They resumed walking, and the princess let out a slow sigh. "It's nice hearing good news. Things have been far too bleak here." She looked to Tam. "How are things with you and Rivard?"

"Fine." Tam paused, then added, "Perhaps a little better. He's been very attentive the last few days."

"I'm glad." Jayveh tightened her hold on them both, and the flush of joy she suddenly felt was powerful. "Things are going well for all of us, then. I have some news to share . . . I'm expecting."

Amryn's surprise was echoed by Tam's, but she was quick to embrace Jayveh. "Congratulations!"

Jayveh beamed at her. "Thank you. It happened fast, but . . . I'm so happy."

"Does Argent know?" Tam asked.

"I told him last night. He was shocked at first, but when I realized I was . . ." Her voice drifted, and a hand settled on her still-flat belly. The surge of love, wonder, and anticipation she felt made Amryn's own chest swell. "I was surprised, too," Jayveh said, her grin wide. "But Argent and I are both ecstatic. Frankly, I knew I needed to tell you today, despite the funeral, because Argent will only be able to keep from screaming it from the rooftop for so long."

"How long have you known?" Amryn asked.

"I realized I was pregnant just before we left for Zawri. I decided to wait and tell Argent, though. If he'd known, he would have been worried about me the whole time." She sighed, though excitement remained in her eyes. "We'll announce it to everyone soon; we just wanted to wait until after the funeral. But I couldn't wait to share this with you both."

Amryn's throat was suddenly too thick. She'd never had close friends, but when Jayveh smiled at her, it was clear the princess reciprocated Amryn's friendship fully.

On impulse, she hugged Jayveh again, though she was mindful of not squeezing her too tightly. "I'm so happy for you, Jayveh. For you and Argent."

While they embraced, Amryn used her empathic sense to probe a little deeper, and there, nestled inside Jayveh's happiness, she could feel new life. Brushing against the purity and gentleness of that small soul brought tears to her eyes.

When Jayveh and Amryn finally pulled back, Tam took her turn to embrace the princess. "Congratulations, Jayveh." Though Tam's words sounded sincere, there was an undertone of sadness; maybe even regret.

Amryn could imagine what had caused that. Even if Rivard had been more attentive since Zawri, their marriage was nothing like the loving match between Argent and Jayveh.

When Tam pulled back from Jayveh, she groaned. "Argent will be impossible to live with now. He'll probably declare an empirical holiday—for every day of the pregnancy."

Jayveh laughed, but Amryn was fairly certain Tam wasn't joking.

In the light of such happiness, Amryn could only smile.

32

CARVER

ARGENT CLAPPED A HAND ON Carver's shoulder. The wide grin that split his face hadn't ebbed all evening. "I'm going to be a father!"

Carver chuckled. "So you keep telling me."

Argent somehow managed to keep smiling even as he took a drink of brandy.

They stood on the edge of the sitting room where everyone was sharing drinks and conversation after dinner. Argent and Jayveh had made their official announcement tonight, though Carver had learned about Jayveh's pregnancy last night.

Argent had sought him out to share the news, even though it was quite late. Carver had never seen his friend so happy.

Amryn had already retired to her room, but with Argent's excited voice booming in the suite, it wasn't a surprise that she'd come out. She'd been wearing a long white nightgown, her red hair arranged in a thick braid that trailed down her back. She had smiled as she'd embraced Argent, offering her congratulations.

Carver had never been jealous of his friend. Until that moment.

When she'd—finally—pulled back, she continued to smile at Argent as he grinned and talked about having a boy or a girl—he didn't care—and how excited he was to tell his grandfather . . .

Carver couldn't take his eyes off Amryn, standing there in that nightgown.

He hadn't been able to get the sight out of his head all day.

Amryn was currently standing across the room with Jayveh. Her hair was arranged in an elaborate pile atop her head, and she wore a deep teal, off-the-shoulder dress that fell silkily to the floor.

Another image he wasn't likely to forget any time soon.

He'd been avoiding confronting her. About the seals, and the rebels she'd *known* were tracking them on Zawri.

He hadn't shared any of this with Argent, and that was wrong. If he'd learned these things about anyone else . . . He would have arrested them by now.

With Amryn, he couldn't even form his questions. He dreaded asking her anything; he didn't want lies, but he feared the truth.

Saints, he didn't want her to be a rebel. He didn't want her to be his enemy. He just wanted her to be *his*.

"Carver, do you have a moment?"

He twisted to face Marriset. She wore a dark green dress with black accents. She was still favoring her side after being injured on Zawri. She looked paler than Carver had ever seen her, and with a good deal less makeup on her eyes and face.

Argent cleared his throat, his smile falling for the first time. "I'll give you a moment."

After he'd moved away, Marriset edged a little closer to Carver. "I was hoping you would join me for a walk in the garden tonight."

"That won't be possible."

"Why? I've missed you." She reached for his hand, and he took a quick step back. Her eyes narrowed. "You think I've lost access to Darrin's kingdom so I'm no longer worth seducing?"

"No. I just can't do this with you."

"You didn't seem to have a problem before."

"I'm sorry." And he was. Manipulating her had always been the goal, but he didn't like hurting her.

Marriset swallowed hard. "Darrin was murdered in front of me. I was *attacked*." Her words came out a little hoarse, and her fingers tightened on the small glass. "I need comfort. I need to feel safe."

"The high cleric has increased security. Guards are patrolling the halls—"

"I don't want more guards." She cut in. "I want *you*."

"I'm sorry," he said again.

A shadow passed over her face. She pulled back from him, and her eyes darted across the room to Amryn. When she looked back at Carver, her jaw was set. "We don't always get what we want. Do we?"

She turned on her heel and strode away, headed for the nearest door. The high cleric and Chancellor Trevill both noted her quick retreat, and they glanced back at Carver. Trevill had a curious look on his face. The high cleric just looked suspicious.

Carver looked pointedly away from them, turning to find Amryn watching him.

As was often the case, he couldn't read her expression.

"You're done with Marriset, then?"

Carver's grip on his glass tightened as he faced Rivard. "What's that supposed to mean?"

Rivard rolled his eyes, keeping his voice pitched low. "You weren't always subtle. Rumors spread." He lifted one shoulder. "Obviously, it was part of your investigation, so that's all I was implying; you've cleared her as a danger."

"I don't believe she's a rebel."

"Since she was attacked by them," Rivard said dryly, "I think that's a solid conclusion."

Carver forced himself to take an even breath. "What of your investigation?"

"It's slow. There are a lot of clerics. But I did learn something interesting about your wife."

His stomach lurched. He fought to keep his expression clear and his tone level. "What about her?"

"She makes frequent trips to the library, and she seems to always look at the same book: *Zerrif's Voyage.*"

No, no, no . . .

Rivard continued. "The clerics I spoke to also said she often talks with a cleric named Felinus, and they seem to always meet around where that book is shelved. By all accounts, Felinus generally keeps to himself, so the other clerics thought it odd." His gaze drifted across the room.

The back of Carver's neck itched as he followed the man's stare—right to Amryn, who was still talking to Jayveh.

"I admit," Rivard said softly, "I find it odd as well. I thought you should know. I'll talk with Felinus, and you can talk to Amryn."

"I will." His lungs felt too tight. "Tell me what you learn from Felinus."

"Of course. I look forward to your report as well." Rivard's eyes were sharp. "Finding a connection between a reclusive cleric and one of the Empire's Chosen is a promising lead."

He strode away without another word, and Carver was left standing alone. Tension coiled in his shoulders, and panic curled inside him. If Rivard learned that Amryn was a rebel, he wouldn't keep that from Argent.

Saints, Carver shouldn't be keeping this from his friend, either.

He'd delayed too long. He needed to confront her before Rivard could expose her. He needed a chance to find out *why*. If she was being forced to help the Rising, like Jayveh, then maybe he could help her. Save her.

Or maybe he would learn that she had no desire to be saved. That she wanted to kill him, Jayveh, and Argent.

Either way, he would find out tonight.

"Is everything all right?" Amryn asked, her voice echoing softly on the stone walls as they walked back to their room.

It was late. While everyone else had slowly left the room to retire, Argent and Jayveh had been too excited to sleep, so Amryn and Carver had lingered.

Admittedly, he hadn't been in a rush to be alone with Amryn.

But once Jayveh started yawning, Argent had insisted that she go to bed. The prince and princess had just gone down the hall that led to their room, leaving Amryn and Carver alone except for the guard that trailed them.

"Fine," he said, in answer to her question.

Amryn frowned. "Was it something Rivard said to you?"

Yes.

"No." He was aware of the guard behind them, and he didn't want to have this conversation here.

She bit her lower lip, making it clear she didn't believe him. Her skirt whispered over the floor, shimmering in the glow of the hall lamps.

Carver unlocked the door to their apartment and pushed it open, letting Amryn step inside first.

Perhaps that was a mistake, because their bodies brushed as she passed him, and the smell of her unique perfume tried its best to unravel him.

He closed the door and locked it, then turned to face her.

She was waiting for him in the center of the room, the dark balcony behind her. A servant had lit some of their lamps, and the soft light cast shadows over her pale face. Her hands were clasped in front of her, and her bare shoulders were tensed.

She was braced for his questions. She knew what was coming.

A stone dropped in his gut.

"We need to talk," he said.

She didn't even blink. "About what happened on Zawri."

The skin around his eyes tightened. "About a lot of things."

"All right."

Her voice was fragile, and he hated the undercurrent of fear in those two words.

He took a slow breath. "I need you to tell me the truth. Are you—?"

A scream ricocheted beyond their room, blood-curdling and sharp.

Carver cursed. "Stay here."

He darted from the room, following the guard who was already bolting down the hall.

The screaming continued, growing more frantic. It was coming from the floor below them.

Footsteps pounded the floor as guards ran toward the piercing sound, and someone was shouting.

Carver reached the staircase and took the steps three at a time. When he landed on the next floor, he saw that all the doors in the hall stood open, and a crowd had gathered in front of one of the corridor's alcoves.

Tam was the one screaming, and she was being held by Sadia. The two women stood slightly away from the crowd, but Tam's haunted eyes were fixed on the alcove—trapped by something she couldn't even see anymore, because of all the guards blocking her view.

Carver's pulse tripped.

Amryn had followed him, of course. She hurried to Tam's side, her face leached of all color.

Carver pushed through the crowd. His stomach dropped when he glimpsed what lay crumpled in the alcove.

Rivard, lying in a pool of his own blood, a dagger in his heart.

"I was on my way up to our room," Tam said, her voice shaking as much as her hands, which were folded on her lap. "I-I turned the corner, and . . ."

Amryn laid a comforting hand on Tam's shoulder.

"Take your time," Trevill said gently.

They were in Tam and Rivard's suite, the sitting room brightly lit with every available lamp. Amryn and Jayveh sat on either side of Tam on a long settee. Trevill was in the chair angled toward them. Carver, Argent, and the high cleric stood slightly apart, observing.

The rest of the crowd had been ordered back to their rooms by the high cleric. Tam had clung so fiercely to Amryn and Jayveh that Trevill had allowed them to stay.

Rivard's body was still in the hall. The note that had been clutched in his hand was in Trevill's pocket, but the words were seared into Carver's mind.

Vengeance is mine.

The tone and wording of the message was too similar to the one found with Cora, and they'd both been killed with a dagger through the heart. The handwriting seemed alike as well, though that would take a closer study to be sure. Still, it seemed likely that their murderer was the same.

Tam took a deep breath, and that seemed to steady her a little. "At first I didn't even realize he was dead. The shadows were thick in the alcove, and . . . I thought maybe he'd drunk too much brandy. He—he's done that before. I called out to him, but he didn't answer. And then I saw the blood, and . . ."

Trevill leaned forward. "Tam, this is important. Did Rivard mention feeling afraid, or nervous?"

"N-no. But we really didn't talk much." Fresh tears swam in Tam's eyes. "I-I'm sorry."

Trevill's tone was endlessly patient. "That's all right. When was the last time you saw him?"

"In the sitting room, after dinner."

"He spoke to General Vincetti," Zacharias said. "And he left the room directly after."

Trevill twisted to Carver. "What did you and Rivard discuss?"

"Nothing of importance," Carver lied, even though his insides knotted. Rivard had just shared his suspicions about Amryn and the cleric from the library, Felinus. Was that a coincidence?

"He walked out rather quickly," Zacharias said. "And it's no secret there is animosity between you."

Argent groaned. "Not this again. You accused Carver of murdering Cora, and now you think he killed Rivard?"

Zacharias angled his chin. "I'm sorry, Your Highness, but these questions need to be asked." He looked back at Carver. "For all we know, you were the last person to talk to Rivard. And you nearly killed him once before."

Carver's throat dried.

Zacharias looked far too triumphant. "Rivard told me everything. I know all about the history between you. How you nearly beat him to death three years ago."

Tam sucked in a breath. Jayveh's eyes flew wide. Amryn just looked worried.

Trevill straightened in his chair, his brows lowering as he viewed Carver. "Is this true?"

"Yes," Carver answered, his tone stiff. "But I didn't kill Rivard."

"Rivard was very open about what happened," Zacharias said. "How his actions set your brother on a path that nearly led to his death. And you can't tell us that it's all in the past and you've forgiven him, because you clearly haven't. You attacked him on the training grounds."

Carver bristled.

"This is insane," Argent snapped.

"Is it?" Zacharias glanced to Trevill. "Rivard confided in me. He sought forgiveness for his past sins, but Carver would not forgive him. That weighed on Rivard. He told me he intended to keep working for his forgiveness—no matter how long it took."

"I didn't kill Rivard," Carver repeated, more stiffly than before.

Zacharias ignored him, his gaze still on Trevill. "Carver saw Cora's body. He knew about the dagger in her heart, and he saw the message her killer left. He could have replicated those details to disguise Rivard's murder."

"Everyone learned about the note," Argent cut in, irritation thick in his voice. "And how Cora was killed."

Zacharias opened his mouth, but Trevill spoke first, his eyes on Carver. "I need to know what you and Rivard discussed tonight."

Carver's thoughts raced. He seized on the first believable lie he could think of. "He wanted to talk about the past. I didn't. He soon gave up and walked away."

"Perhaps you followed him," Zacharias pressed. "After drinking a little more, perhaps your anger won out."

"Carver was with me the entire time," Amryn said. Every eye turned to her, but she didn't shrink under their scrutiny. "We left the room together—long after Rivard—and we haven't been apart since."

Despite everything, Carver's heart warmed at her defense of him.

Zacharias was decidedly *less* moved. "Perhaps he compelled you to say that. You're afraid of him, aren't you?"

"*What?*" Carver, Amryn, and Argent all said together.

"Of course not," Amryn said quickly. "And Carver didn't

compel me to say anything. We were together the entire time."

"I'm afraid you vouching for your husband isn't exactly compelling," Zacharias said. "You can't truly account for his whereabouts at all times when you don't even sleep with him."

Amryn's face flamed.

Fury blasted Carver. "You don't need to embarrass her. *Or* interrogate her."

"The servants have reported that your sleeping arrangements haven't changed," the high cleric said, looking back to Amryn. "If you won't share a bed with your husband, you clearly don't feel comfortable with him. So I ask again: is he compelling you to lie for him?"

Amryn's eyes narrowed. "No."

Carver growled. "Stop questioning her."

"Are you afraid she'll break?" Zacharias challenged.

"Enough." Trevill stood. "Zacharias, you need to let this prejudice against Carver go. He has an alibi. For *both* murders."

"But no one else here has such a strong motive to kill Rivard," the high cleric argued. "And to be honest, I'm not entirely convinced he didn't have something to do with Darrin's death as well."

"Blazing Saints," Argent muttered.

Carver might have laughed if the topic wasn't so serious. "Is this because I accused you of orchestrating that attack? Or is it really just because you're threatened by me?"

Zacharias's silver brows slammed down. "I'm not threatened by you."

"By your own admission, you've been against my presence here since the beginning."

The high cleric's mouth opened, but Trevill spoke first. "Carver didn't kill Darrin. Marriset witnessed his murder."

Argent snorted. "Not to mention the fact that Carver was with me when we found them."

"He wasn't always with you," Zacharias pointed out.

"Why would I kill Darrin?" Carver demanded.

"Perhaps because of your recent attention toward his wife? Before going to Zawri, you were seen with Marriset in the garden."

Guilt soured in his gut—along with frustrated regret. "That was nothing."

"Truly?" Zacharias made a disbelieving sound in his throat. "Infidelity is a terrible sin. And, being one of the Empire's Chosen, it could be construed as treasonous. The emperor chose your bride, and if you turn to another, that is akin to rejecting the emperor's will."

"You go too far," Argent snapped, authority ringing in his voice. "This line of questioning ends now."

Zacharias's eyes flashed. "Your Highness, jealousy is a powerful motivator. If Darrin challenged Carver—"

"Argent is right," Trevill overrode him. "You've become far too focused on Carver. You can't even see another possibility."

"As if your investigations have led to anything? You haven't found Cora's killer, and it's been *weeks*."

Trevill glowered. "Things would go a lot more smoothly if you didn't keep throwing around accusations as part of some personal agenda."

The room was charged with flared tempers.

Jayveh stood, drawing every eye. "If this conversation must continue, it can do so elsewhere. Tam needs rest."

The woman looked a little lost, still seated beside Amryn on the couch.

Trevill bowed his head. "Of course, Princess." He twisted

to the high cleric. "Please come with me."

"Why?" Zacharias asked. He looked like a petulant child.

Trevill's expression firmed. "I'm going to examine Rivard more closely, and then I'd like you to order your guards to take care of his body."

The high cleric didn't say anything to that. He just followed Trevill toward the door.

"Zacharias?" Argent called out.

The high cleric paused, then twisted back to face the prince.

Argent's face was hard. "If you come after Carver like this again, I will tell my grandfather how incompetent you really are."

The high cleric's expression revealed nothing, but his hands rolled to fists. He bowed stiffly, then followed Trevill out.

After the door closed, Jayveh's eyes went to Argent. "I'm going to stay with Tam. She shouldn't be alone tonight."

"I'll stay as well," Amryn said. She'd spoken quickly, and she didn't meet Carver's gaze.

He didn't know what to think of that. He didn't think she was afraid of him, as Zacharias claimed, or perhaps she was just afraid of their conversation that had been interrupted.

"Of course," Argent said to Jayveh. "I'll bring your things."

"Thank you." The princess looked to Carver. "You'll bring Amryn's things?"

He nodded, the motion cursory.

Carver and Argent left the room together, and it hit him for truly the first time.

Rivard was dead. A man he'd once called a friend. A man who had betrayed him and his family, and destroyed his brother. A man who had possibly been on the brink of learning that Amryn was a traitor.

He had no idea what he was supposed to be feeling right now, but when he saw servants wrapping Rivard's body, Carver only felt cold.

As he and Argent climbed the steps up to the next floor, Carver whispered, "Rivard knew his killer. They walked right up to him. There were no signs of a struggle; they struck before he realized the danger. He didn't have a chance to fight back."

Argent exhaled slowly. "This is bad, Carve."

It was.

Carver looked to his friend. "You shouldn't have threatened the high cleric like that."

Argent's expression darkened. "I'm bloody sick of him. He's fixated on you, and I'm pretty sure it's my fault."

Carver shot him a look. "What are you talking about?"

"I ruined his illusion of total authority here. I've done it more than once, and in front of an audience every time. He can't punish me, so he's coming after you."

There was merit in that conclusion, but even if that influenced the high cleric's decision to target Carver, it wasn't the main reason. "I've irritated him from the beginning," Carver said. "He even told me I wasn't a good candidate for such an important arranged marriage. Besides, he's desperate to stop these murders so he can save his reputation. The easiest solution is to pin the murders on me. Two birds, one stone."

Argent huffed. "He couldn't throw a stone and hit the side of this bloody temple."

It wasn't that funny. And considering everything that had happened tonight, it was wrong to laugh.

But Carver did.

33

AMRYN

AMRYN STOOD IN THE HALL OF SAINTS, a gallery in the museum with marble sculptures of famous saints. The statues stared at her, lining the long, empty corridor.

The message she'd found in *Zerrif's Voyage* the morning after Rivard's death was short.

Hall of Saints. Cyrin. Midday.

Her heart pounded an uneven tempo and her lungs felt too tight in her chest. She stood by the statue of Cyrin, one hand in her pocket. For once, it wasn't her mother's prayer coin she clutched with nervous fingers. Instead, it was the amulet with the black gemstone. The now-familiar hum she felt from it wasn't as comforting as usual.

She'd been waiting for this in-person meeting ever since returning from Zawri. But now that it was upon her . . .

Footsteps approached, and her tension flared. She sensed the emotional aura of the person before she saw him, and she felt a stab of surprise.

Samuel rounded the corner and strode toward her. His face was smooth, no hint of the boyish smile that normally lifted his features. Unease ribboned through him as he scanned the area carefully. Some of his tension ebbed, but not all of it. "You're alone."

"Yes."

His eyes settled on her. "You've grown close to Carver. I wasn't sure if you'd bring him."

Her stomach twisted. "Of course not. I haven't betrayed you."

Samuel glanced around them, his nerves tight. "It's dangerous for us to meet in person, but after everything that's happened, I allowed your request. However, this meeting must be brief."

She lifted her chin. "Were the attacks on Zawri made by the Rising?"

"Yes. The high cleric's outing was an unexpected opportunity to kill our most dangerous enemies. We couldn't pass it up."

She swallowed hard. "So the goal is to kill Argent and Jayveh here?"

"Yes. And Carver."

The hard edges of the amulet bit into her palm as her hand clenched around it. Her words dried in her throat as she stared at Samuel. She felt his inflexibility. His determination. It bordered on desperation, and she knew he would not be swayed by anything she had to say.

Her fragile plan of convincing the rebels that Argent and the others didn't have to die shattered.

She somehow kept her expression smooth. "What about Cora and Rivard? Did they have to die?"

His mouth tightened. "The Rising isn't responsible for their deaths. I already conveyed that to you after Cora was killed. There's someone else at work here."

His fear rippled through her, chilling her blood. "Do you know who?"

"No."

She tried a different track. "The Rising targeted everyone on that mountain—including me. Darrin was even killed. Why?"

Samuel shifted his weight. "You would never have been harmed. The rebels weren't opposed to killing those who support the empire."

"Ivan doesn't, and he was nearly killed."

"He doesn't support the empire, but he doesn't stand with us." Samuel shook his head. "We don't have time for this. We'll be missed soon, and there is much I need to say. With a murderer among us, we don't have as much time as we thought we would. We can't stay here, just waiting to be killed by someone who clearly has their own designs. Have you located the empirical seals?"

"Yes."

"Have you made copies?"

"Not yet."

"I need you to do that before the Feast of Remembrance." Amryn's stomach clenched.

The Feast of Remembrance was only five days away. The religious holiday was a celebration of the Divinities—a chance for people to remember the divine, and recommit to living better lives. Even in Ferradin, the celebration lasted hours— usually halfway into the night—and it always included food, dancing, and the wearing of masks. The masks represented what life would be like without the Divinities—no identity, no soul, no purpose. To end the festivities, the masks were all removed and a prayer of gratitude was offered. The clerics had already started decorating the giant ballroom, and Ahmi was hard at work putting the finishing touches on Amryn's dress and mask.

Whatever the Rising had planned for the Feast of Remembrance, Amryn knew it wouldn't be anything to celebrate.

"Why?" she asked, her voice a little hoarse. "Why do I need to have the seals copied by then?"

"Because during the celebration—at midnight—Argent will be assassinated, along with Jayveh and Carver."

Her heart stopped.

Samuel continued, speaking in a rush. "The emperor's entire scheme will have failed, and we will leave here together, along with a few other friends. All I need you to do is get those copies and go to the ladies' tea room a quarter before midnight. That way, you won't be anywhere near the strike when it happens. Once they're dead, I'll come for you and we'll make our escape from Esperance with the others. Don't pack anything except those seals—we have supplies for the journey stashed outside the compound. You'll be back home in Ferradin within a month, and all of this will be a memory."

The pang in her chest stole her breath, but she managed to ask, "How will you kill Argent and the others in the middle of a ballroom?"

His jaw tightened. "Leave that to me. You just need to worry about getting those seals. Do you understand?"

"Yes."

"Do you have any questions about your role?"

"No."

Samuel nodded once. He glanced around them, but no one

was near; Amryn couldn't feel anyone except Samuel.

"Don't worry," he said quietly. "This will all be over soon."

Those words rang in her ears as Samuel walked away, and they continued to echo in her mind as she left a few minutes after him.

Her pulse raced as quickly as her thoughts. But one thing was clear.

Carver. She needed to find Carver.

She started down the long corridor that would take her to the exit closest to the training field. She knew he'd gone there after lunch, and he should still be there. She could—

She froze.

She couldn't go straight to Carver. Not after that meeting with Samuel. What if someone was watching her? Watching *him*?

She needed to be cautious. She would have to wait until he came to their suite to prepare for dinner.

Then she would tell him everything.

She didn't get to talk to Carver before dinner.

He entered their suite too late; Ahmi was there, helping Amryn with her hair, which prevented them from talking. And when Carver took her arm to escort her to dinner, she couldn't risk having this conversation in the hallway.

Dinner was excruciating. Sitting beside him, desperate and terrified to talk to him. Hearing Samuel talk to Argent so easily. Feeling utterly helpless.

Carver seemed to realize something was amiss. As every-one else rose from their chairs and moved into the adjacent sitting room, he touched her arm, stilling her movements.

"What's wrong?" his voice low, his blue eyes almost wary.

She stared at him, her heart hammering. This was the moment.

There would be no going back.

"I need to talk to you," she whispered.

Carver's jaw flexed, and his gaze shuttered. "Not here." He took her hand, and if he noted the way she trembled, he didn't acknowledge it.

He made their excuses to the others, saying Amryn had a headache, then he led her from the dining room and through the quiet halls. He didn't say anything, and his emotions were muted in that way that was uniquely his.

All too soon they were in their suite, standing in the moonlight that spilled through the open balcony doors.

He released her hand and took a step back. The fierce hold on his emotions cracked when he met her gaze. She could feel his anxiety, and his suspicion wound around them, nearly choking her.

He'd felt much the same last night, standing in front of her in this very room. He'd been two words away from finishing his accusation, phrased as a question only because he wanted to hear her confirmation.

"Are you an empath?"

Her knees shook. Last night, Tam's scream had interrupted him. Saved her from throwing out denials in an effort to save her life.

Now, she was about to forfeit everything with an admission of treason.

Carver crossed his arms over his chest. "What do you want to tell me, Amryn?" His voice was low and a little rough. A dread pulsed from him.

Or perhaps that was all her own.

She met his stare, her heart thumping so hard against her ribs she didn't know how they didn't break. "I need you to listen to me."

His chin lowered slightly, his gaze firmly on her. "I'm listening."

"I'm sorry. I need you to know that, too."

His tension climbed, his fingers digging into his folded arms. "What have you done?"

Her eyes stung with moisture. "I didn't know what was going to happen. I didn't know the plan. But I *did* come here intending to help the Rising."

"I know."

She stared. "You . . . know?"

His dark eyebrows slammed together. "I've suspected for a while. I've known since Zawri."

The whole world tilted. She retreated a step, which pressed her back to one of the tall stone pillars. "You . . ."

"It was the only explanation for how you knew those men were hunting us on the mountain."

Well, not the *only* explanation . . .

Her thoughts faltered. *Saints.* He'd thought she was a rebel all this time—not an empath.

And he hadn't arrested her. It had been days since his suspicions had been confirmed, but he hadn't done anything.

Except nearly kiss her.

Her breath caught. "You've known I was a rebel this whole time?"

"Yes."

"Why didn't you . . .?"

"I didn't want it to be true." A muscle in his jaw ticked. "I need to know what you've done. What's coming."

Her mind spun, but she forced herself to focus. "They plan to assassinate Argent at the Feast of Remembrance. At midnight, during the festivities. They want to kill Jayveh, too." She swallowed. "And you."

Carver's intense expression didn't change. "Why tell me?"

It wasn't a question she'd expected. "I . . . I can't just stand back and let them do this. Argent doesn't deserve to die. I might have thought that before, but now that I know him . . . He's the only hope the empire has. And Jayveh is my friend. I won't let them kill her and her unborn child. And you . . ." Her voice fell. Trapped by the force of his gaze, she couldn't say more than a whispered, "I can't let them kill you."

Carver said nothing for a long moment. Just stared at her. Then, "Why did you join them?"

"W-why?"

"It's not a difficult question. Why did you choose to betray the empire?"

"I . . . I don't know what you want me to say."

"I want the truth." His voice was hard. Uncompromising.

The crack in her chest made her voice break. "The empire betrayed *me*. Ferradin. Every kingdom it has conquered. The empire is everything I hate."

She swore she saw him flinch, but it was so fast it may have been a trick of her watering eyes.

She slowly shook her head. "When I was told the empire would steal my life by making me come here and marry a stranger . . . Why *wouldn't* I have joined the group that promised me freedom? Freedom for Ferradin, and every other enslaved country?"

His eyes shadowed. "So you weren't forced?"

"No. I made my choice. Just as I am now choosing to betray them."

Carver twisted away from her without warning, one hand shoving into his hair as he stalked across the room.

Her heart was in her throat. "Carver—"

"I need a moment," he gritted out as he paced. "I need to think."

She clamped her mouth shut. It was difficult to read his emotions when hers were an ongoing explosion, but she tried— and they only confused her more.

Fear. Pain. Regret. Resolve. But not anger.

It was the absence of that emotion that helped rein in her need to break the strained silence.

Finally, he paused near the settee, and his eyes pinned her once more. "What was your part in the plan? What have you been doing for them?"

Her voice came out a little hoarse. "They asked me to make copies of the empirical seals, which are in the museum archives. That's all."

"When did you learn of the Rising's plan to assassinate them?"

"This afternoon." She swallowed. "I asked to meet them in person—we've been communicating through notes in a book, but after what happened on Zawri . . . I wanted to know what was happening, and I thought I might be able to persuade them away from any further violence. But then I learned their plan."

"It was an in-person meeting?" he clarified.

"Yes. With Samuel."

Surprise sparked. "Samuel is a rebel?"

She nodded.

Carver seemed to process this, then set it aside so he could ask his next question. "Is Cleric Felinus a rebel?"

"*What?*"

"Has he been working with you?"

"No. He's just a friend."

"What about King Torin and your uncle Rix? Are they aligned with the rebels?"

"They don't—they have nothing to do with this." Saints, she should have realized she'd be asked that question.

Carver's eyes narrowed. "Let me hazard a guess. King Torin is the one the rebels approached. Then he and Rix approached you."

She could only stare.

He made a sound in his throat. "You're not the first person to betray the Rising. We've known all along that the rebels had people inside Esperance. It's one of the reasons the emperor asked me to come here. To find them."

A chill skated down her spine despite the warm stone at her back. "And you found me."

He said nothing.

She swallowed hard, her stomach sinking. "What happens now?"

Carver moved around the settee, not stopping until he was right in front of her. She had to lift her chin to keep his gaze.

Her heart pounded as she waited for him to declare her fate.

His throat flexed as he swallowed. "You chose to forfeit your life by coming to tell me this. You risked everything to save Argent and Jayveh. To save me."

"Yes," she whispered.

His emotions flared, a potent mix she didn't have time to decipher, because suddenly his hands framed her face. When his thumbs skated over her cheeks, she lost the ability to focus on anything but that touch. That swell of heat and spike of desire.

His mouth descended slowly, giving her every chance to stop him.

She didn't.

His lips brushed hers once, a hesitant touch that branded her, body and soul. Her pulse stuttered, and when he moved to draw back, her fingers curled in his shirt and pulled him closer.

His mouth melded with hers, all hesitation gone as he pressed her back against the column. His lips were a fascinating combination of soft and hard. Powerful and gentle. And when he changed the angle of the kiss, deepening it, her knees weakened.

His fingers delved into her hair. His chest felt as solid against hers as the stone column at her back. His tongue touched her lips, coaxing them open, and her breath caught.

She'd never been kissed. She had no idea what to do.

Carver did.

His tongue swept against hers, and she couldn't hold back a moan as she melted against him.

Their breaths came out sharp and fast, and their hearts raced; she could feel his beating rapidly against her hand. And when one of his hands slid down the curve of her side, tugging her body until it was flush against his . . . Saints, thinking was impossible. *This kiss* was impossible.

All she could do was bask in it. Memorize every part of it. The feel of the stone column behind her, and the hard body in front of her. The sandalwood and spice scent of him, which was accentuated from the time he'd spent in the training yard earlier today. The taste of him, intoxicating and warm. The curve of his neck under her palm—because her hands had wandered without her permission. While the fingers of one hand played with the dark hair at the nape of his neck, her other hand was at his waist, grasping his shirt.

Her fingertips slipped beneath the soft cloth and brushed the bare, heated skin of his side. He groaned, and the sound shot delicious tingles all throughout her body.

His teeth grazed her lower lip as he broke the kiss, his blue eyes burning, his desire flooding her senses. She was surprised by the strength of it—the depth of it.

She stared up at him, her chest rising and falling too quickly. "What are we doing?" she barely managed to ask.

His swollen lips pressed into a firm line. "We're going to save your life."

34

CARVER

CARVER GRIPPED AMRYN'S HAND as he marched to Argent's suite. Thank all the Saints the prince was there.

"Dismiss your guards," he said.

Argent sat on the settee with an open book, which he promptly closed once he got a good look at Carver's expression. He gestured to his bodyguards, who moved into the hall without a word.

"Is Jayveh here?" Carver asked.

"No, she wanted to see Tam settled in her room." Argent pushed to his feet as the doors thumped closed, his eyes darting to their joined hands. "Do I need to get her?"

"No, we can catch her up later." Beside him, Amryn trembled. He squeezed her hand. "Amryn has something to tell you, but first she needs immunity and a full pardon from the empire."

"Done," Argent said, no deliberation or questions.

He loved his best friend.

He turned to Amryn. "Tell him everything."

She seemed a little shocked by Argent's immediate response, but she managed to find her voice.

As she laid out everything, Carver was torn between watching her and watching Argent. But since looking at Amryn while she talked only brought his attention to her tempting mouth, he quickly settled for watching Argent's reaction.

His friend's expression hardly altered as he listened, until Jayveh and their unborn child were named as targets. Then his eyes darkened.

When Amryn finished, Argent moved for her.

She tensed, but he only took her free hand in both of his. "Thank you."

Her shoulders loosened. "Of course. I couldn't stand by and let this happen."

Argent dropped her hand and looked to Carver. "What now? Do we arrest Samuel?"

Carver shook his head. "I'm not sure that's our best option. We could arrest him, but we don't know who else is involved, and there's no guarantee he'd tell us."

Argent's expression turned grim. "We could make him."

Ice filled his veins, but he fought to keep that from his expression. His friend was watching him closely.

He knew what Carver had been through in Harvari.

Carver cleared his throat. "We could torture him. But we don't know how long it would take to break him, and as soon as we arrest him the others could strike out, or bolt."

Argent frowned. "You want to turn their trap on them."

"It makes sense," Carver said. "With Amryn's knowledge of what the Rising has planned, we'll be prepared to capture them. The rebel threat in Esperance will be over, and we can ask them any questions we want about the rest of the Rising, once they're in prison."

"Wait." Amryn stared at him. "You want to let them go through with their assassination plan?"

"Obviously we'll take precautions and be on guard, but, yes. We can catch everyone involved and turn the tables on them."

Argent grunted. "It's not a bad plan."

"Of course it's a bad plan!" Amryn took a step back so she could view them both. "What about the threat to you, Argent? And Jayveh?"

"Oh, Jayveh won't be anywhere near that room," Argent said.

Carver shot him a look. "Neither will you."

The prince rolled his eyes. "Jayveh can be barricaded safely in an unspecified room due to some ailment, and the rebels will still try to kill me. But if I'm not there? I think they'll notice."

"No, they won't." Carver folded his arms across his chest. "Because I'm going to be you."

Argent frowned. "We're not exactly lookalikes."

"No. But with the feast masks on . . ."

Amryn's eyes narrowed. "You can't seriously suggest that our best plan is for you to become a walking target for a bunch of assassins?"

Considering everything, it was probably an inappropriate moment to remember how those pursed lips had tasted. He shook himself. "It makes tactical sense."

"No it doesn't," she argued. "It doesn't make *any* kind of sense."

"They *did* mention wanting to kill you, too," Argent reminded him. "While I appreciate your willingness to pretend to be me, it won't work. They would still choose to strike with only Jayveh missing, but both of us . . . Besides, if only one of their targets is in the room, they might become suspicious that their plans were leaked." He looked meaningfully at Amryn.

Carver tensed. Argent had a point. Still . . . "You're right. I can't be you, since I need to be there as myself. But there's someone the Rising would never see coming, because they don't know he exists."

Argent's confusion faded in the space of a blink. "Ford."

Carver dipped his chin. "Ford."

Their friend would agree to the plan, no matter the risk. They both knew that.

"We can take advantage of the masks, just like our enemy is trying to do," Carver said. "We can make the switch close to midnight, so no one will have a chance to see Ford isn't you. You'll be safe with Jayveh, and we'll catch the assassins." He looked to Amryn. "We're going to make fake copies of those seals, and you're going to act like nothing is wrong. If Samuel or anyone else is watching, they'll never guess the truth."

"If you're sure this is our best move, I'll support it," Argent said. "But for the record, I don't love the idea of you and Ford taking this risk. Especially because I'm assuming you don't want to inform anyone about this."

"Correct." If they told the high cleric, or alerted anyone but Argent's trusted bodyguards, they ran the risk of the rebels finding out.

Argent sighed. "Well, I guess we have a plan, then."

"I'll sneak out and tell Ford tonight," Carver said.

The prince nodded, then focused on Amryn. "Thank you again for coming forward. You have my deepest gratitude, and I will write up your official pardon tonight."

Amryn bit her lip. "I'm grateful that you're pardoning me—truly—but . . ."

"Rix and Torin," Carver said, easily guessing where her thoughts had taken her. "You want protection for them, too"

"They were only doing what they thought was right," she said. "They're not embroiled in all of this."

"I can't promise a full pardon for either of them," Argent said with a small frown. "Especially King Torin, since he holds such power. But I'll be sure they're given a fair trial, and I'll do all I can to speak for them."

Some of the tension dropped from her shoulders. "Thank you, Argent."

The prince nodded once, then glanced between them. "Confessions of treason and murderous rebels aside, I have to ask . . . Have you two bloody kissed yet?"

Amryn flushed.

Carver punched Argent's arm, but he couldn't stop his grin.

The doors opened behind them and Jayveh walked in. She blinked when she saw them all, and one eyebrow slowly lifted. "I missed something, didn't I?"

Carver climbed over the balcony railing, his body aching from climbing the walls of Esperance. It was still a couple of hours before dawn, and he hoped to get a little rest before then. His night had been eaten up with a visit to Ford; he'd needed to update his friend on everything they'd learned from Amryn, and tell him their plan to trap the rebels at the Feast of Remembrance. Before Carver could even ask if Ford would take Argent's place, his friend had offered.

After plans were discussed, Carver thanked Ford for protecting Amryn on Zawri. This led to a cheeky grin from Ford, and some very personal questions Carver had avoided by leaving the cabin. But despite how tired he was, he couldn't stop smiling the entire walk back to the temple compound.

As he slid quietly through the balcony doors and entered the dimly lit sitting room, he instantly honed in on Amryn, who was curled up on the settee, her head resting against the arm of the couch as she breathed deeply in sleep.

She'd come looking for him.

The thought warmed him, but was quickly followed by a worry that she'd needed him while he was gone.

He padded his way over to her, lowering himself onto the edge of the short table in front of the settee. No lamps were lit, but the moon gave off enough light to see by. She wore her nightgown and blue wrapper, which had been tucked around her folded legs. She looked even softer and more fragile now than she did when awake, which was a feat. His chest expanded, his protective instincts flaring even as liquid heat pooled inside him.

He set a hand on her bent knee. "Amryn?"

She stirred, her neck twisting as she lifted her head. She blinked, but the sleepiness didn't leave her pale green eyes. "You're back." Her voice was husky with the dregs of sleep.

The sound tightened something inside him, and it was a struggle to find his own voice. "Yes." His palm still rested on her knee.

He didn't move it.

Amryn yawned, and her eyes watered, making her look even more tired than before. "How is Ford?"

"He's fine." He cleared his throat, hoping to drive away the low roughness of it. "What are you doing out of bed? Is anything wrong?"

"No. I was just waiting for you."

Blazing Saints, that made his chest swell.

She pushed up into a sitting position, and only then did he let his hand drop.

He missed touching her immediately, but he held himself back as she re-settled on the couch. Her sleep braid shifted against her neck, and his fingers itched to play with the loose curls at the end.

"Did Ford think your plan was incredibly dangerous and idiotic?" she asked, sounding a little more awake now.

The corner of his mouth twitched. "No, actually. He likes it."

She huffed. "I don't know him well, but I think it's a safe bet that if Ford likes a plan, that plan may just be reckless."

He chuckled. "That's a decent bet. But he helped me refine the idea. This is our best option for catching the rebels off guard."

She sighed, her shoulders dropping as she folded her arms around her drawn-up knees. "Jayveh thinks it's too dangerous."

"And you agree."

"You *don't* think it's dangerous?"

"I think sometimes you have to take strategic risks if you want to win the battle."

Amryn bit her lower lip and the sight snared him, re-awakening the hunger from their earlier kiss.

He held himself back, just as he'd done ever since they'd left Argent's suite. The hardest moment had been when she'd told him goodnight in this very room, and he'd had to watch her disappear into the bedroom.

In this moment, it was hard to remember why he was fighting the pull to touch her. To hold her. To taste her. But he didn't want to overwhelm her.

The bravery she'd shown by coming to him . . . he was in awe of her. And so incredibly grateful, because it would have been so much harder if she hadn't. If he'd had to be the one to accuse her.

"I should let you get some sleep."

Her soft words brought him back to the present, and he straightened his spine. "You, too."

She didn't move.

Neither did he.

She studied him in the darkness. "Why did you want to save me?"

Clearly, her thoughts were far from his own.

He pulled back a little, ordering his body to cool. "I don't think I understand your question."

Amryn's cheeks pinkened in the silvery moonlight. "Why didn't you just arrest me? Why did you insist that Argent pardon me?"

"Because you told me the truth."

"That doesn't erase everything, though. I still despise the empire, and that's not going to change. I'm still . . ."

"You're still what?" he asked gently.

She glanced away. "I'm still your enemy."

"*Are* you?"

Her eyes darted back to his, and the uncertainty and confusion in those pale green eyes made his heart squeeze. "I don't want to be," she whispered. "But I can't change who I am."

"And who are you?"

She said nothing.

Carver leaned forward, his forearms resting on his spread knees. "I'll tell you what I know about you, Amryn. You're good. You're kind. You have strong morals, and you won't compromise them—no matter who asks you to do it. You are brave. You came to me, regardless of the consequences, because you didn't want people to die. You chose to give up everything in order to save people you once considered enemies, because you valued their lives more than you valued a cause. Because you clearly believe that true peace isn't gained in death, but in understanding and trust. In friendship. Amryn, you are the most incredible person I've ever known. I don't see you as my enemy. Saints, I *never* want to be your enemy. We might disagree on things, but I want us to be allies."

"You've lost so much to protect the empire," she whispered. "But I've lost virtually everything *because* of the empire. How are we supposed to compromise on that?"

"I don't know. But I'm willing to find a way." He paused, choosing his words carefully. "I know the empire isn't without fault. But I *do* know what life is like outside the empire. I've seen the wars waged by neighboring countries. The senseless death. I've buried the bodies of children, and I will never understand how men can kill such innocence, just because that child speaks a different language or believes something different. And I will give every drop of my blood to make sure that horror never touches this empire. My family. You. *That* is what I'm fighting to preserve." He met her gaze. "What do you see in the empire?"

"Death." Her voice was hollow. "A loss of independence. The loss of religions, and cultures, and languages. When the empire took Ferradin, they slaughtered Torin's family in front of him. He was only fifteen."

"I'm sorry." He could try to defend that action—try to explain that there must have been a reason. Saints, his own father had probably been the one to give that order. But that wasn't the point of his asking for her view of the empire. He didn't want to make her see things his way. He wanted to understand *her*.

She slowly shook her head. "Everything that makes our kingdoms unique and strong, the empire steals it or makes it a criminal offense. I grew up knowing that the emperor could order any death he wanted. Justify any action, no matter how heinous. Hunt anyone he wants to hunt . . . And no one can stop him." She pulled her legs more tightly to her chest. "Do you know how afraid of him I've been my whole life? He was more monster than man. And meeting him, seeing him in reality . . . it just makes everything he did more awful. He's just a man. An old man who laughs and eats and loves his grandson. And yet he has the blood of thousands on his hands." Her eyes bored into Carver's. "There are no longer wars between our kingdoms, that's true. But how many people died to create that peace? A peace that is fragile, by the emperor's own admission—that's why he ordered us to come here." She exhaled slowly. "Carver, you see the empire and you see peace. I only see death. I don't see any compromise there."

He was silent for a long time. "You think Argent can make things better?"

"I hope he can."

"Then that's where we start. That's our compromise. Because I believe in Argent, too. Can you meet me there? Can you trust me that much?"

Amryn eyed him, and his pulse pounded as he waited for her answer, because he knew it would change everything.

"Yes," she finally whispered. "I trust you."

35

AMRYN

"I TRUST YOU."

It shook Amryn to the core to realize she meant that. Somehow, she trusted General Carver Vincetti.

Saints help her.

Carver stared at her. His features were shadowed, but the moonlight caught in his blue eyes. His jaw was strong, and stubble had crept in, darkening his bronze skin. He smiled a little at her words, and his lips . . . She flushed at the memory of what those lips had felt like against hers. Soft, but hard. At once coaxing, then demanding.

She wanted to kiss him again. And that would be the most foolish mistake she could ever make. While she did trust him, that trust could only go so far. She could never allow herself to get too close to him, because if he learned the full truth about her . . .

Empaths were regarded as monsters. Inhuman. Dangerous. Vile.

He might be able to forgive her for joining the Rising. He

would *not* be able to overlook the fact that she was an empath.

"I trust you, too," Carver said.

The words stung. He couldn't really trust her—not when he didn't even know what she was.

Tears pricked her eyes. Not for the first time, she wished she didn't have any abilities. She wished she could respond to the desire inside of her—the desire thrumming inside of *him*—and climb into his lap. Kiss him again. Lose herself in him.

Saints, it would be so easy to fall in love with him.

But she couldn't. So, she stayed curled up on the couch as she said, "I might be able to get more information out of Samuel."

Carver drew back just a little. "How?"

"I could ask him to meet me again. I could ask more questions."

"I think it would be dangerous to call another meeting, especially if you have nothing to report, only to ask him more questions about their plan. He might find that suspicious. We need to continue exactly as before."

In truth, she agreed. And she was more than a little relieved that she wouldn't have to meet with Samuel alone again. However, that reminded her . . . "Samuel said that Cora and Rivard weren't killed by the Rising. He said there's someone else acting in Esperance."

Fine lines cut into Carver's brow, and she fought the impulse to reach out and smooth them away with her fingertips. "We've known there was possibly another enemy in Esperance for a while now. I guess I just hoped they'd be one and the same." At her confused look, he explained, "Ford, Argent, and I think there's an imposter among the Empire's Chosen. And I'm fairly sure this person killed Cora and Rivard—especially if the Rising is denying it." He told her about the pile of scorched bones that were found in the jungle, and he shared that, while they could personally vouch for most of the people at Esperance, they didn't personally know *everyone.*

"Did you know any of the Chosen before coming to Esperance?" Carver asked.

"No. Sorry."

He nodded once—almost as if he'd expected as much—but she did feel a pulse of disappointment. "There's no need to be sorry. I'll figure it out." He shoved a hand through his dark hair, and his exhaustion was unmistakable.

He'd been up all night, and here she was, keeping him awake. Her cheeks warmed. "I should let you sleep." She set her feet on the braided rug, but, sitting on the low table before her, he was too close—she couldn't stand without bumping into him.

He didn't move. His boots remained planted outside her bare feet, and his arms were still braced on his thighs. "I've operated on much less sleep than this."

Truth rang in his words, along with heaviness.

He was talking about Harvari. The war.

"I'm sorry," she whispered.

He lifted one shoulder in a half shrug. Then, "I'll let you go to bed." He stood, briefly invading her space before he sidled to the corner of the table. Then he extended a hand.

Her skin tingled even before her palm fit against his. At the actual contact, her entire body ignited.

He tugged her to her feet. His expression was smooth, but she could feel his reaction to their touch. It was almost as powerful as her own had been.

His thumb skated over the base of her thumb.

A shiver threaded down her spine. Desperate to fill the heavy silence, she blurted, "I don't know how you've slept on this couch for so long. The bed is much more comfortable."

His dark eyebrows raised.

Her entire face burned. Why had she blurted *that* of all things? It had sounded like an invitation! "I-I didn't mean that," she stammered. "Not like *that*, I mean. I just—the couch is uncomfortable, and—I'm sorry. I mean, I'm grateful, I just—"

A long finger touched her lips, stopping her flood of words. His wide lips twitched. "Amryn? Go to bed."

Her blush was painful. The calloused pad of his finger brushed against her lower lip as his hand fell, and his shining blue eyes were all she could see as she said quietly, "All right."

But her thoughts were far too errant, and her mouth tingled from his casual touch. It reminded her of other touches that had *not* been casual, but deliberate, scorching, and all-consuming.

It was far too late at night, and her tongue was loose in the dark. Staring at him, she whispered, "That was my first kiss."

Something in his eyes changed. Heated. His desire flared, flooding her senses.

Her blush wasn't as fierce as before, but it was still very present. Saints, was that the sort of thing she was supposed to admit? Probably not.

Self-consciousness bled in, but she tried to force that back as she said, "I just . . . I wanted to tell you. To thank you. Because it was a very nice first kiss."

His blue eyes had never looked brighter as his fingers tightened around her hand.

Her breath caught as he leaned in, but his lips only touched her forehead before he drew back.

When he spoke—though the words were the same as before—his voice was lower and rougher. "Amryn? Go to bed."

This time, she obeyed.

But even after she climbed into bed, she didn't fall asleep for a long time.

If Carver's emotions were anything to go by, he didn't, either.

36

CARVER

TOMORROW WAS THE FEAST OF Remembrance. It had been four days since Amryn had trusted him with the Rising's plan, which meant it had also been four days since Carver had kissed her. Every day that passed without another kiss killed him.

Amryn was holding back. It wasn't a hesitancy born of newness, either; she'd never been kissed before, but she'd enjoyed it. She'd even *thanked* him.

No, she seemed to be holding back from *him*. And he didn't know why.

When she'd come to him and confessed everything, he'd been so bloody relieved. And after he'd returned from visiting Ford and she'd been waiting in the sitting room for him . . . They'd spoken about important things, and she'd even said she trusted him.

He should have just kissed her again that night. *Really* kissed her, not that innocent brush of his lips against her brow.

Of course, it had only been innocent in the sense that he'd avoided her mouth. What he felt when his lips touched her skin was decidedly *not* innocent.

The couch had been *very* uncomfortable that night.

He had to keep reminding himself why he hadn't truly kissed her that night. His emotions had been too strong; that stone bridge he normally anchored himself on was nowhere to be found. Not when there was moonlight in Amryn's eyes, and her scent filled his lungs, and she was standing there in a long white nightgown, her feet bare.

Kissing her the first time had been an unstoppable impulse. Sheer relief, mixed with pure elation. But if he'd kissed her again outside that bedroom door . . . it felt like he would have been taking advantage of her vulnerability.

She was beautiful, sweet, and innocent. She'd started that evening thinking he was going to arrest her—or worse.

So he hadn't kissed her again. And, honestly, he still thought that was the right decision. But after four days of nothing between them, he was getting desperate. He wanted to hold her again. Taste her. Swallow every moan she offered while he tangled his fingers in her fiery red hair.

His entire body tightened just thinking about it.

And in his distraction, Argent disarmed him.

They were on the training field. Argent's bodyguards were on the edge of the grounds, chatting as they watched over the prince.

They were otherwise alone.

Argent made a sound in his throat. "Well, that hasn't happened in years. I never manage to disarm you."

"Sorry. I'm a bit distracted."

A twinkle sparked in his friend's eye. "This distraction wouldn't have anything to do with your wife, would it?"

Carver leveled him with a look. "You're a worse gossip than

Elowen."

"Your sister isn't a gossip," Argent said, stooping to pick up Carver's fallen practice sword. "She's just informed."

"Her words, I assume?"

"Yes, I just like them."

That sounded like Elowen. Carver grunted.

Argent offered the wooden sword to him hilt-first, and as Carver took it, the shine in his friend's eyes dimmed. "Is something wrong between you and Amryn?"

"No."

Argent cocked an eyebrow.

"Not wrong," Carver amended. "Just . . ."

"Different?"

He shrugged.

The corner of Argent's mouth lifted. "Of course things are different, Carve. She risked everything to tell you the truth. Not only that, but you finally started kissing your wife. That's bound to change things between you."

"We haven't kissed since that first time." He wouldn't have admitted that to anyone else, but talking to Argent had always been easy. And, clearly, his friend was much better at being married than Carver was—he could use his insight. "I feel like she's pulled back, or put up a wall."

"How so?"

He exhaled slowly. "We're barely alone—the high cleric's incessant schedule sees to that—but when we are, she doesn't sit as close as she used to. And she hurries off to her room as soon as we return to our suite every night. It's like she's afraid of me." Now that he'd said the words out loud, he realized just how much the thought had bothered him. He eyed Argent. "What am I supposed to do if she's afraid of me?"

His friend's face softened. "She was nervous around you in the beginning. How did you break down those walls before?"

He considered briefly. "We talked."

The prince tipped his head. "Then you do that."

"But she's avoiding me."

"If you found a way when she was a rebel and you were nothing more to her than *General Vincetti*, I'm fairly certain you can find a way now."

That was a good point.

Still, he sighed, slowly rolling his wrist so the sword in his hand spun gently. "I probably shouldn't even worry about this right now. We have other things commanding our attention."

They'd finalized their plan to take down the Rising in Esperance, but they couldn't afford to lose focus. They knew Samuel was watching them, and there were other rebels. They couldn't risk tipping their hand.

"We do have a few things going on," Argent allowed. "But I still think you can start breaking down some of those walls. You don't want them to get too thick."

It was good advice.

His voice came out low as he said, "I think I understand now."

Argent's head cocked to the side. "Understand what?"

"How you could trust Jayveh, even after her brothers tried to kill you. How you could trust her when she suddenly appeared back in your life and told you about a rebel plot."

Argent smiled faintly. "Despite your somewhat resigned tone, I'm happy for you, Carve. You deserve every happiness, and Amryn . . . Well, you're perfectly suited."

Carver didn't get a chance to respond. Movement at the

edge of the field caught his attention, and he had to force his face to remain neutral as his eyes met Samuel's.

He'd seen Samuel several times since learning the man was a rebel, and each time he'd managed to put on a pleasant smile and interact normally. This could be no different. They needed the Rising to stick to their plan, and he needed to keep Amryn safe.

Still, Samuel's smile didn't seem as effortless as it used to when he called out, "I hope I'm not interrupting. I was eager for another sparring lesson, if you have time."

Carver matched the man's smile. "Of course."

The afternoon passed as the general and the rebel sparred, and the prince of the empire watched.

No one said a word of what was to come.

AMRYN

THE FEAST OF REMEMBRANCE arrived. Amryn stood in front of the looking glass in her room and ran her hands down her dress. It was a silver sheath with black threadwork that brought curling accents to life. The sleeveless gown flared just below her hips and fell to the floor in a rippling wave. A small, slightly hidden pocket that she'd inserted herself held her mother's prayer coin and the old amulet—two things she didn't like to be without. Her long hair was twisted into an elaborate knot, with some ringlets falling to brush against her bare shoulders. The red of her hair looked all the more vivid because of the silver and black dress. She honestly didn't know how Ahmi had made something so beautiful out of the plain silver dress she'd had to work with. Her talent was incredible.

Amryn hadn't brought much jewelry to Esperance, but she had a silver chain with a single diamond—a gift from Torin and Rix for her eighteenth birthday—and that was currently resting beneath the hollow of her throat. Ahmi had brushed varying shades of purple and silver powder over her eyelids, and kohl lined her eyes, darkening the edges and making them vivid for once. A light dusting of powder had muted her freckles, and a faint blush touched her cheekbones. Her lips were scarlet, thanks to lip stain, and as Amryn peered into the looking glass in her room, she actually felt beautiful.

If only she could rein in her nerves.

The days leading up to the Feast of Remembrance had only increased her anxiety. Pretending that nothing was amiss so Samuel—or any other rebels watching—wouldn't become suspicious had taken its toll. Sadia had grabbed her just today to ask about her mask's design, and Amryn had struggled to keep the tightness out of her voice. The whole time the other girl chatted, Amryn stared at her and wondered, *Are you a rebel, too? Do you know what your husband plans to do tonight?*

Sadia's emotions were dominated by excitement for the night to come, but Amryn only sensed her emotion—she didn't know the cause. Was she excited for the festivities, or the Rising's attack?

It was driving her mad, not knowing. Everyone looked like an enemy to her.

It was probably for the best that the high cleric's schedule kept them so busy. Especially for poor Tam.

She was struggling with Rivard's death more than Amryn would have imagined. She wasn't grieving—not exactly. Instead, Tam felt sparks of anger and ripples of melancholy, though shock remained dominant. "It seems so wrong," she'd whispered once. "I was with Rivard for his final days, but not my own mother? Haven't enough of us died here? Why won't they just let us go home?"

Amryn never knew quite how to answer, but Jayveh was always quick to offer words of comfort, or some activity they could do to distract Tam.

Amryn needed distractions as well. If she had too much time to think, she began to wonder what she was supposed to be feeling now that she'd betrayed the rebels—betrayed Rix and Torin. Would they understand, or would they blame her?

Then, of course, there was Carver.

They hadn't kissed again since that first time. It wasn't from a lack of desire—for either of them. She could feel Carver's want every time he looked at her, but he was holding back, because *she* had pulled away.

Putting distance between them was necessary. She didn't know how to be vulnerable with him while also protecting her secret. She could sense his concern and confusion, but his patience had been infinite. She wondered if that would change once he didn't have the distraction of preparing for tonight.

At that thought, nerves tightened in her belly. And it was all the more alarming when she realized not all the nerves came from fear. She *wanted* Carver to kiss her again. And that was dangerous.

Knuckles rapped on her door. "Are you ready?" Carver asked through the wood.

Just hearing his deep voice made her shiver. She mentally shook herself. "Yes," she called out. She took a last look at herself, then moved to the foot of the bed to lift the mask she'd discarded there.

The door pushed open, and she twisted to face Carver. He stilled at the sight of her, his eyes tracking every inch of her. She felt his appreciation, and it made her heart pound. While he studied her, she took in the sight of him.

He wore black with subtle silver embroidery threaded in simple designs across his shoulders and chest—her opposite, and yet her perfect match. The jacket he wore fit like his empirical uniform, enhancing his broad shoulders and narrow waist. His dark hair was combed into perfectly tousled locks and his blue eyes were bright. He'd recently shaved—she could smell his spicy sandalwood soap, and his firm jaw was smooth. Carver Vincetti was the most handsome man she'd ever seen.

And he was looking at her like she was the only thing in the world worth seeing.

Her cheeks warmed. "You look nice."

"And you are stunning," he said, his voice heavier than normal.

She played with the ties on her mask, the corner of her mouth rising. "Thank you."

He crossed the short distance to her. "For you to wear a mask is criminal." He stopped in front of her, and she could feel anxiety break every other emotion. "Maybe you shouldn't come tonight."

Feeling his genuine concern for her, she smiled softly. "You're the one who's walking into a trap."

"It's a calculated risk with precautions," he argued smoothly. "But I don't like that you'll be alone—even for a moment."

"If I don't go to the feast, Samuel will be suspicious."

"You could have a headache."

She lifted one eyebrow. "Isn't that Jayveh's excuse?"

"You can both have headaches."

She shook her head. "You said I need to act like I'm still a rebel. Like nothing's wrong. I need to be exactly where I'm supposed to be tonight—at the celebration, then in the tea room a quarter before midnight. Samuel said he'd meet me after the assassinations, which means if everything goes according to plan, you and Ford will catch Samuel and whoever else tries to assassinate you before any rebels come to meet me."

"And if things *don't* go according to plan and Samuel or another rebel comes to you?"

"Then I tell them we need to use the south exit, because I overheard you tell Argent that it's the only one without an increased guard tonight," she said, reciting the plan he'd drilled into her. "The guards you stationed there will capture him, and keep me safe."

Carver's eyebrows tugged together. "I wish there was a way to have a guard on you at all times."

"There's not, though." Since Amryn was required to leave the ballroom before the strike, she couldn't deviate from Samuel's instructions in any way. She couldn't be trailed by a guard, and they couldn't even risk planting guards in the adjacent rooms, in case the rebels scouted out the meeting place beforehand.

Amryn moved to her vanity and found the small black purse with the fake wax copies of the seals. She secured it to her wrist with the attached silk ribbons, then twisted back to face him. "Are you ready to go?"

"Almost." From his back pocket, Carver pulled out a small knife and sheath. "I know this breaks some rules, but I'll feel better if you have this."

She eyed the blade hesitantly. "I'm not sure if I could actually use that."

"I guess we'll need to increase your time on the training field so you feel more confident." They'd only had a few scattered matches on the training field during their time at Esperance, and while she'd enjoyed her time with Carver, she didn't like to think of actually using any of her newly acquired skills in a fight. It had nothing to do with confidence, and everything to do with being an empath.

"I assume you'll be armed?" she asked.

"I've got a few hidden blades." Carver handed her the sheathed knife, and she had to appreciate how lightweight the blade and holster were. He nodded to her leg. "You can wear it on your calf."

She moved to the bench at the foot of her bed and set her foot there, then gathered up the hem of her skirt. Unfortunately, holding the silky material while also fumbling with the sheath didn't work well—especially with the purse hanging on her wrist.

"Here." Carver was suddenly there, and her breath caught when he took the sheath from her hands. He bent and wrapped the leather straps around her calf, securing the blade onto the outside of her leg. His fingertips ghosted over her skin, and she swayed. Her hand dropped instinctively to his nearby shoulder, to steady herself. The heat from his body bled into her palm, and muscles beneath her hand flexed as he worked.

He peeked up at her. "Is that too tight?"

Saints, he was so close. And there was something about having *him* looking up at *her* that made her stomach flutter.

Her cheeks were warm, but she managed to meet his gaze. "No, it's fine."

He dipped his chin and finished securing the sheath.

When he straightened, he cupped her elbow, which kept her balanced as she dropped her skirt and planted both feet back on the floor.

She didn't feel altogether steady, though. "Thank you."

His grip on her arm tightened briefly, then fell away. "You're welcome."

"No, really—thank you." She pursed her lips, and her heart beat a little too fast as he met her stare. "No matter what happens tonight, I'm grateful that you trusted me."

His eyes softened. "I'm glad you trusted me, too. But nothing bad is going to happen tonight."

"I know." The words were quiet, but weighted.

She felt his slight tug of hesitation before he shifted closer, his hands lifting to frame her face. "This isn't a goodbye, all right?"

Her chest tightened. "All right."

Carver leaned in, and his anticipation amplified her own. His breath teased her skin a second before his lips swept over hers, slow and gentle. His hand curved around the side of her neck, holding her close.

Her pulse pounded. She melted against him, her toes curling as he changed the angle of the kiss.

He was right, this wasn't a goodbye. It was a promise. And when he pulled back and looked at her with bright eyes, she knew it was one she would carry with her for far longer than tonight.

Saints help her, she was in love with her husband.

Amryn tugged on the edge of her mask. It covered the top half of her face, a silver and black affair with imitation diamonds. Ahmi had outdone herself, but it looked like all the maids had been busy—everyone looked elegant, and the air was festive as she and Carver stepped into the vaulted ballroom.

Clerics with musical talents played an assortment of instruments in the corner, and just the sight of a cello made Amryn's fingers ache to dance across the strings. The room itself was brightly lit and decorated with potted fronds and bright flowers from the gardens. Perfumes scented the air along with sweet pastries, diced fruit, fresh bread, and savory meats. There were tables and chairs on one end of the room, and most of the seats were taken by clerics and off-duty servants. The crowd of masked dancers was thicker than Amryn had expected, as not only the Empire's Chosen but also clerics danced. Food, wine, music, dancing—everything about the atmosphere was festive. The darker edge Amryn felt was certainly not perceived by everyone in the room; most of the people on the dance floor had no idea what was coming.

Amryn kept running the plan through her head.

A half hour before midnight, Jayveh would retire to her room with a headache; in reality, she would be escorted by her guards to the library. Argent hadn't wanted her in the ballroom at all, but she'd insisted that not putting in any sort of appearance could make the rebels nervous and disrupt all their plans for the night. Carver had agreed, and Argent had been outvoted.

Just before a quarter to midnight, Amryn would make her way to the ladies' tea room.

Ten minutes to midnight, Ford—who was waiting in a nearby room—would exchange clothes with Argent. He'd return to the ballroom as the prince, with Argent's bodyguards around him. Disguised in simple masks and nondescript clothing, Argent and his remaining guards would join Jayveh in the library.

At midnight, the rebels would strike—and Carver, Ford, and Argent's bodyguards would catch them.

"What if they use an arrow or something to shoot you from afar?" Amryn had asked.

"They won't," Carver said, utterly confident. "A bow is too large to smuggle in, and there are no good vantages in the ballroom. They'd be shooting through a crowd, and that is doomed to fail. It will be close, with a small blade—probably one they'll hide up their sleeve."

She didn't quite see how getting stabbed was any better than being shot, but at least Ford and Carver would be watching each other's backs.

"If possible, they'll try to attack as a group," Carver had continued. "Samuel will probably attack me, and his rebel friends will attack the guards. They'll be relying on the element of surprise—which they no longer have—to make a clean strike, and then to flee. Their plan won't work."

Carver made it all sound so easy, but Amryn knew countless things could go wrong. She needed to stop thinking of everything that could fail, or she'd drive herself mad.

"Dance with me."

Amryn turned to Carver, who stood at her side. His mask had also been designed by Ahmi, and it was similar to Amryn's—no doubt on purpose, so they could match. It covered the upper part of his face in black with silver accents. His strong jaw was visible, as was his mouth. His blue eyes glittered like gemstones.

Still reeling with the realization that she was in love with this man, Amryn tried to adopt a casual smile. She wasn't sure she succeeded. "You know, I think it's customary to *ask*."

The corner of his mouth twitched. "And risk the chance of you saying no?" He took her hand and tugged her onto the floor. Amryn caught sight of Jayveh and Argent, who looked magnificent dressed in matching crimson and gold. She spotted Samuel and Sadia on the other side of the dance floor, wearing blue and white.

Carver gathered Amryn into his arms, turning her gently to face him. His palm pressed against her lower back, his other hand enfolding hers. Her same hand also held up part of her skirt, and she was grateful that it was so long and wide that it easily kept her hidden blade covered.

She rested her free hand on his shoulder, her heart beating a little faster now. "I'm not a very good dancer," she warned him.

The corner of his mouth lifted. "Don't worry. I am."

He led her fluidly into the sweeping steps of the waltz, his steps capable and sure. His fingers tightened as he spun her around, and the lights, colors, and sounds blurred. He guided her through every movement, helped her sweep across the floor with an ease and grace she'd never experienced before.

She'd always avoided the large parties at the castle, and dancing had never been a lesson she needed. It put her closer to people, which put her in an overwhelmingly large crowd with far too many emotions to handle comfortably. But with Carver as her partner, she had to admit dancing wasn't so bad.

They danced for a couple of songs, until a deep voice asked, "May I steal a dance?"

Ivan stood beside them. Even with his blue and gold mask, it was obviously him. No one else had hair that blond, or eyes that icy—or a strong Sibeten accent.

Carver's grip on Amryn tightened, but she was already nodding. "Of course."

She could feel Carver's worry, as well as his edge of annoyance and a hint of possession.

She shot him a look that said, *We're supposed to act naturally.*

His look clearly said, *I don't care.*

She sent him a smile as she retreated a step. "Could you get me a glass of wine?"

Carver's eyes narrowed slightly. "Of course." His attention slid to Ivan as he told Amryn, "I'll have it ready for you after this dance."

She squeezed his hand. "Thank you." Then she took Ivan's offered hand, and he pulled her into a dance.

He was not as talented as Carver, but he still moved smoothly as he led her through the steps.

"Your leg must be feeling better," she said.

"It's healed very well, actually." He looked down at her, and their eyes locked. "The physician believes the cut wasn't as deep as I thought it was. He said I would have bled out if the damage had been that severe."

Her throat felt a little dry under his scrutiny. Saints save her from blue-eyed men who looked too closely at things. "I'm glad it wasn't as bad as it looked," she said.

"*Yenn*," he agreed, still looking at her far too intently. "It was miraculous."

Suspicion, curiosity—it floated from him, making her heart race.

"Thank you," he told her suddenly.

Her stomach hollowed. "For what?"

"For helping me. For stopping the bleeding."

"I didn't do much."

"I disagree."

"I fainted."

"I know." His head listed to the side. "You saved my life. I owe you for that, *il mishka*."

She had no idea what he'd just called her, but his tone was gentle. Almost reverent. Her cheeks warmed. "You really don't owe me anything."

He ignored that. "I will repay this debt whenever you have need—no matter what you need."

"Thank you." She wasn't sure what else to say; he was clearly determined to offer.

He dipped his chin.

The song ended, and they stepped apart. She offered him a curtsy and he bowed, a fist held against his forehead. When he straightened, his eyes drifted past her. "It would seem your husband does not like to share."

She twisted to see Carver standing on the edge of the dance floor, two wineglasses in hand and his gaze trained on them.

Saints only knew why that heated every part of her.

Ivan escorted her back to Carver, tipped his head in a silent goodbye, and left them.

Carver eyed his retreat, even as he handed Amryn her glass of wine. "What did you two talk about?"

"Nothing much. He thanked me for helping him on Zawri." She took a sip, and the intense flavor exploded on her tongue.

"He gave you the Wolf Salute."

She glanced over at Carver. "The what?"

His expression was neutral. "The Wolf Salute. It's a sign of respect between warriors. The highest, in fact. It's usually only exchanged between fellow Wolves."

She blinked. The bow had seemed oddly significant, but she hadn't expected *that*.

"Is there something that happened on that mountain you didn't mention?" Carver asked.

"No. But he's convinced I helped save his life."

"Well, according to Ford, Ivan was bleeding a lot, so you probably did." He fingered the stem of his glass, his attention shifting to the clock on the far wall.

She followed suit, noting that it was almost time for Jayveh to leave.

Fifteen minutes later, it would be her turn.

Her stomach dipped.

Movement at the corner of her eye made her turn slightly. Sadia was pulling Samuel up to them. "Carver," she said cheerfully, "I need your help settling a little debate Samuel and I have been having. In Westmont, the ports are primarily . . ."

Amryn couldn't focus on Sadia's words. Not with the forceful barrage of emotions coming from Samuel.

The crowded room had made it impossible to get a read on him before, but now that he was standing right next to her, she was able to feel his nervousness. Sweat beaded on his upper lip, but the rest of his face was covered with his mask. He felt a rising panic and dread, and she could tell it concerned Sadia, but she couldn't discern *how*.

Samuel's eyes darted to Amryn, then flashed away. His body was stiff, and she wondered how she hadn't known he was a rebel before. He wasn't a very good actor, especially under pressure.

The bells rang. It was a half-hour to midnight.

Across the room, she saw Argent place a quick kiss to Jayveh's brow, and then she and her guards swept from the room, her hand on her temple.

Five minutes later, Sadia and Carver finished their conversation, and she looped her arm through Samuel's as they drifted away to talk to Tam, who stood near the refreshment tables. Tam's dress was the same shade of red as the wine that rested beside her, and she looked beautiful. The chaos in the room made it difficult to get a good read on her emotions, but Amryn felt a peaceful sort of contentedness from her friend, and that made her own nerves settle just a little.

The minutes leapt by, and all too soon, it was Amryn's turn to leave.

She finished her wine, and Carver took her glass. "Be careful," he murmured. His tone was warm, calm, and strong. Just like he was, standing beside her.

It helped steady her pulse. "You, too."

She didn't linger. She could feel eyes on her. She wasn't sure if it was Samuel or another rebel, but the back of her neck prickled as she skirted around the people gathered between her and the door.

She spied Marriset on her way out, flirting with a guard. The guard's rapt attention told Amryn that Marriset's charms were definitely working.

She stepped out into the hall, and the cooler air raised the fine hairs on her arms. She shivered, and felt a sudden pulse of anxiety from Carver as he lost sight of her.

Her own alarm spiked when she could no longer feel him.

She didn't stop walking down the hall, though.

Her footsteps were loud in the quiet of the deserted halls, and as she neared the tea room, she felt like the shadows were watching her. It was unnerving, and she was grateful to finally reach the room and escape the shadowy halls.

The moon shining through the tea room windows gave her enough light to find her way to the nearest lamp. Once lit, she stood in the pool of light facing the room's only door.

Her heart pounded as she waited.

Samuel had said he would come to her after Argent, Carver, and Jayveh were dead. Since Carver and Ford were prepared to spring their own trap for the rebels, the only person who should walk through that door after midnight was Carver or one of Argent's bodyguards.

She fiddled with her mother's prayer coin, tucked in her pocket. The low hum of the amulet was by now familiar, but for once, it didn't help settle her nerves.

The knife strapped to her leg felt suddenly heavy, though she'd nearly forgotten it until now. She removed her mask and set it on the side table beside the lamp. The purse on her wrist swung a little, the false wax copies of the seals barely weighing it down.

It had only been a few minutes when she heard footsteps.

She felt Samuel's presence before he opened the door, and her chest tightened.

It wasn't midnight yet. He wasn't supposed to be here.

Samuel stepped into the room, his gaze easily finding her in the dim light of the lone lamp. His emotions were chaotic. Extreme.

She couldn't stop her wince—his feelings were overwhelming. "Are you all right?"

He didn't answer, just stepped farther into the room.

Her scalp tingled in warning. She took a small step back, ordering herself to focus—to play the part of a rebel. "You're earlier than I expected. Is it already done?"

Samuel peeled the mask off his face and tossed it onto the nearby settee. "I'm sorry," he whispered. His wave of guilt, sadness, and regret hit her hard.

Fear curdled in her gut. "Sorry for what? What's going on?" Her anxiety sharpened when she became aware of others gathering outside the room—too many to easily specify based off their emotions, which were a mix of all things lethal, hard, and eager.

Her lungs seized and she looked to Samuel. "What have you done?"

Pain cut across his face, and through the air. "It will all be over soon."

The door was prodded open, and a familiar voice slithered in. "Oh, I think the ending is exactly what Amryn is afraid of."

Shock stole Amryn's breath. She *knew* that voice, but it was wrong—all wrong. It was dark, edged with harsh humor and tinged with bitterness. The woman's emotions felt equally as wrong, but there was no doubting *who* she was.

The only thing Amryn didn't understand was *why*.

Tam stepped into the glow of the lamp, her dark red dress trailing behind her as she plucked the ties of her mask loose. "Amryn, you look so surprised. You really had no idea, did you?"

"Tam?" A thousand questions lived in the single word. Confusion tore through her.

Behind Tam, three men wearing Esperance guard uniforms stepped into the room, hands on their belted weapons.

Tam tossed her mask onto a chair and rolled her shoulders. "Frankly, I can't believe you didn't figure it out. Especially in light of your, shall we say, *unique talents*."

Ice dropped down Amryn's spine.

No. There was no way Tam knew she was an empath.

"You don't know how many times I've fantasized about telling Carver the truth about you these past few days," Tam went on. "He might have forgiven you for being a rebel, because he wants you. But he won't want you once he knows what you truly are."

Samuel darted a look between them. "What are you talking about?"

"Oh, nothing you need to worry about." Tam strolled forward and scooped up Amryn's discarded mask. She fitted it onto her own face, but didn't bother tying it. "I hope it was worth it, Amryn. I hope your time with Carver fulfilled every fantasy you ever had, because you won't be seeing him again. You won't be seeing anyone after tonight, actually." She threw the mask at Amryn.

She flinched as one of the ribbons whipped her cheek before the mask tumbled to the ground.

Tam's fury was blistering. "You betrayed us for *him*. For a murderer with blood-soaked hands, you sold us all out."

Amryn fought to find her voice, her cheek stinging. "I don't know what you're talking about. I didn't betray the Rising."

"Save your lies," Tam snapped. "I watched you become enamored with him, and it was absolutely disgusting. For a brief moment, I thought you'd remembered who he is—what he's capable of—during Trevill's insipid debate about the war in Harvari. And when he started flirting with Marriset . . . Saints, you saw them in the garden!" She shook her head. "After Zawri, when you told Jayveh and me that you had forgiven him . . . How could you be such an idiot? How could you forget our cause for someone like *him*? I knew I couldn't trust you after that. And your demand to meet in person felt like a trap— one that I could turn on you." She gestured to Samuel. "I sent him to meet you so you would think he was your contact. It wouldn't have mattered to me if you'd killed him, or had Carver there to kill him. And he wouldn't have told you who I was, because he knew the consequences of that."

Samuel was shaking. "Please. Let me go to Sadia. You promised she didn't have to be in the room when it happens."

Tam ignored him, her focus purely on Amryn. Her eyes were filled with a terrifying light. "I was watching you, Amryn. After your meeting with Samuel—where he said everything I prepared him to say—I saw the shifts in your behavior. I also know you and Carver went to Argent's suite after dinner that night. You told them everything. You betrayed us."

Amryn's heart pounded. "I didn't."

"Stop lying!" Tam slammed a hand on the table, rattling the lamp and making Amryn and Samuel both jump.

There was a beat of silence, then Tam sucked in a breath and straightened her spine, grasping at her anger in an effort to rein it in. "I know you told them everything, but don't worry. It was the plan I wanted them to hear."

Amryn's lungs were too tight. Fear gripped her completely. *No, no, no . . .*

Tam smiled. "I suppose I should thank you for distracting them so well. They've done exactly what I wanted them to do— divide and isolate. I knew Argent wouldn't want Jayveh in the ballroom once you warned him of the danger; it was an easy matter to have one of my spies trail her tonight to the library. I assume Argent will be joining her soon?" She didn't wait for an answer. "But that's not all you're doing, is it? Carver wouldn't let Argent take undue risks, and the masks give the perfect opportunity for the use of a double. I assume Carver is still in place as himself, but some guard has switched places with Argent." Tam shook her head. "Too bad Carver won't see his death coming."

Amryn's ears rang. She needed to get out of here. She needed to warn Carver. Argent. Jayveh.

"What about Sadia?" Samuel asked. "You promised she would be safe."

Tam rolled her eyes. "Saints, you never shut up about her." She glanced at Amryn. "Samuel's resolve also weakened as he fell in love, but at least that gave me a weakness to leverage. One threat against her, and he's willing to do anything." She snorted. "Both of you are pathetic. Your dedication to the cause wasn't strong enough. Not like mine. I guess that's why I was placed in charge of this mission. I have allowed no distractions to sway me from doing what needs to be done."

Amryn slipped a finger under the ribbon of the purse that dangled from her wrist, slowly loosening its grip. She hoped it looked like nervous fidgeting.

She just needed to distract Tam. And it seemed like keeping her talking would be the easiest way. "Did you kill Cora?" she asked.

"No," Tam said, frowning slightly. "I don't know who did that."

"You coordinated the attack on Zawri, though," Amryn said. "The one that killed Darrin."

"Yes."

"Did you kill Rivard?"

Her face softened. "Yes. I killed him."

Nausea twisted inside her. "Why?"

"He wasn't a good man, and he supported the empire—those were reasons enough. I knew I could model his murder after Cora's, and of course no one would look twice at sad, quiet Tam—the woman who found her husband's dead body. As for why I killed him when I did . . ." She shrugged. "He'd been sniffing around you. And even though at that point I knew your feelings for Carver were real, I didn't want Rivard to unveil you as a traitor. Not when it could destroy our entire goal here, and certainly not when you could still be useful to me. Besides, the high cleric obviously hates Carver, and I was fairly sure he'd accuse Carver of Rivard's murder. I thought there might be a chance that alone would remind you of what Carver is capable of. What evil he has done in the name of the empire. He—"

Tam cut off her own words, surprise flashing as Amryn ripped the loosened purse off her wrist and snatched up the lantern. She stepped back quickly, and the flame in the lantern sputtered within its glass walls.

"Let me go," Amryn said, "or I smash both of these into the wall and your empirical seal copies melt."

Tam's shock settled and she lifted an eyebrow. "Do you really think I trusted you to get those for me? I had Samuel do it yesterday." Her lips curved. "So go ahead, Amryn. Start a fire. I'd love to see Esperance burn."

Amryn stared at Tam, hardly recognizing her friend. The soft-spoken, quiet, depressed woman who was always on the edge of the room, longing for home and her mother. She knew none of that had been a lie, but Tam had used it as a mask. She'd always known to be careful around Amryn, because her emotions could betray her. And when a strange emotion had surfaced, Amryn had always thought up a reason for it. She'd never questioned Tam.

She'd been so stupid. So blind. And now, everything was falling apart.

She couldn't afford to fall apart.

She hurled the lantern at Tam, bracing for whatever pain the impact would bring her. Tam shrieked and darted away, and the lantern shattered on the rug. Oil splattered, and one small flickering flame ignited into a roar.

The guards rushed around the fire, but Amryn was already at the window. They were on the first floor. If she could just get outside—

A hand snared her wrist as soon as she freed the latch.

She screamed and prayed that someone would hear, even as she struggled to escape the man's steely grasp. Another rebel threw his arms around her from behind, pinning her arms to her side. She kicked once, but when the guard tried to snatch her ankle, she stopped.

She couldn't let him find her knife. She might be able to use it later.

The man who held her spun her back to face the room.

Samuel was beating out the flames with a lap blanket that had been thrown over a couch.

Tam's chest rose and fell quickly in the silver moonlight, her shock, pain, anger, and betrayal all twisting together as she stared at Amryn. "You would have killed me." She actually looked surprised.

"Please, Tam. You don't have to do this. You don't have to kill anyone. Argent is not the enemy—"

"Spare me your delusions," Tam ground out. "Everything is already in motion. Esperance will be the most noteworthy failure of the emperor's life. This whole place is going to be a tomb. Everyone who doesn't walk out with me is already dead. They just don't know it yet."

The malice, the sick cunning, the glee . . . it made Amryn's stomach heave. "What have you done?"

Tam's eyes glittered in the silver light that streamed through the windows. "I hope you enjoyed the wine, Amryn. I'm afraid I didn't get a chance to sample it."

Amryn's stomach dipped. "You *poisoned* us?"

"I couldn't leave anything to chance. You'll probably start feeling the effects of it soon." Tam's slow grin was chilling. "Carver will die, waiting for an assassin that will never come. And while I want to kill Jayveh with my own hands—and *oh*, do I have plans for Argent—it really doesn't matter if something stops me from personally killing them. Because regardless of what happens next . . . they're already dead. You all are."

Samuel's breath caught. "Sadia." He jerked toward the door, but one of the guards pulled out a wicked-looking knife. Samuel stilled, his empty hands clenching at his sides. He turned on Tam. "You lied," he hissed. "You said Sadia would be safe if I did everything you asked—"

"That's not exactly what I said," Tam said, lifting a finger. "I said I'd let you be together. And you will be—when you're both dead."

Samuel's devastation was crippling. "You said only a few people had to die. That's all you ever said!"

"Hmm . . ." She tapped a finger against her lips. "You know, I think you're right. I did say that. I guess I *did* lie."

"You're a monster." Samuel vibrated with hatred and fury and terror. "You're insane—the Rising wouldn't want *this*!"

Tam's eyes sharpened. "Don't you *dare* presume to tell me what the Rising would want. You're as much a traitor as Amryn is!"

"He's right," Amryn said, her lungs feeling crushed beneath the arms banded around her. "The Rising had a methodical plan. Copying the seals—"

"My plan is better," Tam cut in. "In fact, I wish I would have deviated sooner. I might have killed the emperor while he was still here. But he did have a heavy guard, and I suppose this works better in the end. I'll still get the seals, and I've taken a few other things as well. It doesn't matter that the Rising didn't ask me to kill *everyone*—they can't argue the fact that this will be a blow to the empire. Families will revolt after so many nobles and heirs are slaughtered here, and the kingdoms will fracture further apart. The Rising will be perfectly poised to destroy the empire once and for all. But enough talk." Tam swept a hand over her skirt. "It's time to end this."

Samuel lunged for her, his empty hands clawed.

A guard rushed forward before he could even touch Tam.

A knife flashed in the moonlight before it was buried in Samuel's gut.

Amryn doubled over from the pain, a shudder wracking her as Samuel fell, clutching the knife still lodged inside him.

His breaths were sharp, panicked, and filled with agony.

Tam sighed. "I suppose you'll be the first to die tonight. Don't worry. Sadia will join you soon." She looked to the man holding Amryn. "Bring her. I want her to witness the end."

38

CARVER

FORD STOOD BESIDE CARVER, SIPPING wine as he tried to look taller than he was. He wore Argent's scarlet and gold mask, and he'd re-entered the room dressed as the prince only moments before.

It was almost midnight.

Music still played. The roar of conversation and laughter rang against the high ceiling. The crowd was as lively as ever, despite the lateness of the hour.

"I don't see Samuel," Ford murmured. They were both doing their best to be seen, but not look overly approachable, as if they were attempting a short reprieve from the celebration. This would hopefully keep anyone from discovering that Ford wasn't Argent.

Carver sipped from his own wineglass as he scanned the room.

He spotted Sadia talking with the high cleric, but Samuel—who had been beside her all night—was nowhere to be found.

"What does this mean?" one of the bodyguards asked, his

voice pitched low.

"Maybe he slipped away in order to signal the other assassins," Ford said. He glanced at Carver, and within the mask, his eyes had turned grim. "Or he never planned on staying for the killing, and he's meeting Amryn early."

Carver hated everything about that. "Stay alert," he ordered quietly.

The men nodded, obviously attuned to the room—some peered at the edges of the ballroom while others kept an eye on the closer crowd.

Carver's tension built with every second that brought them closer to midnight, and the wine in his stomach soured, making him feel a little nauseous.

The music continued loudly, drums and strings and flutes colliding in a rhythm that matched his thudding pulse. The laughter in the room was sharp; a woman shrieked, and Carver jerked around only to see a female cleric throwing her head back as she laughed, her glass of wine sloshing and her cheeks splotched with color.

He saw Trevill and Ivan talking on the edge of the dance floor, and it was difficult to say who looked more annoyed.

He couldn't see Tam, but Marriset was sauntering this way.

Saints, he didn't need this right now.

She grinned at both men, a glass of wine dangling from long fingers. "Your Highness, where did Jayveh go?"

"She had a headache," Carver said, before Ford had to.

"Oh, what a shame." Marriset's eyes twinkled in the glow of a thousand candles that hung from the ceiling in elaborate chandeliers. The lamps on the walls played with the shadows on her face.

She was undeniably beautiful, but there was an unreal,

almost counterfeit quality to it. Her beauty was a facsimile of the real thing; her smile didn't touch her eyes and her smooth skin was too perfect. There wasn't a single freckle.

"I admit I've been hoping for a dance, Argent."

"I'm afraid I'm too tired," Ford said, switching his timbre in an effort to imitate Argent's voice.

She frowned—Carver wasn't sure if it was from Ford's negative response, or because she'd picked up something in his voice.

They'd never know.

A scream split the air, a continuous cry that others echoed.

It was coming from the main double doors.

Carver, Ford, and Argent's guards moved as one toward the door. When they finally broke free of the crowd, Carver stopped short.

Samuel stood weakly in the doorway, his shoulder propped against the doorframe. Sweat streaked his pale face and blood coated his hands, which clutched his bleeding middle. He was shaking, and his eyes were already glossing over in coming death. His breaths were weak and wheezing, and when he caught sight of Carver, his mouth trembled open.

"Help," he croaked. "Carver . . ."

Nothing about this made sense. The fact that Samuel—the leader of the rebels in Esperance—was standing there, bleeding out after clearly being attacked—made no sense. Unless this was a ploy?

But no. That blood was real, and so was the ice in Carver's veins.

Something was terribly wrong.

Samuel grunted and doubled over. As he started to topple, Carver lunged forward and caught him before carefully lowering the rebel onto the floor. He was wracked with spasms, and agony twisted his face as he rested his back against the doorframe.

Someone—the high cleric?—yelled for a physician, and Argent's guards formed a perimeter, ordering people back from Carver, Ford, and Samuel.

Carver's fingers dug into Samuel's shoulders as his eyes flashed over the wound. He had plunged his hands into a dying man's gut more times than he cared to remember, and he knew it never did any good. It was a slow and painful death, and nothing could save Samuel's life now.

"What happened?" Carver demanded.

Samuel's bloody hand gripped Carver's wrist. He was shaking so hard, even his teeth clicked together. Tendons stood out of his neck as he struggled to speak. "Trap," he rasped out, his voice barely carrying to Carver's ears; Ford leaned closer to hear. "Wasn't—me. Tam . . . She made me—tell Amryn— everything. Tam poisoned us. All of us. The wine. We're . . . dead."

Carver stared at him in shock, denials cutting through him. No words could come out of his sealed throat.

Tears burned in Samuel's eyes and spilled out from the corners. "Sorry. So sorry. She . . . promised. This wasn't supposed to—happen. Sadia . . ." His head listed to the side.

Carver squeezed his shoulder. "Samuel, what does Tam know? Where is she?"

"She . . . knows you switched—places. Went to—library. Took—Amryn."

Carver's ears rang. *Amryn.* She was in danger. So were Argent and Jayveh.

They'd all been manipulated. By *Tam.*

A shudder wracked Samuel and he cried out, clutching his bleeding stomach.

"Samuel!" Sadia screamed his name and shoved against the guards that held her back.

Samuel's eyes skipped to her, and his breath caught. "I'm sorry . . ."

Sadia's eyes were wide as she took in the sight of her husband, covered in blood.

Ford made a sharp gesture, and the guards let her through.

Sadia stumbled forward, tearing off her mask as she crashed to her knees before Samuel, her blue skirt billowing around her.

He stared up at her, eyes glassy, lips barely moving as he said, "I love you."

Sadia was crying. Samul was dying.

Carver stood, stumbling back one step as his mind raced. *Tam* was their real enemy, and she'd poisoned them all.

There was a low burn in his stomach, and somehow he knew. "The wine." He looked to Ford. "Tam poisoned the bloody wine."

"She must have had help in the kitchen," Ford said tightly.

This was a disaster. They'd all been poisoned, and Tam wasn't done. She had Amryn. And she was headed to the library. To Argent and Jayveh.

She could already be there.

Carver ripped the mask off his face, and Ford followed suit. They both ignored the gasps as people realized he wasn't Argent.

Carver grabbed Argent's nearest guard. "Secure the room. No one leaves." He lowered his voice. "We've all been poisoned. I think it might be the wine. Question the kitchen staff—figure it out. If there's an antidote, get it to everyone *now*. And don't let anyone eat or drink anything else."

The man's eyes were wide, but he jerked out a nod.

Carver's blood roared in his ears, and he swore the sweat on the back of his neck was from the poison coursing through his body. But he couldn't think about that right now.

He ignored the sharp whispers of the crowd, the shouted questions. He ignored Sadia's sobs as she tried to stop Samuel's bleeding, and he didn't linger to hear Samuel's fractured good-byes as he died.

There was nothing he could do right now about the poison inside of him. But there was another fight he refused to lose.

Carver looked to Ford and the rest of Argent's guards. "You're all with me," he barked. "The prince is in danger."

39

AMRYN

AMRYN'S WRISTS WERE SECURED IN front of her by one of Tam's men, and he had a firm grip on her elbow as they moved down a dimly lit corridor. They'd left Samuel to die in the tea room, and now Tam led the way to the library. With the Feast of Remembrance going on, they didn't pass any servants or guards in the halls.

They were nearly to the library when Tam said suddenly, "I expected you to ask how I know what you are."

Considering Tam had turned the tables on them, poisoned them all, and taken Amryn prisoner, the fact that she knew Amryn was an empath seemed almost inconsequential at this point.

Tam looked over her shoulder, her eyebrows lifting at Amryn's silence. "Or perhaps you've already guessed who shared your secret?"

The list of people who knew she was an empath was far too short.

Rix, who would *never* betray her.

Her father, wherever in the Scorched Plains he was. And . . . *Tiras.*

Just thinking his name made her pulse quicken. Took her back to the room where her mother died. Blood, all over her. His horrible smile. *"I made them nothing."*

Tam exhaled sharply, and the sound snapped Amryn out of her nightmarish memory. "I thought you'd be curious, but clearly I was wrong." Tam twisted back around, her footsteps quickening.

"Who told you?"

The question came out soft. Desperate. And far more tortured than Amryn had wanted it to.

Tam glanced back at her, smiling faintly. "Maybe I'll tell you before you die."

Frustration, fear, and desperation knotted inside Amryn. Her fingers itched for the comfort of the prayer coin in her pocket, and she tried to find comfort in the soothing hum that came from the amulet. Her gut clenched as she thought of her last kiss with Carver, and she just wanted to go back to the beginning of this horrible night.

The library doors were closed. There were no guards stationed outside, which was odd, since Jayveh was inside.

Tam opened the door and pushed inside. Scattered among the tables of the great study area lay the bodies of Jayveh's guards. Jayveh was a prisoner, guarded closely by five rebels. The princess's wrists were bound in front of her, but her split lip, an already-forming bruise on her cheek, and the rip in her crimson sleeve showed evidence of a fierce fight. Still, she did not look defeated. Even with blood streaking her mouth and her hair a knotted mess, she stood with shoulders thrown back and her chin held high. She looked every inch the empress she was destined to be, and the towering bookshelves behind her—cast in thick shadows because there were only a few lamps lit—made an imposing backdrop.

Jayveh's eyes narrowed on Tam. "You will die for this." Her fury was potent, blistering the air around her. She also felt betrayal and sadness, but they were muted by her sheer rage. Then her eyes darted to Amryn, and a wave of concern washed from her. "Are you all right?"

"Fine. You?"

Jayveh's jaw worked. "I'll be better once Tam's dead."

"I'm not the one dying tonight." Tam motioned for Amryn to be moved to Jayveh's side, and then she drew out a dagger. Her voice was perfectly level and chillingly cold. "Your uncle warned us you might not be fully committed to the cause, Jayveh. You fooled me for a while, though—I thought your adoration of Argent was a ruse. But it wasn't, was it? You've been working with him from the start." She shook her head. "Even if you hadn't betrayed us, I'd have to kill you. You have Argent's spawn growing inside of you, and I can't allow that thing to live."

Amryn grimaced. Tam's hatred, her lust for revenge—it was physically painful.

Or perhaps the poison was beginning its work, because there was a horrible pinching in her gut, and she could feel sweat sliding down her spine.

Jayveh's bound hands fisted in front of her stomach. "I swear to you, Tam, I'll—"

"What?" Tam cut in. "Give me riches if I leave you alone?"

"No." Jayveh's eyes darkened. "If you try to harm me or my child, I'll kill you."

Tam almost smiled. "I think I'd enjoy a fight with you. But

I'm afraid I'm far too busy. Your husband will be here any moment." She turned to two of her men, who were dressed as Esperance guards. "Stand guard at the doors. We don't want Argent seeing anything amiss until it's too late." She eyed Jayveh and Amryn. "And don't bother screaming any warnings. If you do, it will be the last sound you ever make. And why risk an earlier death when you won't even know if he's close enough to hear you?"

Amryn's throat burned with panic, but she needed to do something—even if it was only distracting Tam. "The poison you used tonight; is it the same one you used to poison our tea?"

Jayveh jerked. "Poison?"

Tam ignored the princess as she eyed Amryn. "I didn't poison that tea. Do you really think I would poison myself?"

"Yes. If you knew it wasn't lethal and it helped the cause."

"I'm actually flattered. And it's true, I'm committed to the Rising completely. But poisoning all of us didn't do any good. It might have destabilized things here in Esperance—just as Cora's murder did—but it wasn't me. Maybe Cora's murderer also poisoned the tea." She shrugged. "I guess we'll never know."

The leather cords bit into Amryn's wrists, but she tried to work them loose. She still had her knife belted on her leg. She just didn't dare reach for it yet, with the guards standing so close.

She tried to keep Tam engaged, her focus pulled away from the doors as she waited for Argent to arrive. Maybe he'd realize something was wrong—hear them talking, and hesitate. "How could you do this, Tam?" she asked. "Jayveh and I have been your friends—"

"No. You really haven't been. You both betrayed me when

you turned to your husbands instead of upholding our cause."

"So your response is to kill us?" Jayveh asked, her eyes flickering to Amryn. She felt a stirring of hope; she'd picked up on what Amryn was doing, and she thought Amryn had a plan. Jayveh attempted to do her part to keep Tam talking.

Tam cocked an eyebrow. "What else am I supposed to do with whores of the empire?"

Jayveh snorted. "Saints, you're insane."

Tam twisted the blade in her hand as she turned toward them. "*I'm* insane? You both lost sight of *everything*, but *I'm* the one who's insane?"

"You poisoned a ballroom full of people," Amryn said.

Tam didn't respond to that.

Jayveh's head tipped to the side, making her half-fallen bun look even more crooked. "I'm trying to decide if anything you told me was true. Is your mother even sick?"

Tam's face flushed. "Don't you *dare* mention her."

Amryn tensed. But Jayveh clearly had her own plan, now—upset Tam to the point of an outburst—because she kept going. "Oh, so she *is* really dying? How sad. Unless of course she's like you, then her death will be a good thing."

Tam screamed and flew at Jayveh, her fist cracking against Jayveh's nose.

The princess fell back against the guard behind her, and though Amryn felt her pain as blood spurted from her nose, she also felt a flash of triumph. "Does screaming help?" Jayveh asked.

Tam's chest heaved as she growled. "I'm going to enjoy killing you. You're—"

Something banged against the doors a second before they flew open. Argent and his guards rushed in, and Amryn caught a quick glimpse of other guards fighting Tam's rebels in the hall.

Whether Argent had heard Tam's scream, their raised voices, or didn't recognize the guards, it didn't matter. He'd known something was wrong, and he and his guards were ready. Argent had a knife in his hand, and when he saw his wife—bound and bleeding—he snapped. He ran for Jayveh, dodging blades and men as his guards converged on the rebels.

Amryn was shoved into the table beside her as her guard entered the fight. Pain blasted her hip, but it was almost lost in the torrent of other emotions that flooded the room. She gasped as she felt someone die, and her stomach lurched. She doubled over and grasped the blade strapped to her calf. Tugging it free, she cut at the bonds that tied her, trying to break them.

Argent roared, and the blade slipped in Amryn's hand and nicked her palm. Sweat streaked her brow as she looked up and saw Tam had grabbed Jayveh from behind, and she had a knife resting against the princess's abdomen.

"Stop or she dies!" Tam screamed.

Argent jerked to a stop five paces away. He strangled the knife in his hand, his anger and fear swelling. "Don't hurt her."

"Order your men to stop and drop their weapons!"

"Weapons down," Argent called out.

His guards hesitated.

The prince shot a look around the room. "Put your weapons down *now*!"

Blades clanged and rattled as they hit the stone floor, and again when Tam ordered them to kick the weapons aside.

Tam's eyes flashed to Amryn's knife, and she dropped it

as well. Thankfully, the sharp blade had made a deep tear in her bindings, and with a quick tug she was able to finish freeing her hands. She wasn't exactly free, though. She was frozen with the rest of the room as Argent turned back to Tam and tossed his own knife aside.

The prince held up both hands. "You've got me, Tam. Let the others go. Jayveh, Amryn, the guards . . . they don't need to be here. You want me."

"I want you on your knees," Tam hissed.

Argent's knees hit the floor at once, his hands still lifted, his palms out.

"Argent," Jayveh breathed, a catch in her throat.

The prince's eyes were focused on Tam, but Amryn could feel the depth of his love for Jayveh as he said, "Release her, Tam."

"This feels so good," Tam said. "Too long, you've had my people—my family—on their knees. You controlled everything. Now, I control your whole world." Her hold on the knife shifted; it cut through the material of Jayveh's dress and broke skin; a thin slice of blood appeared alongside the blade.

Jayveh sucked in a breath.

Argent's face tensed, and a muscle in his cheek jerked. "Please don't hurt her."

"I guess you're worried about your child, too, aren't you?" Tam clicked her tongue. "I really do have you, don't I? You'd slit your own throat right now if I asked you to."

"Argent, don't—" Jayveh's soft plea was broken when Tam actually pushed the knifepoint slowly into Jayveh's side.

The princess gasped, her face twisting. Fear for her child punched through everything, stealing Amryn's breath.

Argent snarled, his calm breaking. "Let her go, Tam. *Now!*"

Tam nodded for one of her guards to step forward. The moment he was close, she shoved Jayveh at him. The man caught the princess, banding his arms around her to keep her immobile.

Jayveh hissed in pain, blood dripping from her wound, but her desire to fight only sparked brighter as she saw Tam advance on her kneeling husband. She began to struggle.

Argent shifted an open hand toward Jayveh. "Stop," he ordered.

She halted, breathing through her teeth. "Argent—"

He jerked his head, and she fell silent.

The whole room was frozen. Tam stood a pace away from Argent. His bodyguards were barely breathing, and Amryn was so tense she didn't know how her spine didn't shatter.

Argent eyed Tam. "I assume you're the rebel in charge here."

Her knuckles whitened against the knife. The edge of the blade was stained with Jayveh's blood. "Yes."

"I didn't ever suspect you," he said.

"Your arrogance blinds you, just as the emperor is blinded. He thought Esperance would bring hope. Peace. But it will be his darkest hour."

"I suppose there's nothing I can say to change your mind."

Tam sneered. "No."

"Very well." Nothing outwardly changed, but Amryn tensed along with Argent. "*Now.*"

One of his guards ripped a metal star-shaped blade from his belt and hurled it. It thunked into Tam's chest and the girl flew back.

Argent shoved to his feet and tackled the man holding Jayveh, the three of them going down hard. The soldiers all leapt back into action.

Amryn was overwhelmed by the pain she felt in Tam and others, but she managed to snatch up her discarded knife. She stood just in time to see Tam pluck that metal star out of her chest and reach for her knife.

Amryn ran and pounced, slamming on top of Tam.

Tam roared and threw her weight to the side, rolling them. Amryn's temple knocked against the stone floor. Her vision blurred.

Tam's fingers dug into her piled hair and yanked. Her scalp burned and pins snapped free as Tam snatched a handful of her hair and pounded her face into the stone.

Amryn's cheekbone exploded with pain.

"Amryn!" Jayveh screamed.

Instinct had Amryn jerking aside, and she heard Tam curse even as the tip of her knife struck the ground.

The blade would have gone through the back of Amryn's neck.

She kicked out at Tam and scrambled back. Arms caught her from behind and hauled her to her feet, and Amryn struggled until she heard Jayveh hiss in her ear. "Run."

The princess's hands were no longer bound. She dragged Amryn away from Tam, who was pushing to her feet. Blood poured from the wound high in her chest and she was shaking with the force of her rage.

Amryn and Jayveh ran, bolting down one of the narrow aisles. Tam snarled and ran after them.

Amryn took the lead, grasping Jayveh's hand as they darted down another aisle. The library was a maze. If they could lose Tam, they could double back and run for help. Carver needed to be warned—not just of Tam's attack, but of the poison. They needed to figure out what had been used if they had a prayer of finding the antidote in time. Amryn didn't know if the twisting in her gut came from fear or the poison, but she knew they were running out of time.

"Jayveh!" Argent's scream chilled Amryn's blood, and the princess's hand jerked inside hers.

"Argent!" Jayveh tried to turn back, her free hand pressed to her side, which dripped blood, but Amryn tightened her hold.

"No! Jayveh, we have to—"

Argent stumbled around the corner, pale and frantic. His eyes landed on Jayveh—saw she was all right—and the wave of relief he felt nearly knocked Amryn off her feet.

"Jayveh." Love burst from Argent, intense and all-consuming.

And then Tam slid behind him.

Jayveh screamed as Tam shoved a blade into his side, all the way to the hilt.

Argent jerked and stiffened. His eyes flew wide and his nostrils flared.

"Jayveh's been poisoned," Tam hissed near his ear. "But I have a vial of the antidote in my pocket."

Argent froze—or perhaps he was rigid because Tam still gripped the knife that was buried inside him.

Jayveh took a step forward, and Tam twisted the blade slightly.

Argent groaned, and sweat dotted his forehead.

"Stay back!" Tam snapped at Jayveh. "The prince and I are talking." Her fingers flexed around the blade still buried in his side, her other hand clutching his arm as she used him as a shield. "Things haven't exactly gone according to plan. So, let's improvise. You get me out of here, and I'll give Jayveh the antidote."

Argent's body shook, and his voice was laced with pain. "Done."

Jayveh choked. "Argent, no!"

"Oh, *shut up*." Tam released his arm to fish in her pocket and she drew out a small vial with a pink-tinged liquid. She held it out on her palm. "Amryn, lose your knife, and come take it."

Amryn's fingers clenched over the hilt of her small knife, but she passed it to Jayveh and walked forward. When she stood right in front of Argent, she couldn't help but meet his gaze.

His eyes were strangely peaceful, even though she could feel his pain. "Take care of her," he whispered. "Make sure she's safe."

Amryn swallowed hard. She could only nod.

"Amryn," Tam snapped.

She took the offered vial and slowly retreated back to Jayveh's side.

"I love you," Argent said, his voice horribly calm as he stared at his wife.

Jayveh's face was streaked with blood and tears, and she gripped the knife like it was a lifeline. "Please don't do this."

Regret slashed through him. "I'm sorry," he whispered.

Tam twisted the knife again, making Argent grunt. "Follow us or try to stop us, and I'll gut him in front of you." She pulled him back down the aisle, and the last thing Amryn felt from Argent before he was forced away was a soul-deep peace.

It was buried in Jayveh's grief, rage, and helplessness. "We need help," Jayveh seethed. "Someone to stop her at the gate—she'll kill him as soon as she no longer needs him." She started moving.

"Wait!" Amryn snatched her wrist and held up the vial. "You need to drink this. The baby—"

Jayveh's eyes burned. "I—I think the baby's already gone. I was kicked, and . . ."

Amryn's stomach dropped. She could feel Jayveh's pain—her body was covered in it. But there, buried in her womb, was a gnawing, tearing pang.

The baby *was* dying. The poison had weakened the baby, and Tam's knife hadn't helped, but Amryn could feel the bruising already starting around Jayveh's stomach. The kick must have been brutal.

That baby wasn't going to survive. Even Amryn's healing abilities wouldn't be strong enough to keep that small soul in its tiny body.

Tears stung Amryn's eyes. "Jayveh—"

The princess wrapped Amryn's fingers around the vial, and her gaze was fierce. "If there's only one antidote, Argent gets it—even if I have to pour it down his throat."

40

CARVER

CARVER BYPASSED THE BODIES strewn on the floor in front of the open library doors. He darted blindly into the room, heedless of the danger. He craved it. *Needed* it.

If there was someone to fight, it meant he wasn't too late.

His gut was burning, and he was dizzy. The poison was taking its toll, but he shoved all that aside as he scanned the room.

More bodies were stretched out on the floor among the study tables, and Ford muttered a curse beside him.

He didn't see Amryn among the dead. Or Argent, or Jayveh. Or Tam.

"Spread out," Carver ordered.

None of them made it far before footsteps pounded toward them.

Every guard tensed and looked toward the hulking book-shelves.

Amryn and Jayveh—both of them bleeding and disheveled—burst out from between the shelves.

Relief slammed into him.

Amryn spotted him first. "Carver!"

He ran to her.

As soon as he reached them, Jayveh snatched his arm. "Argent," she gasped. "Tam has Argent. Did you see them?"

Panic cut him. "No, the halls were empty."

"Is there another way out of this library?" Ford demanded.

"Y-yes," a weak voice croaked.

They all turned to see a male cleric pushing up from the floor. He'd been lying in the corner, and he was pale and shaking. Blood stained his robe and he was clutching his stomach.

"Felinus!" Amryn darted toward the cleric, hurrying to kneel beside him so she could help him sit with his back to the wall.

He sucked in a brittle breath, and his eyes were cloudy. "I tried—to stop them."

Carver knelt beside Amryn. He wanted to hold her, to reassure himself that she was really all right, but there wasn't time. "Cleric, which way did they go?"

"To the back. Past the special collections . . . there's another exit."

"I know where that is." Jayveh straightened. "But we need to alert the perimeter guard. Tam has a knife in Argent's side, and she's using him as a shield."

"On it." Ford bolted out the main doors.

Carver shoved to his feet. "Amryn, Jayveh, stay here."

Jayveh didn't even bother to argue—she just started running toward the back of the library, her hand still pressed to her side. The guards fell in behind her, and Carver muttered a curse.

Amryn squeezed Felinus's shoulder. "Help will be coming soon. Just hold on."

The cleric made no response as she stood and darted after Jayveh and the others.

Carver fell into step with her, and he didn't miss her wince. "Are you all right?" he asked.

"Fine. Well," she snorted, "not really. Tam poisoned the wine."

"I know."

She shot him a surprised look. "You're rather calm about it."

"I'm good at prioritizing."

They tore past rows of darkened bookshelves, heading toward the back of the library. Amryn's breaths were heavy as she said, "I've got one dose of the antidote in my pocket. Tam offered it to Jayveh in exchange for Argent's compliance, and he didn't hesitate."

Of course he hadn't.

"Jayveh hasn't taken it?" he asked.

"No, she—" Amryn doubled over with a sharp cry.

Carver caught her as her knees gave out. His own stomach burned, but whatever she was feeling was clearly much worse. She was smaller—perhaps it made sense the poison might overtake her first.

Terror gripped him. "Amryn? Amryn!"

Distantly, he heard Jayveh scream in agony.

Tears rolled down Amryn's cheeks as she peered up at him, her body wracked with spasms. "Take the antidote—to—Jayveh."

Everything was happening too quickly. They were losing Argent, the poison was attacking, and he didn't know if anyone in the ballroom had figured out a cure.

The woman he loved was dying in his arms, and she wanted him to give away the only thing that could save her.

"Pocket," Amryn gasped. "In—my—pocket."

He searched for her pocket. It was small and hard to find, but he managed to tear out the contents.

A tarnished coin, an ugly amulet with a black stone, and a vial of liquid that was far too small.

He made a split-second decision.

"You can share it with Jayveh." He dropped the coin and amulet, which landed on the floor beside Amryn. Then he popped the cork and brought it to her lips.

She twisted her head aside. "Not—enough. Tam only kept— for herself. One dose."

She shuddered against him, and he ground his teeth as his heart fractured.

Saving Amryn was the selfish choice. And, Saints, he'd never wanted to be selfish more in his life. But Jayveh carried the heir to the empire. And while Ford might be able to rally enough guards to save Argent, the poison was going to finish what Tam had started.

His friend was probably going to die either way. And that tore something deep inside him.

Jayveh needed to live. Argent's *child* needed to live.

Carver pressed a kiss to Amryn's temple. "I'll be back," he promised. "I'll be right back, and I won't leave you again."

He laid her on the floor, and she curled into a tight ball, her breaths fast and uneven, heavy with agony.

Carver stood, and a stabbing pain ripped through his middle and seared his insides. The burn had become an inferno in one devastating wave.

He staggered and knocked into the nearest bookshelf, struggling to keep the vial upright in his hand.

"*Carver!*" The pain in Amryn's voice was even more extreme than before.

He fell to his knees, one arm banded around his middle, the other shaking with the antidote.

He'd never reach Jayveh. Not like this.

I'm sorry.

The words were for Argent, Jayveh, Ford, his family, the emperor—everyone.

He crawled back to Amryn, each movement taking all his willpower. When he reached her, it took the final dregs of his strength to tip the vial against her lips.

She swallowed the antidote, not even seeming aware of doing so, her eyes hazed with agony.

He didn't know if it would work. If it was too late. But as soon as the vial was empty, he dropped it, and it clattered and rolled across the stone floor.

He dropped next to Amryn, his gut on fire and his world going fuzzy as his vision clouded. Nausea churned. His head hit the floor, and he couldn't lift it. He reached blindly for Amryn, and when he found her fingers, he clenched her hand in his.

"Carver?" He felt her body shift beside his. "Carver!" Her free hand swept over his brow. "What did you do?" Pain still clutched her words, but it sounded different.

Or perhaps that was wishful thinking—that the antidote would work quickly, and that she would live.

Please, let her live.

"*No.* No, no, no, no, no . . ."

She pulled back, and he groaned, his head rocking as he strained to feel her hand against his face again.

Then one of her hands was on his abdomen, and Carver felt a strange tug. It reached all the way to his spine, and his back arched off the floor.

He was blind with the pain of this torturous death, his thoughts scrambled, but he felt another pull—and then another.

The stabbing pain in his stomach diminished somewhat.

His eyes snapped open.

Amryn was crouched over him, her eyes closed and her face screwed up in concentration, or agony—or both.

Her hand tightened against his stomach, and he felt another tug.

She flinched.

Another pull.

Her shoulders jerked.

His breaths came a little stronger now. His vision slowly cleared. The pain was no longer a roaring flame, but a smoldering burn.

"What's happening?" he rasped. "What are you doing?"

Amryn didn't answer, but that strange tug happened again. The hand on his abdomen trembled, and her grip on his fingers turned strangling. But a little more of the burning in his gut dimmed.

He didn't understand what was happening, but Amryn . . .

Somehow, she was taking the poison from him.

And it was killing her.

41

AMRYN

"STOP," CARVER GASPED. "AMRYN, *STOP.*"

She could barely hear him.

She didn't know if she was going to survive this. Empaths couldn't heal themselves, but he'd given her the antidote, so there was a chance they could both survive this.

Unless healing the damage inside of Carver would take too much of her energy, and by trying to heal him, she was only dooming herself.

It didn't matter. She couldn't stop. She couldn't let him die.

Jayveh, Argent, and everyone else . . . there was nothing she could do to help them. But Carver was with her. She could make sure he lived.

From the corner of her eye, she saw her mother's prayer coin, discarded by the amulet. Seeing the coin gave her a measure of peace. If her mother's religion was right, she would soon be with her again.

Carver wasn't shaking as much, his pain no longer all-consuming. But he was still weak as she fought to heal him.

He was fighting, too. He released her hand, only so he could lay it over hers, which was pressed against his ridged stomach. She didn't need to touch the actual wound in order to heal someone, but touching as close to the damaged area as possible helped her focus her efforts.

Carver tried to pry her hand away, but he was too weak. "Amryn," he cracked out, his voice breaking.

Saints, she didn't want to die. She didn't want to leave him.

She didn't stop dragging the poison out of him, and into herself. She could feel her energy draining. Her empathic gift was burning through the poison, but it was killing her.

Wanting the comfort of her mother's coin, she reached out with her free hand. Her outstretched fingertips grasped the pendant of the necklace by mistake, and the black gemstone flared, changing to a blinding crimson.

The amulet *woke up*. There was no other way to describe it. The muted hum that had always been there became a roar. Power—hot and pure—rushed up her hand and settled in her chest.

She didn't understand it, but she didn't question it.

She embraced it.

She clutched the pendant in her palm, and she *took*. From the glowing gemstone, and the poison inside Carver. She dragged the poison out of him, and the wrenching she felt in her own stomach wasn't as painful as it had been a second ago.

It wasn't only her body that felt stronger. It wasn't even just her healing ability. It was *everything*.

She could feel everyone in the library with a precision she'd never experienced before. She could perfectly read Jayveh—who was indeed dying. And that small baby inside her was almost gone. Both fought desperately to survive, but they would fail.

Unless she helped them.

She pulled their pain into her own body, and the power inside her swallowed it up.

One guard stood with her, a sentinel who'd volunteered to stay behind with his dying princess while the others continued after Tam and Argent.

Tam. Argent.

She searched for them, but her new power was overwhelming. It widened in a circle, rather than choosing a direct path. She felt Felinus, each beat of his heart heavier than the last.

She healed him, too.

A couple of guards who were slowly bleeding out in the hall . . . healed.

She didn't have to touch them. With the amulet, she only had to *feel* them.

Her circle of awareness reached the ballroom, and she shuddered at the pain. Even with the buffering strength of the necklace, a hundred people were all dying from the poison inside them. And Samuel, who was on his last breaths. He'd only held on because Sadia was with him, and she was desperate for him to stay. He didn't want to hurt her.

"Amryn?" Carver's voice was pinched, and suddenly *he* was holding *her* hand.

She was so focused on everyone in the ballroom, she could barely see Carver. He'd risen to his knees, and he clung to her.

The amulet inside her fist pulsed.

"Amryn!" Carver's fingers dug into her upper arms as he shook her.

Her fingers loosened.

The power inside her *screamed*.

The pulse of the gem had a voice now, and it threaded through her mind.

More. More. More.

"Amryn." His hands were on her face, his thumbs skating over her cheeks. "Amryn, look at me. You need to stop. Whatever you're doing—you need to stop."

She couldn't stop. *Why* would she stop? She was *power*. She was *unstoppable*.

The poison from a hundred people rushed into her body, and the power burned it easily.

In the back of her mind, a thought niggled. She could feel everyone—but not *everyone*. Who was missing?

Argent. Tam.

That was right. She'd been searching for them. She refocused.

While the healing in the ballroom continued, she widened her circle of awareness.

Yes. Yes. Yes. That pulsing voice said. *More. More. More.*

Beyond the temple, beyond the yard, an essence she knew at first brush.

Tam.

Her men were with her, but Argent . . .

She couldn't feel him.

Argent was . . . gone.

Anguish crushed her—but only a small part of her, and she was so big now. The power was a flame inside her, growing brighter and brighter.

The smallest part of her was aware of her body quaking. Weakening.

Her body wasn't meant to hold this much. Stretch this far.

The power was killing her. She was dying, and she couldn't even scream. She felt locked in her own head. Her own emotions were . . . *irrelevant.*

Calloused fingers on her cheeks. A forehead pressed against

hers. A breaking voice, deep and rough and beautiful. "Come on, sweetheart, I need you to stop. *Please*, Amryn. Stop."

More. More. More.

NO.

That voice was hers, and she began to pull back.

No! The power inside her cried. *More!*

She ignored the pull of the power. Tried to shrink back inside herself. To *be* only herself.

The power churned inside her, fighting against her. Wanting to *be her*, even if it killed her.

She didn't know where to send the power, but it had to go somewhere.

The amulet vibrated in her hand.

She shoved the power there, and it rushed out of her.

She crumpled into Carver's arms.

"*Amryn!*"

She couldn't speak. Her vision blackened, and her heart stuttered in her chest. She dropped the necklace and it hit the floor, the blood-red stone shining brighter than ever.

As her consciousness fled, Amryn heard that voice in her head that wasn't her own. It said only one word.

AWAKE.

The first thing Amryn became aware of was the scent of spiced sandalwood. It was followed closely by the realization that her head was lying on something hard, and one of her hands was moving in a steady rhythm of rise and fall, rise and fall. And she was warm. *Too* warm. A blanket was tucked around her, and a strong arm lay over her.

Her eyes cracked open.

She was in a dimly lit room—*her* room. A lamp glowed on the nightstand, barely illuminating the body beside her.

Carver.

He was on his back, and her head was tucked on his shoulder, one hand on his stomach. He held her with one arm, the other thrown up above his head. He was asleep, and he looked far too pale. Though he held her, he was angled toward the door and any potential threat that might burst into the room.

Even in sleep, he was protective.

Beneath her palm she could feel the rippled muscles of his abdomen, lifting and sinking with each breath.

He was alive.

And so was she.

She curled into him and drifted back to sleep.

This time, oblivion was restful.

Fingers brushed her cheek, and Amryn stirred.

"Are you finally going to open your eyes so I know you're all right?" Carver's throat sounded dry, making his voice rougher than normal.

She instinctively read his emotions.

He had a pretty good hold on them, as he often did, but she detected threads of worry, confusion, and relief.

Slowly, she pried her eyes open.

Carver was lying next to her on his side, propped up with an elbow so he could see her. Her scalp tingled pleasantly, and she realized his fingers were playing gently with her loose curls that swept over the pillow.

"There you are," he whispered, searching her eyes. "Saints, you terrified me."

She blinked up at him. Sunlight streamed around the edges of the curtains, telling her it was morning. She shifted slightly, and realized she was in a nightgown—something she hadn't noticed the first time she woke up. She assumed Ahmi must have changed her last night—

She stiffened.

Last night.

Her heart tripped as it all came flooding back.

The ball.

Samuel.

Tam.

Argent.

The poison.

The healing.

The amulet.

That voice.

She shuddered.

"Easy," Carver murmured. "You're safe."

She pushed up into a seated position. He followed her, shifting so one shoulder was braced against the large wooden headboard.

A furrow dipped between his dark brows as he studied her face. "Are you all right?"

"I . . ." She pinched her eyes closed. "I think so."

Though there was no way she should be.

Unless the poison had made her hallucinate? Perhaps the necklace, the voice, the flood of power—had it all been in her head?

She opened her eyes, easily meeting his gaze. "What happened?"

"To be honest, I was hoping you could tell me." Carver reached for a pitcher of water and a glass on the nightstand. He poured a cup and passed it over.

She took it and eagerly swallowed the tepid water. The action made her aware of the swollen, bruised state of her cheek, from where Tam had slammed her face against the floor. The pain was dulled, which made her think she'd been given some form of medicine. Clearly, however great the power she'd wielded, she still hadn't been able to heal herself. Which meant the antidote Carver had given her had saved her life.

Carver set aside the pitcher and re-settled against the headboard, his focus on her. "What do you remember?"

More. More. More.

She had been able to feel everyone in Esperance. And that burning poison . . . The horrible red-glowing gem.

AWAKE.

Her fingers pressed harder on the glass. "We were dying. The poison . . ." Her stomach burned at the mere memory of that pain. "We survived."

Carver watched her closely. "We did. So did everyone else."

Not a hallucination.

Ice slid down her spine.

Misgiving rose inside Carver, but his tone remained careful. Calm. "You did something last night. To the poison. I could feel it leaving me, and going into you. I know how that sounds, but . . . I know what I saw. What I felt." The skin around his eyes tightened. "That necklace—the one with the red stone. It was glowing."

Her throat felt suddenly tight as his misgiving flared. "What happened to the amulet?" she asked.

He studied her with unrelenting scrutiny. "It's safe. I decided to keep it hidden until I could ask you about it. I don't know what it is, but it was unnatural. I couldn't pry it away from you. I don't think you could even hear me." Undercurrents of remembered fear and vulnerability wavered from him.

"I heard you," she whispered.

His jaw flexed. She could feel the shift of his focus—he was still concerned about the amulet, and he would demand answers—but desperation suddenly clutched him. "You weren't responding. Your eyes kept fluttering closed. You wouldn't stop shaking." His pain, his terror—it threaded the air around them. "I've seen men die more times than I want to remember, but that . . . that was the most terrifying moment of my life.

Her heart swelled. "Carver . . ."

"You saved my life," he said. "You saved all of us. I just don't know *how*."

"I don't know how, either."

"You don't know how you healed us?"

"No."

Doubt swirled. "You expect me to believe that?"

"I . . . I don't know what happened. That amulet—"

"It wasn't the amulet. Not at first. I might have been dying, but I *know* you started healing me *before* you touched that thing." His throat bobbed. "Who are you, Amryn?"

Who.

Not *what.*

The difference for him might have been inconsequential, but to her, it was everything.

She was at a crossroads. She could lie and continually dodge his suspicion, or . . .

She could tell him the truth.

Panic clamped around her chest. She knew the pain of betrayal. Her own *father* had sold her to the Order of Knights. Carver could easily do the same. Once, she would have been *certain* of it. Now . . .

Carver leaned closer, twining his fingers with hers. "You can trust me," he whispered.

Trust.

It was a choice. Jayveh had said that once.

She wanted to trust Carver. The desire to do so was so powerful, it was an ache inside her chest.

She made her choice.

She took a slow breath. "I don't understand how I healed everyone. I was only trying to heal *you*."

He stared at her. "How?"

Words she'd never uttered were slow to come. "I . . . I'm an empath."

His emotions stirred—then scrambled. "You're an empath?"

"Yes."

His shoulders tensed, but he didn't draw back. She did feel a flicker of fear, though.

"I'm not going to hurt you," she said. "I healed you, remember?"

Confusion etched his face. "But that's impossible. Empaths can't *heal* people."

"I can. So could my mother."

He shook his head slowly. "How did I not know that?"

"There are a lot of things the church has hidden about empaths."

Carver shoved a hand through his dark hair, his thoughts clearly racing. "This is . . . *impossible*. I can't . . ."

She set a hand on his bent knee. "I know this is a lot to

process. And I'll answer your questions, but I need to know if you told anyone about what I did."

"No." There was a hint of humor in the word, though it felt desperate. "Who would believe me? Everyone thinks we just got lucky. That the poison was too diluted to kill us."

Despite her best efforts, she trembled a little as she asked, "Are you going to report me to the high cleric?"

Carver's eyes slid to her, and his emotions narrowed into one determined wall. "No."

She was frozen, unable to find her voice.

Carver misread her silence. "I'm not going to betray you." His gaze narrowed and he braced his shoulders, his expression resolved. "Go ahead—delve into my mind and see for yourself."

Despite everything, her mouth twitched. "Empaths aren't mind-readers. I can't read your thoughts or know your intentions. I only feel your present emotions."

Slowly, his body loosened. "All right. What do you feel from me, then?"

He relaxed his tight hold on his emotions, and without those defenses, she felt everything fully. Desperation. Sincerity. A little uncertainty and apprehension. Burning curiosity. Gratitude. A quiet grief, but that was muted—it had nothing to do with this moment.

Protectiveness. Loyalty. Affection. Friendship. Trust.

Love.

The sheer intensity of that single emotion stole her breath, and tears filled her eyes.

Carver cursed. "What is it? What's wrong?"

Her throat was too tight for words, so she threw her arms around him and buried her face in the curve of his neck.

His arms banded around her, confusion and concern billowing.

"Thank you," she managed to whisper.

His grip on her only tightened.

42

CARVER

"IS JAYVEH ALL RIGHT?" AMRYN ASKED.

Carver had a thousand questions for his wife, but in truth, he wasn't even sure where to start. So he would answer hers. "Physically, she's fine. You healed her. The physician is worried about the baby, though. He said there's no way the baby should have survived that poison."

"I felt the baby."

Such a simple statement, but it boggled his mind. "You did?"

Amryn nodded. "The baby *was* dying, whether from the poison or a blow Jayveh took when she was fighting Tam, but the healing touched him."

"Him?"

"I'm not sure, but I think so. The baby's essence feels male."

It was unreal. Incredible.

"I should go see her," Amryn whispered.

"She's resting with a sedative. She was . . ." *Inconsolable.*

Carver's own emotions were raw. Jayveh had told him what

had happened in the library. That Tam had stabbed Argent. Tam had taken him, but she'd only used the prince so she could get out of Esperance. Beyond that, he would have served no further purpose for her. She would have killed him then—if he hadn't already bled out.

Staying numb, skirting denial . . . it was the only way Carver was staying sane. Until they found a body, Carver couldn't believe that Argent, the heir to the empire—his best friend—was dead.

"I didn't feel him," Amryn whispered. "When I was reaching out, I . . . I felt Tam. But I didn't feel Argent." Pain bloomed in her eyes, and the thin hope he'd been clinging to snapped.

The knot in his stomach pulled taut. "I can't believe he's gone."

Amryn's hand settled on his knee. Tears welled in her eyes. "I'm so sorry, Carver."

"Ford is still out looking for him," he whispered. "Tam and the other rebels have disappeared, but we're still looking. Ford hasn't found any sign of Argent yet—not even a body." Of course, if an animal had gotten to him first . . .

He felt sick.

"You want to be out there. You want to help find him. And Tam."

He eyed her. Saints, she actually *knew* how he felt, didn't she? "Yes," he answered her. "But I couldn't leave you. Not until I knew you were going to wake up."

"You should go now," Amryn said.

"Ford is supposed to report in at noon. I'll join him then." There was a short silence, then he said, "Jayveh is convinced Argent is still alive. That he survived the poison like us, and that Tam would have treated his wound. That she abducted him." Saints, he wanted to believe that, too.

Pain bloomed in Amryn's eyes. "I can't believe he's gone, either. But I didn't feel him, Carver. He wasn't with Tam—he wasn't anywhere."

His lungs felt caught in a vice. "We can't tell Jayveh what you felt."

She shook her head. "I wish we could, but . . ."

It would betray Amryn's secret.

Carver glanced away. "I know you didn't feel him. I know what that means, but . . . I think I need to see his body, too. I just can't believe he's gone. Not fully."

"I know." Amryn squeezed his knee. "I'm so sorry, Carver."

He inhaled slowly, then exhaled even slower. "Tell me everything that happened after you left the ballroom."

She did.

Everything she said only made Carver more furious with Tam. He touched Amryn's bruised cheek, silently swearing that if he ever got his hands on Tam, he would strangle her.

When Amryn finished, there was a brief silence, and Carver knew he wasn't the only one sorting through everything that had happened last night.

"When I was healing everyone," Amryn said, "I felt Samuel with Sadia."

"He made it to the ballroom and warned me about Tam's trap."

"He was being forced to help Tam. He joined the Rising before coming here, but . . . he fell in love with Sadia. He didn't want to help the rebels anymore, but Tam forced him by threatening Sadia's life."

Carver felt a flash of sympathy for Samuel. "Jayveh hasn't ordered his arrest yet, but he's under guard."

Amryn's lips pursed. "I'll speak for him."

"You don't need to do that." Samuel knew Amryn had been a rebel, too—not that he could do anything to hurt her. Not when she'd been pardoned by Argent.

Determination lived in her gaze. "I'll still speak for him. He was filled with regret, Carver. He was trapped. He didn't have anywhere to turn—not without risking Sadia's life."

There was a soft knock.

Amryn's eyes flicked to the closed door. "It's Ahmi," she whispered.

He blinked. What would that be like? To know a person was there without even seeing them, only *feeling* them?

"I have so many questions," he muttered, even as he pushed off the bed and strode to the door.

Ahmi's relief was obvious when she saw Amryn had finally woken. The maid had a tray of fruit and some light foods, which Amryn started eating right away. Then Ahmi turned to him. "The high cleric and Chancellor Trevill are requesting your presence in the high cleric's office. I can sit with Amryn until you return."

He hesitated; even though Amryn was awake now, he didn't want to leave her.

Amryn looked up, her expression softening. "I'll be fine. Go."

The bruises that covered her cheek made her seem all the more vulnerable, but she was safe. Even if Carver still felt the panic and fear of almost losing her . . . she was alive. He hadn't lost her.

He crossed back to the bed and leaned down, dropping a soft kiss to her brow. "We're not done discussing things," he said, his voice low.

He still had far too many questions; about her, about the strange amulet that was shoved in his pocket . . .

There was so much he didn't understand.

He'd grown up on horrific tales of empaths who could read minds and kill with a thought. He knew they were exaggerations—they had to be—but he'd never given much thought to empaths as an adult. By then, the church had killed most of them. Empaths were merely ghosts that haunted the empire's past, and the nightmares of children.

Amryn didn't fit any of those stories. She wasn't evil, or a killer. Nothing like the empaths who'd killed Argent's parents and grandmother.

Carver had a lot to process, but as he left her, he knew there was one thing he didn't have to doubt: Amryn was good. She was a *healer*. And he was going to protect her.

Trevill and Zacharias were locked in a heated debate when Carver walked into the high cleric's office.

Zacharias stood behind his wide desk, and a vein bulged in his forehead.

Trevill was planted on the other side of the desk, his arms crossed and face locked into a fierce expression.

The chancellor cut a look to Carver as he closed the door. "General Vincetti. I'm glad you're here." The man had deliberately used his title, making it clear he wanted Carver's help in circumventing the high cleric's authority—something Argent had done whenever the situation warranted.

Argent's absence was a blade in Carver's gut, but it cut deeper right now.

Zacharias straightened. "Yes," he said quickly. "I'm afraid the chancellor isn't interested in listening to reason, so I could use your voice."

Trevill's eyes narrowed. "The high cleric seems to be under the misapprehension that there's any debate at all."

Carver's temples pounded. "What seems to be the debate?" he asked.

The high cleric jabbed a finger at Trevill. "He thinks Esperance is done. That we should send everyone home and deliver our report to the emperor."

"Esperance *is* done," Trevill bit out. "Argent is gone—probably killed by Tam—and half of the Chosen are dead. There's no point in staying here any longer. We failed. We must accept that."

"We don't know that Argent is dead," the high cleric argued. "We haven't found his body."

"He was stabbed by Tam," Trevill said. "Jayveh witnessed it."

"The princess is *also* certain he's still alive."

"She's a grieving widow," the chancellor snapped. "Of course she thinks he's still alive!" He twisted to Carver. "You can't think it's the right decision to remain. We can continue the search for Argent's body, but we need to report to the capital. We need to tell the emperor what has happened, and we need to hunt down the Rising and destroy them."

"We'll break the seal and send a message to the emperor," Zacharias said. "But we can't just send everyone home. We can't be done."

Carver squeezed the bridge of his nose and pinched his eyes shut.

Argent was dead. So was Cora, Darrin, and Rivard. Tam was

gone. Only Marriset, Sadia, Samuel, Ivan, Jayveh, Amryn, and Carver remained.

Just over half of them.

The emperor's peace at Esperance *had* failed. The Rising had won this fight.

But they wouldn't win the war. There would be other battles, and Carver was determined to win.

He opened his eyes and let his hand fall. "Esperance is done. We can't send everyone home yet, though. The emperor will have questions for everyone. We should all go to the capital."

"The emperor put me in charge," Zacharias said, that vein bulging once more. "And I say—"

"No."

They all twisted as Jayveh pushed into the room. Bodyguards were huddled behind her, but they let her lead. Her hair hung loose around her shoulders in a tangled mess, and exhaustion was in every line on her face.

"Princess," the high cleric said, softening his tone at once. "You should be resting. We're taking care of everything—"

"You're not in charge," Jayveh interrupted him.

His shoulders drew back. "Excuse me, but I—"

"I am the future empress of Craethen," she interrupted curtly. "I supersede the authority that was granted to you by the emperor. You are going to listen to me now." Her chin lifted, and she scanned all three of them. "Argent is alive. I know it."

Trevill sighed. "Princess—"

"I would know if he was dead." Jayveh focused on Carver. "Has Ford found his body?"

"No."

Jayveh nodded once and turned back to the older men in

the room. "He's alive."

"Forgive me, but that's wishful thinking," Trevill said, his tone carefully metered. "Tam already tried to kill him once, on that mountain. And in the library, she stabbed him right in front of you."

Jayveh flinched. "I know. But he would be an invaluable bargaining piece for the Rising. Tam would have reasons to keep him alive."

Trevill sighed. "You've clearly given this a lot of thought," he began.

He got no further, because Jayveh simply said, "I have." Then she looked to Carver. "Has Amryn awakened?" When he nodded, her eyes sparked with relief. "Good. She might be able to tell us more about Tam's plans."

"How would *she* know Tam's plans?" the high cleric asked.

Trevill's eyes rounded as the only real answer manifested. "She was a rebel," he breathed. "Like Samuel obviously was."

"*What?*" Zacharias hissed. "They should *both* be arrested at once!"

Carver's back straightened. "Amryn came forward to warn us about the Rising's plan. Argent gave her a full pardon."

"One I have in writing," Jayveh added. She glanced to Carver. "He was going to give it to you, he just hadn't had the chance yet."

The high cleric's eyes narrowed. "You both have a lot of explaining to do. *Now.*"

"We'll tell you everything," Jayveh promised. "But first, I need to make things clear. The search for Argent will continue. I want men crawling over this jungle, searching for him and Tam. Meanwhile, the rest of us are going to the capital to make our report to the emperor, and determine our next steps.

We leave tomorrow."

Trevill nodded once. "A good plan."

The high cleric gritted his teeth. "I'm not sure that—"

"Nothing more can be accomplished here," Jayveh said firmly. "Argent needs our help. So, we're going to the capital, and we will wage war against the Rising. We will find him, and we will save him."

The high cleric bristled, but there was little he could do in the face of Jayveh asserting her authority, and he knew it. Esperance was his domain, but it was in shambles. "Very well," he said stiffly. "But my report will clearly outline how Trevill failed as well."

The chancellor frowned. "What do you mean?"

"If you'd been able to lead a successful investigation into the deaths of Cora and Rivard, you would have found Tam before all of this happened." Zacharias straightened, speaking to the room at large as he said, "I won't carry all the blame for this."

Trevill scowled.

"Blame should be the least of your worries," Carver said, disgusted by the miserable excuse for a man in front of him. He'd never respected the high cleric, but now . . . "People died here," he continued. "You would think you would be more concerned about the loss of their lives."

The high cleric's mouth thinned. "Of course I care. But clearly it's not my fault all of you were not properly vetted. Someone like Tam should never have been allowed here."

Carver felt a stab of guilt at that. *He* should have done a better job. He should have realized something was wrong with her. Saints, she'd more than likely been the imposter. If he could have found her sooner, he could have prevented all of this.

"We can sit here debating the past, or we can actually *do* something," Jayveh said, folding her arms over her chest. She looked every inch the empirical princess as she asked, "What preparations are needed so we can leave at dawn?"

43

AMRYN

"SOMEONE IS HERE TO SEE YOU," Ahmi said, walking back into the bedroom after responding to the rap on the suite's outer door.

"Jayveh?" Amryn asked.

Ahmi shook her head. "Cleric Felinus. He said he works in the library."

Amryn was surprised by his visit, but it was actually quite timely. She had questions, and he might be able to answer some of them.

Ahmi helped her change quickly into a simple blue dress and they walked out together to find Felinus standing near the balcony. His wariness and tension as he met her gaze lifted the hairs on the back of her neck.

"Can I fetch you both some tea?" Ahmi offered.

"That would be lovely," Felinus said.

Ahmi left before Amryn could decide if she should protest. She didn't really want to be alone with Felinus when his emotions were so odd. He'd never felt like this before. He was anxious. Almost . . . afraid.

She felt an echo of that fear in her own chest.

She knew two guards were posted in the hall, but Amryn felt alone as she faced the bald cleric in the otherwise empty sitting room.

"I'm relieved you're all right," Felinus said.

She sensed truth in that, but his relief was horribly over-shadowed by his fear.

"I'm glad you're all right, too," she said. "I didn't expect you to be walking around yet."

He touched his stomach. "Yes, I . . . I must not have been as wounded as I thought. Shock does strange things to a body." His eyes lifted until they locked on hers. "At least, that's what I told the high cleric when he visited me last night."

A chill swept through her. "I don't understand."

Felinus's resolve sharpened as he stared at her. "Where is the stone, Amryn? I know you have it."

Her pulse tripped. "What?"

The skin around his eyes tightened. "The bloodstone. You have one. Where is it?"

The amulet.

Her suspicion was confirmed, then. The powerful gem in the necklace was indeed a bloodstone.

She just didn't know how Felinus knew she had it.

"The healing," the cleric said. "That kind of power . . . it wouldn't have been possible without a bloodstone. You used it last night, so I know you have it. Where is it?"

She took a step back. "I don't know what you're talking about, but I want you to leave."

"No." Felinus's jaw tensed. "And you won't call for the guards, because you won't want them to hear this. I know what you are, Amryn. I've known since the first moment I saw you."

Her stomach dropped. "I don't—"

"You're an empath. I can sense your ability, even without my bone ring."

Everything in her went cold.

Bone ring.

Only knights were given bone rings.

Felinus was a knight—an empath killer.

Her heart clenched.

"I used to be a knight," Felinus said, his voice quiet, though his hard gaze didn't waver. "I was very good at my job. Even after I retired and turned in my ring, I could still sense empaths. I think the ring changed me—gave me a gift. Or perhaps I always had a gift, and I just didn't know how to use it until the knights taught me how to harness it. But I know the truth. I know what you did last night."

Sweat broke out over her body, and a tremor started in her legs. She locked her knees, hoping to hide any sign of dread. "I don't know what you're talking about—"

Felinus shot forward and grabbed her arms.

A cry pinched in her throat, but she silenced it—she didn't want the guards coming in. They couldn't know. They'd kill her.

Felinus was going to kill her.

She tried to jerk away, but his grip was like iron.

"Amryn, listen to me," he hissed. "I'm not going to hurt you. I'm not going to turn you in. I left the Order because I learned the truth—that not all empaths are monsters. The things I did . . . *I* was the monster."

Regret, self-hatred, horror, pain—all of it slammed into her, stealing her breath.

The old cleric's eyes were tortured. "Divinities know, I've tried to cleanse my sins. I don't know if I'll ever be free of it all, but I left them. I left that life. I became a cleric. And never *once* have I considered turning you over to them. You have to know that."

She was terrified, but she didn't sense any malice from him. She never had.

Felinus watched her, his face lined. "I do not fear you," he whispered, still grasping her arms. "But I fear what you did last night. That power is not meant to be. The bloodstones are an abomination."

That voice.

AWAKE.

It was wrong. *Evil.* Amryn had felt that.

Fear—cold and deep—bled through her. "What *is* it?"

"What I told you about the bloodstones before was true," Felinus said. "I don't fully understand them—I'm not sure anyone does. They were created by empaths through unspeakable means. All I know is that stone must not fall into evil hands. We must find a way to destroy it, and you must flee."

Her pulse roared in her ears. "Why?"

"Because the high cleric knows an empath is here. Too many of us were mysteriously healed last night. He's sent for Knights. He'll want to keep everyone here in Esperance until they can finish their search—and they will find you." His grip tightened. "I can help you escape, and—"

Pain.

Searing, horrible pain made her double over.

Felinus clutched her, and her name echoed as he called it.

Snap.

A life went out.

Snap.

Another.

Amryn gasped, her mind frantic and her body shaking.

The double doors to the suite pushed open.

Felinus whirled, still holding Amryn up.

Marriset strode into the suite, a bloody knife in her hand and the two guards lying dead in the hall behind her.

Surprise flickered as she saw Felinus. "I didn't realize you had company, Amryn."

"Marriset?" Amryn gaped, fighting to straighten in Felinus's arms. "What are you doing?"

"I feel like I could ask you the same thing." Marriset spun the blade in her hand as she looked them over. "Isn't he a little old for you? And a *cleric*?"

Amryn managed to stand, though the torture of those two deaths still rang through her. Felinus dropped his hands from her as she faced Marriset.

The woman's emotions were honed with a cool edge. She didn't feel hate or fear. She didn't feel much of *anything*. Yet she'd just killed two men.

Marriset nudged the doors closed with her heel, never taking her eyes off them. "It's really too bad you're not alone. I was just going to kill you, but I guess we can have two bodies." The corner of her mouth lifted. "I wonder what Carver will think of finding you with a cleric. Maybe he'll be open to my comfort. I miss playing with him."

"Guards!" Felinus shouted. "Help!"

Marriset chuckled. "No one is close enough to hear you, old man."

Amryn and Felinus retreated as Marriset slowly advanced.

"It was you," Amryn said, her thoughts churning. "You

killed Cora."

"I did. And though the Rising took credit for Darrin's death, I'm the one who *actually* killed him. He was getting suspicious. And jealous. The attack by those rebels was the perfect excuse to kill him." Her head tilted to the side. "I didn't kill Rivard, though. I'm guessing that was Tam, and that she tried to frame me. Not that she knew it was me, of course. I fooled all of you."

Amryn lifted a staying hand. "Marriset, you don't have to—"

"I'm not Marriset."

Amryn stared at her. *Of course.* She was the imposter Carver had warned might be among them. Amryn had completely forgotten about it in the madness of last night.

"I did a good job being her, though, didn't I?" Marriset asked. "It's too bad it can't be a permanent thing. Outside this temple, someone is sure to know the real Marriset."

"You killed her," Amryn whispered in horror. "And her entire escort."

"Very good, Amryn." She sighed a little. "Someone was *bound* to notice eventually when Marriset's father didn't return to Palar, but people disappear on long journeys every day. Who knows what might have happened to poor Lord Navarre? But with Esperance being sealed off from the rest of the empire, we were fairly confident no one here would learn about his disappearance until the year was out."

"*We?*" Amryn asked, seizing on that vital word.

Marriset—or rather, the woman who had *pretended* to be Marriset—smiled. "Myself and the man who hired me."

"Who hired you?"

Her chilling smile only widened. "He's paid me a great deal not to share that information."

Amryn fought a shiver. "Who *are* you?"

"I'm whoever I'm hired to be. At the moment, I'm the person who's going to kill you and leave this haunting little message." She plucked a piece of paper out of her pocket. "*This is not over.* A little overdramatic, but I'm just doing what I was paid to do. Make a scene. Disrupt everything. Create discord among the couples. Destroy this entire venture."

"Did the Rising send you?" Felinus asked.

"No." She flicked the piece of paper onto the chair beside her. "Let's just say it was another interested party. And I've been told this is my final job. Apparently, the fear is that Carver might want to cling to Esperance and the emperor's dream, since he's such a perfect soldier. But if his wife is killed?" Marriset lifted a shoulder. "He's just enamored enough that he'll want revenge—he won't care about the peace anymore."

Amryn glanced toward the bedroom. Her knife was there—she'd found it in the bottom of a trunk while searching for the amulet. Carver must have hidden it there. If she could reach it . . .

Marriset looked between them. "Who's first? I don't have a preference."

Felinus grasped Amryn's wrist and yanked her behind him.

Marriset rushed forward.

There wasn't time to get a knife.

Amryn darted around Felinus, ready to tackle Marriset, but the door was kicked open, and Ivan ran in, blades out.

Marriset whirled, snarling as she attacked Ivan.

Blades flashed in a vicious flurry as the two fought violently. Amryn felt the pain when Ivan's arm was cut.

Marriset was an assassin.

Ivan was a Sibeten Wolf.

It was a vicious, brutal fight, but it ended the moment Ivan's blade slammed into Marriset's gut.

Amryn gasped as Marriset cried out.

Ivan's eyes blazed, his emotions just as fierce. "That's for Cora."

Marriset's knees buckled. She slumped against the wall, the hilt still sticking out of her stomach. Her breaths rattled, and the blood slowly drained from her face as she peered up at him. "You . . ."

"I figured it out." He sank to one knee in front of her, still holding one blade. "It didn't make sense that Tam killed Cora. It bothered me all night. Why would the rebels have so many different plans? Why didn't they have just *one* goal? Why be so disorganized in their attacks?" He leaned in. "Unless someone *else* killed Cora and left that note. Just as someone else poisoned the ladies' tea. *You.*"

Marriset choked. "Why would I have poisoned myself? That was Tam."

"No," Amryn said. She fought to keep her voice clear, though her lungs felt too tight due to Marriset's pain. "Tam said it wasn't her."

Marriset's brow grew lined. "Then who . . .?" Her words drifted as footsteps crashed down the hall and a crowd burst into the room.

Carver ran to Amryn, even as he took in the scene.

Jayveh was close behind him with her guards, as was the high cleric and Trevill.

Carver's hand closed around Amryn's. "Are you all right?"

She managed a short nod.

He looked to Ivan. "The guard you sent said Marriset killed Cora—and that she was going to kill Amryn next."

The Wolf didn't take his gaze off Marriset. "I went to Marriset's room to confront her. She wasn't there, but I found a collection of daggers." He demonstratively lifted the knife in his fist. "They match the one that killed Cora."

Carver still held Amryn's hand as he eyed Marriset, who was slowly bleeding out from the wound in her stomach. He looked back to Ivan. "How did you know she'd attack Amryn?"

"Samuel and Sadia's rooms are under heavy guard, and so was Jayveh's. Amryn was the most vulnerable target. As I ran here, I passed a guard—I sent him to the high cleric's office, to sound the alarm."

"Do you have a confession?" the high cleric asked Ivan.

"She confessed," Felinus said quickly. "She killed Cora and Darrin, and she was going to kill us."

"She isn't the real Marriset," Amryn added. That drew every eye to her, but she focused on Carver. "She's an imposter."

"*You.*"

The fury in that single word vibrated through Amryn, but it wasn't directed at her.

Everyone turned to look at Marriset.

Her eyes were on Trevill, who stood at the edge of their group. "You poisoned the tea," Marriset rasped. "You poisoned *me.*"

The chancellor frowned, his expression confused. But under the surface, dread, fear, and guilt spiraled. "You're mad."

"You hired me," Marriset choked, "and then you *poisoned me?*"

Trevill stiffened. "I don't know what you're talking about."

Amryn squeezed Carver's hand, her eyes hard on Trevill.

Carver's fingers tightened in response. "Chancellor, I think you have some explaining to do."

Panic flared inside Trevill. Outwardly, he huffed a hard

laugh. "You can't think anything she says is fact? She's spinning lies to confuse us—divide us." When he was greeted by silence, he singled out Jayveh. "Princess, you can't believe this? It's an insane accusation! I came to Esperance to help the peace succeed."

Jayveh looked to him, then Marriset. "Did he hire you?"

"Yes," she gasped. Her strength was fading. "I'll tell you everything, just get a physician to save me."

Jayveh gestured to one of her guards, who darted from the room. Then the princess stepped closer to Marriset. "Help is coming, but you need to keep talking. Tell me what he hired you to do."

"Turn you against each other. Inspire hate, confusion, jealousy—fear." Marriset leaned weakly against the wall, her pallor white as the snow that tipped the mountains of Ferradin. "I was told I could kill anyone except you and Argent. I started with Cora because she was an easy mark."

Ivan's fury was like ice.

Marriset's eyes rose, focusing blearily on Trevill. "He hired someone else to play Marriset's father. He hired guards as well. They helped me kill the real Marriset and her escorts—they never made it to the temple. Trevill said no one would know. That I looked enough like her, and no one here had seen her in years. But he never told me he would poison us." She coughed, the sound guttural and painful. Her voice was more of a wheeze as she said, "I guess I wasn't making enough chaos for his liking."

"This is insane," Trevill repeated tersely. "The ravings of a madwoman!"

"You never did make good progress in your investigations," the high cleric said. "You kept blaming me—my people, my clerics. But you knew who it was all along, and you deflected everything away from the killer because *you* hired her."

"There is absolutely no proof of any of this," Trevill ground out. "No proof at all!"

"He wrote the notes," Marriset whispered. "They're in his hand. The same handwriting on the letter in my room—a piece of correspondence that will prove he contacted me for my services."

Amryn felt the second Trevill made his decision to run, but he didn't make it more than a step before Jayveh's bodyguards grabbed him.

"Zacharias," the princess said, her eyes hard on Trevill. "Does this temple have a prison?"

"Yes, Your Highness." The high cleric smiled, and his flicker of glee was a little nauseating as he said, "It will be my pleasure to see it put to use."

44

CARVER

IT WAS LATE BY THE TIME Carver finished helping Jayveh make arrangements to leave Esperance in the morning.

Frankly, Carver couldn't wait to leave this accursed temple behind forever.

When he finally stepped back into their suite, he wondered if Amryn would be asleep, but he saw the glow of a lamp around the bedroom door.

She was waiting for him on the bed.

Her trunks had been packed, along with his, and she sat on the center of the bed reading from a small book.

She looked up as he entered. "Has Trevill confessed?"

"No."

She bit her lower lip. "He's guilty, Carver. I felt it."

"I believe you." He sat on the edge of the bed, every part of his body feeling heavy. "Marriset didn't make it."

"Jayveh told me. She came by to check on me earlier." Her brow furrowed. "She also said Ivan found the letter Marriset mentioned."

He nodded. "It's pretty damning. Trevill might not need to actually confess at this point. We've compared his handwriting to the note left with Cora, and the one Marriset was going to leave here." After she killed Amryn.

Risidual fear knifed him, and he had to push it aside.

Amryn was safe.

"What about the message left after the tea was poisoned?" she asked.

"The script is messier than his journal, which we used to compare—almost like he wrote the notes in his non-dominant hand. But the similarities are unmistakable. It was him."

She shook her head. "It doesn't make any sense. Why did Trevill want to ruin the peace? He wasn't part of the Rising."

Carver tipped his head, allowing that because it was unlikely Trevill had been part of the rebels; Tam would have probably mentioned him in all her ravings to Amryn, if he had been. And while his goal may have aligned with the Rising's, he had certainly gone about things in a bloodier way. "The Craethen Council was essentially replacing him and the other chancellors as the emperor's primary advisors," Carver said. "We were taking his place—his voice, and his power. In our first meeting as a council, Trevill told us the chancellors would be our advisors, but by default that meant he would no longer be as important to the emperor. He didn't want the council to be formed, so he hired an assassin to make sure everything here failed."

He took a breath. "When I laid out these possible motivations to Trevill, he denied them vehemently. He said he'd agreed to come here to help the council succeed, and he claimed he wouldn't have come at all if he didn't want the council to exist. But it only makes sense that he came here *because* he wanted things to fail. He knew the emperor couldn't be swayed, so Trevill must have decided to appear to embrace the idea. Saints, he may have even volunteered to come here, just to make sure everything failed."

Amryn released a slow breath. "How could he do such evil things just to keep his power in the emperor's court?"

"Some men crave power more than anything. For an ambitious man like Trevill, losing even some of his influence would have been enough to make him desperate." Carver reached out and brushed a curl from her bruised cheek, tucking it behind her ear. "I'm just glad Ivan figured out Marriset was the killer, and that he didn't hesitate in coming to protect you." He frowned. "Why was Felinus here?"

Amryn closed the book in her hands. "I'm not sure you're going to like the answer."

Well, he certainly didn't like *that*. "What happened?"

She sighed. "He knows I'm an empath."

Denial ripped through him. "That's impossible. He can't know that."

"He used to be a knight. He could sense my empathic ability the moment he met me. But that's not the worst part."

Apprehension tightened his voice. "There's a worse part?"

"Felinus doesn't want to hurt me. He could have turned me in long ago, but he didn't. He came to warn me. He said the high cleric has been asking questions about the number of people who were miraculously healed last night." Fear sparked in her eyes. "Carver, when I was healing everyone, I wasn't thinking. I was just using the power, and . . . I healed people that should have died. Felinus was only one of them. I've never done anything so reckless. I don't know why I didn't think about the fact that someone would notice. But the high cleric knows there's an empath here. He's already called for the Knights."

His body locked. The Order of Knights defended the church and trained empath hunters. Rivard's brothers were knighted, and he'd told stories of some hunts they'd been on. They learned ways to detect empaths, though Rivard had never known the details.

If they were coming to Esperance, looking for an empath . . .

Carver reached out, twisting his fingers around hers. He hated how cold her hand was. "It's going to be fine. We'll be gone in the morning. We'll miss them."

"But if they don't find an empath here, won't the high cleric have us all checked once we're at the capital?" Her voice shook, her words coming too fast. "Carver, I can't go to Craethen. It's the heart of the empire. I can't go with you."

He leaned in, making their eyes level. "Amryn, listen to me. I know you're afraid. But we're not separating. I'm not letting you go, and I'm not going to let anything happen to you."

"Carver—"

"No." He gripped her hand more tightly. "I can protect you."

"Not from this. Not from them." Her eyes were frantic, but her words were horribly sure. "If they find me, they *will* kill me. And they'll have the emperor's blessing."

"That won't happen." He wouldn't *let* that happen. He wasn't going to lose her. Not to the Knights, or the Rising, or her fears.

They were staying together.

She met his gaze, and he swore he could hear the pounding of her heart. "I can't stay in the capital."

"Then we won't."

She blinked. "But, we're all supposed to report to the emperor—"

"We will. But we won't linger. We'll leave as soon as we can—before any knights can be summoned."

"And go where?"

"Westmont." There was no debate there. He needed to know Amryn was in a safe place, and his family offered that security.

Amryn didn't look convinced, but she must have decided to accept it for now. "We have another problem. Felinus told me that the strange gem in that amulet is a bloodstone." She flipped up a hand, stalling his question. "I don't really know what that is, so I can't explain well. Felinus doesn't know much, either." She pointed to the book beside her. "I found this in the museum archives. It belonged to Saul Von."

That was a name he knew. "The empath who killed Argent's parents and grandmother."

Amryn nodded. "He was a terrible man, and his journal is mostly incoherent. But he was documenting everything he could about bloodstones. He was trying to find them. There are supposed to be five of them, and Felinus said they're a weapon that empaths found a way to make." She looked right at him. "Where is the amulet?"

It was suddenly heavy in his pocket. He pulled it out, along with her odd coin. He knew that tarnished coin meant a great deal to her, because she relaxed the moment her eyes fell on it.

She took the coin first, her fingers rubbing across the worn surface before she pushed it into her pocket. He wanted to ask her about it, but that would have to wait. She took the necklace.

As soon as she touched it, it glowed bright, then dimmed to a more natural crimson sheen.

"What *is* it?"

She glanced at him. "I really don't know. I found it in a cave on Zawri. It . . . sort of hummed. Like it was calling to me. I don't understand it, but it's like I can sense something from it. Like it's alive, but not."

He eyed her. "And you decided to bring something like that home with you?"

Her cheeks colored. "I didn't think too much about it at the time."

"Considering everything that's happened, we should probably think about it now." He took the amulet back from her—there was no glow when he touched it, though the gemstone remained red. "You said when you touched it in the library, you felt a flood of power, right?"

"Yes. I also heard a voice in my head."

"A voice? From the bloodstone?"

"Yes."

His eyes narrowed. "I don't like that."

She gave an almost laugh, though it was weak. "Neither do I."

"Did you hear any voices just now when you touched it?"

"No, but . . . it feels different than it did when the gemstone was black. And it never glowed like that before when I touched it. Not until last night, when I was using my healing ability." She studied the amulet in his hand. "It did more than amplify my powers. It's like it . . . woke up inside me. Almost like there was more than just me inside my body."

"I'm not finding any of this comforting," he told her.

She met his gaze. "Felinus said we should destroy it. But I'm not sure we should—not until we learn more. I don't even know if we *can* destroy it."

"What do you mean? I could toss it in a fire. Melt it down."

She shook her head slowly. "I don't think that will work. The necklace is tarnished, so I think that could be destroyed, but whatever a bloodstone is . . . it's alive. I think it was asleep when I found it, but now it's awake. And I don't think it's going to die without a fight."

These supernatural matters were far beyond his realm of experience. "Whatever you think we should do with the disturbing bloodstone, I'm with you."

She took a moment to consider things. "I think we should learn more about it. And we need to keep it a secret. It can't fall into the wrong hands."

"Done." He set it on top of Von's journal. "Can I ask that you avoid touching it, though? I don't want any voices or entities in your body—only you."

She shivered once. "I don't know why, but before now, nothing about the amulet scared me. The hum I felt from it was comforting. Now . . . there's a pulsing. Almost like a heartbeat."

Now he was sort of wishing he'd thrown it in the fire.

"It's strange," she said, her voice musing. "I had the bloodstone with me when I healed Ivan, but nothing strange happened then. No rush of power, no voice—nothing but the soft hum. And there was nothing as I was healing you until I touched the stone. That's when it changed colors, too."

"Wait." Carver's spine straightened. "You healed *Ivan?*"

She nodded. "On Zawri."

Saints, this woman would be the death of him. "Does he know you healed him?"

She looked a little sheepish. "I don't know. I haven't confirmed anything, but . . ."

"The Wolf Salute." He muttered a curse as he remembered

that moment on the dance floor. "He may not understand how, but he knows you saved his life. And that means he could turn you in."

"I don't think he will. He said he owes me a debt. Although, since he helped save me from Marriset, he might consider us even now."

Carver rubbed his aching temples.

The corner of her mouth lifted. "You're worried about me."

He grunted. "You've taken years off my life already."

"Sorry." But she was still smiling.

He shook his head. "You don't look sorry."

"It's just . . . I never thought you'd be worried about me. Not after you knew the truth."

Despite all the fears, worry, and uncertainty, he felt his features soften. He leaned in, moving slowly because this was still new and fragile.

She met him, their lips brushing gently.

Heat shot down his spine and pooled low in his gut. He cupped the side of her neck, his thumb stroking her soft skin as he broke the tender kiss.

"I know there's still a lot we need to figure out," he whispered, his forehead pressed to hers. "But you're not alone in this. All right?"

"All right."

He eased back, his hand still resting against her neck. He could feel her thready pulse, and it grounded him.

"If I'm going to keep you safe," he said, "I need to know who else knows about you. Besides Felinus and possibly Ivan."

She sighed. "Tam knows."

Saints. "That's bad."

"The worst part is, I don't know who told her. She taunted

me with it, but never actually said. But only three people knew about me before I came to Esperance."

At least it was a relatively short list. He just didn't like her rising tension. "Who?" he asked.

"My uncle Rix, but he wouldn't have told anyone. He's never even told Torin."

Carver wasn't ready to dismiss Rix out of hand, but he nodded to her. "Who else?"

She hesitated. "My father."

Carver stilled. "You said your father was dead. That you lost your parents, and Rix was your only family."

"He's not." She bit her lower lip. "My father isn't dead. At least, not as far as I know. He just left me for dead a long time ago."

Carver had questions—so many questions—but he didn't ask them just yet. "And the last person who knew about you?"

A tremor went through her, and beneath his palm, her pulse quickened. Dread was in her eyes as she met his gaze. "Tiras. My brother."

Carver stared at her. Confusion and shock mingled inside him, broken only by a slice of hurt. "You told me you didn't have any siblings."

A faint wince traced over her pale face. "I lied. But that's not what's important."

It felt pretty bloody important to him. She'd lied about her father's death, and her brother's existence. But he tried to wrestle aside his own feelings so he could focus on her.

"Tiras is an empath," Amryn said. "But he's not like me."

The small hairs on the back of Carver's neck rose. "What does that mean?"

"I told you about my mother's murder. That I was there.

That someone saved me that night. It was Tiras." Her voice was threaded with unmistakable fear. "He killed them. Four powerful men, and Tiras *destroyed* them. He was twelve years old."

Carver stared at her. He had no words, only a growing sense of horror.

Amryn swallowed hard. "It's because of empaths like Tiras that the rest of us are hunted. He is the reason everyone thinks we're monsters. And if he's the one who told the Rising about me . . . If he's one of them . . . We're all in grave danger."

THE STORY WILL CONTINUE IN
BOOK 2 OF THE ESPERANCE TRILOGY

Acknowledgements

The seeds for this story were planted years ago, and this book has gone through some big revisions to get to this point. I have a lot of people to thank for their endless support and encouragement, and I'm sure to miss someone. Just know that I am extremely grateful!

I want to first thank my Heavenly Father, who gave me a love of stories and the unrelenting desire to become an author.

I also need to give a special thank you to my extremely early readers who read the first incarnation of this book and loved it, while also daring me to make it better. Rebecca McKinnon, you saw the magic in Esperance from the very beginning, and you haven't let me lose sight of it. Thank you! Michalla Holt, you have been keeping secrets for years now (sorry!) and even though you have to keep another big one for a while longer, thanks for helping me see the light.

K.M. Frost, thank you for being a sounding board, a beta reader, a cover designer, and an amazing sister. I love you!

Kevin Frost, thank you for an incredible map that really brought this world to life!

Thank you to my amazing beta readers and proofreaders who helped make this book shine: Laurie Ford, Cynthia Ford, Mikelle Ford, Elyce Edwards, Amelia White, Sarah Hill, Ashley Hansen, Marlene Frost, Anna Brown, Crystal Frost, Stephanie Blue, Amy Cardon, Vi Ki Bjorkman, Heather Coombs, and Jonnie Morgart.

As always, thank you to my family and friends who continually support me in so many ways.

Thank you to the early readers and reviewers who fell in love with Esperance and spread the word. I love you all so much!

And finally, thank YOU for coming to Esperance and reading this story. My dream ever since I was a kid was to write stories that people would love. Thank you for helping to make my dream come true!

If you enjoyed Esperance, would you please consider leaving a review? They help so much.

Thank you!

GLOSSARY

AHMI *(AH-mee)*

Amryn's maid during her stay at Esperance.

AMRYN LUKIS *(AM-rin LOO-kis)*

An empath, and a newly recruited member of the Rising. From the kingdom of Ferradin. Married to Carver Vincetti.

ARGENT VAYNE *(AR-jent VAIN)*

Heir to the Craethen Empire, and grandson to the emperor. From the kingdom of Craethen. Married to Jayveh Umbar.

CAEL *(KAYL)*

One of the central kingdoms. It has many mountain ranges and is known predominantly for mining and metalwork.

CARVER VINCETTI *(CAR-ver vin-SEH-tee)*

The emperor's favored general, also known as the Butcher. From the kingdom of Westmont. Married to Amryn Lukis.

CHANCELLOR AARON TREVILL *(AIR-uhn truh-VIL)*

One of the emperor's advisors. He was sent to Esperance to preside over the newly formed Craethen Council, and to be a mentor to the Empire's Chosen.

CLERIC

A rank in the church. Clerics can be male or female. They are assigned different roles within the church depending on their strengths and interests; they can be teachers, preachers, preservers of knowledge, etc.

CORA AMIN *(COR-uh AH-min)*

From the kingdom of Hafsin, where her uncle is king. Married to Ivan Baranov.

CRAETHEN *(KRAY-then)*

One of the southern kingdoms, and where the empire originnated. The empire's capitol is still located there.

CRAETHEN EMPIRE

The Craethen Empire consists of twelve smaller kingdoms that were united by Emperor Lorcan Vayne.

CREGON VINCETTI *(CRAY-gun vin-SEH-tee)*

High General of Craethen, and Carver's father. Ruler of Westmont, and strategic advisory to the emperor.

DAERSEN *(DAIR-sen)*

One of the central kingdoms, and one of the first to unite with the empire. Headquarters of the church, and an important crossroads in the empire's river trade routes.

DARRIN FYTHEN *(DARE-in FI-then)*

From the kingdom of Vadir, where he is a high-ranking noble. Married to Marriset Navarre.

THE DIVINITIES

The deities of the church. Also known as the All-Seeing Divinities.

EMPEROR LORCAN VAYNE *(LOR-kun VAIN)*

Leader of the Craethen Empire. Created the empire by forcing the other eleven kingdoms to unite. Argent Vayne is his grandson.

THE EMPIRE'S CHOSEN

The twelve men and women selected by the rulers of each kingdom, as per the emperor's orders. They have been tasked with coming to Esperance to marry the spouse the emperor arranged for them, and forming the first Craethen Council.

ESPERANCE *(ES-per-ens)*

A remote temple compound located in the kingdom of Xerra. Esperance is owned by the church, but is considered a joint stronghold with the empire. It is run by High Cleric Zacharias, and it is where the Empire's Chosen are to live for a year.

FELINUS *(FEL-in-us)*

A cleric in Esperance, assigned to the library. He befriends Amryn.

FERRADIN *(FAIR-uh-din)*

One of the northern kingdoms, and the last to be brought into the empire. It has a cool, mountainous climate.

FORD GALLO *(FORD GAL-oh)*

Served with Carver in the war with Harvari. From the kingdom of Westmont. Currently stationed outside the walls of Esperance, to be a contact for Carver during the next year.

HAFSIN *(HAF-sin)*

One of the central kingdoms in the empire, known for its rich farmland.

HARVARI *(har-VAR-ee)*

The kingdom to the south of the Craethen Empire. They have been at war with the empire for years.

HIGH CLERIC

The title held by a high-ranking official in the church.

HIGH CLERIC ZACHARIAS *(zak-uh-RYE-us)*

The caretaker of Esperance. He has been given authority to act in the emperor's name as he presides over the Empire's Chosen.

IVAN BARANOV *(EYE-vun BAIR-ah-nov)*

From the kingdom of Sibet, where his father is king. One of the Sibeten Wolves, the elite fighting group in Sibet. Married to Cora Amin.

JAYVEH UMBAR *(JAY-vuh OOM-bar)*

From the kingdom of Xerra, where her uncle is king. Married to Argent Vayne.

KALMAR *(KAL-mar)*

One of the northern kingdoms in the empire, close to the eastern sea.

MARRISET NAVARRE *(MAIR-uh-set nah-VAR)*

From the island kingdom of Palar, where she is a high-ranking noble in the court. Married to Darrin Fythen.

PALAR *(pah-LAR)*

An island kingdom just off the eastern coast. It is known for spices, silks, and priceless artisan works.

THE RISING

A rebel group intent on destroying the empire. They have actively recruited in most of the kingdoms, and are a growing concern to the emperor.

RIVARD QUINN *(ruh-VARD KWIN)*

From the kingdom of Daersen. Has strong ties to the church. Married to Tam Ja'Kell.

RIX VARDEN *(RIKS VAR-din)*

Amryn's uncle and guardian. Also the chief advisor and best friend to King Torin of Ferradin.

SADIA KAVEL *(SAH-dee-uh ka-VUL)*

From the kingdom of Cael, where her cousin is king. Married
to Samuel Kenton.

SAMUEL KENTON *(SAM-yul KEN-tun)*

From the kingdom of Wendahl, where his father is king. Married to Sadia Kavel.

SIBET *(suh-BET)*

The northernmost kingdom in the empire. The climate is very
cold and there are many snowy mountain ranges.

SIBETEN WOLVES

The Wolves are the elite military force in Sibet.

TAM JA'KELL *(TAM juh-KEL)*

From the kingdom of Kalmar, where her father is king. Married to Rivard Quinn.

TORIN HALVIN *(TOR-in HAL-vin)*

King of Ferradin and best friend to Rix Varden. He helped to
raise Amryn.

VADIR *(vuh-DEER)*

One of the central kingdoms in the empire. There are many
hills and rivers, though it is prominently farmland.

WENDAHL *(WEN-dahl)*

One of the northern kingdoms, known as the crossroads of the north. It has direct river access, and is home to the best universities in the empire.

WESTMONT *(WEST-mont)*

One of the southern kingdoms, and one of the first to join the empire. It is the primary home of the empire's military, and is located on the western coast.

XERRA *(ZAIR-uh)*

One of the southern kingdoms, and where the temple of Esperance is located. It has a jungle climate.

ZAWRI *(ZAH-ree)*

A mountain peak in the jungles of Xerra, located near Esperance.

ABOUT THE AUTHOR

Heather Frost is a #1 Amazon bestselling author who writes YA/NA fantasy romance and paranormal romance. She is the author of the Seers trilogy, the Fate of Eyrinthia series, and Esperance. Her books have been finalists and nominees for a variety of awards, including the Whitney and Swoony Awards. She has a BS in Creative Writing and a minor in Folklore, which means she got to read fairy tales and call it homework.

When she's not writing, Heather likes to read, travel, and re-watch Lord of the Rings. She lives in a beautiful valley surrounded by mountains in northern Utah. To learn more about Heather and her books, visit her website: www.HeatherFrost.com.